The Edge of Darkness Trilogy

VORACIOUS

Book 2

LEIGH RIVERS

Art designed by Zoe Maxwell (@kowai_girl_tattoo on IG)
Cover Design By: Ashlee O'Brien at Ashes and Vellichor Designs
Formatting by Charly Jade *of* Designs By Charlyy

Edited by Laura at Ten Thousand Editing
Proofread by Lauren at PSR Editing

Distributed by Zando

First Edition: September 2026

978-1-63893-547-6 (trade paperback)
978-1-63893-607-7 (BAM signed edition)

10 9 8 7 6 5 4 3 2 1
Manufactured in the United States of America
LAK

PLAYLIST

When the party's over – Billie Eilish
Spiracle – Flower Face
From Now On – The Greatest Showman
Kings And Queens – Thirty Seconds To Mars
Crawling – Linkin Park
Bathroom – Montell Fish
Swim – Chase Atlantic
Can't Help Falling In Love – Tommee Profitt (Dark Version)
Taylor Swift – You Belong With Me (Taylor's version)
Spanish Sahara – Foals
Pumped Up Kicks – 3TEETH
Porcelain – Moby
Feel So Close – Calvin Harris
11 Minutes – Halsey and YUNG BLUD

The Edge of Darkness Trilogy playlist can be found on Spotify.

CONTENT WARNING

As this is a continuation of Insatiable, I highly recommend reading that first to avoid any major confusion.

Voracious comes with several triggers. As well as having sexual and violent content with multiple kinks like mask and primal play, praise and degradation, ass play, and light breeding, it also has some extreme triggers that should be taken seriously. There are multiple counts of sexual assault, sexual and physical abuse, rape, gang rape, drugging, torture, child loss in the second trimester and attempted suicide.

This story ends on a cliffhanger.

1

STACEY

"Do you need anything, Miss Rhodes?"

I stare out the window, watching the wing of the private jet cut through the air, tears soaking my cheeks, some already dried on my skin. I sniff, using my sleeve to wipe my nose. It's been all but three hours since we took off, and I can't calm my somehow beating heart as it races in my crippled chest.

The last few hours run through my head – from the moment Kade rushed me onto the motorbike, to being chased through the streets while gunshots fired, to finding out he's being blackmailed, to that last kiss – and I can't breathe.

Barry stands beside the small table, hands folded in front of him.

"I'm okay." Lie. I'm not. I'm anything *but* okay.

I'd begged them to turn around and help him, but Barry said

they have orders they can't go against. Kade made sure that no matter what happened at the hangar, they'd get me into the air. I was to be protected at all costs.

I'm far too terrified for Kade's safety to think about my own. Or what waits for me at home. I'll deal with Chris later. My mind is on fire with traumatising thoughts of what could be happening to Kade right now.

He could've come with me. He could've taken my hand and left this behind. We would've worked out how to get him out of this – together. His parents would've protected him.

It's over. It's been over for two years.

He's wrong. If it was over, then what the hell has this entire trip been? The sex. The kiss. The need to hold me. We aren't done.

Kade told me not to speak to his father about what's going on, but I have no idea how else to help him. What will telling Tobias actually do? Would it just cause him to spiral? Luciella said he's been doing really well with his health and behaviour.

Telling him might jeopardise that.

But what else can I do?

Does it make me selfish that I'd risk destroying Kade's dad's life to save his? Do I speak to Aria? Luciella?

I'm lost.

"We need to do something," I whisper, looking up at Barry.

"The police can't help, so don't bother calling them. No one can interfere."

"There must be someone who can help him?"

"No."

It's a solid answer that I refuse to believe.

"Will they hurt him?"

Barry averts his gaze, shifting on his feet. "He'll be fine."

"Someone hit him on the head. You saw it too."

"Miss Rhodes..."

"Stacey," I reply. "Please call me Stacey."

"It's nothing he can't handle, Stacey," Barry replies. "You should sleep."

They thought I was asleep in the car – like I'd actually be able to pass out under those circumstances. I heard every word they said –

I'm too innocent; I'd be in danger if we spent time together – and Kade saying I should have stayed out of his life, but I was always there.

An hour later, my thoughts are still wild. Barry hands me a glass of water, which shakes in my grasp. He sighs and drops into the seat in front of me. He looks tired, as if he hasn't slept in days. He does a lot for Kade – cleans up his messes and deals with him when he's drugged up or drunk out of his mind.

I'm starting to think Kade is forced to take drugs too, because he hated them when we were teenagers.

I manage to gulp down three mouthfuls of the water then place the glass on the table between us. "I have a question. Do you work for them? Or Kade?"

He clears his throat, straightening his already flat tie. "Mr Mitchell is my boss. He pays my salary and bonuses. But I'm very aware of the Sawyers and his position with them."

"Who's the wife?" I ask, leaning my elbows on the table. "Her name and everything else you have on her."

"There's no reason for you to know. You can't do anything. No one can. Do what Mr Mitchell said – move on."

A tear slides down my cheek. "How can you just sit back and watch these people control him?"

"Do you care about your family, Miss Rhodes?"

My teeth grind together. "Partially."

"Then understand that if you keep digging, your family will suffer the consequences. Stop while you're ahead. That is my only piece of advice."

"Will you go back for him once I'm home?"

"No. I'm to monitor you for the foreseeable."

"Can you please go back for him?"

He wipes his face, exasperated. "We land in four hours," he replies, changing the subject, and my heart sinks. He really isn't going to do anything? "Once we land, contact your brother to pick you up. I'll follow behind. Don't tell him about any of this or pay any attention to me or my colleagues. We're ghosts to you."

My stomach plummets. What if they see Chris?

Regardless of the twisted feeling in my gut, I nod. "Okay."

He gets to his feet and buttons his suit jacket. "To put your mind at ease, if the order comes in, then yes, I'll go back for him once I know you're safe. But I doubt we'll hear from Mr Mitchell for a while. He's blocked all comms to his phone and deactivated the system. He's untraceable. The last time that happened, he was gone for three months."

My lip trembles. "Kade wasn't always like this. I... I'm so worried about him. They could be hurting him right now. I feel useless."

The lights dim, and he refills my water.

"Mr Mitchell has been in a lot of situations where his life has been at risk. Trust me when I say this is minor. He's too valuable to be killed. Many have tried and failed. He's good at what he does because of what he's gone through." He gives me a tight smile and gestures to the cockpit. "I'll be right through there if you need anything. Get some rest. Miss— Stacey."

I'm not sure how much time passes; the music playing from the speakers is all I have to focus on. "When the party's over" by Billie Eilish is on, and my heart sinks with every lyric. Memories rush through me. Me inverted on the hoop; Kade kissing me upside down while this song plays. He often used to interrupt my routine to kiss or touch me. Other times he'd sit to the side and watch me, as if he was watching me dance for the first time.

I knew that version of Kade was in love with me. I could see it in his eyes.

I'm not sure I'll ever see that side of him again.

I go to use the bathroom. My eyes are swollen from crying, my headache teetering on the edge of a full-blown migraine. I stop outside the cockpit door, hearing Barry's voice.

"A girl?" he asks in a happy tone. "What else did the midwife say? Yeah. That's awesome. I'm so sorry I couldn't be there, baby. I'll be home in a few weeks. Work is a bit hectic." Then there's a long silence. His partner must be talking.

"Honestly, she's not what he described. I think they need their heads knocked together and to actually talk it out. Yeah. I miss you too. I'll be home before our wedding anniversary, I promise. I love you too."

I move away and stop eavesdropping on Barry and his wife. It's good to hear people still have joyful moments, even when it feels like the world is swallowing me whole. I remember how excited me and Kade were when we found out we were having a girl. We'd impatiently waited until the sixteen-week mark and paid for our own ultrasound instead of waiting the extra four weeks.

It stayed a secret until I figured out a plan to escape Chris without risking Kade's life. I used the excuse of not wanting Luciella to know yet. I took it easy with dancing and told my friends I'd torn my rotator cuff, so I couldn't do rigorous exercises; that I couldn't drink on nights out because I was on certain meds, and they bought into the lie.

So many lies.

I had the faintest swelling at the bottom of my abdomen that I blamed on bloating when around Lu and Ty, but despite how small I was, the midwife said everything was perfect. We started planning even more. Where we'd move to, the house we'd build, how many children. Listing names.

Kade was mortified with half the names I suggested. *I am not fucking calling my daughter Vixen.* And then: *Georgina? Really? She's not ninety.* My favourite was: *You're trying to fucking annoy me now, Freckles. That's a dog's name.*

Disaster struck barely a week later, and it was the beginning of the end.

Right now, I'm so confused about everything. Kade said it was over, yet he kissed me. I can still feel his lips on mine as I run my fingers over my mouth. I wish I'd let him kiss me before. I wish we'd done it the entire trip.

Do I still love him? Yes, without a doubt. Am I *in* love with him? I have no idea.

Feelings suck sometimes. They're my best friends, but they're also my worst enemies.

I manage to fall asleep, and when we land in Glasgow, Barry waits outside the airport bathroom while I try to remain calm and call Tobias on the number Aria gave me, but he doesn't pick up. I send a message to let him know I landed back in Scotland.

Kyle tells me he's parked at arrivals, and I've to move my ass.

I exit the bathroom. "Can I tell my brother? About what

happened?"

Barry stares at me in horror. "Absolutely not. Did you not hear what I said on the flight? Consequences, Miss Rhodes."

"Stacey."

"Unless you want your brother dead, keep your mouth shut and get on with your life. I won't interact with you. I'm just here to make sure the Sawyers aren't hunting for you."

They'd never find me. Chris is a cyber-freak. I don't think the police could even hack into my phone or the Fields' manor security system. After begging him last year, he removed the tracker and stopped reading my messages, but only because I agreed to stop locking my room door. I did, but only for a little while before paranoia kicked back in.

I sacrificed one form of privacy for another.

Barry leaves my side and goes to his black SUV, which is waiting a few cars behind the white Range Rover Kyle bought a few months ago. My brother grins at me and puts my bags into the trunk, and I climb into the passenger side, my nerves shattering when I see Chris glaring at me from the back seat.

2

KADE

FLASHBACK

Whoever decided it would be a fucking fantastic idea to go camping as a family needs to die. Preferably before the tents are pitched and I'm lying in mine bored as fuck.

We were supposed to celebrate my brother Jason's birthday with a party in the manor, and as much as I hate parties, I would've been able to drag Stacey into a spare room or closet and devour her face until we couldn't breathe.

I despise any sort of social gathering. But this? Spending the weekend close to Stacey but not being able to kiss or touch or even speak to her? Way worse. It's torture.

I have to maintain this facade that she does my head in because apparently it'll look suspicious if I randomly stop calling her names and making her life hell.

Last night, when everyone went back to their tents while Ewan and Base got into a heated debate about the blueprints of the Eiffel Tower, we texted for hours before she fell asleep. The last message was me asking if she was still awake, and I've had nothing from her all day.

All. Fucking. Day. It's brutal. Being so close but not being able to do anything. I'm sharing a tent with Jason, Dez and Base. Ewan and Mum are in their own tent, and Luciella, Stacey and Tylar are in the other a few spaces away.

I can hear my sister giggling, and it irritates the fuck out of me. How is it fair that she gets to have Stacey to herself?

It's been an entire month since we left London, since I woke up with the smell of her vanilla-scented hair in my face, her body on top of mine, her soft breaths hitting my neck. It felt different, maybe because we'd just had sex for the first time. I felt the butterflies intensifying, especially when she woke up and smiled at me.

I'm not afraid to admit that I stayed in that position for fucking hours, stroking her dark hair, tracing the ink on her shoulder blades, wondering how long it would last before she got fed up with me.

We've been going slow when it comes to sex, or any other acts for that matter. I don't mind at all. We aren't in any rush. But the five times we have fucked, it's been careful, safe and always ends with me holding her until we both fall asleep. I usually wake to her gone.

We're still learning from each other. I think, along with her as a person and how beautiful she is, I'm also drawn to how understanding she is. None of this is easy for me. Emotions I've never been in touch with are surfacing whenever I'm around her. She's patient with me, and I think that alone makes me comfortable around her.

Call me insecure, but I second-guess everything. It's impossible for a person to be as happy as I am and not have the other shoe drop like fucking thunder. She doesn't even want me to meet her family yet, for fuck's sake.

We aren't in a relationship. Nothing has really been established. We haven't spoken about how we feel, except for the odd time she tells me she likes me, and I need to hold back on telling her I think I might be falling in love with her.

Might be.

I'm not sure if the need to see her, speak to her or even fucking smell her is an obsessive trait, one that may turn into a dangerous need for control or make me manipulative. I can't wake up without her on my mind, and when I go to sleep, all I can think about is her.

When I'm not with her, I check my phone every five minutes, intentionally going to the kitchen when I know Luciella is there to see if Stacey is with her. I'm always on her social media, her tagged pictures and checking if she's following anyone new.

My heart literally sinks when she takes forever to respond to me. But it also explodes in ecstasy when she smiles at me, when she cuddles into my side and tells me she doesn't want to go back to my sister's room.

I haven't heard any noises from the other tent in a while. Would it be psychotic of me to sneak in, kidnap Stacey and drag her to the woods to kiss the living daylights out of her?

Debatable.

I sit up in my sleeping bag and grab my phone.

Me: Still awake?

Three dots appear, and I internally sigh with relief and lie back, holding my phone up to my face while I wait for her reply. I pull the strings of my hoodie, tightening the hood around my face.

Freckles: Yep. I can hear Ewan snoring from away over here! I would've suffocated him with a pillow by now if I was your mother. Wait. Is that Ewan or Aria?

Could be either of them. In all fairness, Stacey snores as well. I won't say that to her though. She's in denial about her singing voice – imagine I commented on her snoring too? I'd be the one suffocated with a pillow.

Me: It sucks being so close to you and not being able to do anything. How is it possible to miss you, yet you're right here?

Was that too forward? Fuck it, the message has already sent. Dad told me to be honest, so I'm being fucking honest.

Freckles: I miss you too.

I smile and type a reply.

Me: I have a question…

Freckles: You may ask.

How the hell do I ask about exclusivity without asking her to be my girlfriend? I reckon the latter will scare her, considering how secretive she wants us to be, so I won't mention us being in an actual relationship.

Me: I know we spoke about this when I was in America, but do you want to see other people?

She types. Deletes. Goes offline. Comes back online and types. Offline. Online. Types and deletes.

Freckles: Ummmm…

Fuck me, my heart is rattling in my chest. What if things have changed since London and she's been seeing other people, and I've completely read this wrong?

My left eye twitches, an unsettling, violent feeling sinking into me at the thought of someone else kissing her. Seeing her smile. Hearing her giggle. Watching her dance and falling asleep with her in their arms.

I'll find out who and I'll hurt them. Threaten them.

Wait, no, fuck. No.

Freckles: Have I misjudged this? Without sounding needy, I only want you. But if you're wanting to see other people, then please tell me. I'm not into sharing.

Is the heavy weight lifting from my chest what relief feels like?

Me: I only want you too. Come here and I'll prove it.

Freckles: Do you forget the part where you're sharing a tent with your brother and friends?

Me: They're drunk and asleep. Come keep me company.

I shut my screen off when she goes offline, and I check to make sure they're definitely asleep. It's three in the morning – I doubt anyone will be awake. Base has his arm over his eyes, mouth open with deep, sleepy breaths, mumbling in Russian. Dez is face down and keeps twitching in whatever dream he's in. Jason is motionless, a sure sign he's in a deep sleep.

I throw one of Base's protein bars at them, and none threaten to kill me.

Definitely asleep.

The zipper of the tent slowly moves up, and her head appears. Her hair is mostly pulled back with a clip. Her face, from what I can see in the moonlight, is make-up free, but there's a slight sheen on her lips where she's put on lip balm before coming here.

In a hoodie and baggy sweats to keep her warm in this frigid weather, she climbs into the tent, zips it back up at the speed of a snail then crawls over to me as quietly as she can.

It's kind of pathetic how my heart skips a beat over her willingly wanting to spend time with me. The excitement I feel that she's sneaking away from her friends, sneaking around mine and sliding in beside me in my sleeping bag is unmatched by any thrill I've ever had.

That's just it with Stacey. She could be singing a musical horrendously off-key with food all over her face, and I'd still see her as my own fucking angel.

"Hi," she breathes as I turn on my side to face her, mirroring her position. "This is risky."

I look over her shoulder at my friends then look down at her, pulling my sleeping bag up to hide her from them. I half-smile and tuck a stray strand of hair behind her ear. "Risky is fun."

"They won't wake up and tell Luciella I'm here?" Her voice is so quiet, so sweet and soft.

"Not if they want to live, no. It's just Base and his big mouth though. He's a fucking gossip."

We whisper as low as possible, talking about anything and everything – what she's been up to this week, the classes she's been teaching, the sketches I sent her one night when I was bored. After she saw them, she asked if I'd design her a tattoo.

Stacey is already a work of art. The idea of having my drawings on her skin makes mine tingle. I'm no pro, but my therapist has started encouraging me to doodle often, since it helps when I'm overwhelmed or need to express myself in a way I struggle with.

She wraps her arms around my neck, hiking her leg up to rest on top of my hip. "I can't fall asleep here," she tells me. "But I want to cuddle for a bit."

I tighten my hold on her waist, bringing her knee up higher to my ribs. "Then cuddle me, Freckles. It's been brutal not being able to do this with you."

"I love how romantic you are," she says. "I know you keep saying you're not, but you really are. You're just as needy as me."

I squeeze her ass. "I'm not romantic." Needy? Yeah, I'm fucking needy when it comes to her.

She hums quietly. "Is that why you researched all the side effects to my pill and restocked your minifridge with things to make me feel better? Or when you bought me a hot-water bottle the morning after our first time, because I was sore?"

"The side effects are a little intense. I was being nice." I raise my shoulder. "I need to take care of you somehow after how well you take it."

She slaps my arm, and we both silently chuckle.

Most of the time, we just do this whenever we're together. Cuddle and talk.

Stacey being a cuddler has been unexpected. Without a doubt, this is one of my favourite things about her – whenever we sleep, she always has to touch me.

Her head is always on my chest, and whenever I wake and we're tangled as one, I can't seem to move. I don't want to move. It's moments like those – this – when I try to figure out if my dad ever felt this way about my mum, and at what point it all turned sour. At what point did he decide it wasn't enough and start using manipulation and coercion to keep her for as long as he did?

He still does. In a way. Her life, twenty years later, still revolves around my dad like fragile glass. She loves him – a part of her can never not love him. They remain in this toxic bubble, where she lights up around him, and he conceals every vicious urge to keep her happy.

I know that takes a lot for him, and sometimes, when Mum needs space from dealing with his bad days, my dad ends up in solitary confinement for being an enraged psycho.

One thing I will say, and fuck if my parents ever found out, but I never want them back together. They're truly toxic. Plain and simple. She's married, and I honestly think I'd go with Ewan if they split up.

Personally, I think Ewan deserves better. He should find someone who can love him the way he loves her.

I'm the worst son ever for thinking that.

Stacey brings me out of my head fuck by cupping my cheek. "Hey. What's wrong?"

I shake my head. She doesn't need to know where my thoughts go sometimes. "Nothing. I really do miss you."

Base is definitely asleep. Because he'd be snorting and trying not to laugh if he heard me.

She grins and gives me a chaste kiss. I go in for more, but she presses her middle finger to my lips. "I'm right here."

Yeah, she is, but I can't kiss her or hold her or fucking even look at her ass without chancing us being caught. Her shitty rule of keeping this all hush-hush is starting to piss me off. I'm trying to be patient, but fuck me.

I'm not patient.

And I'm also starting to despise my sister.

"You know what I mean," I say against her finger.

She moves her hand and slides it between us, gripping the waistband of my grey sweats. "We're going home tomorrow. I'll see you after my hoop class. I'm teaching until nine."

I sigh deeply and lower my forehead to hers. "Not enough."

Stacey shakes slightly in a silent laugh. "What are you going to do when I go to Hawaii with my family in January?"

"Burn your passport before you can leave."

She curls her fingers into my waistband and whispers, "I keep it in the drawer beside my bed. You'd need to sneak into my room and get it."

"Sneaking into your room isn't impossible." Her dad has tightened security since I showed up at their door, but that won't stop me.

Stacey bites her bottom lip, sucks it and releases it slowly. My eyes are drawn to her mouth, and I want to taste those lips, to slip my tongue inside and roll her beneath me.

"I want you to sneak into my room."

Jesus. "You do?"

Her hand slides below the waistbands of both my sweats and boxers. "Uh-huh." A groan drops from my mouth as she wraps her fingers around my hardening cock and begins stroking me from base to tip. "Next week when my... family is away. I want you to sneak in through my window and climb into my bed and wake me up with your face between my legs."

Fuck. Fucking fuck. My dick swells in her hand with each movement, images in my head of me between her legs and sucking on her clit.

"That," I say, stopping as she swipes her thumb over the tip, smearing my precum, "can be arranged, Freckles."

"Good," she says, capturing my bottom lip between her teeth and sucking on it. It pops back, and she tightens her grip around me, making me fight an audible groan.

Dez and Base and Jason are right there, and her hand is wrapped around my cock, but I don't care about them, just her and the way she watches me with each stroke.

With one last glance at them sleeping behind her, I lower my head, nudging her nose with mine. I release her thigh and grab the nape of her neck, crushing our mouths together in a kiss.

I tilt my head and shove my tongue past her lips. The kiss becomes hungrier – more demanding each time she twists her wrist at my swollen head.

My hand vanishes from her hair, dropping between us and into her panties. She's wet – really fucking wet – and I roll my hips into her grip as my thumb presses to her clit.

She quietly whimpers into my mouth, gasping as I push two fingers inside and fuck her with them. I curl them against her warmth, feeling her tighten, her hips rolling into my hand.

I ease them out of her and yank her sweats down while she completely frees my cock from my own sweats. As quietly as possible, we get one of her legs free of material and hike her knee to my hip.

We lie on our sides again, facing each other, and my dick presses between her thighs. I rub the tip against her entrance then lower my head with a mouthed fuck. "I don't have a condom."

She grinds against the underside of my dick. "The pill would've kicked in by now."

I lift my head to look at her. "You want me to keep going without one?"

"Only if you want to. I only had to wait seven days before having unprotected sex. It's been three weeks."

Just for further permission, I ask, "You're sure?"

"Yes." She rocks her hips, her wetness sliding all over my cock. "Please, Kade."

Note to self: Have Stacey moan my name while fucking her. Preferably not while sharing a tent with my brother and friends.

I nod, gulping before caressing her lips with a gentle kiss. Without breaking our mouths apart, I grab her thigh, holding it to my hip as I line up and push into her with ease. The warmth of her tightness has my eyes closing, has me holding in the noises threatening to leave my throat at how perfectly her pussy is gripping my dick.

Without the barrier of a condom, I can feel everything. From how wet she really is, to the addictive heat, the way her inner walls accommodate my length, the slight pressure from still being new to sex. I already thought sex was amazing, but without the barrier, I think I might die from how good it feels.

Just this once, I'll enjoy this. As much as fucking her bare for the rest of my life sounds like a day in heaven.

Stacey – flushed with parted lips and dilating eyes – grips on to me for dear life as I sink deeper. I slide out, keeping the tip in, then thrust in again. And again. And again. Until I'm swallowing each shattering sound from her lips with a solid kiss and holding on to her as she matches each thrust. My tongue is on hers, my fingers digging into her flesh, and I glance at the bodies beside us to make sure no one has woken up.

I devour her mouth, tasting her, feeling her under my fingertips as I *explore every inch of her body.*

I'll never get used to this. Her.

"Mine," I say against her mouth.

No one else's.

I kiss her shoulder, the area where she has a rose and skull tattooed on her skin, then I drag my mouth to her throat, where I want to wrap my hand around it. An impulsive thought, one I'll never act on.

This is the sixth time we've had sex; I doubt she'll be comfortable with me grabbing her throat while fucking her.

I stop moving when I notice she's trying to take control. Her little breaths and the way she can't take her eyes off mine have me cupping her face in both hands, slamming my mouth on hers and letting her take the reins.

She digs her nails into my scalp, tugging my hair to use as leverage to grind on me. Each thick inch is cradled by her wet pussy, and she hooks her heel to my thigh so she can fuck me harder. If we weren't in a tent with people, I'd allow myself to moan and not bite my lip to stifle each sound.

My balls squeeze, tingling from electrifying sensations at my spine, and I'm so fucking close to exploding inside her, but I'm not ready for this to end.

I pull out completely. "Turn around."

She does, giving me her perfect ass. I cradle a cheek in my palm, squeezing as I kiss a wet trail up the side of her throat to her ear then nudge through her entrance from behind. It's tighter from this angle – I hold her leg up as I fuck into her pussy.

It's a slow and torturous rhythm that I want to speed up; I want to ignore the others sleeping so close to us and slam into her harder, faster, to hear her moaning so loud she wakes all of the wildlife in this campsite.

"Oh God," she breathes, backing into each thrust, making me go deeper and hitting that sweet spot that has her writhing. I cover her mouth before she can get any louder as I pick up the pace.

I drop my chin, whispering against her ear. "Close your eyes. I don't want you looking at my friends or my brother while you come from me fucking you."

A perfectly acceptable demand. In my head anyway. She shuts her eyes and digs her nails into my wrist, my hand still on her mouth as I thrust harder.

Skin slapping skin and heavy breaths echo around the tent, but they don't stop me from driving into her, or Stacey from arching her extremely flexible back and giving me a new angle.

"You're doing so good, Freckles," I say, kissing below her ear as I thrust harder. My voice is shaky, but I keep praising her. "Taking it so fucking well."

I can feel my dick swelling, the head throbbing from how much she's tightening around it. I reach in front of her, dropping my hand between her legs and pinching her clit.

She bites into my palm as she clenches around me, her walls strangling my dick as her orgasm crashes into her. Each pulse, each time she swallows me with her euphoric spasms, I start to lose my vision. Blurry. Hazy. Like I'm happy drunk or on uppers, my own fucking drug as my balls pull.

I bury my head into the crook of her neck, sucking on the skin there as my thrusts quicken – until I stop completely, stilling deep, my cock twitching as I fill her with each drop of my cum.

I've no idea how long we lie here, cuddling, trying to catch our breaths. Long after we fix our clothes, Stacey stays in my arms. We hear birds chirping, the lapping of the water nearby and the pattering of rain against the tent.

She eventually goes out to pee, because apparently that's a thing after sex, but comes straight back to me.

"I should go," she says quietly. "People might start waking up."

I stroke her cheek with my knuckles. "Come for a smoke with me first."

"We should make a deal to quit," she says, narrowing her eyes. "It's bad for us."

"I will if you let me see you more."

She rolls her eyes but smiles. "Maybe."

We sneak out, making sure not to wake my heathen friends or brother, and I follow her into the woods. She leans against a tree, the canopy of branches guarding us from the rain. I hand her a cigarette, light it for her and spark my own.

I've never been attracted to smoking, but anything Stacey does is fucking hot to me.

She blows smoke above us and tilts her head. "Why are you staring at me?"

I shrug and inhale deeply. "You're cute," I say as smoke releases from my lungs.

Shaking her head, she blushes and takes another draw. "Did you mean it when you said you only wanted me?"

I nod. "Did you?"

She nods too. "Yeah."

"Great."

"Great," she repeats, smiling hard.

So beautiful and mine.

"Sit next to me in the car ride home."

She hums. "Why?"

"So I can hold your hand." I shrug and press my mouth to hers. "Or your thigh. Whichever is more accessible."

"In your mum's car?"

"I'll put my hoodie over our hands. Happy?"

"See! You are romantic! That's kind of like when we were in your living room, when we were watching that dreadful movie Lu chose. We held hands under the blanket."

I remember that night. I couldn't get the image of her beneath me out of my head for weeks. "For the billionth time, I'm not romantic."

"You are!"

I roll my eyes and lift her into my arms, carrying her in the opposite direction from the tents to a nearby picnic bench, settling her on top of it. I stand between her legs, and both our heads gravitate to the side, mesmerised by the sight before us.

The sun rises over the Torridon Hills, illuminations cracking the sky and atmosphere with orange and yellow hues. Flocks of birds fly over the water. I look at Stacey, and her eyes dance with the colours reflecting, her cheeks and nose red from the cold.

She's like my own sunrise. Beautiful. Perfect. She fills a part of me that's been empty and dark for as long as I can remember.

Maybe I am *falling in love with her. Should I tell her? Would that scare her?*

I see her chitter a little, so I yank off my hoodie and pull it over her head. Hers is thin and small. Mine drowns her body, nearly coming down to her knees. "Thank you," she says, fisting the cuffs and holding them to her cheeks. "It smells like you."

"Don't steal this one."

She grins. "I'll need to take it off before we go back to the tents, but I'll steal it later."

I smirk, pulling her closer to me by the knees. She buries her head in my chest. We stay like this for God knows how long. In a comfortable silence I'd like to stay in. But then the annoying thoughts start to run wild, so wild I'm shocked she can't hear my heart slamming against my chest.

Gulping nervously, I allow myself to be honest by asking something that's been bothering me for a while. "Does it not worry you? Who I am?"

Her head lifts. "What? Why would I be worried?"

"I'm the son of a psychopath who kidnapped his own girlfriend and killed multiple people. Does it not scare you that I might be the same as him? It's genetically possible. You know how much I struggle with emotions."

Without hesitation, she shakes her head. "You aren't Tobias."

"Then why can't I stop thinking about you? What if it's the start of an obsession like he has with my mother?"

She grins and pulls me to her, hooking her ankles behind my thighs.

She brushes her fingers through my hair. "I can't stop thinking about you either. Does that make me a psychopath?"

I scoff. "Of course not."

"Then there's your answer. Can you kiss me now? I made it look like I was in my sleeping bag with blankets and a pair of headphones, but it'll be noticeable now, so I need to go back."

I chuckle and pull her lips to mine, doing as she says until our tongues are numb. We part ways, our fingers slipping free as she sneaks back into her tent, and I climb into mine.

3

KADE

Blinking under the bright light, I rub my eyes and try to sit up, failing when dizziness knocks me onto my back. I'm not in a sleeping bag or in a tent or in my goddamn dream, I'm in a hotel room, the bed far too soft, with red hair dangling over my face. It isn't dark and smelling of vanilla. It's like straw and smells of cigarettes.

The butterflies aren't there either. The only sign of humanity I have left, that I only feel when I think of *her*.

Fuck.

I rub my eyes again, needing to fall back into one of the many memories I escape to when I'm in these situations.

Bernadette leans over me, grinning widely. "Oh, good. I thought you passed out on us. Did we dose you too many times?"

There's a voice to my left, close – really close – but I don't try to turn my head to see who it is. Bernadette speaks to them while she leans over me, stroking my cheek like I'm her little petting lamb. Her nails scrape against my stubble, and when I attempt to sit up, she shoves me in the chest and presses her palm down.

I'm far too weak to fight her. My veins are burning with whatever they injected me with.

I'm in and out of consciousness from the drug, but that doesn't stop them – something jabs at my arm, and a rush of heat spirals down my spine, gathering in my balls. She keeps stabbing me with shit that makes me hard, and no matter what I do, I can't stop it. Being forced to have a hard-on for weeks is starting to hurt. I want to cut my dick off.

We came back to Scotland a few days ago, staying in a hotel up in Inverness while she signed some deal with new clients. She sold me to a married couple for two days then had to clean the mess up because I killed them both. I don't remember skinning them alive, but apparently I did the wife first while the husband watched. Neither of them got near me.

I'm nearing my limit, even with all the consequences looming over my head. I'm the son of Tobias Mitchell, for fuck's sake. I'm not a fucking toy – but in order to protect those I love, I need to pretend to be one. A pet. A killer. A warm body that she sells off, even though she has more money than fucking sense.

Barry better be keeping Stacey safe. I've done everything possible to distract Bernie while she hunts for both Stacey and my team. I'm surprised she's still not dug into her little system and found my ex – it's like she doesn't exist at all. It's... concerning. Someone is messing with her existence. It could be the reason Barry and I were never able to hack her home security or her phone – all I ever got was her previous address and the death certificates of her parents.

If she hadn't told me about her stepbrother Kyle, I wouldn't have known he existed. We live just far enough apart that our paths probably wouldn't cross.

Bernadette did catch the tail of some of my guys in Australia – they were dissecting a terrorist group planning on attacking a high school, but I sidetracked her by causing an issue in Inverness.

I've been lying in this bed since yesterday morning. Somewhere near Glasgow. My body is starting to go numb. No food or water – she has fluids going into me through a vein yet still insists on jabbing me with needles.

Bernadette tells her bodyguards to get out and find Archie, and after she locks the door behind them, she pulls off her nightdress and smiles at me. "I know I said I'd give you two weeks off, but you're coming to a party with me and Cassie next weekend. Then you're going to take my daughter to the hotel room there, and you're going to be at least a little more compliant than you are now. She needs to think you *want* to be there with her."

I stare at the monster, and I guess my expression speaks volumes, since I'm too fucked to string words together.

"My daughter can be sensitive to our world. She'll get used to it, but I need you to be by her side throughout. Archie is still insisting on marriage."

My empty stomach curdles, and I grit my teeth as she pulls her hair into a ponytail then twists it into a bun.

"Your father is in solitary confinement, and he will stay there until I find who was working for you. Is his life no longer enough? Will I pay your sister a visit next?"

"No," I grit, my voice strained.

"Will you behave and marry my daughter then?"

I try to glare, but whatever drug is pumping through me has me dizzy. It seems she doesn't care for a response as she straddles me.

I close my eyes and sink the back of my skull into the pillow, revulsion and murder crashing into me. I think about dark hair, a soft voice, the way she feels under my fingers and ignore my body betraying me. It makes me sick. No matter how much I fight it, the drugs she's given me win over my denial. I'm not attracted to Bernadette. I hate her more than anyone I know.

Death would be better. But me dying risks everyone else.

If I'm dead, how the fuck will I keep her off Stacey's tail?

Barry could protect her – I trust him the most out of everyone – but he's due to have a kid. Will he leave Stacey alone when his wife gives birth? Who will keep Stacey safe?

Fuck, my heart is racing again – the beginnings of a panic attack. I try to breathe through it, think about something calming.

Stacey is safe. She's fine.

I haven't laid eyes on her in so long and it's killing me inside. Before, I could sneak away and log into my laptop, watch her on the cameras while she danced, or in the manor with my sister, or I'd park my car near the studio and wait for her to leave so I could see her face.

I can still taste her on the tip of my tongue. Just one fucking second of her, one drive to the studio for one goddamn look, that's all I need – it's fucking torture. Maybe worse than my current position.

Bernadette grabs my throat and squeezes. "Eyes on me, boy. Think about *me*."

I don't look at her, even as she crushes my airways. I look right through her – dissociating like I always do.

I'm too weak to snap her neck. Too fucking useless as I keep my eyes unfocused and imagine I'm somewhere else. A tent. My bed. On my motorbike with Stacey's squeals of excitement in my ear while I speed through traffic. The look on her face when I showed her the tattoo I made for us both. The first time she told me she loved me.

My fingers mentally trace over imaginary paper as I stare at the last ever drawing I made of her – unfinished. Gathering dust in my apartment, locked away in my safe where all my drawings are. I once drew what I assumed our daughter would look like – my most prized possession.

I fist the sheets at my sides when Bernadette leans down to kiss my throat, breaking my focus. I'm not sure where the energy comes from, or how I manage, but I drive my forehead into her face. Her screams are the last thing I hear before she gets off my dick and stabs me with another needle, and I welcome it now, because I can go back to where I want to be in my mind.

4

KADE

FLASHBACK

Leaving Stacey in my bed this morning is a struggle, but when I kiss her forehead and untangle her limbs from mine, I know it's going to be worth it. She's wearing a hockey top my dad sent over from America, and it's fucking huge on her. She seems to have claimed half my wardrobe.

Sweats and a top to hand, I lean down and kiss the tip of her nose, grinning as she groans and rolls onto her front. I check the time on my phone, seeing four messages from Base and Dez, both of them in Russia for some family party.

Dez sends an SOS with a picture of a guard standing with a gun, and Base accidentally sends me a message that was clearly meant for my sister.

Sebastian the Third: Aw please don't cry. Don't be worried, princess. I get why you're scared, but you don't need to be. If you need to chat until you feel better, then you know I'm always a phone call away. You're going to fucking smash it over there, and anyone who gets to be by your side is lucky. Safe flight and let me know when you land xx

Sebastian the Third: Fuck. Of all the fucking people, I send it to YOU. I will hang your ass if you screenshot that.

Any other time I'd give him hell, but the fact that he's trying to make my sister feel better, to comfort her while on the other side of the world, is fine with me. Hell, he has every force under him to keep her safe and could crush a skull with his bare hands if he wanted to. Luciella couldn't have landed with a scarier yet more caring guy. If only she'd rearrange her moral compass and give him a chance.

She won't.

Which is probably why Stacey is even more scared for her to find out that we're seeing one another.

Freckles has been on the pill for two months now, and the side effects are starting to get to her. Her tits are swollen, her face is breaking out and she has a constant craving for ham sandwiches. Tylar asked her why she was gaining a bit of weight, considering she works out twice a day and is usually very careful with her diet.

Stacey called me as soon as she left the studio in tears, paranoid that I'd lose interest if it didn't stop.

It took me days to convince her that I wasn't going anywhere. It took me another few days to finally have Stacey believe that regardless of how she looks, she's beautiful.

Now she keeps putting her tits in my face and trying to suffocate me with them.

So yeah. Losing interest in Stacey is impossible.

I sneak out of the house and off the grounds before the sun beams over the Munros, making my way to Glasgow to pick up our new fluffy friends. I'm excited about her reaction. She'd said her favourite dogs were large ones. And I want a Dobermann. It just so happens that I'm rehoming two after the shelter posted online that they were in need of a home urgently.

When I reach the shelter, I sign too many forms and set up the back of the car, opening up the carriers. While I wait for the assistant to bring the dogs out, I inspect the large dent in the side of Jason's car.

I took the blame, but it's safe to say Stacey needs a hell of a lot more practice before she can drive on a normal road. I've been trying to teach her how to drive for weeks now, but no matter what, I end up with whiplash, and she ends up in my lap.

"Mr Mitchell?" A voice pulls my attention to the front door. "Thank you for doing this. We had nowhere for them to go as all of our kennels were full. They've been sitting in reception for the last two days after being abandoned in the middle of nowhere. We have all the essentials in this bag." He hands me said bag, a tote with their shelter logo on it. "The smaller one has an upset stomach from stress, but he should be fine in a few days."

"Right." I place the bag in the car and take the leashes. "You need anything else from me? Did the shelter receive the donation?"

He smiles warmly, his glasses resting on the bridge of his nose, grey hair messy in the wind. "We did, thank you. You're very generous. If you struggle, or need to rehome them, we can give some assistance."

I lift the dogs into the carriers and lock them, slowly closing the trunk. "Thanks. I'll be keeping these little guys for good."

"That's nice to hear. We'll give you a call in a few weeks to see how they're doing."

I nod, shake his hand and head for home.

On the way back, I turn off my radio and tell them about where they're going to live, that I have a sister who'll most likely run away from them and a huge indoor pool for them to swim in. "I also have this girl at home, and she's going to love you both. I reckon I let her name one of you." I look at the smallest one through the mirror. "You can be The Destroyer."

He tilts his head at me, looking all cute and adorable.

By the time I get back to the manor, the sun is fully up, and the house is awake.

Mum squeals when she sees them, Ewan pats their heads and Luciella leans down but cowers when they let out a stream of high-pitched barks at her.

"What kind of dogs are they?" she asks, rising and sitting back down to her breakfast. "They look like Dobermann pups."

"Yeah, they're Dobermen." She raises a brow, and I realise my mistake. Fucking Stacey and her made-up vocabulary. "You know what I mean."

"We need to leave in five. Will I ask one of the staff to look after them?"

I shake my head. "They can go in my room until I'm back."

I take the carriers and bag full of things to my side of the manor, up the spiral stairs to my room.

Stacey could sleep through a riot. She doesn't make a sound or wake when I slip them into the bedroom, set up a puppy pen in silence and quickly run down to the kitchen while Luciella is sorting out her plane bag. We leave sharpish and quickly say our goodbyes at the airport.

For some reason, it takes Stacey two hours to message me in panic, the total opposite of what I expect.

Freckles: OMG, Kade!!! Why are there two dogs in your room??? Can you hurry up? Please? PLEASE?

Freckles: You got two Dobermann pups? They are going to eat me! I'm too young to die!

Next is a picture of her under the bed, capturing the two of them staring in the phone's direction, heads tilted, captioned, This will be the last thing I see before I die. At least they're cute. When I'm gone, you're not allowed to have sex with anyone else. My ghost will get jealous and haunt you.

I laugh and shake my head. Mum nudges my arm and tells me to hurry up and drive. I quickly send a response.

Me: I just dropped Luciella off at the airport. You'll survive another hour until I'm back.

Freckles: Well, when you come back and I'm ripped to shreds, you better fucking miss me.

Me: So dramatic, my little Freckles. They're only pups.

Freckles: Your little Freckles is going to be a lump of flesh by the time you get back to bed. I think I'll actually stay under here until you're home. They look like evil villain dogs who want to dissect me with their extremely sharp teeth.

"She was the one that said she loved large dogs," I mutter to myself.

"Huh?" Mum replies, and I shut off my screen with a snort and pull Jason's car out of the parking spot. Mum is wiping her eyes in the passenger seat while speaking to my dad on the phone. "I can't believe my little girl is finally going to university," she sobs, her voice shaking as she places my dad on speaker. "What am I supposed to do now?"

Dad laughs, the smile evident in his tone. "Sweetheart, you'll see her every month when you visit."

"It's not fair that you get to see her every day." Mum sniffs. "I'm officially jealous."

"Of me being locked up in here? You would hate the early rises and the food. And that's if she chooses to visit me. She hates visitations. Plus, she's two hours from me."

Luciella going away to study shouldn't have our mother this upset, surely? She should be glad that she's getting some peace from her. I sure the fuck am.

It's a week into the new year, and I'm done with the celebrations. The parties weren't too bad, since I got to sneak around with Stacey and steal a kiss from her just as the clocks turned twelve. But then Luciella and Tylar decided it would be a cracking idea to go out clubbing, and I had to pretend not to look at my phone every two seconds while sitting with Base and Dez.

I worked my ass off with Ewan for the last two months to make sure I could get Stacey the perfect Christmas present. We went to Dublin the day after celebrating with my family, and we got drunk in the Temple Bar before I dragged her back to the hotel and learned more about her body.

She cried when she opened the little dancer charm for her bracelet and held my hand while we got matching tattoos – a design I'd worked on for weeks. Our initials intertwined and distorted to make them unrecognisable, with the words so small and vine-like, not even Stacey knows that they say "I choose who I love, and I choose you".

It's a little deep, considering how fresh we are and still not official, but I don't know, it seemed right. She was more than happy to get the ink, and I'd do anything to see a smile on her face.

I'll tell her what it says one day.

It took me a lot to admit to myself – and a lot of convincing from my parents – that I wasn't a raging psycho who wanted to claim her and keep her to myself, but even though I still think there's a possibility, I know how I truly feel about her.

It's an emotion I had no idea I was capable of. Or my own twisted version of it anyway.

I've fallen in love with Stacey Rhodes.

I wanted to ask her to be my girlfriend while we were in Ireland, since my dad said it was the next step for us, but when I'd hyped myself up and tried to push the words past my lips, I froze. My chest had gone tight, I had black dots in my vision, and Stacey said we'd go back to our room and watch movies when she noticed I was losing it.

It worked, because the pain and anxiety were gone, and I had her in my arms for hours until we needed to catch our flight home.

The calmest I've ever felt in my life is when I'm with her. The voices are quiet, my heart slows to a healthy pace and I can sleep.

The panicking and overthinking and obsessive thoughts haven't calmed completely – if anything, they're worse when she's not around. Mainly me going through every scenario of things ending.

It's stupid, but I'm paranoid. I think about her as soon as I wake up, immediately checking my phone, and I'm either ecstatic she's texted or confused when there's no message. When my friends come over or arrange a day of smoking at Base's, I ask Stacey if she has plans, just to make sure there isn't a better option. Most of the time, to my disdain, she says she's busy, and that we'd make plans for when she's either at the studio or staying with Luciella.

So when my twin sister announced she was going to study in the States, I was fucking buzzing that I'd have more of Stacey. But that would make me possessive surely? Wanting her to myself and hating others who have her attention? We were in Edinburgh and a guy opened the door for her while I was at the ATM, and I imagined his body in a morgue and me behind bars.

Dad thinks it's normal. But he would say that, wouldn't he?

My new therapist has been a lot of help, and even got me on better meds to control certain impulses and negative thoughts.

They're always there, regardless, but sometimes I feel like I can actually breathe, and it's when she's with me. I worry that I'll hurt her, or that she'll end up scared of me. I might become someone she doesn't want, a demon in her closet waiting to attack. A guy she fucks when she wants, someone who does everything and anything for her.

Stacey is taking over my life and we've only been at this for a few months.

I want her to be my girlfriend, and maybe then we can stop sneaking around and tell the world that we belong together. Maybe, with the blessing of her family and her seeing it from mine, things will get better.

Not that things are bad. I love being around her, on her and in her. I love hearing her atrocious singing and her laugh, especially when I cause it. I can hear it now as I drive, the little pig snorts when she belly laughs, exaggerating it with a hand slapping whatever is closest to her. I watch her sleep, because I always wake first, her face relaxed and at peace as she dreams about – hopefully – us.

Fuck, I'm in deep. But I want to be deeper. More. I need more of her.

Mum finishes her conversation with my dad and hangs up, giving me a tight smile. "Are you okay?"

The frown I have on my face deepens as she stares at me. "Why wouldn't I be?"

"She was your twin!"

I try not to laugh as her eyes water again. "Jesus, woman. She's not dead."

Ewan leans forward, head poking between the two seats of his son's car. "He's right. And so is Tobias. You'll see her more than you think, *okay? If it'll make you feel better, we can go stay at the lodge in Stranraer for a week."*

She nods. "I'd like that."

Mum pats her eyes with a tissue and turns to me again. "So what's the plan for you?"

I raise a brow. "Drive home?"

For an old woman, her slap to my arm is a tad stingy.

"Are you going to tell Luciella about Stacey?"

"When Stacey wants to, yes," I reply.

Ewan speaks next. "Have you made it official yet?"

I sigh and run my hand down my face. "I tried, but I freaked out. I will though."

"What if you ask her on her birthday? She's nineteen next week, right?"

"Yeah."

She's twenty-three days older than me and won't let me live it down. She keeps saying she feels weird fucking someone younger than her. It always earns her a spank and being tickled into a fit of coughing.

"I'm taking her out on the boat – is that alright?" I ask Ewan. He taught me how to drive a boat years ago, and I have the perfect image in my head of taking Stacey into the loch and asking her then. "On Saturday."

"Sure," Ewan replies. "Ah! Pull into McDonalds."

I do, and we munch our food, setting aside a Big Mac for Stacey. But by the time I get home and get to my room, she's asleep on top of the bed with one of the dogs cuddling into her, the other asleep at the foot of the bed. She's got blankets over her and is cradling the Dobermann pup into her body.

The small one's head pulls up, ears flopping. He hurries over to me and licks my cheek when I pick him up.

I take a picture of Stacey and the pup, putting the meal, my phone, car keys, cigarettes and lighter on the bedside unit before pulling the duvet aside and climbing in with them, keeping the other pup between us. Somehow, I fall asleep, and if I had to give up everything in the world for this, I would.

I'd give it all up for Stacey.

5

STACEY

It's been weeks since I got back from America, and although Barry and his colleagues are everywhere, neither of my brothers notice them. When Kyle drives me to the studio, he doesn't realise the SUV nearby is watching us, and when I attend functions with Nora and her sons, no one sees the suited-up men and women keeping their eyes on me.

We were at a family party in Dunfermline – Nora's sister hitting fifty – and Chris kept his hand low on my back when his mother and brother weren't looking, but I knew Barry could see. When I went to the bathroom, Chris followed and waited outside like a possessive boyfriend, then forced me to take his hand when he wanted a drink from the bar. I knew better than to fight him.

That night, Kyle went to his girlfriend's house, Nora vanished and I was left with Chris. He'd been punishing me ever since I got back from America, so I was at the point of listening to whatever he said. I downed drinks, swallowed pills he forced into my hand and didn't fight back when he beat me. Or when he crawled into my bed hours later and held me until he fell asleep. Fighting makes it worse. It only makes his cock hard and his smile wide.

When he tries to kiss me, I refuse, accepting the punches to parts of my body hidden by clothes. When he tries to touch me, I sink my nails into his wrist, accepting the way he cuts off my air until I pass out.

All I can do is accept the pain.

Barry can't see what happens in the manor. I'm thankful. Imagine the war it would cause if Chris knew about my week with Kade and that he had bodyguards trailing me?

"You're not going to class tonight."

I look up from my book, staring at an angry Chris standing in my doorway. "Why? I have to go. I'm an instructor."

"You're going for a drive with me."

"Are you going to hurt me?" My voice doesn't even shake when I ask.

He shrugs. "Depends. If I need to make you compliant, I have some of those pills left from the weekend."

I roll my eyes and continue reading. "One of these days, I hope whatever you drug me with kills me. Then I'll be free of you."

He rushes forward, grabs my book and launches it out the open window, glaring at me. "I'll still fuck your corpse."

Bile rises in my throat. Nora is at the family lodge and Kyle is out, and if I refuse, Chris will make me.

When I get dressed, he smiles at me as I walk down the stairs. It's strange to think I was at my happiest just over a month ago, riding on a motorbike and laughing and spending time with my ex, just being in the now.

He grabs his car keys from the bowl next to the garage door. But then he presses his hand to my chest to stop me, lifting my chin. "Don't look so depressed, baby. This will be an educational trip."

"I'm not your baby."

"You've been my baby since you walked into this house."

Scoffing, I pull my face away from him. "Yeah. When I was

fourteen, you disgusting bastard. I didn't want you then either."

He snatches my hair and drags me into the garage. "Get in the fucking car."

Barry isn't on shift tonight. It's some other guy who's always on his phone. I was watching him out my window earlier, the car tucked away behind trees, where they always sit while I'm at home. He's older, maybe in his forties, and smokes like a chimney.

When Chris pulls out of the estate, the bodyguard surprisingly realises and trails us, far away and out of sight. However, Chris is acting stranger than usual. His eyes haven't softened the way they do when I give in to his demands, and he's speeding.

He never speeds.

My stepbrother firmly settles his hand on my lap, and I jump and push it off. "Don't touch me."

He tuts. "The more attitude you give me, the worse this drive will get."

I cross my arms and stare forward. He has the radio playing heavy metal music as he strums his fingers on my leg. His other hand grips the steering wheel like he's trying to strangle it. He's angry, and I'm growing nervous.

My phone vibrates in the back pocket of my jeans. I mentally think of everyone it could be to keep myself sane.

Tobias hasn't once replied to me or tried to call me back. His phone is turned off. I found out yesterday that he's been in solitary confinement for weeks. Kade hasn't reached out, but I expected as much. I can't try to contact him in case they have his phone. It could be Tylar calling because Luciella told her I couldn't make the studio tonight.

Either way, my phone stops vibrating, and my heart rate increases as Chris veers left, the streetlights and buildings vanishing as he drives us into a farm road.

Into the darkness where no one can see us.

I glance at the mirror, and I don't see the car following us.

I gulp, my voice low as I ask, "Where are we going?"

"You'll see," he replies.

There's nothing up here but fields and narrow roads for tractors, so where could he be taking me?

"Calm down and sit back."

When I don't, he shoves his hand against my chest and pushes me against the seat.

"I've asked this before, but I think I'm done with you refusing to answer. Why did you keep blocking me when you were in America? Who were you with?"

I frown. "I told you. My friend and her family."

He slows but keeps driving. "Who else?"

I can already tell by his voice that he knows, and if I don't get out of this car, I'm done for. "Chris—"

"Fucking tell me!"

My bones rattle all over my body, and I stare at him, counting to three in my head.

It's dark out, but I quickly unclip my belt and grab the handle, fully intending to jump out and run through the fields to get away from him. But he grabs me by the hair and pulls me back before the door can open.

"Let's try this again."

He forcefully grabs my hand and doesn't let it go as he drives. It's painful – he's crushing my middle and forefinger together, tightening his hold.

"Seat belt."

My shaky free hand clips it in, my jaw sore from how hard I'm gritting my teeth.

"I'll ask the easiest question. Because you're pissing me off. Why did you keep blocking me?"

I shake my head, my heart rate picking up its pace. "You're delusion—"

My words cut off as he twists my fingers, and my teeth dig into my lip to hold back a scream. That's what he wants. He wants me to feel pain and to be loud about it. It gets him off when I make a sound of distress.

"Why?" he asks again.

"Fuck. You."

He lets go of my fingers, and the side of my head smacks into the window. Burning hot pain shoots through my skull, ringing in my ears.

I screw my eyes shut as he smashes my head into the window again. "S-Stop."

"I already know why. I'm giving you the chance to confess before I bleed it out of you. Start from the hotel in Edinburgh, the private jet, then everything that happened in America."

My eyes ping open, and my lungs seize. Of course he knows. He's a cyber-freak who would've been tracing my steps from the moment I left the house. I'm shocked he didn't fly to America and rip me in half then burn Kade alive.

I stay silent, my skull throbbing, a lump already swelling at the side of my head.

We're driving deep into the back roads now when he swerves into a passing place and throws open his door. I gasp and unclip my belt again, trying to climb away when he opens the passenger door and yanks at my feet. He's a lot taller and stronger than me – I don't stand a chance. My body flies right out of the car, and I land hard on my back.

Winded, I cough, my vision already blurring; I can barely see the moon given how crowded the trees are above me. It's nearly pitch-black here, silent except Chris pacing in front of me, tugging at his hair and whispering to himself that I need to be punished, then telling himself not to hurt me – that he needs to get in the car and drive away.

I try to turn onto my front, to attempt to crawl to the car when he snatches my hair and slams me into the gravel. He straddles my hips, his eyes wild like he's possessed, face red with rage.

He's going to kill me, and no one will ever know.

Part of me hopes he does. The only reason I need to survive is to make sure Kade gets help. And if that's the only reason, maybe I'm already dead.

"Chris," I choke as he grips my throat. "Pl-Please."

"You blocked me while you were with him. *Him.* Of all fucking people, you go back to Kade Mitchell?"

My face whips to the side as he slaps me, my cheek stinging.

"He is beneath me. He'll never be able to be what you need him to be. I can. I fucking *can.*"

"You..." I can't breathe – there's too much pressure on my neck and face, and my eyes feel like they're bulging. I smack his arms, desperate for air. He releases me enough that I can suck in oxygen, coughing as I try to speak. "You were threatening m-me. I… had to block you."

"So you went to him? If you were a good girl, then I wouldn't need to threaten you. I told you to behave and to keep in contact – you didn't. Did you sleep with him to piss me off? Let him fuck you behind a goddamn nightclub like the stupid fucking whore you are?"

"You need to stop this," I sob, trying to push him off me, kicking my legs desperately and failing. "Please."

He lets go of my throat and presses his hands to the ground beside my face. "Why didn't you tell me someone was trying to hurt you? I could have protected you if you fucking told me!" He's yelling in my face, spit falling from his mouth and onto my cheek. He grabs my chin to make me look at him. "They shot at you, and you told me nothing!"

My face snaps to the side again, a sting on my other cheek.

"It took me weeks to retrace your steps. How can I ever trust you if you keep shit like that from me?"

I clench my teeth as I stare at the trees, the way the leaves blow in the light wind, the little rocks around me. I marvel at how fresh the air is, how the stars glint so brightly.

Another blow, and I taste blood from the fist he smashed into my face.

I welcome each painful smack as he cries, each agonising punch as I lie unmoving, trying to find my safe place in my mind each time he grabs my hair and slams my head into the concrete.

"I was going to wait to do this…" He holds me by the throat, reaching into his pocket with his other hand and pulling out a clear bag filled with little white pills.

My eyes widen, but I'm in no position to stop him forcing who knows how many into my mouth, covering my mouth and pinching my nose until I swallow them all – dry, catching in my throat, making me gag, even though I gulp down blood along with them.

"Give it ten, maybe fifteen, minutes, and I'll be able to do whatever I want to you, and you'd never know."

The mental block I fall into always keeps me grounded. I'll think of memories that make me happy. They'll hold me there just long enough to make me numb to the pain I'm in – and the revulsion.

But right now, I can't find my mental block, and my mouth is filling with blood from him punching me. My hands are shaking at my sides, my body tense.

Until I can't stay still anymore.

It takes everything in me, and I grit my teeth as I use force. My knee hikes quickly, and it smashes between his legs, hard enough to cause a rush of air and a groan to fall from his lips. "Fuck!"

I see the fist coming, but I'm not fast enough to dodge it – he drives it into my jaw, snapping my head back so it hits the concrete.

No one is coming. My head falls to the side and I'm dizzy, silently begging the SUV to appear, or Kade's black Audi, or anyone to drive up the road and stop this as Chris presses his forehead to my temple, spittle dripping from his mouth. "Why are you making me do this?" he asks, his own tears hitting my face. "I don't want to hurt you. I don't want... I don't want to hurt you."

Then stop, I try to say, but I can't form words.

If I can get him off me, I can make myself sick before the drugs kick in.

Something shifts to my right, and Chris is thrown off me as the bodyguard assigned to me tackles him. I lie completely still, not sure if the pain wracking my body is from how tense I am or from Chris hitting me. I feel tired. Exhausted. But if I close my eyes, I won't know if the bodyguard will save me.

The sky is so dark. So peaceful compared to what's going on beside me.

I somehow manage to turn my head.

Him and Chris are fighting. Punching each other. There are gunshots that have birds fluttering from the trees – yet I don't flinch from the bangs echoing in the night sky.

I hear the gun dropping, being tossed aside as Chris kicks the man in the chest, knocking him on his back right beside me. My stepbrother drives his fist into the man's face with so much force, his nose bursts open, gushing with blood, and as the blows continue to rain down, it sounds like he's choking. His jaw is distorted, and some of the blood hits my face, but I don't move.

He doesn't fight back. He's still – like me.

Can he see how peaceful the night sky is?

Chris is covered in blood, wiping his hand down his face. "Shit." Then he looks at me, his eyes wild. Like something chimes in his head, he glances between the two of us then leans down to me. "I'll call an ambulance to save him, but I have conditions."

My lips barely move as I mouth, *What?*

"You stay away from Kade Mitchell. You apologise to me for being a brat. And when I tell you to kiss me, you kiss me."

Tears slide down my cheek, but I don't speak.

"He's one of the guys ordered to keep an eye on you, right? You think I didn't fucking know? I know everything about you, Stacey. *Everything.*" He lifts a brick. "If you don't agree to my conditions, I'll kill him right fucking now."

More tears slide down my cheeks as I stare at the man struggling to breathe, soaking the concrete with blood. He probably has a family at home waiting on him. A wife and children. Brothers and sisters. Mother and father.

People who will miss him.

Chris lifts the brick, and I try to scream through my weakness. "Okay," I rush out on a croaky breath, my voice straining. "Okay, okay, okay."

His eyes narrow on me. "Prove it."

My bottom lip quivers, and I will my body to work. My face is tingling, and I don't know if it's from the drugs or from him hitting me.

He tosses aside the brick and climbs on top of me, and every nerve in my body shrivels at his nearness, my heart racing with the immense fear injected into my veins.

Chris doesn't hold back as he presses his lips to mine, holding his mouth there with a painful grip of my jaw, even as I don't respond. He takes my bottom lip between his teeth, and I wince as he bites down hard. "Kiss me back."

When I still don't respond, sick rising in my throat, he pries my jaws apart and shoves his tongue into my mouth.

Forever forcing. It's what he's been doing to me since I was young. Since I was a child. My last straw snaps, and I find the courage to bite down on his tongue, hard enough to draw blood, but all it does is make him twitch against my thigh, a chuckle leaving his throat.

He tilts my face so he can deepen the kiss, and I can feel him growing even harder as he presses his body to mine. It's revolting, and I refuse to reciprocate. I stay still, my body trembling, my eyes on the sky as he keeps trying to get some sort of reaction from me.

Chris pulls away, scowling at me. "Fine. Have it your way."

The scream I let out is for nothing as he grabs the brick and crushes it into the bodyguard's face. The shock kickstarts my body to work, and I cover my mouth as Chris keeps going. Smashing the head into a pile of pulped flesh.

Again.

Again.

And again.

Each whack, each land of the brick, turns the guard's face into nothing – unrecognisable.

I try to crawl backwards towards the car while Chris is busy mincing this guy's face, but my body is still in shock as I strain to stand.

He gets up, drops the bloody brick and looks at me. "You made me kill him."

I shake my head. "No."

He snatches my throat, and my eyes bulge with how hard he's gripping me.

"I'm going to kill them all. I'll start with Kade. I'll tie him down and make him watch me fucking you. I won't wear a condom and I'll fill you with *my* kid. I'll make him listen to your moans while my name falls from your lips. I'll put him on the brink of death, and the last thing he'll see is you coming all over my cock."

Rage fills me, and I'm not sure where the energy comes from, or the bravery, but I use every bit of strength to throw my fist against his nose with a crack, catching him off guard. He reels back as I hit him again, grabbing his bleeding nose, so I lean up to sink my teeth into his cheek. He doesn't catch my knee as I smash it between his legs again.

He yells and pushes me as he drops to the ground, and I quickly run to the car, slamming the door and locking it just before he can grab the handle.

A bloody palm slaps on the window as I turn the engine on, my hands uncontrollably shaking and sore. Thank God he left the keys in the ignition.

I grip the steering wheel, clench my teeth to hold in how sore my body is, my head aching, and press on the accelerator. I fully intend to run him over when he moves to stand in front of the bumper, but he dives out the way. Seeing his face, the shock and fear and terror, is worth it.

It's an expression I've never seen on him before.

If I want Kade to fight his way out of the deep hole he's trapped in, then that's what I have to do too. I've never stuck up for myself this way, and I don't intend to stop. I'm done with his abuse. I'm done being fucking silent and letting him treat me like his personal punchbag.

I shove the gearstick into reverse, the car screeching as it rapidly backs up, and Chris dodges me again then tries to grab the door handle. The wheels skid on the ground, and I quickly put it in first before slamming down on the accelerator again.

The edge of the bumper clips his hip and knocks him on the ground, and I speed away as paranoia overwhelms me that he'll get the better of me. I pass the SUV tucked away in a passing place, and my heart twists in my chest as I think about what happened to its driver.

I knew Chris was insane, but I didn't know he was a killer.

If I'd kissed him back, would the bodyguard still be alive? Would he have called an ambulance? I feel responsible, and it's gnawing at my conscience.

I search for my phone and swear to myself. It must've fallen out of my back pocket when he tossed me on the ground. Instead of trying to call Kyle or Nora or one of my friends for help, I do the next best thing without a phone.

There's a dead body, marks all over me and more than enough evidence to get Chris locked up for a long time.

I don't stop the car until I reach the police station.

6

STACEY

AGE FOURTEEN

"Are you sure you want to join this dance class, Stacey?"

I look up at the building from the passenger seat of my dad's car. "Yeah. Mum would've wanted me to keep dancing. Can we go inside and ask if there's space?"

Dad huffs and pushes his glasses up the bridge of his nose. "Nora is against this. She'll be mad if I let you join. She wants you to start ballet instead."

My smile drops. "I don't care what Nora wants. She isn't my mother. Why are you letting her control what I do?"

Another huff, and he turns off the engine, unclipping his seat belt. Slowly, he turns his body to face me. "Nora isn't trying to be your mother.

No one can ever replace Marie. Please be patient with her and her sons. They're trying with you. Nora even wants to throw you a birthday party."

"I don't want a party. I don't even have any friends here!" Then I grimace. "And I don't like Christopher. He's weird with me."

Weird is an understatement. The guy is sick.

"He's not. I can see how much he adores you already. You should be happy you have two big brothers to look after you."

I fidget my hands, the words on the tip of my tongue that Christopher doesn't treat me like a sister. It's been months since we moved in, and he keeps sneaking into my room and watching me. He makes me keep my bathroom door unlocked, and he always puts his hand on my thigh while we eat dinner. I tried to remove his palm from my skin earlier tonight, but he twisted my fingers until they hurt.

He's four years older than me. Eighteen and grown up. He won't leave me alone, even though he has a really pretty girlfriend. I can hear them... doing stuff. And then he forces me to watch videos of them the next day. When I close my eyes, he threatens me to watch so I'll apparently know what to expect when he inevitably does the same things to me.

He just wants to wait until I'm old enough. But that doesn't stop him ordering me to touch myself the way his girlfriend does. I always refuse, not only because I have no idea how to but also because he makes me uncomfortable, and then he hits me, usually where no one can see.

A freezing shiver crawls up my spine.

"Can you move me to another bedroom?" I ask instead. "Maybe near yours?"

"Why?" Dad tilts his head. "We've just finished decorating your room."

Because it's right beside his. *And we're the only ones on the top floor. "It's too big. I prefer smaller spaces."*

"No. You're being ridiculous now, Stacey. We can't move into Nora's home and try to change things."

"But..." I chew my lip and try not to let my voice shake. "I think Christopher is going to hurt me." He always does, but I mean really *hurt me.*

For a second, I think Dad might laugh, but instead he sighs and wipes a hand down his face, removing his glasses in the process. "And why do you think that?"

"He—" I gulp, averting my eyes. "He touches me a lot. And... And he

pushed his way into the shower yesterday while I was washing my hair. When I try to get dressed, he tells me to do it slowly and records me. He's—"

I flinch as Dad slams his hand against the steering wheel. "That's enough! Why are you saying this?"

I close my eyes, and a tear slides down my cheek. I've never feared my father before, and he's never made me flinch. Yet now, I'm conscious of his hand, as if he's going to do the same things as Christopher.

"I understand you're having a hard time getting used to being in a new family, but you will not *mess this up with your lies. Christopher is a lovely boy, and he's just as excited as Kyle to have a little sister. You can't make stuff like that up. How dare you? Your mother would be turning in her grave with shame if she knew the way you were acting."*

I sink my nails into my palms.

"Christopher snuck into my bed at the weekend," I continue, needing to tell him and hoping he'll save me from the monster. "When I told him to get out, he put his hand over my mouth and pressed his... thing against me."

Embarrassment floods me that I'm even saying this to my dad, but he's the only one who can protect me. If he knows his daughter is being treated in such a way, he'll leave and never make me go back there. Mum would have already taken a knife to Christopher's throat.

"He's—"

"Stop," he snaps. "Stop lying to get attention. What is going on in that warped head? I'll book you in with CAMHS and they can deal with you."

"I don't need to speak to someone about my mental health. I need you to get me away from that house! Please, Dad," I cry, my vision blurring. I try to grab his hand, but he dodges me like I'm a disease. "Please believe me. I'm so scared of him. Look – I have bruises on my back!"

He snatches my wrist when I try to pull my top up at the back to show him. "Stop it!"

Tears soak my cheeks now, the collar of my top drenched as my body shakes. "I promise I'm not lying. I'm not making this up. He told me he'd take my virginity one day and that I'm already his. He has pictures of me on his phone! Please. Please believe me!"

"You disgust me," he sneers. "We didn't raise you this way. Moving to Scotland is already changing you."

I sniffle, my heart racing in my chest. "Please, just look at his phone. Please. You need to believe me! If you don't help me, I'll run away."

"Get out of the damn car," he demands, throwing his door open and muttering under his breath, "Fucking teenage girls and their hormones."

I exit the car and rush to the pavement, trying to catch up to him marching towards the dance studio. "Please believe me, Dad. Check his phone. I'll even try to record him to show you. He stands at the foot of my bed and touches himself nearly every night. Please!"

He stops abruptly and turns, nearly causing me to smack into him. He glares at me. "One more word and I mean it. Christopher is a good kid. He's in a relationship and has been since he was fifteen. He already has a job offer from a top-end cybersecurity company even though he isn't out of uni. You throwing around accusations like that will only ruin his future. You do that, and I will never forgive you. Neither will my wife. Do you understand?"

I hate the way he says "wife". Mum was his wife.

"But I want you to protect me and—"

"Cut the attention-seeking. Do you understand?"

I lower my head and nod once as a truck pulls up beside us. "Okay."

"Good. Now," he says, plastering a smile on his face, "let's get you back into dancing to clear that head of yours. No more lies. And no more trying to ruin someone's credibility because you can't handle not being the centre of attention by being the only child. You. Will. Stop."

If my dad doesn't believe me, then no one will. I'm trapped. I'm trapped with a brother who wants to hurt me.

"Hold the door!" a girl's voice calls from behind us, and I turn around to see her running from a car. She quickly spins and waves. "Thanks for dropping me off, Jason! Sorry I spilled ketchup on your seat!"

The guy, who looks to be in his mid-twenties, waves back. "It's fine. I'll pick you up at nine, sis."

"Okay. Love you! Bye, Kade!"

I hear a muttered, "Fuck off."

The driver reverses out of the space. It's then I see a boy in the passenger seat. He's wearing a hoodie and looks about my age, his dark hair scooped back in a cap.

When he glances up and says something to the driver, I frown at him – he's lighting a cigarette, which the older one grabs and tosses out the window.

The girl with long blonde hair barrels towards us, asking my dad to keep the door open again. "Hi," she says when she stops beside me, a little taller than I am. "Are you here for the aerial hoop class?"

She's very pretty. She looks like Christopher's girlfriend but a lot younger. I think she might be American, but she also sounds a little Scottish.

And I realise I'm staring.

"Oh, no," I reply, wiping under my eyes and hoping I don't look like a disaster. "Just dancing."

She scrunches her nose. "You have good shoulders. I bet you'd be good at hoop. Why don't you try it? Dance class doesn't start for another hour. I'll show you around. My name is Luciella, but you can call me Lu."

I glance at my dad. Aerial sports aren't technically dancing, and I've never done them before. I did trampolining for a year before my mum got sick and I had to stop. Would he allow me? There's a picture on the door of a stick person on a pole, and another one of a dancer. I didn't tell him about that part of the studio when Kyle and I found it on Google.

"Can I?" I ask Dad. "It's kind of the same as dancing." I think. "I can do two classes?"

He fakes a grin at the girl instead of me. "Sure. She can fill in all the paperwork, and I'll pick her up in two hours."

And then he places his hand on my shoulder and firmly squeezes. It makes me flinch and stiffen my shoulders. Christopher does the same thing to me. And then one word comes out, the same one my insane stepbrother says to me whenever I leave the house.

"Behave."

7

STACEY

The glass door slides open, and I push myself into the building of the town's police station, somehow managing to move my feet. My entire body is shaking uncontrollably, exactly how my heart is beating in my chest. The adrenaline is the only thing keeping me going. I feel so close to passing out, I might fall to the ground at any moment.

The reception is empty.

I lean over the desk to see the computer on and clipboards scattered around. There's a mobile, a packet of cigarettes and a magazine opened on a celeb gossip page.

I nervously tap the counter and wait, my hands jittering. I look down at my palms – at the blood dried on them.

"Can I help you?"

I spin around to see a young officer. "Oh... I... I need to re-

report a crime. I was attacked."

Are my words slurring? I have no idea. I tried to make myself sick on the way here, but I nearly crashed in the process.

The place is so bright, I need to screw my eyes a little to see.

I'm covered in blood, and my hair is a mess, my face swollen. He doesn't flinch at my appearance. I'm certain my lip is split open, but it's too numb to know.

He glances down at the paperwork he's holding, scans the words then looks up at me again as if he's inspecting a crazy person.

Maybe he is. Did all that just actually happen?

The guy nods and gestures to a door. "Follow me."

I hover there for a second, swaying, looking around to see if anyone else is here before I follow. We walk down a corridor, my fingers sliding on the wall as we turn left and enter an office. He tosses down his papers and sits behind his desk.

"Okay," he starts, nodding towards the chair opposite him. I drop into it, gripping the armrests. "Are you feeling well?"

I stare at him – I think I nod.

"You want to report a crime. Tell me what happened."

I gulp, sitting on my hands. The last person I told about Chris was Tobias, and he's been MIA. My dad is dead. And no one else but his deluded friends know how Chris treats me. I glance at his badge – Officer Bennett – then let out a breath.

"My stepbrother attacked me, then... then he killed someone." Even I know my words are erratically spoken.

He's unfazed as he writes the details on a notepad, nodding. "Okay. Tell me from the start. Do you know your attacker?"

I frown – I just told him he was my stepbrother. Or did I not say that?

Regardless of his terrible attention to detail, I let the words fall from my lips, unable to stop the tears or the spittle dripping from my mouth. I tell him everything, like I've found some new courage to speak about it – from when Chris started abusing me at aged fourteen to tonight. I show him my hands, my busted knuckles from punching Chris, gesturing to my face when I tell him about him beating me, then, somehow, I manage another breath.

"Where is the body?" is all he asks. Maybe I imagined telling him everything else.

"The farm road, near Inverkip. You turn left at the park and it's about twenty minutes north." The words sound forced, as if I have to physically push each one out.

"And you're positive he's deceased?"

I nod once. "His entire head was bashed in, and there was brain matter on the ground." Was there? Yes, because I didn't kiss my brother back. "I should have kissed him."

"Excuse me?"

For some reason, I don't remember if I reply. I look at him, and he chews on his lip.

He grimaces as he reads back through his notes then makes some more. "I'll send over someone to have a look."

The officer vanishes from the room to make some calls, and I close my eyes and drop my head to the table. I feel fuzzy, and I come to the horrible realisation that the drugs Chris forced into me are fully in effect, the adrenaline no longer holding them at bay. I'm floating – or rolling down a hill. I'm not sure.

When he returns, I lift my head lazily, wincing from the bright lights again.

"Well, from the location you gave, there's nothing. I had a patrol check everywhere nearby, and nothing."

Did I fall asleep? How did they do that so fast?

"He m-must've moved... moved the b-b-body. Do you h-h-have a nurse or first aider on siiiiite?" I ask, a little perplexed he hasn't offered me any medical help. My face is swollen, and I'm covered in blood. I could use a painkiller at least. My head aches, and my lids are droopy as hell. I think my voice is cracking too.

He narrows his eyes at me. "Miss Rhodes, have you taken any drugs tonight?"

I stare at him, shaking my head. Or I think I do. I can barely feel anything other than the swelling on my face and how hard my heart is beating.

"I'll have a nurse come over to confirm – you look out of it." He radios to someone, and I can't quite catch what's being said. Something about false reporting and drugs and to contact someone.

My eyes close again, my head drops on the table and I fall into a deep, peaceful sleep.

"I'm sorry about all of this," a voice says. "My sister hasn't been in a good place mentally for a while. She's been off the rails ever since her father died. We're really worried about her."

"That's understandable. Do you know where she got the drugs?"

"I'll find whoever the bastard was. I'll be sure to let you know."

"Thanks, Chris," Officer Bennett says. "I won't book her, since you're my sister's ex and all, but you need to get her help. Maybe a therapist and some rehab. I shouldn't be releasing her in the state she's in."

"Thanks, man. I'll make sure the right professional sees her," Chris says, his voice clearer now. "The bathroom is covered in glass and fake blood. I think she punched the wall until her knuckles bled. My mother's cleaning up the mess now, so we'll get her home and into bed. She'll need the sleep."

"Of course. I'll check in with you in a week or so to see how she's doing. Give Nora my best."

A door closes, and I slowly open my eyes just as Chris leans over and clips my seat belt in, his overwhelming aftershave filling my nostrils. "N-N-No."

"Shut the fuck up," he whisper-hisses, stepping back and slamming the door.

He's still talking with the officer – my body too weak to unclip my belt and run, to slam my palm against the window and scream for help.

My heart sinks when he gives Officer Bennett a sort of bro hug, slaps his back and winks at him, before walking around the front of the car and getting in.

The body was gone. There was no blood. The SUV wasn't there.

Did it really happen?

"W-What did you… you do?"

Chris reverses out the space and out of the station's car park, pulling onto the road. "Officer Miles Bennett is Ashleigh's brother." Ashleigh – his ex. "As soon as you gave him my name, he knew it was all nonsense. He knows how innocent and safe I am, so he contacted me. You're mentally deranged and in need of psychiatric help, by the way. He's put forward a recommendation that I keep you close and ensure you don't get yourself into any trouble, especially falsely reporting crimes."

"But you k-killed him."

"Killed who?" he asks. The smirk he pulls confirms it was real – he did kill that man. "No body, no crime. And another thing..." he trails off, chuckling, before erupting into a belly laugh.

I watch him as he tries to stop laughing. He's a lunatic.

"Another thing?"

"I'll give you a second chance. I won't harm that fucking ex of yours – but you need to adhere to my rules. Got it?"

"W-Why?"

"You pissed me off. You already know what happens when you piss me off." He grabs my chin, forcing me to look at him while he takes his eyes off the road to scowl at me. "You'll kiss me when I demand you kiss me. And eventually, I'm going to fuck you, and you'll enjoy it. I won't wear protection. I'll stuff you with every drop of my cum until you're carrying my child. Then you'll be mine forever – shackled to my fucking side."

He releases my chin, and I stare forward, tears tracking my cheeks.

He drives us home. Parks in the garage and turns off the engine. We sit in a silence that slowly kills me inside – it's deafening.

"What do I need to do?" he asks finally.

I stare at him, giving him a look of groggy confusion.

Sighing, he wipes a hand down his face. "I've tried everything possible to make you feel the same way I feel about you. Nothing, not even forcing you to care about me, works. What do I need to do?"

All I can do is shake my head. He doesn't care about me – he wants to own me. He basically already does. The fear he triggers in me when he's around, the way I flinch when he lifts his hand, or how my body tenses at the feel of his touch on my skin are examples of his sickening ownership over me.

He's already won. He's taken everything I ever had and crushed it. What more does he want?

"If I kill him, would that make you hate me more?"

I nod – the image of the guard with his face bashed in is replaced by Kade lying lifeless. Bile rises in my throat.

Chris blows out a breath. "Then if I let him live, if I leave him be and treat you right, will you hate me less?"

If I say no, then I don't know how far Chris will take this. He might lose his shit and hunt down Kade.

Instead of giving him a reply, I drop my gaze to my lap and dig my nails into my palms, trying to take the attention away from how useless and powerless I feel.

"So you're aware..." I take a deep breath, forcing my words out even though I'd rather go to sleep and never wake up. "So you're aware you don't t-treat me right?"

"I know I can be a bit hard on you."

A bit? *A bit?*

"You'll learn to love me back, Stacey," Chris says, almost sounding sad. "Mum and our dear older brother will understand."

I try to shake my head, still drowsy from him drugging me. "I'll n-never love you."

Chris grits his teeth and snatches my hand painfully. "Unbuckle my belt," he orders.

I try to pull my hand away, but he's too strong. I shouldn't have said that. Now he's mad.

"Do it – or else."

Closing my eyes, I turn my head away from him as he takes his own belt off then unzips his jeans. My chest tightens with disgust as something warm and hard hits my hand, and he manipulates my fingers around it with his own.

"Imagine I'm him," he breathes. "If you need to, pretend I'm him."

He's moving his own hand on himself but with my fingers trapped beneath, and I feel bile rising in my throat as he starts to let out soft whimpers, telling me sickeningly how he's imagined me doing this since I was fourteen.

Sick, perverted asshole.

Every time I try to pull away, it makes him swear under his breath and tighten his hold on my fingers while he thrusts upwards. I flinch as he grips my thigh with his free hand, digging his blunt nails into my leg as he finds his horrible release, messing his steering wheel.

He keeps my hand there, and I try to ignore the warm liquid dripping onto my skin.

"This is only the start, Stacey," he tells me, letting go of his cock to grab my chin with his cum-covered fingers. "Open your mouth."

I refuse, but he forces his fingers past my lips anyway, sending a shock of pain through my system as he rips my burst lip further, filling my mouth with his horrid taste.

He pulls away just before I vomit all over his car.

8

STACEY

The following two weeks are a nightmare.

I don't leave the manor to see my friends or attend the studio. I don't even step onto the grounds because Nora has therapists coming in and out, my phone confiscated, and Chris refuses to leave my side. Everyone thinks he's being a sweet, caring big brother; he even told Kyle he'd take time off work, so he doesn't need to.

My body is healing. The swelling on my face is gone, my lips are no longer cracked and split, and the bruises that are visible are barely there. He hasn't beat me further, but something far worse has replaced his punches and slaps. Something that has me contemplating death.

His touch. His pleads for me to love him back. Forced kisses and holding me while he falls asleep in my bed. Every. Single. Night.

Despite physically being okay, I'm contemplating not being here anymore.

I've thought about dying once.

Once.

I stood at a bridge, wondering if I'd die on the way down to the cold water below. It's usually a lie when they say someone dies on the way down. They had a heart attack, so they didn't feel pain – it's more of a comfort to the loved ones than anything else. But that's not always the case. When someone jumps, they hit the water with such a force that it's just like hitting solid ground. They break their bones, shatter their skull, turn the water red with their blood, and if they're unlucky enough, they'll survive just long enough to feel it all.

That could've been me. But someone talked me down.

I don't think anyone could talk me down now. I wish I'd leaped off when I had the chance, but knowing my luck, Chris would follow me to hell itself and still force me to touch him.

My bedroom door opens, and Chris walks in with a tray of food, setting it down on my bedside table. "Eat up. You're going back to class tonight and then we're going out."

"You said I wasn't going to go back," I say – monotone. "You even made me tell my friends I was going away for a month before giving your mother my phone."

"She's *our* mother. And I couldn't be fucked with them trying to find you. You're mine – no one else should be vying for your attention."

I roll my eyes, which earns me a scowl.

"Don't start your childish bullshit. Eat, get dressed and I'll drop you off. The hour of class is the only courtesy I'll grant you. Tell your friends you were at the lodge."

Chris walks to my wardrobe and starts tossing clothes out before landing on something that has him pausing. "This one. Wear this dress."

It's short and red and revealing. "What kind of party are we going to?"

"It's a little fancy, an adult entertainment-type place. But I want you in this. I want easy access."

My stomach curdles. “You said you wouldn’t touch me there without my consent.”

It’s the only thing he’s giving me control of. I have no say when it comes to him finding his release using my hand. He’s taken a liking to repeating what happened in the car, which usually results in me vomiting or slapping him across the face.

He told me to get on my knees last night, and the only reason he didn’t succeed in shoving me to the ground was that one of his friends called about a party – I assume the one we’re going to tonight.

“I’ll be drunk. I’ll probably forget about that little rule when I see you in this.”

He hangs the dress up next to my vanity table then pulls off his shirt and tosses it aside. He ruffles his blonde hair and pushes it back, gesturing to my bathroom door. “I’m going to shower. Come with me.”

My lips flatten. “No.”

He sighs and unbuttons his trousers, siding them down his legs and kicking them off. I look away as he removes his boxers, and I stare at the fork on the plate of food he brought me and contemplate sticking it in his neck.

Knowing him, he’d survive and make my life even more hell.

An hour later, he takes me to the studio, but I’m already late for class. He issues his usual command to behave and says he’ll pick me up while tucking a lock of hair behind my ear. I knock his hand away and give him a stern look. “Don’t touch me.”

He smiles. “Watch your tone. See you soon, baby.”

Everything within me recoils when he calls me that, and I snatch my bag and slam the car door with more force than necessary. I don’t look to the right in case I draw any attention to him, but Barry is leaning against a wall across the street, talking on the phone.

Chris won’t drive away until I’m inside, so there’s no point waiting around to try explaining anything to Barry. What would I even tell him? That his colleague fell and smashed his face into a brick and disfigured himself – that he's dead?

Luciella isn't in tonight – she's doing a placement in the labs at the Royal Infirmary, but Tylar screams and claps when she sees me. "Thank God! You've not answered one single text. I thought something bad had happened!"

I fake a laugh. "I told you; I was at the lodge and had no signal. I left my phone there." I fake another laugh. "I'll get it back soon." Probably a lie.

She hugs me anyway and tells me about the past few weeks. Her and Dez are officially together, and she even posted about it online. He's become attached to her hip, and they're talking about going travelling together. Backpacking, to be exact.

She sounds so happy, and she's smiling so hard, it's infectious enough to make me smile. I haven't in a while, and I love that I got an hour to see my friend and dance.

"What about you and Kade?"

"What do you mean?"

She smirks, nudging my shoulder. "You know what I mean. You left the airport to see him, and you two have been close again. Dez told me what he knows, but you know you can tell me, don't you? I'll help you tell Luciella, if that's the problem. You two are good for each other."

I avert my gaze in an attempt to tamp down my annoyance. Not with her but the situation. I miss him. I miss him, and I'm worried about him.

"We're too busy and too different."

She rolls her eyes, laughing. "When you're ready to really talk to me about your hot, American fling with your bestie's twin brother" – she winks – "I'm all ears."

I shove her arm, somehow smiling. "Shut up and teach the class."

We're doing pole class tonight. My students are doing a photoshoot soon and want to perfect their poses. I spot them, catching ones who fall, then direct them to point their toes, to arch their backs and to stop looking like they're taking a painful shit.

By the end of the hour, I feel myself deflate at the thought of having to leave. I can't even text Chris and beg for more time. That's how low I've sunk – I'd actually beg my stepbrother and be thankful if he said yes.

Not that he would.

"What are your plans tonight? Do you want to lie in bed and watch movies and eat loads of pizza? Gossip? Sleep until ungodly hours?"

Tylar looks at me hopefully, grinning as if I'm going to say yes like I always do. I'm a sucker for movie night with my friends, but my shoulders drop as I shake my head. "Sorry. I need to go home. I'll hopefully be at class tomorrow night though, so I'll see you then?"

Her smile drops. "Oh, okay. Are you still helping out with Festival of Fright Night? A lot of the students were looking for you to help make up routines, and I could use the extra hands on production."

I bite my lip. I want so badly to say yes, to nod, to scream and say, "Of course!"

"I'll let you know?"

"Are you okay?" she asks, giving me a warm smile. "Really, are you okay?"

No. I'm slowly dying inside, and I think my soul is shrinking into a black box that's locked away in a deep closet, and only Christopher has the key.

"Yeah. I'm just tired."

"Well, Dez is outside. I'll see you tomorrow maybe?"

I nod, and she smiles and kisses my cheek. "I missed you."

"I missed you too," I say, my voice cracking.

As soon as I walk out of the studio doors, a firm hand snatches at my arm and yanks me into the alleyway beside the studio entrance. "What the fuck happened to Emmerson?"

I blink up at the man, realising who it is. "No. No, Barry. You need to go. *Now.*"

Barry frowns. "What? Why?"

"Please go." *He'll kill you too, and you have a baby on the way.* "Please."

"Tell me what happened to Emmerson first."

I move past him, and he catches my arm again. "*Stacey*."

"If he sees you—"

"Problem here?"

My heart sinks into the ground at the sound of Christopher's voice.

"Want to tell me why you're manhandling my girlfriend?"

Barry looks between the two of us, his brow furrowing. "Girlfriend…"

I gulp, averting my eyes to the ground as Chris grips my hip and pulls me to him.

"Yes. Girlfriend. I'll ask again. Is there a problem?"

Barry steps back, eyeing Chris. But when he sees my wide eyes, he shoves his hands into his pockets. "Not at all. My little sister goes to this studio, and I was asking Stacey here where she was."

"Go ask someone else." His voice drips with the threat, and I cringe inwardly.

Barry stares at Chris, a smile playing on his mouth. "I didn't catch your name?"

"The only thing you'll be catching is my fist across your face if you don't fuck off away from my girl."

The air around us seems to vanish, and I try to tell Barry silently to back off, that this isn't a fight he needs – nor one he can win.

He retreats a few steps before turning his back, walking across the street and down a side street.

As soon as he's out of view, Chris shakes his head and glares at me. "Who was he?"

I shrug. "His sister must be in the—"

"You're about to lie to me again. He works with those bodyguards of Kade's, doesn't he?"

I stay silent – he already knows.

Chris drives me home, and I can tell he's irritated with me. Usually, he'd grab my hand or grip my thigh, but he keeps both hands firmly on the steering wheel, driving faster and rougher than usual.

He doesn't even smile at me when I walk down the stairs with the dress on.

Not that I want a smile – but I know my night is most likely about to become one of the worst of my life.

Chris orders me to stand by the door then lifts his phone to take a picture of me. I raise a brow, and he smirks through his annoyance. "You look pretty. It's a shame you're going to resemble a fucked whore by the end of the night."

I pause, wide eyes on his. "What does that mean?"

"It means it's time for your punishment. Did you think I was going to let you off with everything? My friends have been waiting for years to have a shot of you again."

My breathing suddenly grows heavy, and my eyes sting. "For someone who doesn't like me being with others, you don't mind sharing me. You contradict yourself."

"Use that tone with me again and I'll bend you over. I'm being patient with you, Stacey, and I'm waiting until you willingly give yourself up to me, but I can revoke that at any point. I won't hesitate to stuff you with my cum until you're carrying *my* child and not some other loser's."

God, I hate him so much. "I'd rather die."

The back of my head hits the wall, and burning pain sears through my face. Chris keeps his fist raised, readying to punch me again.

I wipe the blood from my mouth, glaring at him.

Pretty soon, he'll drug me, and I can float around by his side and not understand what's happening.

If I'm lucky, he'll make me overdose.

9

STACEY

Chris keeps his hand low on the small of my back as he ushers me to the front entrance of an extravagant-looking building. It looks like it's worth a billion pounds – even the front doors are gold. Chris's friend is a rich dickhead whose family works in this place, and he got VIP passes for us.

Chris hasn't told me which friend we're meeting – he just smirks when he mentions how great the night will be. I've to behave, do as he says, and if one of them wants me to sit in their lap, I sit.

My eyes are cast down, but I glance up just before we walk through the entrance, and my gaze clashes with Barry's for half a second. And just to make things a million times worse, while we stand, Chris talking away to someone I don't recognise, I see someone else.

Through the crowd, among the chattering people and laughs

and drunks waiting to get their seats in front of the dancing women, is Archie Sawyer. The sight of him has my heart dropping.

I tug at Chris's sleeve, making him look at me mid-conversation. "What?"

"Can we leave?"

He frowns like I've just asked him to jump off a building. "No." It's a simple, straight-to-the-point response that has my bottom lip trembling.

Archie doesn't see me – I'm too far away, and I can only just make him out through the shoulders of tall people. He's smiling as he talks to a woman with wine-red hair, a younger, slimmer blonde woman beside her. I can barely see them, but I see enough to tell me the woman could be his wife.

The reason for Kade's entrapment.

Someone shifts in front of me, revealing them fully, and my insides twist when I see who else is here – his hand on the older woman's back, her hand on his chest as she smiles at Archie. In a black fitted suit and shirt to match his hair, his tattoo peeking out from his collar, Kade stands completely still – a statue – as his companions chatter.

The lady with red hair leans up and whispers in his ear then takes his earlobe between her teeth.

"Are you okay?" Chris asks me, his voice filled with concern even though he's a fucking psychopath. "You've gone pale."

"You threatened to sell me to your friends the entire drive," I grit, dragging my eyes elsewhere. "Don't expect me to be in a good mood."

"Such a fucking brat," he replies, shaking his head. He takes my hand and pulls me into the room on the left, away from Kade and Archie and who I assume is the wife. The younger one might be the daughter? Or maybe another poor soul trapped in their web?

However, all my thoughts stall when Chris leads me to where we're sitting, a mini stage in the middle of a semi-circular leather booth. But that's not my issue – my issue is that I recognise the faces of the men waiting for us.

I try to stop walking, but Chris crushes my hand and drags me. "If you thought what happened the other week was bad, you're going to wish you were dead. Now fucking walk."

The last time I saw them was when Chris drugged me, sold me and ultimately destroyed my entire life by having each of them beat and rape me while I was in a relationship with Kade.

Chris pulls me down on his lap, wraps his arms around me as he greets his friends then slips pills into my hand. "Take them," he orders. "Unless you want to make a scene where I force them down your throat followed by my cock? No one will help you here."

I gulp, folding my fingers over the little white pills before swallowing them. The dryness of my throat makes them catch, and Chris offers me a drink to wash them down.

I'm not sure how much time passes, but I'm hot, a layer of sweat on my skin, trying to stay conscious as Chris laughs with his friends, who keep asking me if I remember them.

They want me to dance. They want me to cry their names. They want me to show them between my legs again.

"How much for an hour?"

"Fuck off," Chris replies, laughing and shaking his head. "She's mine tonight."

"She's yours every night. Three grand? I can wire it across right now and we'll be back with her in thirty minutes."

Chris tightens his hold on my hip. "No."

For some reason, Chris tells them to fuck off again and doesn't laugh at their jokes or pay attention to anything they say. He's stroking my side with his thumb, turning his head to whisper in my ear, "I changed my mind – consider your punishment done. We're leaving."

"Ten grand?"

Chris glares. "No. This was a mistake bringing her. I'm taking her home."

"If you do that, I'll leak the videos you sent us of her. I'll even add in the other girls you've abused. How many is he at now, Phil? Twelve girls? Thirteen?"

"Fifteen victims, I believe," Phil – I assume – replies, sniggering. "One click and *poof,* all of those incriminating videos out in the world."

My stepbrother freezes. "You wouldn't. You all took part."

"We can easily blur our faces." The first one smirks, a cigarette hanging out of his mouth. He's older, bald, a groomed ginger beard covering most of his pale face, his eyes beady and haunting. I remember the feeling of him on top of me when I was a teenager, him asking if the blood smearing his cock was virginal. Little did he know that I'd lost my daughter a month prior. "Twenty grand. Thirty minutes. That's all we're asking for. You sold her to us before – what's the problem now?"

"We're leaving." Chris holds my waist, and I slip my arm around his shoulders for balance, since the room is starting to spin.

I hate him, but he's currently saying no to them. He's never said no to them sharing me.

"Come on, Fieldsy," the ginger one says, glancing at his friend beside him. "Fine. We'll all chip in and raise it to a hundred grand. Surely you can't pass up that kind of money? It's not like we haven't fucked her before. You're being a spoilsport."

"Chris," I whisper, seeing the change in his expression. "Please take me home."

He closes his eyes. "You send the money now, delete everything you have on me and you can have two hours."

My insides freeze. *No.*

The ginger one grins. "You have a deal."

I won't let them touch me. I'll fight. I'll fight until they have no choice but to kill me.

Phil leans on his elbows and points to the pole. "You can dance. Keep us entertained until I book us a room."

I look at the pole – it reaches all the way to the high ceiling. I don't feel like I'm in any position to refuse. If they can manipulate someone like Chris – scare him into selling me – then they'd do worse to me.

They're violent. I was barely lucid when they attacked me before, but I remember the way they brutalised me until I was barely conscious. There were six of them then, and it's a little warped that I think myself lucky only the three are here tonight.

"What song would you like on?"

I glance around the room, and my breath hitches when I see the bar, and I quickly need to look away before I make it obvious. Kade is sitting beside Barry – they're talking.

I haven't seen him since he forced me onto the jet. Did they hurt him? Did they punish him for rushing me out of the country?

Do they know I'm here? Can they see me? Is Barry here trying to save me? What if Archie Sawyer sees me?

My heart is beating so hard in my chest, I'm shocked none of them can hear it.

"'Spiracle'," I say, gulping through my nerves. "By Flower Face."

Chris points to the pole. "Are you in any state to dance on that?"

I ignore him. I'm not – I already feel whatever he gave me in my system.

When I get to my feet, I nearly lose my balance.

The metal of the pole feels so cold against my clammy, sweating hand. The world blurs together for a few minutes, and I silently beg my heart to stop beating – for my lungs to give up and let me die. If I fall and hit my head, I could pass out – maybe even make myself brain dead from the force of the fall.

Kade is watching me – I can feel the heat of his gaze on me. Chris is too in his own head to realise he's so close to us. He's mad that his friends have fucked him over, and he keeps asking the ginger one if he'll call off the deal.

"Okay, I'm hard and bored," Phil says, slapping his thighs. "You can stop."

I get down, rubbing my arm and staggering to the side a little.

"She isn't consenting to any of this," Chris says, which I find ironic. His eyes are on me as he keeps talking. "You only fuck her, and you'll all wear protection. Don't hit her, and don't kiss her."

"Ah, right. I forgot you said you wanted to get her pregnant." The ginger one is smiling at my widening eyes as all three of them stand, way taller and bigger than me. "I wonder if she'll cry this time – or at least stay awake. I loved her tears before."

The three of them approach me, and Chris takes my hand delicately. "I'm sorry," he mutters under his breath as he kisses my cheek, sliding something sharp into my palm.

10

KADE

This place is pretentious as fuck.

High ceiling with low lighting. Loud music with no one dancing but the people barely wearing any clothes on poles and those suspended bits of material Stacey dances with.

Douchebag men cheating on their wives while waitresses sit in their laps and accept money for touches.

I blow out a cloud of smoke as I stare at my surroundings. To the right of us, there's a bar – but no one is standing at it. All the servers are rushing around, trying to tend to the rich wankers throwing around money like confetti.

For being full of millionaires, the place smells.

I almost want to turn my nose up, but I don't want to draw any attention to myself.

Bernadette sits on my left in the booth, her daughter Cassie to my right, and they chat away like normal mother and daughter while a girl with a white mask covering her face dances to the slow, sensual song.

I don't watch her – it feels wrong to watch. Especially since I know she's drugged. It's very likely that all the employees at this place are on some sort of drug.

My system is pretty fucking messed up right now too, which is maybe why I'm overanalysing my surroundings. Maybe this girl isn't even on the mini stage in front of us?

I look down as both women place their hands on my thighs, still deep in conversation.

Removing them will cause more trouble than I need, but do I want to stub my cigarette out on their hands?

Fuck, yes.

Each booth is large, with leather seats, positioned in a half circle. There are mini pole-dancing stages in the middle of each booth, someone dancing around the pole while people watch – tossing some cash for a flash of tits. Bernadette loves it here – she wanted to bring Cassie, her insufferable daughter – and she's already given me a migraine from talking.

Bernadette is still insisting that I marry her, and obviously, I'm still refusing. My dad is still locked up in solitary because of it though. Usually his punishment would make me give in, but I fucking can't marry Cassie Sawyer.

I won't.

I tell them I'm slipping to the bathroom, huff out a breath and shove my hands into my pockets, needing this night to be over already. Once I take a piss, I go left and head for the bar in the other room. It's busier, louder, and music blares throughout while dancers twirl on poles and move around the groups of people as money is stuffed into the straps of their underwear.

I stop at the bar and order a drink, closing my eyes for a beat while I push through the overwhelming feeling of everything.

A throat clears to my left, and when I look, I see my assistant.

"Don't make it obvious," Barry says. "Look forward, sir."

I grit my teeth and avert my eyes to my glass of whisky. "Please tell me you're here with your wife." He doesn't have friends – he doesn't see the point in them. And if he's not here with Lisa, then that means...

"My wife who's heavily pregnant? No."

Fuck. "Where's Stacey?"

He pauses and takes a drink of his water. "I have it under control, sir. Don't draw any attention to her."

My breathing is already laboured from the drugs, but knowing she's so close, with Bernadette within walking distance? I think I'm about to have another panic attack. "Get her out of here," I tell him in a strained voice. "That's an order. Get. Her. Out."

"I'm trying," he replies. "She's been stuck to her boyfriend's lap all night."

The world freezes – or maybe it's the beats of my heart that stall. "Boyfriend?"

Barry is about to speak again when the song changes.

"Spiracle" by Flower Face plays, and the hairs on the back of my neck rise. The need to look for her wins, and I let my eyes roam the room.

The whisky gets caught in my throat. Am I fucking hallucinating right now? I must be – I better be.

In a tight dress, hair down her back, Stacey sits on some guy's lap. I can't see his face properly from this angle, but he's surrounded by three other guys. All of them are drinking, and the one Stacey is sitting on has his hand low on her back, her arm across his shoulders.

She has her back to me, but I fucking know it's her.

All of them start chanting her name, and the guy's hand leaves her back and gestures to the pole in the middle of the mini stage. The same as the booths in the other room.

Stacey stands – staggers.

When she starts to dance, she throws her head over her shoulder, and our eyes meet. A silent pleading – I can feel it. That's why she put this song on. It's the same one she told me to listen to when we were younger to describe how she felt about me.

I know every lyric by heart.

She knows I'm here – she wants me to save her.

My feet move before I can think, but a hard force yanks me

back.

Barry's hand is on my shoulder. To outsiders, it's a friendly hold, but his fingers dig into me. "You can't go to her."

"Get your fucking paws off me, Barry." I swipe at his arm, forcing him to release his grip, and he steps back. "She needs my help. Don't you dare try to stop me."

"Shut up," he snaps, surprising me. "You were about to make a diabolical mistake. I told you – I'm watching her. I don't know what the fuck is going on, but it doesn't feel good. You marching over there will only make it worse."

I rein in the need to punch him for talking to me like that. "Every reason to go over there and grab her. She needs me."

"Do that and you risk exposing her to Bernadette. She's in the next fucking room, sir." He blows out a breath and shakes his head. "Emmerson is missing – presumed dead. He was on her guard and vanished. I tried to find out what happened, even went to talk to Stacey after she finished dancing – which she wasn't at for weeks, by the way – then that bastard she's sitting with said she was his girlfriend and that I was to fuck off. I think he has something to do with Emmerson's disappearance."

I glance at her again, but we're too far away to see any of their faces. Thankfully, Stacey isn't dancing on the pole anymore; she's just standing there, rubbing her arm – she's nervous as the guy she was sitting on talks to her. I want to wrap her in my arms and run away with her.

Maybe I could do it now. Put a bullet in each one of the guys' heads, throw Stacey over my shoulder and get the fuck out – leave Bernadette and her daughter here and disappear.

Bernadette is drunk – she'll want to leave soon.

I can't leave.

Before we can make an elaborate plan to try to get Stacey away from the group of assholes, three of the men stand, and the one she was sitting on whispers something in her ear, kisses her cheek and slips something into her hand – a small blade.

Wait, a blade?

"I know that fucker's face," I say, fisting my hands – needing to go over there and smash his face into every wall in this place.

"Remember when I asked you to run checks on the guy who was standing at the manor gates talking to Stacey? That's him."

"The records were blank," Barry replies. "I couldn't find a single piece of information on him."

"He might be the same person who called her at the hotel in Edinburgh." When she rode my face and dry-humped me while on the phone to him – fucking bastard.

"You armed?"

"Yes, sir," he replies, nodding as we watch the three guys walk with Stacey. She's heading to the door that leads to all the hotel rooms – the rooms where everyone fucks.

She glances over her shoulder again, and I can see the desperation and fear in her eyes as she looks at the guy who gave her the blade – then her eyes slip to me for a split second.

I try to step forward, but Barry grabs my arm again. "I know you want to go after her. I get it. I would burn this place down for Lisa, but we need to be smart about this. Causing a scene will only draw attention to her. If Bernadette sees her, it's game over. If you think the way she tortures you is bad, imagine what she'd do to Stacey."

I fist my hands at my sides again. "We're following them."

"Of course we are." Barry pulls out his phone and, within seconds, hacks the venue's security system. "A room was booked a few minutes ago."

The guy who Stacey was sitting on rubs his hands down his face, grabs at his shaggy blonde hair and sits at the booth with his elbows on his knees. He's shaking his head and keeps glancing at the door she went through.

Who the fuck are you?

I step forward again, fully intending to pummel the fucker into the ground, but yet again Barry grabs my arm, and I glare at him.

"Eighth floor. We'll get him later, sir. Miss Rhodes needs us more."

And here I thought I was the boss.

I quickly check on Bernadette, Archie and Cassie. They're still sitting at the booth – drunk as fuck and flirting with the waiter. I pull out my phone and shoot her a text to buy me some time.

***Me**: One of your clients is here. She wants an hour with me. What do I do?*

Cassie is insistent that if I agree to marry her – not that I ever will – then I've not to sleep with others, meaning my sexual slavery comes to an end. But Bernadette is still refusing that condition since I make her a lot of money and popularity from it.

She glances down at her phone then grins widely as she shows Archie the screen.

***Bernadette**: What a stupid question. When have we ever turned down a client? I'll have a car pick us up once you're done.*

She'll eventually know it's a lie – the clients pay her directly, and I get a cut. She usually gives them three days to settle the bill after the session. I'll be punished, but I guess it'll be worth it.

We ride the elevator up to the eighth floor, both our guns drawn but hidden within our suit jackets. The hotel-room door is still open, and when we reach it, I lower my aim while Barry swears under his breath and locks the door behind us.

Standing in the middle of the room, splatters of blood all over her, her dress ripped down the middle, Stacey holds the blade, hand raised to the side as tears stream down her face. Her chest is rising and falling, her lips trembling as she gasps.

Fuck.

11

KADE

I drop the gun slowly and approach her – careful steps so I don't startle her, since she seems to be going into shock. "Stacey, it's me," I say gently, and when I step over the ginger guy, I try not to look at the gaping holes in his face.

The other two have their throats cut – one on the bed, his trousers down; the other next to the bathroom.

This isn't a moment to be mega proud of Stacey, considering she's caked in blood and heading for a breakdown, staring at me with wide eyes, but I fucking am proud.

She fought.

When I reach her, shielding the exposed parts of her body from Barry, I lift my hand to her wrist, sliding my fingers under hers to peel them away from the blade.

Her eyes lift to me as I toss aside the blade. "I k-killed them."

I take her face in my hands, and all I see is the trauma in her eyes, the way she's not filling her lungs. "You need to breathe, Stacey."

"They're dead," she says, shaking. "They're… I…"

"Breathe. You need to breathe."

"They tried t-to…"

Her bottom lip trembles, a tear slipping down her cheek as her focus comes back, yet her pupils are dilated so badly that I can't see the beautiful winter forest in her eyes.

"K-Kade," she whimpers, another tear slipping down her cheek. "Kade."

"It's me, Freckles."

She collapses in my hold, and I hug her to me. "Fuck. Are you hurt?"

She shakes her head. "I needed you to s-see me. The song. I… didn't know if you re-remembered it."

I close my eyes and rest my chin on her head, tightening my arms around her. She's taking steady breaths now, each one rattling in her chest. "I heard it. How could I ever forget that?"

"I… I m-missed you."

Fuck do those words feel like she just drove a blade through my heart. Words I can never do anything with.

She pulls her head back and looks up at me with glazed, bloodshot eyes, her pupils the size of a fucking planet.

"They drugged you." It's not a question.

She swallows, and I can tell she's not feeling too good.

I shrug off my suit jacket and wrap it around her, covering her ripped dress, then I gather her in my arms and pull her off her feet. Her face is stained with red splatters, and there's a gash in her palm from where the blade must've cut her.

Stacey buries her head into my chest as I hold her, unable to do much else but whisper my name repeatedly. Barry is already making calls while the girl I sent away nearly three months ago to keep her safe, keeping me anchored in this world without even knowing, slowly goes limp in my hold.

The hotel room is ruined. She must've smashed a lamp over one of their heads too, and there are handprints on the walls from them trying to get away from her.

She'd been here for less than five minutes before we got here. My girl just fought for her damn life, and now I can tell she needs sleep, but not with whatever is in her system.

I kick open the adjoining bathroom, lower to the ground with Stacey in my arms and push up the toilet lid. "I need to make you sick, okay?" I tell her softly.

Barry tells someone to have a car wait out back and to have a medical kit ready.

I shove my fingers down her throat, and she vomits all over my hand and into the toilet bowl. I do it again, forcing her to bring up what's in her stomach until she slaps at my hand to stop.

As I wipe the blood from her face with tissues, the concealer she was wearing comes away too. She has bruises on her face, her throat purple from someone strangling her.

These aren't all fresh – though one on her cheek I can tell just happened. One of them punched her.

I wish my impulsiveness won sometimes, so I could've walked over to the booth when I saw them and beat the shit out of them one by one. But Barry is right – causing a scene would have drawn Bernadette's attention from the other room, and then Stacey would've been on her radar. She would already be strung up somewhere, and I'd need to watch her being tortured.

Barry takes the cup from the sink and fills it with water before handing it to me.

"Drink this," I say, tipping her head back and pouring little bits into her mouth at a time. "Swallow. That's it. You're so fucking strong, Stacey. You're a fighter. You're okay. You're okay." I think I'm saying the last part to myself more than anything.

"Make sure that bastard downstairs doesn't leave. I want him interrogated."

Barry chews his lip as he glances at his phone, searching through CCTV footage. "He already left. I can have him tracked in the car he got into, sir."

Gritting my teeth, I lace my fingers with Stacey's and nod once.

As a little bit of life comes to her, she slouches in my hold, and I brush strands of hair from her face. She's looking up at me, and somehow, her dimple dents as she manages a smile. "You're alive."

"I am," I reply. "I'm kind of hard to kill."

"I w-w-was so worried. Did they..." She gulps, takes a second to breathe then continues. "Did they hurt you?"

I shake my head. "No," I lie. Unless you count unlimited beatings and forced hard-ons.

"Fight back." She can see the lie. "I had to fight. I went t-to the police and they... they didn't stop him after he attacked me – he killed the bodyguard and said if I didn't stay away from you, he'd kill you too."

I hear Barry swear under his breath again. All I can picture is snapping whoever this person is in half.

"Please don't let him find me. Please," she mumbles, panicking as she grips only my white shirt. "He said he wanted to get me pregnant."

My voice drops to a deep, threatening tone. "Who?" I ask her, my teeth clenching so hard they might crack.

She hiccups as her head lolls to the side, and I catch her shoulder as she nearly falls away from me. "Chris." Then she gestures to her busted-up face with unsteady movements. "Cyber-freak and master manipulator. The creator of this wonderful artwork."

"Who?"

"Your boyfriend?" Barry asks, and I want to punch him for even addressing that she's potentially in a relationship.

"No. Chris," she replies groggily just before she passes out, and I don't think I breathe for a good minute while I run through what she just said over and over and over again.

Who the fuck is Chris?

He wants to get her pregnant?

Cyber-freak?

"Now it makes sense," Barry says, a deep line between his brows. "Yet it doesn't. I have no idea who Chris is." His brows furrow deeper. "I think we missed something. I'll do a retrace."

"Whoever it is, I'm going to kill him." Understatement – I'm going to rip him limb for limb and set the cunt on fire.

Barry paces. "I'll see what I can find."

"Take Stacey to the manor – tell my mother everything that happened tonight. Whoever this prick is, she'll issue security alongside ours. Contact Emmerson's family and offer our condolences; give them enough money to be comfortable. And find out who the fuck Chris is when she wakes up."

"On it, sir."

"When you find out who that was downstairs, I want him too."

"I'll ask Miss Rhodes for information on him when she's conscious. Our car is here," Barry tells me. Then he shows me his phone screen. "Bernadette is still sitting at the table with Cassie. Archie is in some debate with another husband. You can make it back without appearing suspicious." He gestures to my shirt. "Do you want to swap shirts with me? You're covered in blood."

"No offence, Barry, but my chest and back are a lot bigger than yours."

He hums, crouching down to Stacey to check her eyes. "I might need to give her Narcan. Do you know if she's allergic to anything?"

"No. No allergies." I shake my head at the fact I need to leave Stacey when she's in this state. I lean my back to the wall beside the toilet, keeping her between my bent knees, her head resting on my chest. "Please keep her safe – I need you to watch her. I'm about to get time off so I can be with her, and you can go and see Lisa. You haven't been home in months."

Barry nods. "You need to go now, sir."

I look down at Stacey, taking in the worried expression she wears even while she's sleeping. The bruises fucking piss me off, and when I get the chance, I'll hunt down the asshole that dared to lay his hands on her.

Reluctantly, I lift Stacey in my arms and pass her to Barry before tightening the suit jacket around her. I stare at her – the beauty of her – and release her hand.

"I'll be back at the manor in a few days. We'll discuss everything then."

Stacey groans and starts tensing up in Barry's arms, and he rushes her back to the toilet to vomit all over again.

"Go, sir. I'll have someone clean up the bodies. Leave before you draw attention."

My phone starts ringing, and I give Stacey one last look, even though I want to be the one holding her hair back and head up in her condition. I want to be the one caring for her.

Instead, I put my phone away and leave the hotel room, going back to Bernadette, her delusional husband and the daughter they want me to marry.

"What took you so long?"

I sigh and lift my drink, not looking at Cassie as I reply, "None of your business."

She leans in and whispers in my ear. "You have blood on your sleeve, and there's a smear of it on your cheek."

I flinch as she runs her tongue up my cheek, feeling her smile at the corner of my eye.

"All gone."

I turn my head to glare at her. "Don't do that again."

Bernadette is arguing with Archie while he declares war on someone who outbid him on some game, leaving me to sit at the booth with their daughter. The daughter who keeps getting closer – thinking I would ever willingly lower myself to go anywhere near her.

"Unless you want my mother to know you were doing something bad, I suggest you tell me the truth."

"Don't threaten me," I snap, gulping down my drink, enjoying the burn. I glance at my watch. Barry will have got Stacey out by now. She needs all the support she can get, because when the reality hits that she's killed three people, her head will be fucked.

Mine was.

Cassie rests her hand on my lap. "Do you want to leave?"

I knock her hand away and blank her, taking in my surroundings. The drunks and the druggies – all standing around a large table flashing their cash. Bernadette keeps looking over at us, either jealous that her daughter is trying to seduce me or calculating how to force me into agreeing to marry her. It's a fucking joke.

"Were you fucking someone?" I can hear the anger in her voice.

"Yes," I lie. "Why do you think there's blood on me?"

Her face contorts with rage. Good. I hope she'll give me some fucking space.

"You fucked a virgin?"

I shrug. Maybe she'll leave me the fuck alone if I tell her that her own mother forces me into her bed. Not that it's anything to be proud of – disgusting, if anything. She already demanded her mother stop selling me for sex, so maybe hearing that she still does offer me to clients and controls me by forcing me to fuck her or watch the people I care about get hurt will stop this incessant need to throw herself at me.

I'm not interested.

All I need is to wait a few days, and when Bernie goes away with Archie, I'll have two weeks of freedom. I'll string up everyone involved in tonight's disaster and have the abdominal cavity of whoever the fuck Christopher is sitting as a trophy on my bedside unit.

Cassie leans in again, whispering in my ear. "You can at least pretend you want me."

I roll my eyes. "Why would I do that?"

"Because I lied and said we were making progress, so your father will be released from solitary confinement tomorrow."

I turn my head. "What?"

"Yeah," she replies, nodding as she licks her lips, moving closer. "So you owe me."

I snatch her throat and shove her away from me. "I owe you nothing."

"Unless you want your sister to be the next target," she says, rubbing her throat, "I highly suggest you act like we're making progress. Stop manhandling me."

Every single time she tries to get close, I either shove her, threaten her or strangle her, and she still doesn't get the fucking hint. She's been mindfucked by her parents, but that doesn't mean I'll go easy and bow to her fucking orders as well.

Bernadette's gaze clashes with mine – she's drunk and mad, which only means one thing. I'll get no sleep tonight. She taps Archie's shoulder then demands we all go home.

When we get to Bernadette's mansion, I go to my designated room and shower, and when I get out, Bernadette is sitting on my bed, a frown on her face.

"There was no client," she says, sounding disappointed as she sighs. "You just don't ever seem to learn your lesson. You don't lie to me, Kade. Ever. What am I going to do with you? I've already lifted the punishment on your father."

I don't get a chance to formulate another lie – someone appears beside me and shoves a taser into my ribs, and when I try to fight back, someone else crashes my head off the wall with such force, I temporarily lose my vision.

Bernadette stays sitting on the bed as I push myself to my feet and tackle their legs, feeling punch after punch landing on my side until they do their usual bullshit and bring more guys in to beat the shit out of me.

12

STACEY

"Is she okay?" I hear Aria ask as someone carries me upstairs – dogs barking behind us. "Is that blood?"

"What the fuck happened?" Ewan. His voice is faded, as if he's a few steps behind us.

Barry's voice is next. "She was attacked. I've given her Narcan, but she needs fluids. She's both in shock and drugged."

"Oh dear," Aria replies, hurrying after us.

Barry isn't waiting around – my head flops as he takes two steps at a time.

"Second floor. My office – I have all the supplies in there."

When I open my eyes, I can see the details of the wallpaper, the swirls of white and sage, the family portraits that line the main stairway that dominates the manor.

Relief fills me that it wasn't all a dream, and Barry really is carrying me through the manor. That I did see Kade. He's alive, but I can't remember if he was okay. Was he? Did they hurt him when we left the airport?

I can smell him – the rich fragrance of his aftershave – but it's mixed with the tang of copper, and I can faintly taste vomit at the back of my throat. I lift my hand to my face to shield against a blinding light as we get to the second floor.

My breath hitches, and I startle myself when I notice my bloody hands.

I can hear the gurgling from Phil as I slashed his throat from behind, and when the other tried to pin me to the wall with his elbow, my reflexes won, and I stabbed the blade Chris slipped me right into his artery.

When I lost control and ended up with the largest one on top of me, ripping my dress down the middle, I kept stabbing him until he went limp on me and fell from the bed. I think his blood hit my face too.

Did I actually do that? Did I imagine it all? Dream it?

Am I dead? Did I kill them?

My stomach recoils, and Barry turns me just in time for me to vomit all over the floor – yellow bile spilling from my mouth and burning my nostrils and eyes. My stomach twists in revulsion at the thought of having three people's blood all over me.

I wipe my mouth with my sleeve and notice I'm wearing a suit jacket.

My mind works for a second – Kade covered me. Wait, my dress is ripped. Did they touch me?

Barry holds me closer again and walks us to Aria's office. It's dark, the sun just starting to rise over the Munros in the distance. She clicks on a lamp, and Ewan brings up towels, a bottle of water and a pile of Luciella's clothes.

Barry sets me down on a soft couch, and I close my eyes again, needing sleep, needing to escape, needing to forget the past twenty-four hours.

Then my eyes ping open. "Where is he?"

Barry stops typing on his phone. "Who?"

"Chris... Did you catch him?"

His eyes narrow. "You need to tell me who Chris is."

I try to sit up, but get dizzy and lie back down again as Aria tells me to relax.

Blinking, Barry frowns and folds his arms while Aria sinks a needle into my arm, connecting IV fluids to a stand and checking it over. "Was Chris the one with you last night? The one who said you were his girlfriend and told me to fuck off?"

I somehow nod, my lip trembling. "Yes. He's not my boyfriend." But before I can say anything, my stomach twists again, and I tip to vomit into a paper bowl Ewan holds up for me.

A hand towel wipes at my face and mouth, and I lift my gaze to see Aria giving me a warm smile. "You're okay, sweetheart." She looks at Barry. "I think we should let her rest, and then you can give her twenty questions."

"Very well," he replies. "But I need you to have the manor on high alert. Every member of security you have needs to be on guard. I can bring in my own team too."

"I'll arrange it all." Ewan grabs his phone and leaves the room.

Aria glances at Barry after checking my temperature. "How did you know to bring her here?"

"Mr Mitch— Kade was the one who ordered— told me to bring her here."

Aria doesn't seem to catch his blunder. "You know him?"

"You could say that," he replies. "We... worked together."

Kade has said from the start that his family can't know the truth about what he actually does for work – or who he works for. When I told Kade about my visit to Tobias, he wasn't happy in the slightest.

Telling them would risk their lives. Would make Kade's job harder.

Barry knows this – that's why he's lying.

"I do have a few more questions for you both because none of this is making any sense, but she needs rest. I'll clean her up and get her into fresh clothes. Thank you for bringing her to us. I could take your number and call you if I need to know anything else."

"With all due respect, ma'am, I need to stay by her side to make sure she's okay. Kade will be home in a few days, and he can take over for me."

Aria smiles and looks down at me. My eyes are practically closed, but I can see a little. They must think I'm asleep. "I always knew they'd find their way back to each other. I'm glad they talked things out."

Barry hums.

I want to cry, because that isn't the case at all. Nothing had changed between us – just him protecting me as usual.

"I do have some work to do, so I'll make a few calls and shower while you see to her. She… she was attacked in a hotel. She fought back. I'm not sure they got the chance to do much else but rip her dress."

"The police should be contacted."

"Believe me, ma'am, that is the last thing she needs right now."

My eyes close fully, and I want to sleep so badly. Everything hurts, and it feels like my skull is cracking – red images flash before my eyes, and I hear their screams again and again until I fall into a deep sleep.

13

KADE

FLASHBACK

I roll a joint while we walk, Stacey holding both leads as we take the dogs around the front of the manor grounds. We have acres of forests and a dug-up golf course – zero chance of walking the full vicinity as planned when we woke from our nap earlier.

Once I finish rolling my joint, I tuck it behind my ear and take a lead.

Stacey is glowing, her face highlighted by the moon, and wears both my cap and a permanent smile that keeps drawing me in. As well as my hoodie, she has on the tightest fucking yoga pants, but, annoyingly, my hoodie drowns her so I can't stare at her ass.

I take her free hand and lead us through the rose garden while the pups sniff around. Before, I would've hated this. Holding hands. I barely ever held my mother's hand or Luciella's when we were kids – it wasn't something I wanted. But I always have Stacey's hand. Either in my lap while I play online games with Base and Dez or when I drive, or interlaced as I push into her.

Once she woke up and saw the dogs hugging into her, she relaxed, and I kept my eyes on her while she played with them. We sat at opposite ends of my room and threw toys at each other – both the pups running between us.

She squealed when I said we own them. Hugged me when I said I'd rehomed them and that they'd be with us from now on.

Us. I said "us" and she didn't correct me.

Not going to lie, they prefer her to me – she suits having them on each side as she walks. I wonder if they'll be around when we have kids.

Woah, slow the fuck down.

"When do their ears point up?" she asks me as she crouches to pick a rose, sniffs it then tucks it behind her ear. "I'm so glad they have their tails. Why do people crop them?"

"I read that some owners dock them for shows or to make them look how people expect. But I also read that their tails are really thin, so they're easily injured. It depends, to be honest."

She nods, and Mum beams ear to ear when she sees me and Stacey holding hands as we walk up the entrance steps, the two pups jumping around happily at her feet.

Ewan takes them into the main sitting room, Mum follows and Stacey's eyes nearly blow out of her head as she whips the joint from behind my ear. "She could have seen this!"

"She didn't," I say. She would've killed me. She knows I smoke, but if she found out how regularly I smoke joints, she would lock me up with my dad.

I snatch it back, tuck it behind my ear then gesture to her to go out the back, and we walk over to the pool house.

It's dark out, but it's not cold. In my shorts and T-shirt, I sit at the bench near the dock, and Stacey sits beside me, both of us looking out over the loch. "I need to go home tonight," she tells me. "I haven't been home in two days."

I groan and roll my neck until it cracks. "Stay one more night."

Resting her head on my shoulder, she huffs. "I wish. My brother would kill me if I stayed out again."

"What's your brother got to do with you staying out?"

She's silent, chewing her lip and then shaking her head. "Kyle will say to my dad, and he won't let me stay over with a boy."

"Maybe I kidnapped you?"

She buries her head into my neck, her body shaking with a chuckle. "Please do." She attempts to take the joint from my ear, and I steal it away. "Let me try it."

"This is a joint."

She gives me a look. "Duh, I know. Let me try it."

I shake my head. "Not a chance. It's weed, Stacey."

She narrows her eyes, and instead of coming across as scary, she's cute. I want to kiss the frown from her face.

"And? You smoke it all the time. I just want to try it."

I contemplate, thinking of ways to stop her, but she takes it from my fingers, gets to her feet and sprints to the dock where Ewan's boat sits.

I scramble up and chase after her, and instead of being pissed, we're both laughing as she hides behind a tree, going left when I go right, right when I go left, and finally spinning and running again when she manages to dodge me.

"You can't even catch me!" she bellows, inches from the dock.

I do catch her, both of us falling to the ground, and I protect her as we roll on the grass, down the hill so we're hidden, both laughing and out of breath.

"Fuck, you run fast." I lie on my back, her doing the same, and we both look up into the sky.

"I train a lot."

"I try to," I say. "Dez made me go running with him before and I nearly died."

I can feel her grinning. "He's got the build for a runner."

My head snaps to the side. "Meaning? Do I not?"

She rolls her eyes. "He has an ectomorph build. He's lean and slender. You have muscle, therefore you're more of a mesomorph."

I feel dumb. "I have no idea what you mean, but by all means, continue."

"I like learning about the human body when it comes to fitness. I'd love to go to uni and do human biology one day. Do you think you'd ever study?"

I shrug. "Ewan wants me to work for him, but I like just doing jobs here and there with him for extra cash. I think I'll look into aeronautical engineering."

She whistles. "Please tell me you'll wear glasses while you're studying?"

"I have perfect vision, Freckles."

The water lapses nearby. "Wear lensless ones then."

"Only if you wear them while riding me."

Stacey tries not to laugh but fails. The first time she climbed on me and sank onto my cock, we both had no idea what to do. It took a few minutes of moving around, her gyrating in all directions, and then me thrusting upwards until we were comfortable.

I say comfortable, but I got a cramp in the back of my thigh, and we had to rub it out and start again.

I think it might be my favourite position now. Her above me, me beneath her, especially as she turns into a bag of bones after her orgasm and falls asleep on my chest.

Last night, she was straddling me, ordering me to go harder and faster, until I was fucking up into her and shaking the bed, the headboard smacking the wall. She screamed my name, and I poured every drop of cum inside her.

My dick needs to stop twitching.

"I like this," she says, her voice soft as her fingers link with mine. "Us lying in the grass and watching the stars."

I turn my head to look at her, her eyes dancing as she keeps them on the moon. I smile, but it drops when she says, "You're usually a moody prick."

I narrow my gaze, pulling at the grass and throwing a handful at her.

"Hey! I was kidding!"

Little shit.

She melts as I cover her mouth with mine, sinking my teeth into her lip teasingly, but then she shoves my chest to get me away, and we settle on our backs again.

"I just mean it's relaxing. I think if I ever took my last breaths outside, I'd like to be able to see the moon." As grim as that statement is, she lets out a peaceful sigh. "It's beautiful."

With my eyes on her, I say, "So beautiful."

I want you forever, I say in my head.

"Have you thought of names for the pups yet?"

I smirk, because I know she's going to kill me. "I named one; you can name the other. The small one is called The Destroyer."

Stacey sits up, eyes large. "You aren't serious..."

"Very. He suits it, doesn't he?"

She disagrees. "He's scared of the TV, jumps when someone sneezes and has fallen over his two front paws too many times to count. No, he doesn't suit it."

"What would be a better name then?"

She thinks for a second, pressing her hand to my shoulder so I lie back again then rests her head on my chest. "Maybe Hopper. He hops around a lot."

I snort. "Fine. Hopper it is. And the other?"

"I had a dog when I was younger, and my mum wanted to call him Milo, but my dad refused and called him Bruce instead." She's silent for a beat. "She died a year later, and my dad rehomed him before I got home from school."

Her dad's a dick. "Milo then."

She smiles, her eyes glassy. "Milo and Hopper."

I curl my fingers into her hair then stroke my thumb against her cheek. I'm not the best at comforting, mainly because I don't experience the emotion that requires it. I know how it should feel, since I witnessed Luciella breaking down when our family dogs died when we were kids, but I felt nothing.

I wanted to, but it was more of an urge to fit in with the rest of the house.

But I want to comfort Stacey, to grieve with her as she tells me about her mother. She got into dancing because her mum was a dancer, played the piano and made Stacey feel like a princess. She was Stacey's best friend, and when she was diagnosed with cancer, Stacey witnessed her mother slowly dying, her father pulling away from the family and having an affair with Nora. And it was Stacey who held her hand while she took her final breaths.

"I want her to see how far I've come with my dancing and for her to tell me she's proud of me. I miss her so much, Kade."

There's a squeeze in my chest as I hear her sniffing and wiping away tears. "Hey," I say, shifting so I can see her, taking her face in my hand

and capturing another tear. "Don't cry." I hate people crying – it makes me feel awkward. But with her I know what to do. "You know she's proud of you. You're talented as fuck and amazing, beautiful and strong."

"I like when you're cute," she says, the corners of her mouth curling up towards her wet eyes. "Keep going."

"You have nice tits and a cracking ass."

She scoffs, but she's grinning, glancing down at her chest. "I wonder if they'll stop growing. I've gone up like two cup sizes in a month."

"Is that normal with the pill?" I ask, trying to tug down the hoodie at the front to see her cleavage then dodging the hand she tries to whack me with.

"I think so. Tylar said she just got really spotty, and Luciella has the implant, so I guess her side effects are different. Her boobs are shrinking if anything."

I grimace. "Less details on my sister please."

"I might change my contraception, I don't like how sick it makes me. I'm nauseous all the time."

I hum. "We can look into other forms and see what works for you. Or I can wrap it."

"I'll think about it," she says, leaning up and pressing her lips to mine in a chaste kiss. "We need to be careful again if I do change. Imagine we fell pregnant? Lu would lose it."

That's her concern?

I stare at her, unsure what to say in response. For a second, the thought of her giving me a child one day flashes before me, and I hope that in years to come, that comes true. We're only teenagers, so I need to not overthink this.

"One day," is all I say.

Instead of running for the hills, Stacey kisses me again, somehow happy with what I said. "One day."

Fuck, I love this girl.

With me still on my back in the grass, she leans over me, her hair a curtain around us. "I'll stay one more night, but promise to drive me home first thing in the morning."

I brush both sides of her hair behind her ears, holding her face as I bring her mouth to mine. "I promise, Freckles."

The taste of her tongue as I push mine through her parted lips has me needing more. I grab her leg and pull her on top of me, deepening the kiss. She lets out a little whimper, and I suck on her tongue.

"I can't fuck you here, can I?" I ask against her mouth, palming her ass and squeezing as I grind her against my hardening cock. "Because I really fucking want to."

She glances up to see our surroundings, hidden by grass and bushes next to the water. "Will anyone walk by?"

"The house guards already did their perimeter check," I say, bringing her mouth back to mine. With one hand on the back of her head, I drop the other between us, cupping her pussy. She gasps against my lips, and I can feel how soaked she is already.

"I want to try again," she says, pulling back to look down at me seriously. "I want to try."

She's not confident with going down on me, and when I didn't come within two minutes of her mouth around my cock, she got paranoid and said she was doing it wrong. No matter how many times I said she was doing it perfectly fine, she refused to believe me.

"It's just practice, so if it's terrible, don't laugh at me."

"You're good at it. And I would never laugh at you for that. You made me nearly pass out the first time my dick was in your mouth, or did you forget?"

Shyly, she shrugs.

So fucking gorgeous and mine.

Mine. I want her to be mine and no one else's.

"You know," I start, swallowing down my building panic, the tightening feeling in my chest gripping my fucking heart like a vice, "you need to be my girlfriend now. You're all I can think about."

Relief fills me as she blushes and giggles. "And that means I need to be your girlfriend?"

"Yep." I take her face and kiss her, stroking my thumbs on her freckled cheeks. "Seems boyfriend-ish to think of someone as much as I think of you."

She pulls away, sliding her body down mine to collect the joint dropped on the grass. She lifts it to my lips, pulls my lighter from my pocket and lights it.

"Are you asking or telling me?" she says. Green eyes lock on mine while she tugs at my waistband and I inhale deeply.

I blow out smoke to the side of her, making sure it doesn't go in her face. "Telling." I raise my hips, allowing her to yank both my shorts and boxers down, completely freeing my hard, thick cock. "But if you prefer I ask, I won't be accepting no as an answer."

"How gentlemanly of you." She takes me in her hand, stroking each inch. My breath hitches as the head of my cock lines up to her mouth. "Good thing I like being told what to do."

She drags her tongue up the underside of my dick, and my entire body tenses, the joint nearly slipping from my fingers.

"What shall I do now?"

I wrap my free hand around her hair, keeping it out of her face, then place the smoke between my lips at the corner of my mouth. "Suck."

"You want me to suck your cock?"

Fuck. The innocent voice and the way she's looking at me... fuck.

I give a firm nod, my teeth clenched as my chest rises and falls heavily.

"Fine." She smiles, and my heart stutters in my chest. "Since you're my boyfriend."

14

STACEY

Milo and Hopper are by my side as I walk through the grounds, hands stuffed into the front pockets of the hoodie Aria gave me. It's Luciella's, and when she gets home from America tonight, I'll be sitting both of my friends down and telling them everything, and I'm terrified that our friendship might end.

I've told them so many lies, how can they ever trust me again?

Not even just about Kade. I lied to them about everything when it came to my life.

And I also killed three guys. I can still feel all of it – the warmth when their blood splattered on me, the way my heart beat so fast from the adrenaline, how I couldn't stop stabbing that last one. I can still hear the sounds they made.

I cover my mouth and close my eyes, steadying my breaths. Aria said that the initial shock would stay for a while, then I'll start to overthink, but she'll be with me.

Like the mother I lost.

She's been amazing. After she washed me then got me redressed, she sat on the chair beside the bed she'd moved me to and slept there for two nights until I stopped crying, until she was happy for me to go to Kade's room to sleep with the dogs.

Will my friends be as compassionate about what happened? With their friend being a killer? A liar? A whore who sleeps with their best friend's brother even though she knows he hates her?

Tylar will probably freak out about it all, but she already knows about Kade. But then... Luciella.

How do I tell my best friend – someone who was always against anyone going near her twin brother – that I've not only been sneaking around with him since we were eighteen, but that we were also in a relationship and months from being a family of three, all while keeping it a secret from her? That we split up because he thought I cheated just weeks after losing our daughter? That we'd steered clear for two years but broke the dam by fucking each other's brain out yet again?

Deep breaths.

I was never scared to tell her before. Kade always said it was up to me when we told her about us. My excuse was that I wasn't ready, but in reality, I had a brother at home who would have ruined it all.

Though he ended up ruining it anyway, so I guess it was all for nothing.

There are guards everywhere, standing around with guns. None of them look at me, and I keep walking until I reach a section of grass beside the water. I stare at the spot while the wind whips at my hair – the place we lay years ago and made everything official. Where the guards nearly caught us and we had to hide until we fully dressed and ran for it.

I remember how happy I was – the pain in my cheeks from how hard I was smiling and laughing as we sprinted to the pool house and finished what we'd started. Kade had pinned me to the wall then taken me slow and hard.

Back then, my days were at least a little simpler. I was still worried Chris would find out about Kade and force me to stop seeing him. Hide me away in the Fields' manor for the rest of my life or try to beat up Kade.

There's a ding from my back pocket, and I pull out my phone Barry got from Chris's room. I smile at the screen.

> ***Barry**: Tobias Mitchell is no longer in solitary confinement. He's demanding to talk to you. Are you coming back inside anytime soon?*

I glance over my shoulder to the shadow standing by the outdoor pool. The past week he's been stuck to me like glue. He keeps telling me that Kade will come, that he's getting time off, but I'm starting to think he's only saying it to keep me calm.

He won't tell me anything – who his boss is, what she does, where I can find them. I ask him to call the police, or do something himself, but he tells me to stay out of it for my own good.

I sigh and head back in, seeing each breath I let out in the cold air while I check my messages from Tylar. She's been sending me videos and pictures from Festival of Fright Night, and how great my students did in their performances.

A lump lodges in my throat. I missed it. Ty had to do everything because I was stuck here, recovering, or held prisoner by Chris. They still managed to raise a lot for the studio and our three nominated charities though.

Her next message makes me roll my eyes and laugh.

I show it to Barry as we walk into the manor through the kitchen, and he shakes his head. "That's not a good idea."

I tut. "My friend can be insistent."

Tylar wants to throw a Halloween-themed party in the manor as a joint thing for me and Luciella, since we both turn twenty-two this month. A way to cheer everyone up, because even she can tell there's tension.

She asks me nearly daily if I'm okay, and I tell her I'll talk to her about everything soon.

Which also triggers her to ask more questions.

"I have an offer," Barry says, and I look up at him questioningly.

"I have a lot of connections who could get you a new identity, a new passport and bank account. I could hide you, maybe in America. You're in a lot of danger, Miss Rhodes, and Mr Mitchell won't be happy if something happens to you. *I* won't be happy if something happens to you."

I stop walking. "You could do that?"

He nods. "I can – just give me the word, and I'll get you out. I can come with you. Lisa and our child too. You'd be heavily protected, with no trace to be found." He gestures to the house. "Think about it and let me know."

"Thank you," I say, following him through the manor with my brows knitting together. Leaving everything behind sounds terrible, but to feel safe? To be able to go outside and not worry about my life being threatened? No Chris, no Sawyers.

Aria is sitting on the sofa, her knees crossed, and beams up at me when she sees me. "Oh, there she is now. Do you have time left?"

She nods at whatever he answers. "Don't you dare get caught with that phone, Tobias."

She hands it to me then asks Barry if he'd like some tea, to which he says, "Sure," and they walk out of the room.

I press the phone to my ear and drop to the couch. "Hello?"

"Little one," Tobias says, his voice low. "I wanted to check in with you and see how you are. Aria filled me in on everything."

"I'm… okay." Am I? Strangely, I think I will be. Yes, I took lives, and I still think I imagined that happening, but if I hadn't fought back, I would've been raped… again.

"You sent me fifteen voicemails – in five of them you were crying for over half an hour. Admitting you aren't okay isn't a bad thing."

"Are you?" He'd been locked up alone for weeks. "Aria said she was filing a complaint because you were held in solitary confinement with no evidence of you breaking any rules."

"I got out last week, but I had a few… adjustment issues. But I'll admit I'm not okay. In fact, I want to put my fist through a wall, but I like my hands, so I'm holding back."

He's not even joking.

"How much trouble is he in? I know you lied to Aria about Kade's position."

I shrug, even though he can't see me. "Barry isn't telling me much either."

"The assistant?"

"Yeah," I reply. "He's watching over me just now until Kade makes an appearance."

"You trust him?"

"Who?"

"This Barry. Does Kade trust him? What if he's working for his boss?"

"The Sawyers." I trace my fingers along a blanket, the same one me and Kade shared on this same couch years ago. "I found out Archie is a political leader. He's married to someone called Bernadette. I looked at her pictures – Kade said she was his main boss, but she doesn't seem the corrupt and evil type."

"They never do."

I shouldn't be saying any of this. I haven't even told Barry I did my own research on Archie Sawyer. He has a daughter, my age, and she's honestly so beautiful.

On the outside, they look like a sweet, happy family. They take part in charity events like Nora, and they're the owners of numerous foundations, set up to help people in need around the country – homeless and abused children.

"How is Aria?"

I blink, glancing at the door to make sure no one is there. "She's fine. A lot better now that you're contactable."

"Has she been drinking?"

I shake my head. "No. She's been coming to the home gym with me and tidying the manor. I think she's scrubbed the entranceway on her hands and knees every night."

"Stress cleaning," he says, humming. "She never changes."

Kade stress cleans. He used to freak out if he forgot to put his clean clothes away when I got to his room, then he'd go bright red and try to hide them under the bed, as if I wouldn't notice.

The cute and innocent Kade was adorable.

Tobias tells me about his day, as if we're just two people casually talking. Luciella visited today, and he says the hug she gave him made him feel like he could finally breathe. He hates hugs, but getting one from his little girl meant he was still alive.

My dad hugged now and again, but once he married Nora, it was like the father I grew up with died with my mother.

He tells me about his lunch, and how his therapist was monitoring him after being locked away for nearly three months.

Then, when he finishes explaining the movie everyone in the institution will be watching at movie night, he realises he just talked for a solid fifteen minutes without letting me speak, so he aims his attention back on me.

"Do you know where Christopher is now?"

"He reached out to Kyle the other day – he was getting on a boat to go somewhere and didn't want him to worry."

Tobias scoffs. "Motherfucker."

"Barry has a team tracking him. He keeps buying a new phone and changing cars, and he has some sort of blocker on his bank account, so they can't trace that." I stand and walk around the living room. "He's obsessed with cybersecurity. He builds these trojans and hacks into systems like some tech guru."

"I know you're blaming yourself for all of this, little one – I can hear it in your voice. He's a disease. And he'll be dealt with. You don't need to be silent anymore."

"Barry said he can hide me – get me a new identity and a new life. I could come to America."

He's silent, and then he says, "You're going to annoy me by visiting every day, aren't you?"

"*If* I take him up on his offer, then yes."

"I'd rather spend a year back down in confinement."

I smile at his joking tone. "I think we're becoming friends, Tobias."

He lets out a disbelieving laugh and hangs up on me.

15

KADE

FLASHBACK

I check the time on the boarding passes to Greece, texting Stacey back and forth for an hour before she lets me know her suitcase is securely shut after she jumped all over it and she'll see me after her last class.

She wanted to take my car this morning, but I'd rather punch myself in the balls, if I'm completely honest. She's fucked up Jason's car, which I had to take the blame and pay for, and I refuse to let her do that to my new black Audi R8.

We were practising away from the main roads and any living species. She's not shockingly bad but not exactly good either. She now knows how to drive at least but not safely. I'd trust Base blindfolded and on every drug possible before willingly getting into a car with her on a public road.

Milo and Hopper follow me around as I clean my room for the eighth time, getting rid of any specks of dust. I walk the dogs while smoking a joint, and gather snacks and make Stacey a sandwich.

It's late by the time she finishes work and I pick her up, and she falls asleep on the way to the manor. Her head rolls when we hit the gravel road, and I slow down a little, keeping her hand locked in mine. I glance over at her every few minutes, that warmth in my chest building every day.

She gives me a sleepy smile when we stop on the manor grounds.

The dogs run to her as soon as we walk in the door, me pulling her suitcase along, her carry bag on my shoulder. They ignore me as she lowers to her knees and scratches their ears.

"I told you they love me more," she says, sticking her tongue out at me when I give her the middle finger. "You're just jealous."

Not at all. In fact, seeing the dogs all over her is way better than them being wary, like they are with my friends and even Luciella. Not that my sister ever gives them any attention.

When Stacey gets excited and jumps around, they copy. When she sleeps, so do they. When she cries during a movie or after watching a video on her phone, they cuddle into her for emotional support. When it's time for bed, they wait for her to finish brushing her teeth and washing her face before climbing in with us.

Yep. They definitely love her more.

Maybe they'll change their minds when she sings.

Once we get to my room, she changes into my T-shirt and a pair of shorts that do nothing but tease me. When the movie starts, she's on her front, knees bent and kicking her legs lazily, facing the TV while I sit with my back against the headboard.

I hold her ass cheek, squeezing it, and she giggles then starts humming along to the song completely off-key. I'm distracted, obviously, as my eyes stay on my fingers sliding under her shorts, kneading at her.

"I think you should let me fuck your ass."

She slaps my touch away. "I'll hurt you."

I chuckle and pull her to me. "You could try."

She snorts. "I'll crash your car."

I narrow my gaze on her. "I believe you."

Stacey grins. "Never. I'm such a better driver than you."

"Stacey, you could have lessons for the next hundred years and wouldn't even come close."

She smiles and goes back to watching the movie, and I watch her. I don't think it's even a case of being in love with her anymore. Is there an emotion that's stronger than love? If not, I'm creating one.

It's like a mixture of love and not being able to breathe unless she's around – thoughts that run wild wondering what she's doing, where she is, if she's thinking of me. It's the butterflies that flutter like maniacs when I know I'm going to see her soon.

The Stacey Rhodes Effect.

"Oh my God!" she rudely yells, and both the dogs' heads snap up as my heart restarts. "This is my favourite song!"

"Don't," I warn her as she gets to her knees, readying herself.

"Ready, doggos? Sing with me!"

The first note of "From Now On" she screams has me contemplating ending things with her.

Even the dogs are confused as her voice threatens to destroy every mirror, glass and ornament in the room. I'm surprised the windows aren't smashing in.

I rub my face. "Please stop, Stacey."

But she doesn't.

"Fuck, my ears feel assaulted," I say, covering them as she throws her arms out to the sides to emphasise every word she belts out.

To my horror, Stacey gets to her feet on the bed as the chorus hits, arms outstretched as she jumps up and down, still singing along.

Milo starts howling along with her. Hopper and I stare at each other, silently pleading for help as she shakes her hips and whips her hair at parts that don't even slightly fit the movement.

Against the destruction of my eardrum, I chuckle. "You're supposed to be a good dancer."

She gasps and turns to me, hands on her hips, then jumps off the bed. "Hopper. Up!"

Hopper listens, getting to Stacey's height as she holds his paws to her shoulders, both of them dancing around the room. She does the same with Milo, even though he's giving me a confused look, and still she keeps singing.

She looks cute, so I keep watching her – the grin and giggle, the dazzle in her eyes, the free way she moves around and lives her life.

But her voice is shockingly bad.

She hits a deep note from Hugh Jackman, and I'm impressed. "Right, fine. That was good."

But then she switches to the girl and my ears feel like they might explode again.

She and the two dogs jump on the bed as the song comes to an end, and she attempts to copy the dance moves, kicking her legs out and falling on her ass next to me.

"You're going to break the bed for the completely wrong reason," I say, watching her with my own grin as she tries to catch her breath while the dogs bark to tell her to keep going. "You sound like a strangled cat by the way."

Stacey dramatically gasps, her chest rising and falling, a sheen of sweat on her face. "How do you know what a strangled cat sounds like?"

I look at the invisible watch on my wrist. "I just witnessed it for the last five minutes and forty-nine seconds. Seriously, why the fuck was it on for so long?"

She turns and places her palms on my chest then rests her chin on them, forest-green eyes looking right into my broken soul. "We're getting married to that song, so the longer the better. Maybe not a walk-down-the-aisle song, but definitely one we can do a duo dance routine to. Can you dance actually?"

"After that horrendous performance, you think I'd marry you?" I smirk and glance at Milo and Hopper, who are both staring at us. "Even the dogs are traumatised. I fear for our future children."

"If there are ever any future children, they'll be blessed with your looks and my personality, especially my voice, and you'll love them for it."

My mouth stretches wide, my eyes wrinkling at the corners as I smile. "The world would need to hide if we ever had children. They'd undeniably be heathens."

She tuts, shaking her head, then shifts up to kiss me. "Our little heathens."

On the drive to the airport, Stacey keeps changing the songs on the radio, so I grab her wrist and lace our fingers together. "Why are you nervous?"

"I'm not," she replies, but I'm not in the slightest bit convinced by the shy tone she uses.

"We don't need to go if you don't want to. I know we've travelled a lot the past two months."

"No! God, no. I want to go," she says desperately, turning her body to face me while I pull onto a back roads. "It's just..."

I raise a brow. "What?"

"Don't laugh at what I'm about to say, okay?"

I can't promise that. "What's wrong?"

Her lips flatten, and she drags her gaze out the window to the trees passing us by. "Idon'tthinkyoulikemeanymore."

I frown. "Eh?"

She huffs and drops her head against the headrest. "Is it because I'm gaining weight?"

I pull into the side of the road, cut the engine, rest my hand on her seat and turn to her, completely dumbfounded. "Excuse me?"

"You haven't touched me in nearly a week." She raises a shoulder, her voice low. "I thought, maybe, it was because I'm changing? The pill is messing me up so much, and I'm so, so goddamn moody. I blew up at you the other day, and it was over nothing. I keep thinking you're losing interest in me, which is fine if you are, but I'd rather know."

I literally asked her hours ago if I could fuck her ass. "I could never lose interest in you," I say instead. "Where is this coming from?" Did I do or say something?

"So you're still attracted to me?"

I smirk, tucking a strand of hair behind her ear. "'Attracted' is not the label I'd use when it comes to you. It's way more than that. You're beautiful, in all your moodiness – I think you're the most amazing person in the world. And you're all mine." I lean forward and capture her lips in a claiming kiss. "Mine."

"Yours," she whispers, grabbing my face and sinking against my mouth. Everything else ceases to exist as the tip of her tongue swipes across my lips, and I part mine, both of us tasting, licking and sucking as we deepen the kiss.

I unclip our belts and drag her into my lap. "Never doubt how I feel about you again, got it?" I snatch her bottom lip between my teeth, sucking on it until I let it snap back. "Do you want me to prove how I feel about you?"

"Yes," she whimpers as I pull her hips down, grinding my hardening cock against her.

"This is what you do to me," I tell her as I use my grip on her to rock her hips on me, the underside of my dick rubbing against her entrance and clit through the little black dress she's chosen to travel in.

She devours my mouth, hands in my hair as she moves against me, and I palm her ass, making her ride me through our clothes. She gasps as she finds the perfect rhythm, gripping the steering wheel from behind to use as leverage.

"Fuck," I say, my brows furrowing in concentration as she pulls her dress off and tosses it in the passenger seat. Her thong slides against me with each grind, and I can see how soaked the small piece of material is.

I move it aside and sink two fingers into her, and she lets out a soft cry.

"Ride my fingers, Freckles."

She does as she's told, her hips rolling, her nails sinking into my shoulder as her mouth silences any more words that might want to fall from my lips.

Her pussy is warm and tight, her walls wrapping around my fingers as I start fucking her with them, curling them and thrusting knuckle deep. She moans in my ear, and if I don't get my cock inside her now, I'll come in my pants.

We both work fast to free me from my shorts, and waste no time as she lifts her hips and slowly lowers onto me, my cock disappearing inch by inch into her wet pussy.

She rides me until she's moaning and shaking in my arms. When she struggles to keep grinding, I thrust upwards at the same as I yank her hips down, fucking into her in a way that has her tits bouncing in my face. I capture a nipple with my teeth, sucking, then grab the other and pinch as I feel her strangling my cock.

"Oh God," she breathes. "Oh God."

I throw the door open, making sure I stay inside her as I lift her up, holding her against me as I lower her onto the front of the car. I push her chest so she lies back, and I ease out slowly, before thrusting hard and making her scream.

Thank fuck it's dark and no one is around.

I watch each inch slide out of her, coated with her arousal, the thick head nearly out before I thrust deep. I take the back of her knee and put one of her legs on my shoulder, giving me a better angle to fuck her.

She kisses me as I lower my body onto hers, both of us on the car now, pressing my pubic bone into her clit while I slide in and out of her slowly.

We're surrounded by trees, and her moans and our heavy breaths are probably echoing in the wilderness, but neither of us seems to care. She sucks on my tongue, and I bite her lip, grabbing a handful of her hair and tilting her head to the side to kiss down her throat.

Her entire body quivers as I suck on the sensitive spot under her ear, so I do it again, harder, licking and biting and letting out a deep moan as my balls tighten again.

I flip her over and ease into her from behind. Her pussy is soaking, dripping down her thighs as I fuck into her again, all the way to the hilt.

The angle I'm hitting and the way her ass is shaking has me seeing stars. Black spots crowd my vision as I grit my teeth, wrapping her ponytail around my fist and using the leverage to fuck her harder.

There's only the sound of slapping skin and her moaning my name, then Stacey lets out a pleasurable cry as her pussy strangles me through her orgasm. It crashes into her like a tidal wave, but I don't stop. I keep the pace, yanking her hips back so she only has her hands on the car. I lean over her and drop my hand down from her waist to between her legs, and coat my fingers in her arousal.

She screams as I go faster, circling her clit with equal speed.

My cock throbs inside her with each hard thrust. "Fuck, Stacey," I growl as I screw my eyes shut – then go completely still as I come inside her, my orgasm nearly decking me. "Fuck."

It takes us a few moments to come down from our highs. I ease out of her slowly, mesmerised by the sight of my cum leaking down her thighs. Turning her around to face me, I grab her jaw and kiss her while still attempting to catch my breath.

"Does that prove I still want you? That I'm attracted to everything about you?"

All she can do is nod, dazed, her eyes completely dilated.

"Good. Remember that when you have any doubts. You're stuck with me, Freckles." I raise her chin to look at me when her head drops and kiss her again. "Get used to it."

I help her get dressed, and we stop at the closest bathroom so she can use the toilet. We grab food, and once the car is parked at the Ride and Fly, we do some shopping. I buy her a Kindle and perfume, and us both a camera, before settling in the pub while we wait to depart.

"Your cum is leaking out of me," she randomly tells me as she takes a picture of our boarding passes. The group of grannies nearby give us a horrifying look. "No, I'm serious. When I sneezed? Boom."

I choke on my beer. "Sometimes I wish you'd keep this shit to yourself."

She sips her fruity cider. "You love it."

I love you, I want to say. But instead, I laugh and say, "Drink up. We board in twenty minutes."

Greece is hot as fuck considering it isn't peak season.

On the first day, we explore the area and book matching tattoos for the last day. I drew us a dead rose with some lyrics from The Greatest Showman *mingled into it.*

We eat, drink and go to the beach. I watch Stacey as she sunbathes in a tight little bikini. Try not to get hard as I rub sun cream over her back and legs, and try not to push into her as I carry her in the water.

A few days later, while we're sitting in a restaurant, a little girl, about four years old, has lost her parents. Stacey asks if she's okay, and when she starts to cry, I take her small hand and we search for the parents. When she gets really upset, I carry her through the restaurant, asking the owner if he's noticed anyone looking for their kid.

She's starting to burn, so we buy a high factor of sun cream, and Stacey lathers her with it while I jump into other shops and ask if anyone lost a kid.

An hour later, she's asleep in my arms, and I'm hunting on my phone for the nearest police station, since it's nearly midnight.

Stacey is looking at me with a strange expression, and I raise a brow. "What?"

"Seeing you with kids makes me feral," she says in a whisper.

I chuckle and take her hand, still managing to carry the little girl while we walk towards the station. Stacey keeps silently screaming that I suit being a dad.

The parents are running towards us when we reach the station, and thank us while hugging their kid. They're crying and tell us she ran off while they were talking to other holidaymakers.

I give the kid a high five, and an officer thanks us again before we leave. But Stacey is still going. She keeps informing me that she'll come off the pill in exactly five years and can't wait to see me with my own kids.

Wishful thinking, right? She must feel the same way about me as I do her surely?

I love her, and I want to tell her I love her, but what if I'm being too pushy?

Maybe I should tell her how I feel and see her reaction. Maybe it'll be good to know we're on the same page. She is my girlfriend after all. I should be honest about my feelings.

On the fourth night, we spend all day at a pool with a swim-up bar, and we're smashed and kissing in the water. People can see us, but who cares?

You see this girl here? She's mine.

"You need to stop," she says, giggling. "You're hard and there's like thirty people in this pool with us."

"Maybe they're into voyeurism." I wiggle my brows as I rock her against my dick, which is, definitely, without a doubt, harder than steel. "Will my Freckles be a little exhibitionist and fuck me in front of all these people?"

We're drunk, happily bobbing around in the water, enjoying time together like other couples here. I like this. No, I love this. I love her. I love her so fucking much.

"I have a better idea."

I hum and kiss her throat, on my tiptoes to keep us above the surface. "I'm all ears."

"Let's go to the beach."

"I'm not into getting sand in my ass crack," I say as she takes my hand and leads me out of the water. I wrap my arms around her as we walk to the sunbeds. "But I won't refuse a blowjob."

"Shut up."

I shut up.

Once dried and clothed, Stacey takes my hand again, leading us past the fire dancers that usually have her mesmerised, down the narrow lane that opens up to the beach. We're staying along to the right.

I grin and watch her as we pull off our shoes and walk in the sand with our bare feet.

Music plays in a nearby bar, and I spin her around twice, pull her into me to take her waist and slowly dance her backwards until her back hits the wall of a cave, water crashing just behind it.

"I always fancied you – did you know that?"

She wraps her arms around my neck. "You had a strange way of showing it."

I lick my lips, alcohol clouding the anxiety that might stop me from talking. "I wanted you from the beginning. I wanted you so fucking much, it drove me insane. I hated you because you were my sister's best friend. I knew you couldn't stand me."

Stacey's lips part, and she silently studies the serious expression that matches my tone.

"When I got dared to kiss you, I begged myself not to fuck it up."

She slips her fingers into my hair. "Me too."

I want to smile, but the nerves are kind of catching up to me. "It's only been half a year, but it feels like longer. You're everything to me, Stacey. Everything. I think about you constantly, and I get excited when it's time to see you. I've never been attracted to someone before; did you know that? Never. Not once did I come across someone I found attractive. I thought I was broken, that my emotions were limited, but I just hadn't met you yet."

Her eyes water, but she just listens.

"I want it all with you. I want to go home and tell everyone that we're together, that we're going to have kids and grow old together. Do you want to know why?"

"Why?" she asks, so softly.

I take her face in my hands, stroking hair behind her ears. "Because I love you. I've been in love with you for ages – it's been all I've thought about. And I keep falling more in love with you every single fucking day."

A tear slips down her cheek, and I swipe it with my thumb. "You love me?"

"I do. I'm in love with you, Freckles."

Her bottom lip trembles, her body easing against mine. Voice shaking, she whispers, "I'm in love with you too."

My heart explodes in my chest as I lower my head, pressing a tender, loving kiss to her mouth. "Are you going to be my forever, Freckles?"

She nods, and we both break into a smile, giggling, and kissing as I press her against the cave wall before dragging her back to where we're staying.

"Are you recording me?"

Stacey grins, her phone raised while I try to dry myself.

"And here, ladies and gentlemen, is my wonderful boyfriend Kade Mitchell." She zooms in on my abs. "He's new to the gym, but look at these!" She slaps my sunburn, and I contemplate throwing her off the balcony of our hotel room. "How lucky am I?"

I rub my hair with a towel while she records the room only wearing my black top, no fucking underwear, her hair wet, dragging the camera over the large bath we spent hours in last night. Then she goes onto the balcony to show the camera the view.

The sun is setting over the sea, the sky an orange glow that we've watched every night for the last six days. One more night and it's back to reality.

"And over there" – she points to the cave next to the beach – "is where Kade told me he loved me for the first time."

I laugh and pull on my shorts, following her onto the landing.

"He said I was everything to him, and that we were going to grow old together and have loads of babies." She pouts. "He was drunk, to be fair. So maybe he doesn't love me."

So needy. "I do love you." My arms wrap around her waist. I was drunk when I confessed my feelings, but they weren't lies. "You're exaggerating, Freckles." I place a soft kiss on her neck. "'Loads' wasn't the word I used. If I remember correctly, you cried and said you loved me too."

She taps something on her phone, and our faces appear on the screen. "We're cute."

I raise a brow, and she flinches when I try to tickle her. "Stop calling me cute."

"But you are! You put cream on my back and carried my beach bag all day."

"I was trying to get my hole," I reply, and she slaps my arm.

"I'm recording this and you keep being dirty!" My girlfriend gives me a look while I slowly work my fingers under her top, skin on skin. She tilts her head to me, so we're cheek to cheek. "Stop it." She bats my hands away from groping her tits then changes the subject by saying, "Tell the world, Kade. Who's the best driver?"

I snort. "This again? Considering you nearly crashed my new car, I'd say you lose this one."

She rolls her eyes, leaning into me. "What nineteen-year-old has a black Audi anyway? Such a goddamn predictable rich boy."

"You weren't complaining when I had you bent over it."

Stacey groans and lowers her phone. "Hey! I can't show this to our future kids if you're going to say things like that!"

I laugh against her neck, hugging her tighter to my body.

She'd asked if I ever wanted kids, albeit we're only nineteen and nowhere near ready or in a position, but the idea of having a family with her seems so... right. Not now obviously; no one knows we've been dating for months, but in years to come, having children with Stacey Rhodes, definitely.

I reckon Mum and Dad and Ewan would rip me apart if I made them grandparents before they're fifty.

Once we're ready, we head to the karaoke bar near the hotel. Stacey's hand is soft in mine, her freckled skin more defined by the sun, her hair shiny and falling down her back in dark waves. She documents everything, videoing our fingers interlocked, the view, the smile on my face when she says something ridiculous.

Fuck. She's so beautiful.

We've come to this bar every night, always ending up smashed and singing on the stage with a dozen older couples. I'd usually be disgusted by my behaviour, but this holiday is different – we aren't sneaking away just to have time together like we usually do; we're an actual couple – in love and preparing to tell our families about our relationship. I can finally tell my friends everything too.

She claims to have softened me, but that's impossible – I'm always hard.

Her family won't like me. I'm Tobias Mitchell's son after all. I already met her dad, and he wasn't happy with me breaking into the yard. Her stepbrother Kyle will have something to say, but I don't give a shit. My main concern is Stacey and how she'll feel when everyone tells her she can do way better than me, that she shouldn't be with the son of a psychopath.

Regardless, we're in Greece, enjoying the sun, sea and sex. Everything else can fuck off.

Seems like "King and Queens" by Thirty Seconds to Mars is our jam for the night. Stacey asks someone to record us, and I swallow my fifth shot of vodka and follow her to the stage like a lost puppy.

My throat burns from how loud we're yelling through the chorus. I kiss her in front of the crowd, and they cheer as I lift her into my arms.

When we get back to the hotel room, naked and wrapped up in each other's bodies, we watch the clip, and it's as horrid as I expected. Stacey sounds like a drowning cat, and she keeps giggling at her own voice.

But we look happy.

Her giggles turn into a belly laugh as we keep watching the video, as I lift her from the stage, spin her around in my arms while we stumble out of the bar and fall into the sand. We'd stayed there talking for ages before making it back here. She must've not known the recording was still on.

Dez and Base would refuse to be friends with me if they saw the shit I got up to with her. But she always brings a fun side out of me, like her happiness is infectious, and I'm perfectly fine with it.

Just wait till my dad hears about this trip. He did pay for the first few, to help us vanish from reality for a bit, but I've worked with Ewan a lot to save, and Stacey had some money set aside, so we combined our savings for this holiday. I told him I'd tell her I loved her, and he was excited for me – said he's seeing a new side to me that he never knew existed.

Stacey does that. She showed me at the beginning of our relationship that there was more than doom and gloom, that my low moods were controllable, that the hatred I had for the world shouldn't define who I am.

She taught me everything I needed to fall for her. Even my drawings are getting better.

Stacey sits up on me, thighs either side of my waist, camera in hand.

"Really? More pictures?" I raise a brow when she snaps two more. "Live in the moment, Stacey."

She beams. "I am. I just want to have loads of things to look back on."

I sit up and kiss her. "You say that as if something bad might happen to one of us. I'm going nowhere, and neither are you."

Stacey brushes her fingers through my hair, her eyes still hooded and dazed from her third orgasm of the night. "Can we stay here forever?"

"When it comes to you, Freckles, I'd do anything."

And I mean it. She wants to stay here; I'll make it happen. She wants to move to a different planet; I'll have us on the next fucking rocket out of here.

"Even let me drive your car again?"

"Well..." She giggles as I flip us over, settling between her legs. Her nose is red from the sun, and I press my lips to it gently. "Anything but that."

16

STACEY

When Luciella lands, Barry sends a car to pick her up, and she arrives at the manor in a state of confusion. She glances around all the extra bodyguards, ones with guns and riot gear, and the black SUVs lined up at the front entrance.

I feel Aria move to stand beside me, offering her silent support as I prepare to tell my story.

"What's going on?" Luciella asks, but before I can say anything, Tylar appears at the front door with Kyle trailing behind.

He said he'd pick her up on the way, and it's just typical everyone arrives at the same time. So it looks like I'm going to be doing this now. I kind of wanted to give Lu a heads-up on the subject first, but might as well rip off the Band-Aid and get this over with.

"Can we all sit at the dining table? Or in your office?" I ask Aria.

"My office. I'll have sandwiches and drinks brought up."

Luciella frowns. "Is anyone going to tell me what's happening?"

"I will," I say. "Come on."

The walk to Aria's office is the longest walk of my life. I can't look at anyone, can't breathe properly, silently begging that this goes smoothly. Tobias knows small details about Chris, but the only other person I've told is my dad, who threw it all back in my face.

Barry asks me every day what happened, but whenever I try to formulate actual words, I fall apart and cry – but I think he has an idea. I apparently blurted out that my stepbrother beat me after murdering three people in cold blood.

Forgetting that night is impossible – I see their faces in my dreams. Sometimes, they turn into nightmares, and I don't fight back. No one comes for me – only Chris once everyone else is done with me.

I shiver and blow out a shaky breath. Maybe I'll feel better and will sleep properly once Chris is found.

This will be the first time I tell everyone the full truth. The reason for my lies. My secret stepbrother, the catastrophic abuse, my pregnancy loss and rape, and finally, the whirlwind romance I had with my best friend's brother. My only normality and what kept me going.

Nervous isn't the word I would use, but I am nervous as hell.

This could go in so many directions. What if they don't believe me like my dad didn't? What if Kyle takes his brother's side after hearing everything? Barry told him Chris hit me, that he sold me to his friends the night Barry got me to the manor. He was furious, both with his brother and himself, but everything else his brother did to me is still locked in my mind.

I sit, my hands fidgeting under the desk – Tylar is on my right, and Luciella leans against the windowsill, arms folded, still lost. Aria and Barry sit beside Kyle, opposite me.

Everyone stays quiet while I try to explain everything. I start with Kade – how we started sneaking around, falling into a cycle of seeing each other when we could. I keep glancing at Lu – she's not looking at me. But she's listening.

"I realised when we were in Greece that what we had was dangerous. I wanted to spend the rest of my life with him, but there were so many roadblocks."

"You went to Greece too?" Kyle asks. "How 'together' were you?"

"He was my boyfriend for nearly a year." I shrug. "We went to a lot of places. Going away meant we didn't need to hide."

"Then what happened?" Tylar asks. "Did you love him?"

I take a deep breath and tell them some more, and all the while Luciella stays silent, staring at her shoes. She nods at some parts, shakes her head at others and then finally, she lifts her head. "Why would you lie to me? What harm would it have done if you'd just told me you had a thing with my brother?"

Tylar snaps her head in Lu's direction. "It was more than just a thing. And she was scared her brother would find out!"

Lu shakes her head again. "So you used me as an excuse to stay quiet."

"No," I reply. "You told us to stay away from Kade and his friends. You even made Tylar break up with Dez!"

"Because I was worried about our friendship! Which obviously needs re-evaluated if you need to keep such a thing from me! You even lied that you only had one brother – not two! Who does that?"

My eyes water as I stare at her. "My brother has been abusing me since I was fourteen years old. He would sneak into my room and touch himself, make me touch myself and he recorded it. He'd barge into my shower when I was a minor and watch me. He *sold* me to his friends, hit me and controlled everything I did."

I pull down the front of my top, enough to reveal the scar he left with the key. "I have scars all over me. All in hidden places. He's sick. He killed someone in front of me because I refused to kiss him, and then made me touch him, repeatedly, every single fucking night when I went to bed so he'd stay away from Kade – he would sleep naked beside me and force me to make him—" I stop, lowering my head as my voice breaks. "He is a monster."

Kyle lowers his head in shame. "Fuck."

"I'm so sorry, Stacey," Tylar says. "I wish you'd told us, so we could've helped you."

"I went to the police, and he managed to fuck that up too. They thought I was mentally deranged and in need of psychiatric help. Even Nora took his side."

"If my mum knew the truth, she would have kicked him out."

"I told my dad," I say, glancing at Kyle, who's looking at me like he's seen a ghost. "I told him the things Chris used to do to me, but he called me an attention-seeker. I begged him to help me. *Begged.* And he said I was a hormonal teenager who needed mental help."

"Stacey..." Kyle trails off, shaking his head as his lips tremble. "I'm sorry. I should've protected you."

"It wasn't your fault. Chris acted like the loving big brother around you all, but he was the devil behind closed doors. I told the one person who should've protected me and he... he didn't believe me." I wipe under my eyes. "He looked at me differently after that, treated me like I was a brat... I was slowly losing my dad. How could I tell someone else? I'd risk losing them too."

"I can't believe your dad didn't listen," Tylar sneers. "If he was alive, I'd smack him."

Aria is hugging herself, her eyes wet. "No one should ever go through that. Your father should've protected you. I'm sorry he failed you, sweetheart, but we won't. You have us now. You have all of us around you. If you want him arrested, tell me, and I'll arrange it."

"I don't want him arrested; I want him dead." My words are solid, I don't even hesitate. "I want him dead." I look around me, at everyone on my side. "He doesn't deserve to live after everything he did to me. And I highly doubt I'm the only one."

She nods. "I understand." I know she does. She probably understands the most out of everyone here.

"His girlfriend left him because he said he was in love with someone else." Kyle runs his hands through his hair. "She slapped him in front of me and told him he was sick."

Tylar gulps. "I should have noticed the bruises. Me and Luciella had no idea."

Luciella has been silent the entire time, but then says, "I asked you, and you said you fell. Another lie."

"She had no choice, Lu!" Tylar snaps at her. "Have you listened to a word she's said? She was forced into silence!"

"Please don't argue. I lied to you both. I'm to blame."

Kyle places his hand over mine. "Don't," he says, a tear sliding down his cheek. "Don't you dare say that. You are not to blame for that asshole's actions. I lived in the same fucking house as him, and I… I… Fuck, Stacey. I'm such a shitty big brother."

"I lied to you too."

"I thought he was just possessive of you because he always wanted a little sister. I had no idea he was… doing that. Mum needs to know the truth. I'll call her and make her understand."

Tylar takes my other hand. "You have us, Stacey. You have us."

"There's something else." I hesitate for a second, my chest tightening. "I was pregnant," I blurt out, and everyone looks at me. Aria just lowers her head. "A daughter. I was sixteen weeks pregnant, and when Chris found the ultrasound picture, he beat me so badly, I lost her." I shake, my eyes burning. "I lost our daughter, and then—" I stop, unable to keep going. *I lost Kade and then my father.*

Tylar hugs me, and Luciella swipes under her eyes with her sleeve then walks around the desk, and I let out a sob as she wraps her arms around me from behind. "I wish you'd told me. I'm so sorry I made you feel like you couldn't. No one should go through that alone."

"I couldn't even tell Kade the truth," I cry. "I said I fell down the studio stairs. I lied to him too. I always lie. Always."

Everyone holds me, and the room is filled with sniffs, shaky breaths and whispers of "Sorry" and "We have you" and "We love you".

Tylar, Kyle, Barry and Aria leave us, because I still have to tell Luciella the rest of me and Kade's story. She needs to know all of it – I want to tell her.

She cries when I tell her how we found out we were going to have a baby, that we nearly got to the halfway point before disaster struck. She sobs when I tell her how me and Kade split up, and she declares war on Chris when I tell her the real reason for Kade's strained relationship with everyone.

"When was the last time you were *with* with him?"

I chew my lip. "When we went to America."

Her eyes widen. "That recent?"

I nod. "We didn't speak for two years, but... It just happened again." I leave out the part about Kade rushing me out of the country, or any information about the Sawyers. Barry gave me strict commands that I'd be risking all their lives by telling them, and since Barry has told me some of the ways Kade had been punished, I do as I'm told.

I'm the best friend ever, aren't I? All I can ever do is lie and keep secrets.

Maybe I should disappear.

"Please promise me you won't go to him again." Lu takes my hand. "And I'm not saying that because he's my brother. He's not emotionally stable – he's in such a bad place right now. I don't know what's wrong with him. He's so different, and I need you to promise me that you and Kade are done. He can't give you what you need. He'll break your heart all over again."

"I can't promise that."

"Kade doesn't even know how to love properly. He's... so like my dad it's scary."

"He knows how to love," I say, starting to get annoyed. "He might have some of your dad's traits, but he's his own person, and he loved me."

"It's not real. It's a learned emotion. He taught himself how to feel things he couldn't, but it's not the same."

"I'd take any type of love from him," I snap, pulling my hand from hers and pushing my chair back. "You can't make me stop loving him either."

"If you love him, truly love him, then let him go. Please," she begs me, and my anger ebbs. She's genuinely worried about him. "He needs to come to his senses and work on himself. He won't make you happy. I'm saying this as your best friend, he will *not* make you happy, and I need you to heal."

I manage a nod, but my heart eats away at itself.

"Please don't lie to me again, Stacey."

Barry's offer to make me vanish is becoming more and more appealing as the hours tick forward.

Kade is in France, Chris is a ghost, and when Tylar and Luciella aren't around me, all I can think about is Barry's offer.

If I disappeared, could I live a normal life?

It's been five weeks and four days of constant worrying, feeling sick with anxiety that Chris will appear and blow everything up.

I'm sitting at the dining table with Ty and Luciella while Aria goes through her list of things that need to be done while she's away. Tobias passed his evaluation after his prolonged stay in solitary confinement, meaning he's allowed to have visitors again. So Aria and Ewan will fly over for the weekend so she can log a huge-ass complaint about him being put there in the first place for no good reason.

"How many people did you invite to the party tonight?" Aria asks her daughter, who shrugs a shoulder. "Tylar?"

Ty smiles through her spoonful of cereal. "Don't worry – not too many."

She sighs. "When you say not to worry, I worry more. I can't exactly say no. My girls only turn twenty-two once." She pinches Luciella's cheek then grins at me.

"I promise it'll be a small gathering," Tylar informs her in a tone that instantly reveals she's talking crap.

Aria gives her a sceptical look. "That explains the aerial hoops set up in the ballroom, and the strobe lights, and the garage crowded with alcohol. I mean it. Don't break anything, and if I find out anyone has been in my room, you'll all be kicked out!"

"I don't even stay here," Ty replies. "How can I be kicked out?"

"For the last month, you've been here every day, and you claimed one of the spare rooms as your own years ago." Aria pops her passport and money into her bag.

"I'll call you when I land, honey," she says to Lu, kissing her cheek, and then mine and Tylar's. "Don't do anything I wou—"

"Yeah, yeah," Lu interrupts. "Don't do anything you wouldn't do. Do you forget we've read the articles? Does that mean I can have babies with a psychopath, stab someone eighteen times and sleep with someone I work with?"

Hands to her hips, she spins to face her daughter. "Luciella Mitchell! That's enough!"

All three of us burst into giggles. Tylar chokes on her cereal.

Aria's best friend was killed by someone called Justin, the deceased sidekick of Tobias, and she retaliated by driving a blade into him multiple times. Tobias took the blame, but we all know the truth. No matter how much she fights us on it. Her story has changed far too many times, and even Ewan gave us a nod behind her back once.

Aria rolls her eyes and leaves the kitchen, one of her own bodyguards following to drive her and Ewan to the airport hotel.

Tylar gets to her feet. "I'm going for a swim in your indoor pool. Who's joining?"

"I'm going to walk the dogs," I say, turning to Luciella. "Do you want to come?"

We've been normal – but there is a strain between us. She doesn't trust me, and I'm worried our friendship might be ruined.

"Sure."

Milo growls at Luciella as she walks towards him with the personalised leather harness Kade had made in Paris. She freezes and turns to Hopper with his harness instead, but he also growls. "Nope." She drops the harnesses. "Fuck this. They're going to eat me."

I smirk as I lift the harnesses and both Milo and Hopper run to me to get them on. They lick my hands and face while I clip them and sit nicely while I hook their leads. They're good dogs, they really are, but they also have Kade as an owner. He trained them to be protective of the family, but Lu never bothered with them before and was always away studying, so she didn't build a bond like the rest of us.

Lu stares at me as I pat both dogs, scratching behind their ears. "They really do belong to you and Kade. I never noticed before how attached they were to you. I… I still can't believe you kept this all from me."

I chew my lip. "Will you ever forgive me?"

She gives me a tight smile. "I don't blame you for falling for my brother; I just hate how sneaky you were about it. I... I want to trust you. I love you. You're my best friend, but I think it's going to take me a while. Can you be patient with me?"

I nod. "I am sorry." Not for falling for Kade but for lying. "I asked Kade to stay quiet about it, but it was mainly so Chris didn't find out."

She sighs and holds her hand out. "As long as I'm still your favourite twin."

"Always."

Milo and Hopper stand in front of me, and I reach out to hand a leash to her, but when she goes to take a step in my direction, Milo barks, and she jumps back.

"Nope! No. I'm not doing this. I'm going to get our costumes ready for tonight."

I laugh as she rushes away from the dogs.

Barry rises from his seat at the breakfast bar. "I have some news. And I don't think you'll like it."

"Tell me."

While walking with me through the grounds, the dogs running rings around us, he shows me a photo on his phone – Kade with his hood up, smoking a joint by a jet, waiting for a car. Beside him is a young blonde girl, but I can't see her face.

"Mr Mitchell was spotted coming off a jet this morning at Edinburgh Airport. He's standing with Cassie Sawyer – the daughter."

"Why wouldn't I like that news? Isn't it good that he's back in Scotland?"

He hesitates, and I don't think I've ever seen him so worried. "I managed to access a file on her database undetected. Kade wasn't doing his usual work in France. He was tortured so badly that his sanity was reported to be questionable, and it was recommended he be allowed to rest."

I blanch. "Oh." I gulp. "Is he... okay?"

Barry hums. "He's quite resilient to their torture methods. He's gone through worse, but I'm concerned. It says on the file that he may struggle, especially with having ASPD. He'll most likely experience dream-reality confusion."

"What can we do to help him?"

"He'll reach out soon, and I guess we'll see. I need to go home for a bit, as Lisa's due any day now, but I have on extra security. Will you feel safe enough?"

I try to smile. "You're about to have a baby, Barry. Don't worry about me. Go home to Lisa and have some time off. You deserve it. Chris is nowhere near us, and even if he was, he has no chance of getting past the manor's security."

"Did you think some more about what I said?"

I shrug. "Yeah, but Kade might need me."

"Miss Rhodes, Kade isn't going to have his freedom anytime soon. He'll get a few days off and then he'll leave again. Him needing you is dangerous for you both."

I nod, because I think he's right, even though I wish he wasn't.

17

KADE

I need to see her. I need to hear her voice. I need to touch her skin.

I need to know this is real, that *I* am real.

Her hair is dark. Her lips are pink. Her freckles cluster over her skin. She has tattoos that I drew for her when I was a teenager.

She is… She is…

What was I talking about again?

There's someone beneath me. I can't see the person's face. Their hands are lifting to my hair and tugging at the strands. "I missed you," the voice says. "I missed you. I missed you. I missed you."

Stacey? Is that you? I miss you too.

There's a jolt, and the person vanishes, pain wracks my body, and I'm thrown backwards. The darkness of the room spins somehow, and it feels like all my nerves are being stuck with needles, my teeth gritting so hard, I'm surprised none have cracked.

Then it all stops, and someone grabs my face.

"Is he still alive?"

"Yes, ma'am, just weak. I suggest we put a halt to this method. If we force any more electricity into him, his heart might stop. He's already had two seizures. I fear for his mental state."

"Mum, please, stop," I hear Cassie cry. "You're going to kill him!"

That's fine. Let me die. I'm not too fond of your fucking company.

"Not until he agrees to marry you."

A deep voice interrupts. "This young man won't be in any state to marry someone if we keep going. What you're making me do is a crime!"

Archie laughs. "The little prick killed my right-hand man. He decapitated him. My fucking *friend.* More, or I'll put a bullet in your skull and do it myself."

Maybe if I die, I'll reincarnate into a dog. Stacey likes dogs. She'll cuddle me.

I like her cuddles.

Or maybe I can haunt her – make sure she doesn't meet anyone else.

"Amp it up," Archie orders. "Then I want him treated and freed."

"Why are you freeing him?" Cassie asks, still sobbing. "Put him in my room and I'll make sure he's okay."

I can't wait to see Stacey beat the shit out of Cassie.

"I gave you an order," Archie tells the man sticking up for me. "Up the voltage. That'll teach the little cunt not to fight back."

Stacey fought back, and I wanted to as well.

Is she alright? Where's my phone so I can call her?

I don't think they can hear me.

Wankers.

Cassie screams, Bernadette sighs and tells her daughter to get out, then all sounds are blocked from my ears as electricity shoots right through my skull.

18

STACEY

Music is playing downstairs as more and more people flood the manor.

Before Barry left, he made sure his and Aria's guards knew to check every invite and to search for weapons. I know I should be nervous, but I think the shots Ty made me take have softened my anxiety a bit.

I tried to call Nora earlier, but she declined it then turned her phone off.

Kyle told me to stop. She's on her son's side, no matter what. I don't want any sort of relationship with her, but I don't want Chris to have her blessing either.

Still nothing from Kade. He's back in Scotland, and if Bernadette does what the doctor says and gives him a rest, he might reach out.

Base and Dez are downstairs decorating as per Luciella and

Tylar's demands, both dressed as superheroes. Since Base is huge in both muscle and height, he's wearing the Batman costume, and Dez, slimmer and shorter, is Robin.

All three of us are still in the huge main bathroom, sitting on the stone bench in the middle of the room while we do our hair in the floor-to-ceiling mirror that spans the full wall.

We all have high ponytails on either side of our heads, backcombed and sprayed with glitter, and fake blood splattered over our skin. We wear short tutus and tight corsets, our Pleaser boots from dancing and socks that go over our knees. Luciella is in all white, so the fake blood stands out more – especially in her blonde hair – while Tylar loves being colourful, so she's wearing pink.

I'm wearing all black, and my tutu is so short, I have to wear tight girl boxers to hide my ass. My corset nearly pushes my breasts to my chin.

We fit our Purge masks into place, the purple neon crosses at the eyes and mouth illuminating when we turn off the lights to check the glow-in-the-dark feature works.

Luciella uses a tube of fake blood to splatter her toy rifle, my bat and Tylar's plastic machete, and then she writes on my chest *Touch here.*

I scoff. "Really?"

"It looks good," she replies, laughing, then writes *Hands here* on her chest too.

We take a photo with our fake weapons, and after over fifty, Tylar tells Luciella she's going overboard. We make our way downstairs to the main room, where a DJ booth has been set up in the corner, lasers and strobes lighting up the place, and the hoops sit in the middle of the dance floor, some of our older students playing around on them.

"You did good," I say to Tylar.

"I'm a woman of *many* talents. Now – let's drink!"

We walk into the crowd, and Base beelines straight for Luciella, but his eyes drop to the writing on her chest, and his jaw ticks. Taking a gulp of his vodka, he looks at Tylar. "Dez is like an impatient puppy waiting on you."

She sighs and heads over to him.

Base glances at Luciella again. "Am I still getting the silent treatment, or are you going to talk to me, princess?"

She sucks on her teeth, narrowing her eyes. "Nope," she replies and spins around, walking away from him.

His nostrils flare as he keeps his gaze on her, watching as she vanishes into the dancing crowd.

"She is a nightmare," he says, shaking his head.

"You kind of are too," I reply. "Points for consistency though."

He huffs and finishes his drink, crushing the plastic cup. "Yeah."

"Have you heard from Kade?"

He frowns. "No, why? He's still working on that uni project overseas."

"Oh."

"Does Rhodes have a little crush on my guy?" he teases, and I shove his arm. "You have as much chance as I do with Ella. They're the most stubborn pair. Emotionless assholes."

I laugh. "They're not."

"If you say so," he mutters, his eyes finding Luciella again. She's asking someone to stop swinging on the hoop, and a guy says something to her – I think he's telling her to chill out. Base rolls his shoulders and goes towards them.

I grab a drink and stand aside, watching everyone dancing around. The music is blaring, and my face is starting to sweat under the mask already.

Three hours later, the place is packed with swaying, sweating bodies, dancing to the heavy beat that's making the whole manor vibrate. Dez and Tylar are tangled together and sucking each other's faces off. Lu is ignoring Base while he tries to talk to her, and I'm attempting to not check my phone for the millionth time.

Eventually, my friends and I, and Dez and Base, are jumping among the crowd.

The strobe lights flash faster, and I nearly stop dancing as someone appears at the very back, away from the moving crowd. Someone tall, who wasn't there before, leaning against the wall, watching me intently.

Too tall to be Chris.

Wearing black combat pants, boots and a black hoodie with the hood up, a man with a metallic silver skull mask – tipped up slightly to free his mouth – smokes a joint and watches only me as I move around the dance floor, Tylar twirling me around.

We go for shots, and my chest heaves as I wait for Base to pour each test tube.

I take the shot, and my eyes trace the room to find the person, but he's gone.

When I slip out of the party and freshen up in the bathroom, I check my phone. If that was Kade, he would've texted me, or at least called to say he was okay, right?

I have a message from Barry, informing me that he's boarding the jet now. Kyle wishes me a happy birthday and tells me to enjoy the party, apologising for not being able to make it. Technically, my birthday isn't until tomorrow, but no one wants to throw a party on a Sunday.

When I go back to the main room, Tylar is standing by the DJ booth, the music lowering and everyone turning to face her. She takes the microphone and announces that it's the games hour. She pulls flashcards from behind the booth and reads off them.

"Okay. First one. Down your drink!"

"Boring!" Base boos. "Something spicier, Spence!"

She looks over at Lu; Base is standing beside her with another tumbler of what I know will be straight vodka. "Kiss someone wearing a mask! Anyone who doesn't is eliminated from the game!"

Oh God. I don't want to kiss anyone.

Dez lifts Tylar with one hand gripping the back of her thigh, pushing up both their masks so they can devour each other like they're starved animals. People around me do the same.

Lu's mask is pushed up and she's running away from Base, but she's laughing. He catches her from behind, and I can almost hear her squeal as he lifts her and drags her into a corner. Then the crowd morphs, and I lose sight of them.

Everyone's kissing, and I try to dodge their tangled bodies as I push through the dance floor, aiming for the kitchen to pour another drink.

A shadow appears in front of me, stopping me from going

forward, and I look up to see the silver skull mask, but the mesh over the holes stops me from seeing the wearer's eyes.

Although my insides scream at me to pull the mask up and see who it is, I pat his chest and try to walk to the side of him. "No thanks."

He takes my waist and drags me to him, and I arch my back. "Um. No, sorry." When I push against his chest, he doesn't budge. "I'm not playing."

It's dark in here, but I do notice his gloved hand rising between us, his fingers tracing the writing on my chest. He smears the words with his palm, sliding the fake blood up my throat, blinding me temporarily as he forces my mask to lift then he stops at my cheek. At this point, I'm frozen, even as he smears the fake blood across my lips, dragging my lipstick with it.

"Are you real?"

My heart accelerates at hearing the voice I'm so familiar with, and I try not to smile. "I am."

He pushes my mask all the way up so I can see again. "You're real." His voice is muffled from his own mask, but I would recognise it anywhere.

I nod while he traces my lips with his middle finger, his thumb pressing down on my bottom lip.

He pushes his mask up enough to reveal his mouth. I watch him with wide eyes as he keeps going, the mask disappearing inside his hoodie, hiding his unruly black hair.

His lips part as he stares at me, searching my face, dilated pupils taking me in like he's never seen me before – like he's looking at a fascinating piece of art. I'm speechless. Between his expression of awe, and the bruising all over his chiselled face, I can't speak – all I can do is look at him the way he's looking at me.

He curls his gloved fingers at my nape; my blood turns to ice from the touch, and I'm breathless from the electric current shooting through us. It's a rush of butterflies I've not felt in a while that startles me as he eliminates the distance between our bodies.

"You're going to play this game with me," he whispers against my lips. He tastes like smoke and mint and everything I've missed. "The only person stopping me from pulling my gun out and blowing someone's brain out is you – I need you. I can hear them. Taunting and laughing at me. I can fucking *feel* them everywhere, but I only want to feel you."

A soft moan slips free as he captures my bottom lip between his teeth.

"Make them go away, Freckles."

"Make what go away?" I manage to ask.

"The voices."

I try to speak, to say who knows what, but he silences me with a brutal kiss just as "Crawling" by Linkin Park starts blasting throughout the room – along with some cheering and whooping. I'm already too caught up in the feeling of him all over me to focus on anything else.

Kade keeps his lips on mine as he backs me against the wall, sinking his tongue into my mouth with desperation as he lifts me into his arms and presses me against it. Two solid walls keep me in place as my hands grip at his shoulders and I wrap my legs around him.

I should stop this, stop him from caressing my bare thighs and pushing his palms up to my ass, but I can't. I need him just as much as he needs me – my mind has been going haywire for months, and I want to keep kissing him. And since everyone's too busy devouring each other, basically in the same position as us, I'm not shy about rolling my hips against him.

I feel his teeth, and I melt into the kiss, pressing my lips back to his and wrapping my fingers into the material of his hoodie. He's breathing heavily, gripping my thighs and ignoring his mask slipping off and falling to the ground.

He's hard, and for the first time in so long, I feel like I can let go – all the worries, the stress, the anxiety gone.

"I need you," he whispers against my throat as he nips at the skin there. "I need to know you're real. I need to know you're alive."

"I am," I cry, tilting my head to the side as he leaves a wet trail to my pulse.

I shake through my whimper as he marks my throat, his hands all over my body, not caring that we're in front of hundreds of people.

I halt his hands as he tries to pull down my underwear. "No. We're surrounded by people, Kade."

He lifts his head, confused for a second as he stares at me, and then he's kissing me again, bringing his hands to my waist instead.

Slipping my hand under his hoodie to grip his hair, my gaze clashes with Luciella's, and I freeze in his hold.

She won't know it's Kade groping me and making me soaked between my legs. It's too dark, and he has his hood up and his back to her. Unless they have some sort of psychic twin thing going on like in movies.

We should stop – everyone else is going back to dancing, and some people are looking at us.

Before I can tell him to, he snatches himself away, grabs his mask from the floor and pulls it back on. He backs away as I try to gather myself, my chest rising and falling. I frown in confusion as he keeps putting more distance between us, and then he turns and pushes through the dance floor.

I'm frozen, my heart hammering in my chest, pressing my fingers to my tingling lips. I take a step in his direction. *Where are you going? Come back.* But Lu is in front of me before I can chase him through the crowd.

I'm still touching my lips as Lu asks, "Who was that?"

I pull my mask back into place and walk past her, needing to follow him. She shouts something, but I'm aiming for the door he just slipped through.

My nerve endings are on fire, and my heart is beating so hard, I'm shocked it's not visible through my blood-smeared chest.

As I push through the crowd, I pull my phone from the side of my corset.

Me: *Where are you?*

The pulse in my neck spikes, my heart hammering in my ears as it shows he's read it, but he doesn't type back.

I chew my lip, my feet already carrying me away from the party and into the main entrance, where the grand stairway sits. If I go left, I can go to his wing and look for him, or I can take the grand staircase and check the second and third floor.

My phone dings in my hand.

***Kade**: You looking for me, Freckles?*

***Me**: You can see me?*

There's no one around.

***Kade**: From every wonderful angle.*

I glance up at the security camera, the little red light blinking. There are another three surrounding me at each corner. Kade's watching me through them.

***Me**: Where are you? I want to see you.*

***Kade**: And I want to see you run.*

Clenching my thighs, I look up at the cameras again, my eyes flickering between them all, before my phone vibrates again.

***Kade**: Run and hide. Unless you want everyone to witness me fucking you? Having an audience won't stop me – I'll take you in front of the entire party.*

My lips part as I reread the message multiple times, and I must be insane, because warmth gathers at my core at the thought of Kade chasing me, catching me and then fucking me. I'm even considering not running, just standing here until he comes for me.

But then where's the fun in that?

19

STACEY

I grip my phone, glance at the cameras again, knowing he's watching me, and head for the grand staircase. I take two steps at a time to the west wing, looking behind me as I break into a run, and throw myself into the first spare room.

My chest heaving in both anticipation and from running in heels, I sit on the mattress, dropping my bloody wooden bat on the floor next to the bed. It feels like an eternity since I properly saw him. Yeah, he came for me at the party Chris forced me to go to, but I have no recollection of anything he said, only the feel of his arms around me while he held me on the bathroom floor.

My lips tingle, and I touch them under my mask, needing him to kiss me again.

I can't stop smiling – I haven't felt this... excited in so long. Although I'm being reckless, I blame the alcohol. I should be sitting him down and figuring out what we're doing, telling him the truth, anything.

And I will.

There's a walk-in wardrobe opposite the door, so I hide inside and wait.

A few minutes pass, and I check my phone.

But as I type a message to Kade to provoke him, the door opens, and I hold my breath.

Anticipation swirls in my stomach, and I fight the urge to throw myself out and into his arms.

It's not Kade though. Lu bursts in, with Base following behind her. I move deeper into the wardrobe, peeking out at them from between some coats.

"Then why? What the fuck else do I need to do?"

"I already told you *no.* I've told you to stay away from me constantly, and you won't stop! Why? Why won't you give up?"

"Because I like you," he admits, shrugging. "Is that not obvious?"

"You just want a quick fuck."

He scoffs. "I can assure you, princess, it wouldn't be a quick fuck."

"I don't want you. I don't want to talk to you or to be near you."

Base clicks his tongue and shakes his head. "If you meant that, then you'd actually block me and not message me back. If you really wanted me to stay away from you, you'd stop phoning me when you have a fucking bad day or having me fly all the way to fucking America to sleep in your bed. Do you know how much of a head fuck that is for me? I want you. I wanted you when we kissed during dares. I wanted you when we kissed months later. Cuddling in bed. FaceTiming while we both fell asleep. And I wanted you the night we spent with the other couple. Don't you get that? It's not a quick fuck. I want *you.*"

"We would never work," she says, crossing her arms. "We can't work."

"Why?"

She stares at him, and I contemplate revealing myself. It feels wrong to be here without them knowing. I knew Base was obsessed with Lu, and they do act shifty sometimes, but she never once told me or Tylar she had him fly over and cuddle her in bed, that she cries to him on the phone, that they… I don't even know what he meant by the other things.

"We have very different lives, Sebastian. I would never fit into yours."

"How so?"

"Your grandfather wants you to take over the family business. He wants you to marry a Russian princess. I'm not even Russian! Do your friends know you have strong ties with the mafia? Do you really think my dad or brother would allow me to be with you?"

"Don't use that against me. You know where I stand with it."

"And you know where I stand with it. Therefore, we won't work."

"Tell me why," he says, pulling off his mask and tossing it on the bed behind her. "Give me a good reason and I'll stop. I mean it. I'll delete your number; I'll stop contacting you. You can find someone else to unload on when you're feeling down." He takes a step forward. "I'll give up. I promise. Just give me a good reason."

"It's wrong," Lu says, her voice shaking. "You're my brother's best friend."

"Kade doesn't give a shit. Give me a *real* reason."

Lu drops her head.

"One good reason. That's all I want. I'll leave you alone."

Luciella doesn't respond. Base takes another step towards her, pulling off her mask and dropping it next to my… *Oh God.* I left my bat. This entire night has just plummeted. Instead of Kade hunting me, I'm stuck in a damn wardrobe, and there's a chance I might witness my friend fucking Base.

If they start, I will burst out of here and cover my eyes while spewing apologies.

"Answer me, Ella." Base cups her cheek. "One. Good. Reason."

"Our first kiss was a dare, and the second time was a mistake. Everything else between us was platonic. You didn't touch me during—" She stops, her nostrils flaring, then she pulls away from him, putting distance between them. "Don't touch me."

Base pinches the bridge of his nose. "I don't know what else to fucking do here. Do you just not give a fuck about me, is that it? I'm your shoulder to lean on, right?"

"Don't."

He shakes his head. "Do you want me to stop? Do you want me out of your life for good?"

Silence. *Dammit, Luciella, you know you like him!* I want to yell at her, but I stay frozen in place, watching this unravel. I'm shocked Kade hasn't barged in yet.

Maybe he knows I'm trapped in here and that his sister and best friend are currently in the middle of an… argument? I don't know what this is.

"Tell me right now to stop and I'll walk out that door and forget the obvious chemistry between us. I'll cease all contact. Just say the word and I'm gone."

Lu hugs herself, and I really want to break out of here and cuddle her, to tell her that it's okay. I feel horrible that I'm witnessing all of this without them knowing.

Base goes to her again and tucks a blonde strand of hair behind her ear. "Princess…"

"I can't," she says, closing her eyes. "I can't."

"Then say the words and I'm gone." He strokes his thumb across her cheek gently. "You'll never have to deal with me again."

"I want…" She clears her throat, her jaw shaking as a tear slips down her cheek, and she closes her eyes and presses her cheek into his palm. "I want you to stop," she replies quietly, opening her eyes up to him. "Please."

He lets her go and takes a step back, nodding. "Right."

"I'm sor—"

Base is gone before she can finish, the door slamming behind him.

Lu is silent, chewing on her painted red lips before blowing out a breath, wiping under her eyes and closing them. "God, you're such an idiot, Luciella," she mutters to herself, sniffing and grabbing her mask. "Such a goddamn idiot."

Revealing myself will put her in a position I don't want to put her in. She'll feel the need to explain, but she'll tell me when she's ready. If there's anything to tell.

She walks to the door, stops and takes a few breaths, plants a fake smile on her face before it drops again, then puts on her mask and vanishes.

My phone vibrates as I push out of the closet.

***Kade**: You can't hide in there forever.*

I grab my bat, sneak out of the room and slowly make my way through the wing. The main stairway has a couple at the bottom and a very drunk girl on the phone with someone. I go to the left wing, nervously checking each room – walking in on people fucking and shouting an apology before slamming the door.

The lights in the hallway cut off when I reach the furthest part of the manor. I spin around, unable to see a thing, my heart racing. "Hello?" I call out, getting nothing in return. "Bathroom" by Montell Fish starts playing in the distance, and as I hear a door slam behind me, I scream and run as fast as I can in my heels.

I manage to get to the stairs, but instead of going down, I climb them to the top floor, rushing down the left wing again, my bat still in hand.

There, the lights cut off as well, and I press my back to the wall, breathless and hating how tight my corset is as my heart rate accelerates to a dangerous level. Fear and excitement engulf me, yet between my legs is soaked, and my core pulses as a shadow appears from around the corner.

Deep, dragged-out inhalations, the bright ember of a cigarette burning bright as he comes towards me, blowing the smoke in a cloud above him. I gulp, wet my lips and bite the bottom one.

One step. Two. Another. Slowly, he closes the distance between us, and slowly, butterflies go from fluttering to causing absolute chaos deep within me. But I'm not ready to be found – I'm getting a hot thrill from the chase.

I press the tip of the bat to his chest, stopping him in his tracks, and I back away. "Not yet," I say. "You're not getting anywhere near me unless you put in some effort."

He tilts his head, and God, it shouldn't be hot, the silence from him, but it is.

The more I back away, the less I see of him in the dark corridor.

Until the only things reminding me that he's really there are the sound of his breaths and the bright ember burning.

We've never done this before. Sure, he chased me through the manor grounds once, but not with the intent to fuck me. Plus, I doubt I'm going to be getting it slow and gentle.

Once I know he's going to give me a head start, I run again. I get to the second floor before I need to catch my breath.

My phone dings.

***Kade**: If you keep heading downstairs, people will see us. I think you really want them to witness you getting your ass fucked.*

***Me**: You'd need to catch me first, dickhead.*

I scream and drop my phone as strong arms wrap around my waist from behind and yank me off my feet, pushing me into a spare room and slamming me into the door to close it. Not hard enough to hurt, but enough to show he can dominate me as my chest pushes against the hard surface. He snatches my wrist, squeezing until I drop my bat, and plasters himself to my back.

He grabs one of my ponytails and wraps it around his fist, holding me in place as he slips his gloved hand up the front of my corset, capturing my throat.

"You found me," I whisper, my voice betraying me as it shakes. Instead of trying to get away, I arch my back, pushing my ass against the obvious hardness. "What now?"

He lets go of my hair and grabs my wrist, pinning it above my head, then does the same with the other. He uses one hand to hold them in place, the other sliding down my back, over the tulle of my tutu, and pulling my tight girl boxers down over my ass.

Tingles explode as he lowers his masked face to my shoulder, heavily breathing, letting out a low groan as he kneads my ass cheek, sliding the leather of his gloves between my legs, my clit throbbing as he glides over my wetness, pushing a finger inside an inch then dragging my arousal over my back hole.

I stiffen, even though I want him to keep going.

"Relax," he warns, his voice muffled through the mask.

I let out a whimper as he eases the tip of his finger inside, the tightness making me both moan and tremble. My fingers curl into my palms as he pushes in and out at a slow pace, getting deeper and making my head fall back against his chest.

My body is on fire as he picks up the pace, my moans drowning the faint music filling the darkness of the bedroom. Will he replace his finger with his cock? We only ever tried anal once, and he stopped because I was far too nervous, yet now, I want him to yank me from the door, bend me over and drive his cock so hard into my ass, I'll break my voice box from screaming.

Swirls of warmth wrap around my spine, and I push against his finger with each thrust. My inner thighs are soaked, and after a minute of him patiently waiting for me to relax, he pulls out then pushes two fingers inside. My toes are curling in my boots, and I can barely stay standing.

He pants as he releases my wrists and pushes my skull into the door as he goes harder, faster, deeper. I'm screaming. Begging for more. Crying out for God and Kade and everything as my ass grips his fingers, my pussy pulsing and clenching with each wave as my orgasm nearly knocks me out.

I wince as he pulls his fingers out, and I nearly collapse against the door, but he catches me, turning me around to face him.

He pulls his hood down, his dishevelled hair nearly as dark as his blackened heart – my vision still distorted from the euphoria running wild in my veins. Sliding his mask up, and then mine, his eyes darken with possessiveness. "*Ty moy, Vesnushki.*"

"What does th—"

Kade grabs my throat and kisses me into silence.

Our bodies touch, the vibrations unbearable. It's mind-bending, having him so close to me. He swallows my gasps, tastes the alcohol on my tongue – devouring me.

He kicks my ankles apart, and a shiver scatters through me as he presses himself between my legs. Hard, thick and ready. The heat from his cock is right at my core, and I need all the barriers gone. A moan rumbles between us, and I'm not sure who it came from. I give him back as much as he's giving me, and then he's pulling us away from the door and my back hits the mattress.

Kade's mouth is on mine again.

Pure lust and adrenaline inject into my veins as I lie beneath the devil, waiting for him to consume me until I'm no longer able to breathe, no longer capable of stringing words together. I wait for him to kiss my throat, nip the sensitive flesh with his teeth and fuck me into oblivion.

Kade Mitchell is a glitch in my system. He was never supposed to be in my life. I was never supposed to sneak behind my friend's back to take all of his firsts as I handed him mine. We were never supposed to fall in love and travel the world together. We were supposed to fuck each other until we passed out though. No matter how secretive and messed-up our lives are, holding us both back from what we want, sleeping together without anyone knowing works.

It works pretty well. I can't make myself orgasm the way he's had me submitting and unravelling in the past – taking away every single thought from my mind as he bends my own reality through each thrust and pulse of pleasure. He learned my body language while I was above or beneath him, what angles drive me deeper into the spiral, how my moans and whimpers warrant a certain speed or how hard to pound me.

Anticipation coils in my spine as he straightens his arms and looks at me, taking me in, as he licks his lips and watches the way my chest rises and falls, almost to the muffled beat of the song in the distance.

Desire courses through me as he bites his fingertips and pulls off his glove with his teeth, then reaches for my corset. He stops at the first hook. If he's planning on taking it off me, he'll be as well starting now so we can at least have sex within the next few hours. This thing took three of us to fasten. There must be a million clips.

But his eyes lift to mine. The blue of them shines, but there is an ounce of pain in them too. And need. A hunger so fierce I think he might rip the corset off my body.

"Have you let anyone touch you?" His voice is deep – a threat.

I shake my head.

"Kiss you?"

I sink my teeth into my bottom lip, and his eyes drop to my mouth. "There was this one guy," I say, breathless as he leans down to my throat again. "On the dance floor."

"Yeah?" he says against my heated skin, peppering my pulse with soft kisses.

I gasp as he nips the skin below my ear. "Yeah. He was a terrible kisser though."

"A terrible kisser," he repeats.

I lift my hands and brush my fingers through his dark hair – soft and long enough to grasp a handful for leverage while riding him. "Kade?"

He presses his hands into the mattress, arms straight, looking down at me with furrowed brows, staring into my soul.

"I missed you," I admit.

Kade stiffens above me. Then he stands. "Get up."

"What?"

"This is my father's room," he says, taking my hand and pulling me to my feet. "I'm not fucking you in here."

I wobble in my heels as I look around the room. The lights from the garden gazebo and pool house offer a glow against one wall that's littered with pictures.

Tobias with the kids over the years. Him with Aria. They look to be in their twenties – smiling, hugging. I can see why she was so drawn to him. Kade looks like his father, especially when he was younger. Apart from the tattoos and style of clothing, I might as well be fucking a younger Tobias Mitchell.

I shall never repeat that thought.

Kade is staring at me again, then he's pulling his mask back into place and his hood up. I try to get my mask from the floor, but he captures my hand. "No, I need to look at your face." And then he's leading me out of the room.

The hallway is dark, and I follow him to the stairway. His phone dings, and he quickly checks it before slipping it back into the pocket of his black combats.

"What if someone sees us together?" I ask as his fingers intertwine with my own. Luciella asked me to stay away, and I haven't even lasted twenty-four hours.

Worst. Friend. Ever.

"They won't know who I am." He taps his mask and turns sideways, helping me down the steps in my heels – the same steps I easily ran up not long ago. I don't say that, or tell him I can walk perfectly fine. I enjoy the gentlemanly version of Kade, even if my ass is still sore from him finger-pummelling it while pinning me in place.

"Swim" by Chase Atlantic is playing as we walk along the next corridor to the grand staircase – loads of people are chatting and kissing and arguing at the bottom of it.

The strobes flash from the party as we take each step, lasers zapping through the door from the ballroom. I should be there considering it's half my party, but as Kade tightens his fingers around mine, I know I'd rather be here.

My eyes land on Tylar. Dez has her against the wall, slotted between two marble pillars, both their masks gone. Her legs are around his waist as he drags kisses along her throat. Not fucking – but very close to it. I gulp, looking up at Kade, his mask and hood in place, hiding him.

Then Ty opens her eyes and sees us, and we watch each other as Kade leads me towards his wing. We turn right, and I glance over my shoulder – she's still following us with her hooded gaze as Dez kisses up her neck and along her jawline.

She smiles. And then she winks at me.

20

STACEY

I blush and turn away, silently praying Luciella doesn't appear and ask who I'm with, and why the hell we're heading to Kade's side of the manor – none the wiser that I'm holding hands with her twin brother.

My inner thighs, soaked in my own come, rub together, and when I spot the spiral staircase, my pulse speeds up, butterflies swarming inside me once more. My heart is racing, I'm so excited to have time with him alone. To spend the entire night in his bed, in his arms.

We'll fuck until we can't see straight, and then we'll talk. I'll tell him everything, and then we'll figure out how to move forward.

This far away, the music is barely audible. All I can feel are the vibrations of the base and the tingling of my nerves. They explode as Kade abruptly pins me to the wall by the shoulders.

"This is far enough."

"For what?"

He tugs at my panties under the tutu. "Take these off," he demands through his mask. "Now."

I look down the hallway, unable to see the main entrance of the manor. I swallow, but as my blood sings in my ears, I hook my thumbs into the fabric, slowly sliding them down my legs. They pool at my feet, and I step out of them, then lean down to grab the material and hold them out to him.

He stuffs them into his pocket and takes a step back. "Kneel."

I do.

My ass rests on my boots, the cold leather biting into my skin. I wait, lifting my eyes to his skull mask and watch him slowly unbuckling his belt, unzipping his combats and freeing his cock.

I don't take my eyes off him as he presses his palm to the wall above me, guiding his tip to my lips, sliding his precum across them. My tongue slips out, tasting him, barely grazing the head of his cock.

"Open."

A man of few words, yet they're enough to make my pussy throb.

I part my lips.

His voice is low, tone controlled but deep. "Tongue out."

I do as I'm told, my fingers digging into my thighs in lust-filled anticipation. He guides his dick forward, sliding the head against my tongue, only an inch, in and out, and I can taste more of his precum as it leaks from the swollen head.

"If you need to breathe, tap my leg." Then he shrugs. "Or don't."

Then my head hits the wall as he thrusts fully into my mouth, down my throat, gagging me into silence. My eyes water, and I swallow around the length of him as he groans.

With his metallic skeleton mask looking down at me, framed by the black hood, the view from where I am is terrifying. But does that make me insane to want more? To be turned on by this?

His other hand still on the wall, he wraps one of my ponytails around his leather-clad fist, fucking my mouth, and I'm pinned between two immovable objects as his cock pummels my throat. I try to drag in some fresh air as I hear him groan and mutter a deep, dragged-out *fuck* under his breath.

He gets into a steady rhythm as he robs me of air, and I keep my eyes on him, not daring to look away as tears slide down my cheeks.

Kade pulls fully out of my mouth, and I fill my burning lungs, a string of saliva trailing from my mouth to his tip, before he drives back into my throat and my head is firm against the wall again. His cock swells even thicker between my lips, and my tongue traces each bulging vein.

Deep. Hard. Fast. Everything I want him to do between my legs, he's doing to my mouth. Attacking my throat with lethal rage.

"Always such a good girl when you're on your knees for me. Taking every inch, your throat welcoming me home." He punches the wall above me as he grits out, "Fuck, Stacey, fucking keep sucking my cock."

The fake blood on my chest is smearing from all the liquid leaving the corners of my mouth. The gagging sounds mix with the wet sloshing of each thrust of his cock, and I hear him hiss; see him press the forehead of his mask to the wall as I swallow.

When he goes faster, I want to wrap my hand around the thickness of his cock, but he has it pushed in to the hilt. More saliva gathers in my mouth and drips down my chin, and I'm not sure if that's causing the puddle beneath me, or if it's the slick desire from my throbbing pussy.

I gasp for air as he pulls out again, and before I can wipe my mouth, he yanks me to my feet and pushes me against the wall, dragging his leather-clad thumb across my mouth. The skull glares back at me as my chest rises and falls.

The mask lifts, revealing his good looks, before he lowers to his knees one at a time.

"Part yourself. Show me your pretty little cunt."

I run my shaking fingers up my soaked thighs, pulling the material of my tutu up to reveal my needy core before parting my pussy lips for him.

He stares at how wet and swollen and eager I am for him. I keep myself open as he glides his palms up the back of my thighs, grasping my ass cheeks so hard he's parting them too.

I shake in my heels as he leans forward and kisses my inner thigh, then the other.

I moan as he dives forward, hidden beneath my tutu, sucking on my clit harshly and taking it between his teeth. My fingers slide from the intensity of the feeling that overwhelms me, but I breathe and part myself again around his mouth as he circles my clit with the tip of his tongue.

"Put your leg over my shoulder."

My fingers grab at his hood, holding him in place as I hook my leg over his shoulder, opening myself to him further. I grind against this mouth and whimper, *"Oh God,"* as he swipes at my clit then lowers to my entrance to devour my cunt like a starved animal.

"I knew you were delicious, Freckles," he growls against my clit, taking it between his teeth again and making me jump in shock as his fingertips press at my back hole again. "I just needed a reminder."

My spine twists with pleasure, a coiling heat starting at the lower part of my stomach, but as I try to move against his mouth and chase the orgasm that's so close already, he pulls away.

"I'm going to kill you if you stop again," I pant, the tingling already fading. I'm almost tempted to drop to the ground and get myself off, but as his burning gaze stays on me, I resist. He stuffs his cock back into his combats and leads me to the bottom of the stairs, then pulls his mask back into place and points to the ground in front of me.

"Get on your hands and knees," he says, gesturing to the spiral staircase. "And crawl up them."

Swallowing, I glance up then back over at him. "You want me to crawl up the stairs?"

"That's what I said."

"Is this what you need?" I ask softly. "You need the control?"

Kade stays silent.

But I understand. He's been forced into sex, had zero control over his life for months, so this must be him trying to get it back. I'm more than happy to give it to him.

He waits patiently until I lower myself to all fours, my ass in full view for him as I take the first step. I should be flushing with embarrassment, telling him to fuck off, but my pussy is drenched and needy and desperate.

I feel an intense need to please him.

I can feel his hungry gaze on me as I take a few more steps, his boots walking up two behind. I want to look over my shoulder, but I know his eyes will be on what's waiting for him at the top, seeing how soaked my thighs are and how swollen my cunt is.

I freeze as he tosses his other glove off and moan as he shoves a finger into my pussy.

"Keep going," he orders through his mask, his voice muffled, as he curls that finger inside me, working in and out as I take each step slowly.

"So wet," he says – a deep growl that vibrates in my bones – then presses his thumb to my back hole, ceasing my movements. "I never told you to stop."

My back bows as he nudges his thumb against the tightness of my ass, adding a second finger to my pussy and fucking both. I attempt to move but barely. I try to push back against him to feel more, but he grabs my hair to stop me. "Keep fucking crawling."

"I-I can't."

I wince as he pulls his hand away – his boots are heavy as he follows.

A smack on my ass jolts me, my knees crushing into the metal steps. "Keep going." Another smack, and my pussy clenches at the stinging pain.

My thighs rub together, and when we reach the top, I'm panting and dripping, desperate for another touch, my walls clenching around thin air.

Kade takes my throat, pulling me to my feet. "That's my girl," he groans against my mouth. "I like when you do as you're told."

I whimper his name as he lightly strangles me, and he doesn't stop me as I yank his cock free, taking it in my hand and pumping slowly, feeling my back against his door as he tries to unlock it while I stroke him.

My thumb swipes at his sensitive tip, and his dick throbs in my hand. His knee separates mine, and I grind against his leg while he thrusts himself into my palm.

Kade shoves me through the door, kicking it shut behind him as he lifts me into his arms by my thighs, and he doesn't protest as I grind against his cock, seeking the thickness of him inside me.

His grips my ass cheeks, fingers digging into my skin, bruising and fucking driving me mad as he rolls my hips against him, his swollen crown easing through my soaking entrance.

I moan, hands diving into his hair under his hood.

My back hits the mattress, and without taking off our clothes, or his mask, he abruptly drives his cock into me with such delicious force, I let out a choked scream.

Kade isn't slow or gentle. My back is dragged up the bed with each thrust, and he hikes my leg up to his shoulder to get a deeper angle – opening me for him then fucking me senseless.

The skull watches me as his cock pounds into me, making my eyes roll, my breasts spilling out of my corset.

"Fuck," he blurts out.

Lowering his elbow next to my head, he drives his cock in and out of me continuously, mercilessly, most likely marking my thighs given how hard he's hammering into me.

But I love it. I love that it hurts – mixing with the pleasure and him and what we have.

My hands push into his hood and grip his hair again as I roll my hips into his, meeting each thrust. My teeth sink into my bottom lip as a roaring heat courses through me, as a coiling starts at the base of my spine and has me arching off the bed.

He groans and buries his masked face into my shoulder, snapping his hips against me, each thick inch of him penetrating my core repeatedly – until I'm unable to speak or see or hear, only concentrating on the sweet spot his cock hits that has me tugging his hair as my walls tighten around him.

"You know what I've missed? This," he says, tossing his mask off and dragging his wet mouth down my jawline, my throat, slowly licking at the top of my breasts, covering his face in fake blood. "Feeling your cunt wrapped around me and fucking throbbing while your orgasm builds. You can feel it, can't you? If I keep going, you're going to fucking explode around me."

"Please keep going." Each word is a pleading moan, my ankles around his thighs and drawing him in deeper. "If you stop, I'll hurt you."

"What's fucking new," he mutters against my throat, sucking the flesh between his teeth and releasing my ass, dropping his hand between us to rub my clit. "Let go, Freckles. Strangle my cock while you scream for me."

My lips part, and Kade cages my head with his other arm, capturing my mouth with his.

The kiss is firm but demanding, and as my orgasm builds to unbearable heights, Kade swallows my scream, his tongue delving into my mouth. My spine curls, as do my toes – still in my heels – and my entire body bursts into flames while Kade drags his cock in and out with dominating thrusts.

"K-K," is all I can manage as he groans into my mouth, his tongue stroking my own, tilting his head to deepen the kiss as my orgasm hits its pinnacle. My muscles tense all over, and I can't stop my limbs from shaking.

"Can I come inside you?" he asks, gritting his teeth as he fucks me, the sounds of my wetness intensifying as I feel how drenched the bed beneath me has become. "Fuck. Do I need to stop?"

"Not yet," I pant. "I want to come again."

"So greedy."

I unhook my legs from behind his thighs and shove him, so he falls onto his back, then climb on top of him.

He doesn't stop me as I pull up his hoodie and shirt, tracing his abs with my hands – then he helps me pull them off, tossing them across the room. I kiss across his shoulder blades, holding him down as I align myself with his swollen head.

We both gasp as I sink onto his cock and he fills me with his thick length.

He wraps his hand around my throat and pushes me back, so I'm sitting on him. "You going to ride me like a good little slut?" His words are strained as I lift my hips and roll back down, taking every inch. "Fuck. Keep going." He thrusts upwards. "Just like that."

I bounce all over his dick, chasing my third high of the night as he robs me of air, using his hold on my neck to slam me down on him.

Kade throws his head back with a groan, his Adam's apple bulging, the veins on the right side of his neck pulsing as his cock swells inside me.

"If you don't get off me, Freckles," he says, gritting his teeth and guiding me as he bounces me on his cock, "then I'll fucking come in you. I don't give a fuck if you're on birth control or not. I'll fill you with every damn drop and watch it leak out of your cunt." He fucks up into me harder. "Your choice."

He sits up with me in his lap, bringing us chest to chest, and I keep grinding on him, my clit against his pubic bone as he kisses me again. Soft, gentle, he runs his tongue along the seam of my lips before I part them. I take his face in my hands, fingers curled in the dark hair behind his ears, deepening the sensual kiss with a slant of my head.

Another orgasm smacks into me, and as my walls tighten around his cock in quick intervals, Kade kisses me even harder. I try to whimper, to scream, to moan his name, but he's silencing me with his tongue, snaking his arm around the small of my back and bringing me down faster.

My vision blurs, and my spine twists with each pulse of pleasure, and Kade devours my throat, sucking on the skin as I drop my head back.

Kade's fingers curl into my nape, digging into my flesh and dragging me down harder – then he lets out a deep, guttural moan and stills, his cock pulsing inside me as he fills me up with his cum.

We both collapse as soon as the sensations start to settle, and a low buzz in my ears accompanies the fulfilling feeling. Kade rests his head on my beating chest, arms wrapping around my back and holding me to him while we catch our breaths. Our sweating bodies become one.

"Did I hurt you?" he asks.

My eyes close, and I fall into a deep sleep before I can reply.

21

KADE

FLASHBACK

Dad's version of love comes in the form of obsession; a desire so strong that the only way to have it is to seek, to stalk, to steal and to destroy. He had it all in the palm of his hand and crushed it with one bad decision.

Honestly, he can be a great guy when he tries, but on the inside, he's nothing but hollow darkness wanting to plan an escape, a murder, or to steal my mother away from the world. Or that's what he tells me when he's having a bad day and decides to call me in the middle of one of his episodes.

I've seen images and CCTV footage of Tobias Mitchell in his element. Dangerous. Deadly. A man with a mission, and that mission was to do anything possible to have my mother to himself.

His kill count was announced to the entire world when his case was televised in every country.

He killed two officers and permanently disfigured four others when they tried to arrest him in a hotel room. Let's say his possessive side kicked in, and he lost his shit thinking they were taking Mum. He escaped jail weeks later – and killed a lot of prison guards in the process.

With help from my bitch of a grandmother, he hid for weeks and stalked my mother – until he couldn't watch her anymore. Then he kidnapped her and locked her in a dog crate in an abandoned animal shelter in the middle of the woods.

Yep, a dog crate. Her and her best friend Gabriella were padlocked into them.

The only way to make it stop was for my mum to agree to run away with my dad.

Tobias Mitchell is pure fucking evil. I might love him, but him staying within that facility is the safest option for everyone.

It all started with him tripping her up by accident and thinking she was pretty.

The first thing I thought when I saw Stacey was that she was pretty. I could see myself hurting someone for her.

I have the DNA of Tobias. Therefore, I am capable of destroying Stacey.

A soft hand strokes my cheek. "Hey. You're zoning out again."

I snap out of it and look up at my beautiful girlfriend. "Sorry, I'm jet-lagged."

"Is there something wrong?" she asks, her thumb swiping under my eye. "Did your dad say something while you were over?"

I turn my head and kiss her palm, perching on my elbows on the studio floor. "Nah, I promise I'm just tired."

"Tell me again how your dad was, and why do you think your parents are sleeping together?"

I sigh. "It's just a feeling I have."

She fastens her leather harness at the shoulder, ensuring it's tight enough. "Ewan looks at your mum like she's his entire world."

"Because she is. I can't say she looks at him the same way though. I know she loves him, but my dad definitely has her in his hold still. I think the only way to free her is if he died."

Stacey gasps and tries to slap my arm. "Don't say that!"

"It's inevitable." I shrug. "He's an old man."

She glares at me. "No he isn't. He's in his forties. And fifty per cent of the world's population would fuck your dad."

I tilt my head, confused and disturbed. "What has fucking him got to do with his age?" I lean up and grab her ass, tugging her down on me, so she's straddling my lap in her barely visible outfit, those leather straps everywhere. "Are you part of that statistic?"

She bites her lip. "Maybe. It's the villains that are the sexiest after all. Who wouldn't want a bad boy?"

"He's a psychopath who murdered people."

Her cheeks turn a bright shade of red as she smiles. "Even better."

I groan and attempt not to let the jealousy win. "You're trying to annoy me."

I can hear the teasing note in her tone. "He's Tobias Mitchell."

She stands in her ridiculously high heels and hits my hand away when I try to pull her to me again, continuing to set up for her routine. My eye twitches, but then she adds, "Besides, I prefer his son."

I smirk and decide she'll be mine forever. "Good girl."

She grins over her shoulder at me, then I watch her every move as she sets up.

"Explain this to me," I say, flicking the bucket of liquid while Stacey pulls her hair into a high, tight ponytail, before wrapping it into a secure bun at the top of her head.

"It's a fire-retardant gel to stop my skin from burning."

I tilt my head as she rubs the gel over her hands and arms. I watch her, mesmerised by her beauty while I lie on my side, the studio's LEDs settling on a red glow. Stacey then studies her staffs.

"So you won't go up in flames? Where's the fire extinguisher, just in case?"

She shakes her head with a smile that lights up her face. "I won't go up in flames. The training I've had involves a lot of safety procedures. The flames will simply lick my skin."

"Sounds hot."

"It definitely feels hot," she says. "Are you sure you don't want to go meet your friends? Base might actually hunt you down and force you to go play pool with them."

"He'll survive. I'm sure he's still moping over the fact Luciella isn't replying to his texts. He'll be a bottle of vodka deep and flirting with a wall."

Stacey grins again while she sets up the floor, making sure nothing is in the way, then starts her stretches. "I think she'll give in one day."

"Hmm."

I'm not paying attention to her words as she lowers into a side split and bends her body forward, grabbing her foot and resting her head there. The position makes her ass more defined than it already is, and I want to bury my face between her cheeks.

She won't let me though. Apparently, that part of her body is out of bounds to my face and my dick.

We were each other's firsts for everything, so sue me for trying to take her ass virginity too. I stare at it as she shifts her splits to the other side, then the front. She gets on all fours and pushes back, and I picture myself peeling her little panties down and sinking my tongue deep inside her.

She's been insatiable lately. Even I'm struggling to keep up with her half the time. I'm getting texts to meet in a spare room, a bathroom, in the woods on the grounds, or here in the studio. If I'm not fucking her, my face is between her legs. If she isn't bouncing over my cock, I have her bent over the closest flat surface.

I fingered her in the kitchen while my family was literally outside. I fucked her in the pools, both indoor and outdoor. The latter was fucking freezing by the way – I'm surprised I even got hard. But we were both drunk and fooling around.

She seems to like sucking me off while I'm smoking a joint. We both cut off cigarettes, but as soon as I build a J, she's already tying her hair back and dropping to her knees.

I've been stoned a lot lately.

I've lost count of how many times I've fucked her in my car, and we only got back from Greece two weeks ago. Before I left to spend the weekend with my dad, she crawled under the duvet and sucked my cock until I pinned her down and had her digging her heels into my thighs to push into her tight cunt.

Fuck, now I want to hear her scream.

"I'm going to start now," Stacey tells me. "I used the song you recommended – did I tell you?" She presses play on her phone, and the

dark version of "Can't Help Falling in Love" by Tommee Profitt begins.

A proud smile pulls at my lips. "I knew you'd choose that one. The other was too fast."

Stacey walks to the side of the room to light her equipment as the song plays from start to end very quietly. "I'll try the routine with the fire staff first, then I'll try the dart rope or the fans. I'm not as experienced with the fans though. If I'm going to do this routine in front of thousands, then I want to make sure it's perfect."

My girl makes me proud. She did routines in the background during the show in October and someone spotted her. A few days ago, she received an email, an offer to perform with the Carnival Kraze in London as a fire dancer in May.

She hasn't accepted the offer yet; she wants to make sure it's something she can actually do. Stacey talks herself down a lot, and has a lot of confidence issues, but if she looked at herself the way I do, the way the kids and adults she teaches do, she'd see how fucking amazing and inspirational she is.

Luciella insists daily that she should take the offer, usually with capital letters. She's pushy, my dear sister, but she means well.

She's coming home on Sunday. Five days from now. That's when we're going to tell her about us. Fucking finally. Stacey is ready, and she feels that the first person to know should be her best friend – my twin sister.

I'm ready to tell everyone she's fucking mine and I belong to her. You see that girl there? Mine. All mine.

Dad said I should calm the fuck down when I told him the plan at the weekend.

She stands in the middle of the room with a red LED glow surrounding her, the orange and yellow hues from the flames flickering her shadow around us. Her eyes zero in on my crotch. "Are you hard?"

"My dick has been hard since I walked in and saw you dressed like that. Dance, then I'll deal with it."

Even with the fire and the red lighting, I still see her blush.

The song starts from the beginning, louder this time, and my entire focus is on Stacey. On the burning sticks in her hands, the black polish, the dark hair scraped away from her face. She has minimal make-up on, just a red lipstick I've imagined staining my cock, and her body harness is taut over her lithe form.

She was going to just wear her bra and panties instead of her strapped bodysuit, but lately, Stacey has been majorly against herself. Instead of showing off every curve I've run my tongue all over and worshipped, she covers up her midsection and wears netted tights.

Everything about her to me is perfect. I wish she'd see it – the way her body moves with the music as she twirls and lets the flames flow around her. She's bendy, something I also love about her. When her leg flies up and she points her latex boots to the ceiling, she drags the fire stick against the inside of her thigh, over her pussy, then to her tits before pulling herself back to a standing position.

I gulp and try to pretend my cock isn't painful and twitching in my shorts.

Her eyes find mine as she moves slowly, sensually with the fire. I push myself up and sit against the wall, bending one leg at the knee and attempting to hide how hard I am. I don't want to distract her, even though I want to throw her onto a crash mat and fuck her into oblivion.

The main beat within the song comes, and she speeds up a little, the flames moving faster, the fear settling in my gut when I see how close they are to her face. She's been training fire dance for a while, and I know she'll be fine, but I'm too paranoid.

She drops into a side split and drags the flames all over her. The action makes her ass pop out again, and I itch to touch it.

Would it be inappropriate to have a wank while she dances?

My head snaps into a slant as she tips her head back and opens her mouth, tongue out, and I watch as she slides the fire stick into her mouth. She swallows the flame, and I blow out a heavy breath.

That's... new. And hot. I want her to do that with my dick.

She grabs a ball-and-chain-looking thing and lights it on the small flame in front of her while still in her routine.

Her eyes are dark sins; fierce as the fire she circles around her body. She glides the flaming ball against her arm as she arches to the side, balancing on one foot on her tiptoes and spinning.

I gulp again as she switches back to the staff and turns to face me, spinning the thing between her fingers like a majorette baton.

Stacey eats up the distance with flames twirling around her perfect form, eyes not leaving mine as I try not to let my mouth fall open. I've always found her sexy, hotter than hell itself, and seeing her dance with fire and regard me with a look that begs me to fuck her, my dick gets even harder.

Her heels stop at my feet, and she kicks my bent leg. I flatten it and watch as she lowers into my lap, the flames hot against my skin. She drags the stick down her front, and I keep my hooded gaze on her eyes as she tosses it into a bucket next to us, dousing the fire, the studio darkening.

The song still plays on repeat as she wraps her arms around my neck, rolling her hips with the music, not quite against my dick but close. She needs to lower a bit more for contact. It's killing me so much that my hands shake, but I let her keep going.

"You're killing me, Freckles."

She tugs at my hair so my head drops back, then sinks her teeth into my throat just as she fully grinds against me. I let out a growl as she sucks on my skin, but I don't move. I don't use my hands or try to stop her as she marks my flesh. I don't lift my hips to meet each movement of hers. I give her full control of me as she slowly dry-rides me to the song.

Each drop of the base, I feel my balls tighten, the urge to flip her and fuck her so fucking strong. She licks and sucks at my throat, dragging her lips up my neck to my ear, taking the lobe between her teeth.

The song ends, but then it starts again. Fuck. I'm fucked.

She releases my hair with one hand and slides one side of her black leather harness down her shoulder. But I stop her. "Don't," I whisper, barely able to breathe. "Keep it on." I drop my hand between us, tugging the buttons at the bottom of her bodysuit. "I want this off."

Once I get all the buttons, I freeze, looking up at Stacey. "I don't have panties on," she says with a flirty shrug. "They're annoying to move around in."

Her pussy is wet against my fingers, and I decide I'm taking over. My other hand reaches up to her throat as I cup her fully, rubbing against her entrance and clit.

Her lips part, the red lipstick smudged across her cheek.

She's pulsing against my palm as I caress her cunt. I grit my teeth. "Dance."

One word. One order. One syllable that has her pupils dilating and her hips rolling to the dangerously slow beat. She complies, resting both elbows on my shoulders as she rocks into my hand, coating me in her pleasure, her arousal dripping from her. Through the music, I hear her little gasps and whimpers as I slide a finger inside.

Her inner walls grip me as I add a second, but she only moves more, fucking my hand, my fingers buried deep as her thighs soak with her arousal.

I let go of her throat and free my cock, stroking myself while I watch her. Stacey's head falls back, her body writhing above me.

She wraps her fingers around mine, and I let her take over on my dick while I tug down the front of her bodysuit then reach behind and unclasp her bra. Her precious, swollen tits bounce free, and she moans louder than the song as I take one nipple into my mouth and pinch the other.

I move my mouth to the other nipple, sucking hard while I finger-fuck her.

She moans my name then nearly screams it as her body falls apart above me. Her orgasm smashes into her, and she gasps through it, but I don't stop, pushing in another finger and rubbing her clit with my thumb.

Finally, she falls from the peak of her euphoria and winces as I pull out my fingers, lifting them to her mouth. She licks them clean, and I capture her mouth in a kiss.

"Can I fuck you?" I practically plead against her lips.

Stacey stares at me, breathless. "Do you want to?"

"Yes." I take her throat again, capturing her bottom lip between my teeth.

She wraps her fingers around my dick and rubs the tip against her drenched entrance. Teasing me. Driving me fucking insane.

I let go of her, grab her hips and slam her down on my cock.

The song restarts while she's riding me. I'm not sure if the mirrors are steaming up from the flames she danced with or us. She moans as I rub her clit while she grinds against me, chasing her next orgasm. As soon as it hits her, her cunt strangles me, and I try not to fuck up into her hard and fast since she's obviously found a rhythm that gets her to her pinnacle.

When she comes down from the high, I flip us so I have Stacey on all fours, slapping her ass and pushing into her from behind. I thrust slowly but hard, pulling the pins from her hair so it cascades down her back and around her. I wrap it around my fist, notice the tattoo of our initials on her back and smile.

Wearing my art like a trophy. Branded as Kade fucking Mitchell's property.

I keep my eyes on it while I bring her to another orgasm, and my balls tighten, my spine twisting with pleasure as I still on a groan and empty inside her.

I've lost count of how many times I've come inside her. It's almost like an obsession in itself. My heart rockets, both of us sweating and panting as I pull out and collect the cum sliding down her thigh, shoving it back into her.

She whimpers as I sink my two fingers in to the knuckles, desperate to press my thumb against that forbidden hole. She'll slap my hand away and call me gross, but the need to lean down and swipe my tongue against it is nearly unbearable.

I don't even know why. I've heard too many stories from Base about anal. He loves it. He also preaches that every person in the world should know what an anal orgasm is.

I just want Stacey to feel good.

I tuck my dick away and watch as she rolls onto her back, completely fucked and out of breath. "Wow."

Chuckling, I go over to her phone and turn the song off. "I highly recommend not doing that in your routine in London. I'll end up killing someone for trying to steal my girl."

She rolls her eyes. "Like I'd ever cheat on you."

The sound of the front entrance doors opening stops me from replying. We both turn to the studio doors, and Stacey quickly buttons up her bodysuit and gets her bra back on just as Tylar pushes into the room with a folder.

"Oh." She stops, staring at us. Me in my shorts and T-shirt, hair a sweaty mess, and her in her dishevelled dancing outfit, smeared lipstick, and cum leaking down her legs.

Hopefully she can't see that last part.

Tylar walks into the middle of the room, freezes again and stares between us both. That's right. If you were five minutes earlier, you would have seen me bending her over and fucking her into next week.

She looks at my hair, then at Stacey. "Hi. I needed to bring this down for you to sign. The kids got accepted into the competition in Surrey. Can you sign them off?"

Stacey, with shaky hands, gives her a tight smile. "Of course."

Tylar looks at me again while Stacey does just that. "Did Lu ask you to fix the lights above the mirror?"

I raise a brow and look behind me at the lights. None seem broken, but before I can say no, Stacey hands her the folder again. "Yes. He said he'd stay back and give me a ride home. Right, Kade?"

I simply hum. She doesn't believe us. I can tell. She's going to tell Dez, who will confirm it with what he knows, and Stacey will boot me in the balls for not telling her my friend knows about us. Is it bad that I don't care? Let them all know. What's the big fucking deal?

As soon as Tylar leaves, Stacey sighs and leans her head on my chest. "Sunday can't come quick enough. Luciella should know first. I just hate hiding."

"Me too, Freckles. As much as I love hiding with you."

I kiss her head then sit and watch as she redoes the entire routine.

And this time, she doesn't forget her routine and decide to fuck me.

Sadly.

22

KADE

I'm waiting for it – the abrupt jolt to my brain that pulls me out of this.

I fell asleep. I never fall asleep. I always fuck and leave. I always go to the nearest bathroom, vomit up my guts then snort far too many lines to forget what I just did.

Clients are becoming more frequent, to the point that I'm trying to compromise with Bernadette not to send me, to send someone else. I even offered to pay one of her guards to fuck a client fully masked and pretend they're me.

Why did I fall asleep?

I woke up ten minutes ago with my combats down to my ankles, boots still on, and felt like I'd fallen asleep within a dream and woken up in fucking paradise.

The feel of Stacey cuddled into my side. Her breath on my skin with each fill of her perfect little lungs. Her hand splayed on my chest.

She's alive. She's real. She's alive.

And she's lying on my bed in a ripped tutu, a corset that barely contains her tits and heeled boots she usually only wears while dancing – with marks on her throat, reddened skin on her inner thighs and my cum dripping out of her cunt. I must be dreaming still.

The joint in my pocket is still intact, so I spark it, lean against my dresser and watch her. I watch the glistening liquid seeping out of her pussy, the clear evidence that I just fucked her – my cock is covered in her cum too.

I pace my bedroom again, taking draw after draw, running my hand through my hair, stopping to look at her again.

She's real.

I stub out the smoke, go into the bathroom, soak a towel in warm water and come back out. Then I climb onto the bed, settling between her legs, and start cleaning up her thighs.

She moans as I wipe her pussy, and I freeze, lifting my gaze up to her, but she's still asleep. The last thing I want to do is make her hot and bothered while she's passed out, so I wipe the rest of her thighs then lean forward and place a soft kiss on one.

She moans again, and my cock twitches as if I didn't screw her brains out not long ago.

I pull myself away, rinse the towel, toss it into the basket near my door then clean myself up. Stacey is still asleep. I even check her pulse to make sure she's alive.

I've had enough nightmares of her dying, I check her pulse twice to make sure.

Then I check my phone and find four missed calls from Cassie. My eyes shut momentarily when I see a message.

> ***Cassie**: You aren't in your apartment like you said you would be, and your motorbike is gone. I won't tell my mother yet, but she'll be furious when I do. You have an hour.*

I exit the message and shake my head, nearly crushing my screen as I grip it. Fucking little twisted bitch. What part of "I'm not interested" does she not get? No matter how much shit they put me through, I won't marry her. I'm not even contemplating giving in either.

It must be the drugs, but I feel blood all over my hands. Once I wash them for the tenth time, I stare at Stacey again, not sure if I should wake her up and tell her I need to leave or just… leave.

I can hear the faint hum of music playing downstairs. I wonder if my friends are still there?

I go back into the bathroom, splash my face again and try to make sure I don't look too fucked up. But it's no use. I've taken more lines than I can count tonight, needing something to take the edge off the pain still lingering from all those days I spent strapped to that goddamn electric chair.

Stacey is still asleep as I slip out of my room and down the spiral staircase I made her crawl up. Fuck, did that actually happen? Did she do that? Was it in my head?

I grab the hair at my nape as I walk through the manor, pulling it until it hurts.

If I feel pain, I won't feel everything else.

The party is still going wild as I enter, the smoke machine and strobes making it difficult to see. Some raved-up remix of Taylor Swift's "You Belong With Me" is blasting, and as I get closer, I spot Base – he's topless, standing on one of the hoops hanging from the ceiling, shouting every lyric perfectly while Luciella tries to get him down.

He's singing the chorus to my sister and replacing words to fit their situation.

He's smashed. But I still need to talk to him.

I push through the bouncing crowd until I reach him, and he grins. "Kade! When the fuck did you get here?"

My sister turns to look at me then glances at my black hoodie and combats. Her eyes narrow, and she gives up trying to pull Base down and marches straight for me. "Where is she?"

I arch a brow. "Who?"

"Stacey."

I shrug and cross my arms. "No idea," I lie.

Base climbs down and pulls me in for a hug. Not even a bro hug or a pat on the back – the fucker bear hugs me and lifts me off my feet. His pupils are blown, he's sweating from dancing like a lunatic for hours and he has pink lipstick on his cheek.

Luciella isn't wearing pink lipstick.

"We need to go to a Taylor Swift concert," Base says. "Reckon she'd take me on stage."

"Sure," I say. "Come with me."

"Where's Stacey?" Luciella asks me again. "She isn't answering her phone, and security said she hasn't left the manor. Where. Is. She?"

"Are you deaf? I don't fucking know."

My sister stands in front of Base as I try to grab him away from her, and she glares at me, knowing I'm talking shit, but I don't care. I need to talk to Base.

I shake my head. "Stop trying to control everything, Luciella. I'm surprised you even have any fucking friends left."

I drag him away from the daggers Luciella is throwing at us, and he follows me out of the room, into the kitchen and out back. The cold air hits me, and I feel like I can breathe again.

"Where the fuck are we going? Why did you talk to your sister like that?"

"Just walk," I reply, rolling my eyes at my friend, who's still jumping about to the faint music.

Once we get into the pool house, I pull out a bag and set down two lines of coke. "I need to talk to you about something," I say to him as I offer him a rolled-up note. He takes it and doesn't wait to snort the white powder.

I use drugs because I feel like I'm dying if I don't. After having this shit fed to me for sport, it's a habit now. Base just takes it for a bigger kick than what's naturally within him.

"You haven't decided to take up my offer of a blowjob, have you? I kinda fancy your sister."

I elbow his ribs as he sits beside me on the sofa. "Shut the fuck up. No."

"Do you want me to leave her alone?"

"Only if she tells you to," I say, screwing my eyes shut as I take a line and lie back.

"Then I need to confess to something, and if you hit me, I promise not to hit you back." He leans his elbows on his knees. "I had a threesome with Ella."

My brows furrow. "You what?"

He raises his hands. "I didn't touch her. I promise. It was one of the times I flew over to her dorm when she was sick. She got better and wanted to go out, and yeah… her rule was that I couldn't touch her, only the other guy."

"We're done with this subject. Don't tell me anything else."

"I promise I only fucked the guy while he was fucking her."

"Base," I groan. "Stop."

Sighing, he rubs his face. "Right. What did you want to talk to me about?"

"Your family. The Russian side of your family."

"Yeah?"

"I need them to kill someone for me."

Base laughs, putting another line out for himself, but when I don't laugh with him, he goes silent. "Wait. You're serious?"

My leg is bouncing, and I realise his is too. "What I'm about to tell you stays between us. I mean it. This could get you murdered."

He shivers, the joking tone gone. "Right."

"I need them to kill Bernadette and Archie Sawyer. And their daughter. Her name is Cassie."

My friend frowns like I've just asked him to fly to the moon with me on a fucking unicorn. "What? Why?"

I try to tell him as little as possible. Vague details of how they forcefully pay me to hunt people down, to fuck clients and that they're heavily set on my marrying the daughter. If I don't, some really bad shit is going to happen, and I don't want to find out what.

He's uncomfortable as I tell him more. He's still, listening, a deep line between his brows as he bites his thumbnail.

"So you aren't at uni?"

I shake my head. "I've never been to uni. I applied – that's as far as I got."

"The fuck have you been doing the last two and a half years?"

I tilt my head, and his eyes widen even more. "Shit, man. That's how long you've been stuck with them?"

"Yeah," I say, chewing my lip. "And there's one more thing I need from you."

"Anything."

"I need to go to Russia for eight months with the Sawyers..." I hesitate, chewing my lip as I tap my finger on my thigh. "If your family can't get the job done, I need you to watch Stacey. I need you to keep Stacey safe for me while I'm gone."

Base rubs his face, blowing out a breath. "Are you about to tell me you're fucking Rhodes?"

Stacey is definitely in my bed, right? I didn't imagine everything?

I can feel the tracks of her nails on my back, so I think my mind is just going haywire again. The number of volts they shoved in me is having some annoying side effects.

"Technically, no," I reply, pulling a cigarette out and offering him one. "She's my ex."

"This is too much fucking information for me. I'm not even sober, man. Can't you write all this shit down?"

I nudge him with my shoulder, and he chuckles. "Rhodes. She was *the* ex?"

Taking a draw of my smoke, I nod. "Yep."

"I can't imagine her cheating, not gonna lie. I can't see her fucking—" He stops, sighing. "Luciella mentioned something to Tylar about you two, but I was only eavesdropping. I thought maybe you just slept with her; I didn't know she was the one who broke your cold little heart."

I roll my eyes and inhale another lungful of smoke. "Will you keep an eye on her?" Maybe I'm paranoid, since my guys are also looking out for her, but so fuck. That girl in my bed is everything to me.

"Yeah. But I'll call my grandfather in an hour and see what he can do about that family. The fuckers need dealt with."

I pat his shoulder. "I owe you."

I know it's a long shot, but there's a chance it could work. I can't report them – I can't go public with their abuse without criminalising myself and putting a target on my family from the underworld. My hands are tied. But Base's family have strong ties with the mafia, him being the heir and all.

My phone vibrates, and my heart stops when I remember Cassie's message.

Has it been an hour? Did I imagine the text?

I look at my screen, and my heart sinks.

> ***Bernadette:*** *I have a car coming to pick you up at your apartment at 2 a.m.*

I stand abruptly. "Shit. I need to go."

Base doesn't catch up to me as I rush out of the pool house, leaving my bag of coke with him. He'll probably finish it all and pass out in the damn pool. I get into the manor, through the party, and grab my sister by the shoulder. "Base is in the pool house. Don't leave him on his own."

I'm gone before she can say anything.

I reach my room within minutes and close the door carefully behind me, breathless as I see Stacey still asleep. Real. She's real – in my fucking bed with my cum leaking from her.

I swear under my breath, hating that I need to leave. I can't wait around and try to explain anything. I can't wake her and apologise. I need to grab my motorbike keys and get the fuck away from here.

As soon as Bernadette finds out I'm not in my apartment, I don't even want to know what she'll do.

I pull the duvet over Stacey and kiss her forehead, telling myself over and over again that she's real. She's alive. She's safe. Barry and Base will keep her safe.

Standing back, I run my hand through my hair, checking my phone to see if Barry has replied to any of my texts or calls, but he hasn't. I know his wife is due, so maybe she's in labour.

"Kade?"

My gaze lifts to find Stacey sitting up in the bed, the duvet dropping to her waist. She rubs her eyes, struggling to open them fully to look at me.

I stay quiet as I slide my phone back into my pocket, gripping my keys. The sound of the jingling draws her attention, and she couldn't look more devastated. "You were going to sneak out?"

Now isn't the time. I have a countdown – 2 a.m.

Instead of being a decent human being, I turn and head for the door.

"No! Don't walk away from me again!"

I freeze, but I don't look at her, even as she rises from the bed and walks in front of me, blocking me from the door. "I don't have time for this. I need to go."

"Please stay and talk to me. Please," she begs, her eyes already glazing with tears. "I need to tell you so much, Kade. Please – let me talk."

I try to walk past her and reach for the door, but she grabs my wrist. It pisses me off that I'm about to do this, but I have to. I remove her hand from me and glare down at her. "There's nothing to talk about. Move."

Her lip trembles. "Can we please talk? You can leave right after. Just hear me out."

I back away, putting distance between us. "I don't want to talk; I want to leave. *Move.*"

She goes to step forward and hugs herself instead. "Then you used me."

I scoff. "I didn't use you. You got as much pleasure out of this as I did. What more do you want?" I try to hit deeper, my timer ticking down. "You know we're done. I've told you countless times, and you're still expecting me to forget what you did."

I try for the door again, and Stacey grabs the material at the back of my hoodie. "Please don't walk away."

She's sobbing, and I close my eyes. I hate when she's upset.

Her words are rushed as she tries to pull me to look at her. "I need you to listen to me, Kade. I need you to. I… I have an abusive brother, and he controlled me for years. His name is Chris Fields."

My ears ring with her words. This must be the Chris Stacey mentioned before, and I'm desperate to hear more. I need to hear more. But my phone dings, reminding me I can't. I yank myself away from Stacey as it dings again. I already know who it is, and it only reminds me that I need to hurry and get the fuck away. If Bernadette finds me here, she'll find Stacey.

I try for the door again, and she cries out as she drops to her knees behind me. "Please don't leave me. Please. He's a monster and will come for me. Please don't leave me. Please. He's the reason I was there that night." She's crying so damn loud, it's ripping my heart out. "Please don't go."

Another ding of my phone, and I hate myself for what I'm about to say and do.

I need to hit deep – I need her to stop. I need to leave before I run out of time.

"Stop fucking crying, Stacey. It's pathetic. We aren't together – it was just a fuck. We won't ever be together again. Do you know why?"

She looks up at me with red, bloodshot eyes, and it fucking breaks me that I need to speak to her like this, but I need her to stop, to let me go. I have just over an hour to make a two-hour trip.

Images flash before me, and they add to the venom in my words. "You cheated on me a month after we lost our daughter. Not with just anyone either. You screwed Jason. My *big brother*. No matter how many times we fuck, I will never *ever* fucking forgive you." And then I walk out and slam the door.

I'm not sure how I make it to my apartment in one piece, but I do.

My motorbike hit speeds it's never hit before all the way up the motorway. And I think the number of times I punched myself in the head out of rage, I should definitely have crashed.

My mind is fucked.

I don't even know if everything that happened tonight was real.

The scratches on my back are real.

I focus on them. I focus on that fucking name.

Chris Fields.

The more and more shit I do, the more I see myself as my dad. He's an evil bastard when he wants to be, and I just tore Stacey's heart in two and walked away from her.

You'd think a fifteen-year-old obsessing over his sister's best friend to the point of being blind to every other person in the world romantically would be the first sign that I was like my father. I didn't want to kiss anyone, entertain any of the girls who approached me at school, and whenever I was in the same room as Stacey Rhodes, my heart would speed up and I'd sweat.

And guess what? After teasing her constantly, I finally got her. I *had* her. And she admitted that ever since we met down at the pool house, she's never been interested in anyone else either. It was like fate, but then again, fate is a fucking wanker who pushed her into my brother's bed.

I never wanted to say those words to Stacey. I wanted to tell her that I've already broken rule five. That she can have every fractured shard of my heart, if only she knows how to fix it back together – but I'm an asshole, and I broke her heart instead.

Stacey doesn't know what she means to me, and that's fine. She's safer not knowing and thinking I hate her – that I used her. That I'll never forgive her.

I keep reminding myself that I'm doing all of this to protect her. Because not only is she my weakness, but she's also my strength – my main reason for continuing, the air to my fucking lungs. When I'm around her, I feel like the person I was before – the teenager who fell in love with a beautiful girl and had no idea how to handle the emotion. The kid who always looked at her, even before I kissed her for the first time.

She still makes me nervous, even when I'm following her as she crawls up my spiral staircase, even as I fuck her mouth up against a wall or kiss her moans away.

It hurts to look at her, but I can never stop myself. Denial and bitterness coated my tongue when I told her I wouldn't ever forgive her. In truth, I already have.

But do I want a future with her? Undoubtedly yes.

I could work on my trust issues with her. I never want to step into the same room as her and Jason again, but I would try. For her, I'd try anything. I'd even stop and call my brother right now if I had the luxury of free will and the time to spare.

But none of that is realistic. All I can do is protect everyone from afar.

Bernadette will never find out who she is and what significance she has in my life – past and present.

All I can think about is going back to Stacey and apologising – crawling into bed beside her and holding her against me.

Base pulling through on speaking to his grandfather will sort this for me. If he can get his family involved, maybe Bernadette will see my imprisonment as being not worth the hassle and free me. Who the fuck wants the mafia on their ass anyway?

By the time I pull my motorbike into my garage and haul out the keys, I'm over an hour late. There are SUVs parked outside, which means Bernie got pissed at me and brought her men over.

My phone has no new notifications. I turn most of them off anyway, but there are no angry messages from Stacey, and there's still fuck all from Barry. I quickly message him Chris's full name. Stacey may have already told him, but just in case, he should know.

Hopefully he doesn't kill him, because I want to be the one to strangle the bastard until his neck snaps.

I sigh and disconnect myself from all of my apps and hide them in one of my secure folders. I contemplated tossing my phone while I was driving, but I couldn't risk missing a message from Stacey.

I take off my helmet, toss my keys on the unit and press the button to shut the garage door, bathing myself in darkness until I walk into the main part of the house. It's modern and rather big, a three-bedroom apartment on the outskirts of Stirling. I bought it as an investment – and somewhere to go when Bernadette gave me time off.

I huff and drop the helmet when I see how crowded it is. "Is it really necessary to have all these people here? You're messing up my floor."

One of Bernadette's guards is pointing a gun at my chest, but I don't pay him – or the guy with the syringe – any attention as I raise a brow at her. "I had to go somewhere. What's the big deal?"

Cassie is sitting on the sofa, tears staining her cheeks as she scowls at me.

Her mother tuts, clicking her tongue as she fights a devious laugh. "Who is Stacey Rhodes?"

My eyes widen, and there's a sharp sting to my neck before I'm knocked into yet another memory that I grasp at to stay sane.

23

KADE

FLASHBACK

"Are my boobs getting even bigger?"

I lift my eyes from my sketch of the dogs to stare at her, dropping my gaze to her tits as she stands in the middle of my room. "I'm scared to answer. Is this a trick question?"

She tosses her bunny slipper at me. "I'm serious. My bra is tight, and I look so bloated." Stacey stands to the side, pulls up her top and holds her hands to the swelling of her stomach. "Is this normal with the diet I'm on?"

In all fairness, I understand why she's concerned. She's really swollen. I set aside my drawing pad and pencils and sit at the foot of the bed, pulling her towards me by the waist, and she lets me rest my palm on her. It's hard, and it makes my brows furrow. "Is it sore?"

She shakes her head. "My boobs are though."

I chew my lip. "When was your last period?"

"I don't get periods with the pill I take. The last time I bled was months ago."

We both stare at each other, and I give her a tight smile. "It's possible you could be pregnant."

She pales, and all the blood drains from her face. "Oh God," she says, covering her face and stepping back, her top falling over the small swelling of her stomach. "No."

I stand and pull her to me. I give her a chaste kiss on the lips and rest my forehead on hers. "We don't know anything yet. Breathe. Go back to bed and I'll buy a test, okay?"

She swallows, looking terrified as she nods. "Okay."

I tuck her in and kiss her forehead, whistling for the dogs to cuddle into her while I get dressed and drive into town. It's late, so any pharmacy nearby will be closed. I go to the nearest supermarket and have a headache five minutes in.

Once I buy one of each brand, I hurry home. She's awake and pacing the room when I walk in, and I sit in the bathroom with her while she pees on three of them.

They're upside down while she chews on the sleeve of the hoodie she's wearing – mine as usual. "What will we do if they're positive?"

"Wait and see what they say."

She stays silent for another minute then cuddles into me. "You don't understand how bad this would be for me, Kade. I… I can't be pregnant."

I move hair from her face. "I know, Freckles." Dancing and fitness are her life. She's at the studio or the gym every single day, and when she isn't, she's choreographing or listening to music that she could dance to. "I know."

My nerves kick in when she lifts her head and reaches for the first one – then freezes. "I'm scared to look."

She flips one and gasps as the plastic falls to the ground. I don't even have a chance to see it.

She snatches the other two and turns them. Both have two lines. Two lines that indicate pregnancy. I lean down and grab the digital one she dropped, and it says, Pregnant*.*

We're silent as we stare at all three, a lone tear sliding down Stacey's cheek.

The air in the room vanishes as the light in her eyes shimmers into nothing. "I'm... I'm pregnant." Her lip trembles. "Kade..."

I snake my arms around her, and she shudders in my hold, breaking down as she lets her tears overwhelm her. I stay strong for her, holding her through each gasp for air as she hyperventilates. The tests clank on the floor, the dogs scratch the door to get in and we both sink to the ground.

Stacey buries her head in my chest then looks up at me with bloodshot eyes. "Please don't leave me. Please. I'm begging you, Kade. I can't do this without you."

I kiss her temple, her forehead, her nose and lips and cheeks as I say, "You don't need to beg me, Freckles. There isn't a chance in fucking hell I'll ever leave you."

Stacey wipes her eyes and sits up, leaning her back to the bathtub opposite me. "You promise?"

"I promise, Stacey. Nothing will ever make me leave you. I understand we're young and we had no plans for kids anytime soon, but plans can change. I'm with you, okay? Whatever you want to do."

"Whatever I want to do..." She chews her lip and looks down at the swelling she thought was bloating. "You would be okay if we kept it?"

I furrow my brows. "Why wouldn't I be?"

"I mean, I want to. God, I want so much to keep the baby. But we're nineteen. I have... We don't... I... I thought you had all these milestones you wanted to achieve before you were thirty."

I lean forward and hold her cheek, swiping my thumb against the tears under her eye. "There would be nothing better in this world than having a family with you, Freckles. Ignore our age. Ignore everything else and go with your gut. What do you want to do?" Then I shake my head at myself. "No, sorry, you don't need to decide yet. It's a big decision. Let's go to bed."

She smiles, and a laugh breaks out, a nervous one, as she kisses me. "I want to keep the baby. I want to have a baby with you, Kade Mitchell."

I feel my heart rate picking up, warmth spreading through my chest. "You do?"

"There's no one else I'd rather be with."

I'm already imagining all the journeys we'll have as I take her to bed. We both fall asleep with our hands cradling her stomach, and for the first time in a long time, I'm excited for my future. For our future.

The next day, we call the doctors and hand in a urine sample. The day before Luciella is to arrive home and find out about us, we go for an ultrasound.

We nervously hold hands while the midwife watches the screen. I don't breathe or blink as I see the flutter of our child's heartbeat. Her fingers tighten around mine, but my gaze is stuck on the screen.

"Everything is looking perfect. As you can see, your little bouncing baby has a strong heartbeat. Currently eleven weeks and five days."

Stacey covers her mouth with a whimper. "Look, Kade. Our baby."

"Our baby," I repeat, squeezing her hand. "Stacey's already three months along?"

The lady nods. "Yes, she certainly is. With a perfectly healthy and very active baby. The due date is..." She looks down at something then smiles. "Oh, how wonderful. Christmas Eve. We can discuss further details during the antenatal appointments."

"We're having a baby," I say, turning to Stacey. "I get to have a family with you."

It's this moment that I see my entire future rearranging. In the best way possible. Yeah, I'm fucking terrified. But at the same time, I can't wait.

A mini-Stacey or a mini-me running around with Milo and Hopper following behind. The high-pitched giggle. The dark hair flowing around them while we kiss them goodnight.

My mum's face when she holds her first grandchild, my dad standing beside her. Ewan on the other side with a proud smile. Luciella crying while spoiling them with gifts and kisses and cuddles.

Fuck. I'm going to be a dad. Me. Kade Mitchell.

The lady hands us a picture for us to take home. I look down at Stacey, both of us with watering eyes, and I kiss the woman I get to watch turn into a mother. Into the mother of my child.

"I love you, Freckles," I tell her.

She sniffs. "I love you too. So, so much."

Jason meets me at his house once I drop Stacey off at the studio. I told him it was important and couldn't wait. But now, as I sit on his sofa and my leg bounces with a mix of excitement and anxiousness, I don't know how to say the words.

He might think I'm too young, that I'm an idiot for wanting to keep the kid. Maybe he'll say I'm selfish because I might pass my father's issues to my child, or that I'm barely stable myself.

But I am. The dosage of my meds has been lowered, and I don't have as many bad thoughts anymore. I draw a lot – Stacey has a collection of my designs for tattoos. All I think about is her and the future we have, of the son or daughter she'll give me in a matter of months. This time next year, I'll be a dad.

I still can't believe it – we've known the news for over two weeks now.

Jason hands me a beer as he sits on the sofa opposite, his work clothes still on. "What's up?"

Just get it over with. *"It's Stacey," I say, chewing my lip. "She's—"*

"Did you guys break up? That sucks. You were good for each other, and I actually liked the girl. Did you fuck it up? Do I need to beat your ass?"

I sink into the sofa, my arm slung over the back as I glare at him. "You done?"

He smiles as he gulps his beer. "Depends." He settles the bottle on the coffee table between us. "Did you fuck up?"

"We're fine," I snap, annoyed with him. "She's pregnant."

Jason is silent as he looks at me, his head tilted. "Really? Is it yours?"

"Careful," I warn. "She's my fucking girlfriend. Who else would the father be?"

He bursts out laughing, and I calculate how fast I can knock him out as he gets to his feet. "I'm messing with you, little bro. This is fucking fantastic." Then he stops. "Wait. It's fantastic, right?"

I tip my head back. His happiness irks me for no reason. He's always the cheery one, always trying to get me to be the same. "Right."

He opens his arms wide, waiting for an embrace. I raise a brow, and he huffs. "Give me a hug or I'll force one upon you."

"You sound like Base." He's overly affectionate and wants to hug every fucking chance he gets. I roll my eyes, but a smile breaks out as we pat each other's back and I quickly step away. "So, uh, yeah. Looks like I'm

going to be a dad."

"How far along is she?"

"Just over fourteen weeks."

The corner of his lips pulls up, and he bobs his head. "So you're happy about it?"

"Yeah. It was a bit of a shock when we found out, but yeah, we're happy."

I've become obsessive and overprotective with Stacey ever since we saw those positive tests. She calls me overbearing when I hold her hand going downstairs, and tuts at me when I make a fuss of her dancing for too long.

I don't want to be controlling – I never want to be like that, but I worry. It's in my blood to be a worrier and an overthinker and to be a possessive dickhead – to message her to make sure she's drunk enough water or eaten lunch, even going as far as ordering her favourite food to her house when I'm not with her to make sure she eats.

Mum thinks I need to relax. Dad thinks it's completely acceptable to have anxiety over everything Stacey does and laughs about how my child will have two guard dogs by her side.

Milo and Hopper are good dogs. I've trained them well, socialised them as much as possible in public and training centres around Scotland. Me and Base took them up the mountains the other weekend, where we camped and swam in the loch – I'll keep doing things with them, keep them involved even when my kid is here.

Jason sits back on the sofa and crosses his ankle at his knee. "I thought Giana and I were going to be the first parents of the three of us, but you beat me to it."

Giana wants to get married to my big brother first. It seems me and Stacey will be doing it in reverse. She'll already be the mother to my child; all that's left is for her to be my wife.

Fuck. Imagine that? Stacey Mitchell. It has a ring to it, kinda? Wait, would she even want the same name as my dad?

Maybe I'll take her name. Kade Rhodes.

No.

"Luciella doesn't know about us yet," I say with a sigh. "Stacey says she wants to wait until we know the sex. She thinks knowing it's a boy or a girl will soften whatever blow she'll send her way."

Jason shakes his head. "Keeping secrets never unravels well, kid. It'll definitely blow up. She's gonna be more pissed that you both kept it from her than the fact you're with her best friend. I reckon she'll see how much you love each other and are good for each other and actually be happy for the pair of you."

Is it bad I don't give a shit what my sister thinks? If she's against the idea of me dating Stacey, she can fuck off.

I sigh again. "Maybe. But I'm just going at Stacey's pace. When she's ready, I will be too."

"Where's my little brother? You sound whipped. I never thought I'd see the day you even had a girlfriend, never mind being wrapped around her finger."

I chuckle and get to my feet. "Fuck you."

"Does Aria know?"

I nod. "My dad was kind of mad at me for being careless but said he'd do what he can to help from afar. Ewan offered to set up the nursery and build all the furniture." Fidgeting, I rip the label from the bottle. "I declined though." After finishing my beer, I walk into the open-planned kitchen and toss it in the glass bin. "We want to do everything. I'll build her a house and work my ass off to be the best for them both."

Jason follows me to the front door. "Are you nervous?"

"I'd be a crazy bastard if I wasn't nervous."

He grins. "Do you even know how to wipe your own ass, never mind change a baby?"

I flip him off and walk to my car, raising my hand as I get in and turn on the engine. Stacey will be finished soon – but first, I want to go grab some snacks from the supermarket and get the dogs new bones.

When I get there, I stand in the baby section with the metal basket, staring at pinks and blues and creams, the odd red and green, and decide to buy a little princess dress for a newborn. Stacey is adamant that we're having a girl – has a strong notion that we will – and as much as I don't care about the sex, the thought of seeing Stacey's eyes and my hair surrounding a silver tiara makes me grin and stuff the outfit into the basket.

By the time night comes, and I bring Stacey to my room, she sees all the snacks and the princess outfit in the middle of the bed. I expect her to smile or clap that excited way she always does, but instead, she cries into my chest.

It's only when I lie her down and strip her of her clothes that I notice the bruising on the back of her neck. When I feel murderous, she tells me to calm down, that she hurt it when she was trying to do the neck hold on the aerial hoop.

She promises not to do it again.

The night after, when I sneak into her bedroom through the window, I stop in the middle of the room and watch her silently weep into her pillow. She startles when I climb in, begs me to leave before Nora or her dad comes in and promises to message me in the morning.

It takes a lot for me to go, but I kiss her, make sure we're okay, that she's okay, and spend the night in my own bed alone, texting her for hours until I fall asleep.

Two weeks later, we find out that we're having a girl. Stacey cries in happiness the entire drive home while gripping my hand in her lap.

I'm going to be a girl-dad. A mini-Stacey by my side – my little princess.

When we get to the manor, we tell everyone the news – bar Luciella, since Stacey wants to wait until her best friend is home from uni to drop such a huge bomb. So, really, not everyone. Only Jason, my dad, my mum and Ewan.

I can't even tell my friends yet, but when I do, I reckon Base will fight Dez for godfather duties. Or the title of Best Uncle.

My head is on the small bump that seems to be growing at a snail's pace. I can't wait for her to get bigger, to feel the kicks against my palms and cheek.

Stacey is the opposite. As much as she wants to feel the kicks, she's dreading it. After reading far too many forums for first time mothers online, she thinks she'll be the size of a house. She also thinks I'll become bored – that I'll want someone with slim hips and perky tits.

It seems she has no idea how much I'm obsessed with her. Not just with her looks, but her heart, her fucking soul.

I love her. I love Stacey, and nothing will ever change that. She could cut off my dick and refuse to have sex with me for the rest of our lives and I'd still bend over backwards for the girl.

Kind of whipped, but I don't care.

"Do you think she can hear me?" I ask, resting my head on Stacey's abdomen as she brushes her fingers through my hair. "She might want to

listen to something a little more soothing than your singing voice. Poor girl."

She giggles, shaking me. "You love my singing."

I absolutely do not.

"Regardless, hi." I wrap my arms around the back of her thighs as we lie in bed. "I'm going to be your daddy; do you know how lucky you are? I'm pretty messed up in the head, but I'll go for more therapy before you arrive, I promise. And I'm going to spoil the life out of you, then we'll gang up on Mummy with Nerf guns."

Stacey laughs. "That's kind of cute."

I smile. "I have two dads, Mummy has one, so you get to have three grandfathers. One is a little loopy, but we'll bear with him."

"Hey! That's not very nice." She taps the side of my head then runs her fingers through my hair again, watching me – listening.

"I want to be enough for you, my little princess," I say, choking up for some reason. "I'll never get drunk around you, and I'll stay off the cigarettes. I'll even stop smoking joints when you get here. I'm going to make sure I'm the best version of myself, so I can be a good daddy for you."

Stacey sniffs, her eyes wet as she keeps listening.

"We live in a huge house, but I'll build us our own, okay? You'll have a tree house with a swing, and I'll teach you how to drive." I lower my voice. "Please be better than Mummy – she's terrible."

"I've got so much better," she says, beaming down at me. "Admit it – I'm a better driver than you."

"You're better than Base, and that's all I'm giving you. Now, if you don't mind, I'm trying to speak to our daughter."

She rolls her eyes with a grin as "Spanish Sahara" by Foals plays in the background. It seems to be the song that's soothing her right now.

"Fine. I'm going to listen in though. And no swear words."

"Fine." I shift to get comfortable. "Where was I? Right. You're going to have the best family. I have a big brother called Jason, and his girlfriend will probably try to steal you every weekend. But I won't let her – she can be a bit scary. Oh, and I'm a twin, so I'm kind of glad you're a one-man army, cause fuck having two of you running around."

"Kade!"

I laugh and continue. "My twin's name is Luciella, but Mummy will probably get you to call her Aunt Lu. And there's Tylar, who is absolutely no relation to you, but you'll probably call her aunt as well. Please don't."

Stacey laughs, then I contemplate splitting up with her as she starts listing off the names she loves. My eyes widen with each one.

"I am not fucking calling my daughter Vixen. And Georgina? Really? She's not ninety."

Stacey huffs and crosses her arms. "Both are better than your suggestion."

"What's wrong with Angelica?"

"It just makes me think of the little girl in Rugrats*."*

I scrunch my nose and pull the underwear down her legs, kissing from her thigh to her knee. "I suppose."

She bites her lip as I spread her thighs wide. "What about Daisy?" she suggests.

I slide down the bed and part her with my thumbs. "You're trying to fucking annoy me now, Freckles. That's a dog's name." Then I silence her by slipping my tongue into her cunt.

I devour her, sucking on her clit as I shove her knees to her chest, opening her up to be ravaged by my mouth. I ease two fingers deep. Her back arches, hands in my hair, tugging and urging me to suck harder, to finger-fuck her faster.

She unravels beneath me, soaking my face, and I lick her arousal from my lips as I crawl up her body and settle between her legs. My cock presses against her dripping pussy, so wet and needy.

"Wait. Do you want to go on top? I don't want to hurt you or the baby."

She pulls me to her and wraps her legs around my waist. "You won't. And you didn't do any harm over the last few weeks, so please stop worrying, Kade."

"I just don't want to fuck things up."

We both gasp against each other's mouths as I push into her. "You couldn't even if you tried," she tells me. "Because you love me."

"And you love me," I counter, pushing a few inches deeper.

She nods, biting her lip as I sink to the hilt and put her leg on my shoulder. "More than anything," she says. "Please don't hold back."

I keep my eyes on hers as I pull out to the tip and thrust back in, rattling the headboard.

I haven't fucked her hard since we found out she was pregnant. Every time we've slept together, I've gone as slow and as gentle as possible.

I thrust a little faster, feeling her inner walls clench around me, welcoming my cock with each push and pull. She digs her nails into my back and rips the skin, making me go harder.

"Who do you belong to?" I whisper against her lips.

"You," she barely replies through her whimpers as I hammer into her, plunging deep so my balls smack her ass.

"Try again," I say, gritting my teeth as she lifts her hand to her face and covers her own mouth. Ewan is in, and even though he's miles away, she thinks people can hear us from a different wing of the manor. "Who do you belong to, Freckles?"

"Kade." She moans against her palm, low and inaudible, before I grab it away and pin it to the mattress beneath us. She meets each thrust as she pulses around my cock, breathing out more words. Her free hand grasps at my nape. "I belong to Kade Mitchell."

I press my mouth to hers and say, "That's my good girl."

Once our orgasms settle, I run us a bath, and Stacey hugs me from behind as the water fills the tub. "I'm going to tell my dad and Nora."

"Yeah?"

"Yeah. I'll take the ultrasound picture with me when I leave. I think they'll be okay with me being pregnant. It's just..." She trails off, and I turn around to look at her. "I'm scared."

"Do you want me to come with you?"

Her eyes widen. "Oh God, no."

I frown at her tone and how against the idea she is. If we're going to announce we're together and having a kid, why can't I go with her? I know I have my hands full with her side of the family and that I need to prove myself, but surely me supporting her is a start?

She rests her head on my chest – my automatic reaction is to hug her to me and kiss her head.

She speaks after a few minutes. "Just... let me speak to them, and then we can have dinner with them or something. It'll be okay. I promise."

"Okay," I say, leaning over without letting her go and turning off the tap. "One step at a time, Freckles."

She smiles. "One step at a time."

I'm feeling uneasy. Stacey doesn't answer my calls for an entire day. My messages are going unread, and she isn't at the studio.

I knock on her front door in the dead of the night, but no one answers.

Standing back from the door, I stare up at her room window. It's closed, which it never is. The lights are all off – except for a room at the top left. I have no idea whose room that is, but they might know where she is.

Being the dick that I am, I refuse to wait around until she gets back to me. I search for a stone and toss it at the window.

The curtains ruffle, and a head peeks out, but it's too dark to see. It's a guy, and he quickly closes his curtains and turns off the light. Must be her stepbrother Kyle. I make a mental note to punch him in the face when I eventually meet him for snubbing me.

I look down at my phone – still no response to any of my messages. I type another while I walk back to my car, a pain in my chest as my heart rate fails to slow down.

Me: Did I do something wrong? Please tell me if I did. I'll fix it.

Me: Come on, Freckles. You're freaking me out here.

Hours later, as I sit in the pool house with an unlit joint, I type another while waiting on my dad calling me back. He's as worried as I am – but begs me not to mention anything to my mum yet, since she's still on her way back from dealing with the death of her youngest patient.

I type and retype and finally settle on an immature message.

Me: If you don't respond, I'll take it that you're ignoring me, and I'll ask Luciella or Tylar where you are, and it fucks your plan to tell them the truth when you're ready.

She doesn't answer me all night, and although I want to smoke the joint, I hold back. I go to the home gym for a workout, but I can't focus – I lose my patience and open my chat with Luciella at three in the morning.

Me: Look, you're going to be so fucking pissed at me, but right now, I need you to tell me where Stacey is. I haven't heard from her all day and night, and she's—

I stop texting as the door to the pool house swings open and look up to see Stacey standing there with shaky legs, a burst lip and what looks like a black eye.

I drop my phone and get to my feet. "What the fuck happened to you?"

She holds her hands to her chest as tears fall from her eyes. "Kade," she bursts out. "Oh God. Kade."

I rush to her, and she loses her balance – grabbing her bruised face, her eyes red from how much she's been crying. Her cheek is swollen, blood dried on her chin from the cut on her lip.

"Fuck," I breathe, searching her. She's wearing a dress that shows off more bruises on her leg. "What the fuck happened? Did someone do this to you? Is our girl okay?"

Murderous fucking rage overcomes me at the thought of someone hurting my girls. No one fucks with what's mine. I'm all but calm as she shakes her head and gasps into more tears.

"I fell," she says. "I fell down the studio stairs."

I blink down at her. "Really?"

"I wasn't paying attention and slipped."

They're steep and go on for fucking miles. No wonder she's such a mess.

"I should have been paying attention," she says, trembling and holding a hand to her small bump. "I'm so sorry. So, so, so sorry. She might be hurt."

I try to calm my breathing as I hold Stacey to me. She hyperventilates, weeping into my shoulder. "I don't know..." She hiccoughs, trying to speak while she sobs. "If she's okay."

My eyes sting, burning as I wipe them on my shoulder. "I'm taking you to hospital."

Stacey doesn't fight me as I order one of the drivers to take us straight there, calling my dad on the way and messaging Mum. I hold her to me, refusing to let go as I tug my hoodie over her head and interlace our fingers.

We're seen rapidly, and the doctor asks me to leave while she speaks with Stacey. I refuse, obviously, and sit in the corner while a nurse comes in to help tend to Stacey's wounds.

We're transferred to the maternity unit, where they give Stacey an emergency ultrasound. We both sigh in relief when we see our baby girl on the screen, distorted within the scan, but the fluttering heartbeat makes me close my eyes and tighten my hold on Stacey's hand.

"She's okay," Stacey sobs, her chin trembling. "Are you sure?"

"We suggest being more careful, Miss Rhodes. Everything seems fine, but that doesn't mean something can't happen. Bodily trauma during pregnancy can have a lot of effects. We'll book you in for another appointment next week. But come straight back if you get any pains or bleeding."

She nods repeatedly and wipes her tears.

The lady asks me to leave for two minutes because they have important questions for Stacey that would be better if I'm not present, and since she gives me a pleading look, I agree and wait outside.

When she comes out of the room, I kiss her and take her home. Mum is back before us and tells me to put Stacey to bed and ensure she's comfortable. She makes up sandwiches and fills hot-water bottles, bringing them up to us.

I spend the next three hours with my head on her bump again, telling my daughter how lucky we are, that she'll be painting my nails and making me drink invisible tea with her teddy bears. I'll draw her – I'll teach her how to draw.

She'll travel with me and her mother, and when the time comes and we want another kid, she'll be the best big sister.

Stacey falls asleep first, and I stroke my thumb against her cheek, kissing the bruises on her face. She has bruises on her ribs. Really bad ones. She promised me before she fell asleep that she'd be careful on the stairs and gave in when I said I'd be building a handrail on both sides.

We also agreed that, in the morning, we'll video-call with Luciella and tell her everything. Stacey wants us to run away – to get away from this life – and doting boyfriend that I am, I said yes.

As soon as our daughter's born, we'll start a new life.

With her back to my chest, I fall asleep with my hand on her small, barely there bump, thankful that our pride and joy is perfectly healthy. I kiss her shoulder, telling her repeatedly that she's okay, that I love her.

Stacey's scream wakes me with a start the next morning. It's a strangled string of screams that will haunt me for the rest of my days. She pushes the duvet off us, and my heart drops when I see my worst nightmare.

My hand trembles as I completely yank away the duvet while Stacey grabs my arm, screaming even louder and burying her head into the crook of my neck.

I don't breathe. I don't say a word, even as Mum and Ewan burst through my bedroom door.

I see the princess dress vanishing, the drawer full of outfits set alight, the high-pitched giggles, the dream of having a miniature version of the woman I love in our own house burned to the ground.

The sheets are completely saturated with blood, a haunting sign that we've lost our daughter.

24

STACEY

"Are you sure this is what you want to do?" Tobias asks as I pack my suitcase.

I nod, even though I know he can't see me. "There's no reason for me to stay."

"And you trust this Barry to successfully hide you? How can he change your identity?" I hear him shift on his bed. "You can't fly without a passport."

"He already had a new passport made for me, just in case, and once I have it, I can set up new bank accounts and all the other legal documents."

"You've told him my demands?"

I roll my eyes. "Yes, he's aware you want me nearby. I couldn't talk much since Lisa was in labour. They had a girl by the way. A home birth. Her name is Eva."

"I don't care," he huffs. "I want to know everything. Do you hear me? Everything. Don't you dare leave the manor without security, and you stay by Barry's side. When you all fly over here, I want a meeting set up with him."

Of course he does. Protective ass.

When I don't reply, because I'm violently shoving more of my clothes into the suitcase and trying to close it, Tobias says, "I'm sorry about my son. Kade had no right to treat you that way. You deserve better."

I pause. "I guess it was my own fault. Kade said before that we were done; I just thought it was different this time."

"He cares about you – I know it."

I laugh as I shake my head. "Yeah, he has a funny way of showing it."

"I have some more information on the Sawyers, but I don't want you getting involved. I want you to focus on yourself. Your brother is still out there, and we don't know how far he'll go to get you."

"What do you know about the Sawyers?"

"They're heavily involved in the underworld."

I tilt my head. "What exactly does that mean?"

"Organised crime – a lot of it twisted. They're very dangerous, Stacey. I want you to listen to me when I say this. Do not get involved."

I chew my lip. "But Kade is with them."

"Let me deal with that." Then everything goes muffled as someone enters his cell – he's shoved the phone under his pillow, I assume.

The call cuts out seconds later, just as a message comes through.

> ***Barry****: I have a car waiting for you next to the fountain. Three cars will follow to ensure you arrive at my apartment safely. Try to rest, Miss Rhodes. We don't fly to America until my daughter has had all of her checks.*

***Barry**: I'm sorry it's come to this. Please believe me when I say that Mr Mitchell always goes above and beyond to protect you, and I will do the same.*

***Me**: Thank you, Barry. I'm so sorry I'm doing this when you and Lisa just had a baby. I could stay at a hotel for a few weeks? Or would you prefer I wait here a little longer?*

***Barry**: No need, Miss Rhodes. Lisa is excited to meet you. My job is to protect you, and if you're here, it makes my job easier.*

I sniff and put my phone into my purse, my eyes falling on the ripped tutu I'd pulled off in a tear-filled rage. I showered in cold water to try to stop the panic attack, but all I could do was sob into the frigid water as my back slid down the tiles.

I tried to tell him, and he called me pathetic.

Luciella is in a mood with me because she caught me sneaking out of Kade's room not long after he vanished. She shook her head and said I'd never learn, clearly not knowing my heart was in the middle of shattering.

I tried to call Tylar, but her phone was off.

Kyle picked up on the second ring, but he couldn't talk because he was at work.

Barry answered right away and stayed on the phone with me until I stopped crying – until his wife came on the line, with the softest voice ever, hours after having a baby, and somehow, I calmed enough that I could talk without hyperventilating.

That was when they both suggested I come down to Newcastle to them – that I should take up Barry's offer to make me disappear. So I agreed.

By the time I carry my suitcase downstairs, my music is off, and everyone's gone home. Base and Luciella are in the kitchen, and I peek in just as he takes her hand and says something to her in

Russian, which makes her huff and demand he say it in English.

I back away from them. I can message her and Tylar later and explain. Kyle will be furious, but I have no idea what else to do. Stay locked up in the manor for the rest of my life? Wait on Chris hunting me down?

Or get a new life.

The driver takes my suitcase and opens the car door, and I thank him as I climb in.

"Spanish Sahara" by Foals plays on the radio while we drive through the Scottish back roads, and for once, I don't cry about my situation.

I might be sore from how hard he fucked me, but I don't think of Kade and what went down between us hours ago, the words he threw at me while I begged on my knees for him to stay and listen. I don't even think about the disappointment in my friend's face when she realised I was with her brother after she told me not to.

All the way to Newcastle, to Barry's apartment, I try to think of new things.

Should I cut and dye my hair? Where will I work? Will Tobias get fed up with me when I visit every chance I get?

And finally, will there be a dance studio nearby?

Lisa cradles her baby girl against her chest while she feeds as Barry helps me up the steps to their home. It's already packed up, and they have suitcases lining the hallway.

Barry notices me staring at the luggage. "We've been packed for weeks." He shrugs. "We figured you'd take the offer eventually, and we were already planning to move."

"And you're okay with going so soon after having a baby?"

"Of course. I hate it here anyway," Lisa replies. She has warm brown eyes and her blonde hair looks thick from her pregnancy. "It's great to finally meet you, Stacey. I'm really sorry for everything that's happening, but I promise my husband will keep you safe."

"Thank you."

"Are you hungry? I can defrost lasagne."

Barry laughs. "It's six in the morning, baby."

I look at him, and his cheeks go red. I'm so used to the bossy, fed-up, unenthusiastic side of him that I didn't ever think he'd be sweet. I smile at him, and he rubs the back of his head and follows us into the kitchen.

He goes to his daughter, grinning down at her as she wraps her little fingers around his pinkie, and takes her to get a nappy change.

Lisa dishes up two plates and we sit at the breakfast bar. "I love seeing this side to him. He was always a doting husband, but a father? I think I might need to have ten babies to keep seeing that look on his face."

He does look completely mesmerised by his daughter. Little baby Eva.

It takes an hour for me to get to know Lisa properly. We seem to like all the same things. She's three years older than me, yet she has her life sorted – twenty-five with a loving husband, a baby, enough money to sell a house and buy a new one whenever she pleases. She has her own online fashion business – designing dresses and fabrics.

I'm jealous of the life she has.

I'm about to run away from my life and start afresh, and I have no idea what I'm going to do.

She grabs her laptop and shows me the different places she's been looking at big lovely houses in the city, some on the outskirts, then she gets excited that there's a house near a Starbucks.

I giggle with her when we hear Barry gagging – covering her mouth and nose with his top with a nappy bag on one hand, baby Eva in the other.

I don't hold her when they offer, and Barry understands. Lisa probably doesn't, but I'm sure her husband will explain later.

She goes to rest while Eva's napping, and Barry sits down with me, going over my new identity and how I go about not getting caught – handing me a passport with my picture on it with a completely new name.

He takes my phone, dismantles it, then puts it into a folder. The new phone is the same but with a new number. I've not to use it to reach out right away – I've to be discreet, careful and not use it socially.

Then he places a bank card down and paperwork. "I need you to sign these."

"What are they?"

"Don't make a big deal when I tell you, okay?"

I stare at him, unblinking, and he sighs, pinching the bridge of his nose.

"Kade set up a sort of safety net for you and his family. Each one of you got a lump sum – to be given if he passes away. This is me honouring that deal while he's still alive."

I glance at the paperwork, then my eyes lift to him. "Is this a joke?"

"Nope."

"Kade gave me eighty-six million pounds?"

"Yep," he replies. "Please sign it so we can move along. I've got loads of stuff to go through."

It takes me an hour to sign it, and Barry is close to losing his patience.

A couple of days later, Eva is cleared to fly.

And my next chapter starts.

25

KADE

FLASHBACK

Dad keeps to my side as we walk around the man-made lake, chirping birds sounding from the speakers of the park in the middle of the institution. I kick a stone into the water, numb, unable to form any words, so we keep walking without speaking.

He understands.

I don't.

I don't understand why life can be so cruel to take away such a precious thing. We were happy and ready and prepared, *and an accident ripped everything away from us.*

I should be with my girlfriend right now, talking to my unborn daughter while my head rests on Stacey's bump. Making plans for when she's set free from her nine-month stint.

I shouldn't be walking around the institution like a lost puppy, wondering if the ache in my chest will ever settle. There shouldn't be a bottle of vodka in my hotel fridge, unopened but waiting to be. I shouldn't have smoked a billion cigarettes on the way here.

I'm silent and so is he, but that's alright. We don't need to talk; we don't even need to look at each other to feel the comfortable father–son bond. This is enough for us both.

It's been a month since that horrifying morning. A month since Stacey spent the entire day and night in hospital, refusing to see anyone, even me. She had a procedure done to remove everything that was left of our daughter, and it took three days until the doctors were happy to discharge her.

She had a panic attack two days later and screamed when I tried to help her. My mum had to step in and calm her down.

Mum said she was traumatised and needed time to herself, so I gave her it. I lasted four days before I snapped and begged to see her.

We met by the water at Loch Thom, where she hugged herself and stayed quiet, and I stared at her as the wind whipped her hair around her grief-stricken face.

We were broken, mad and exhausted. But not with each other – I knew that.

Eventually, she rested her head on my shoulder until she agreed to come home with me. She didn't stay the night, but we did watch TV while the dogs made a fuss of her.

We walked them around the grounds – Stacey was drained, so I carried her to the manor on my back. She fell asleep, but she jolted awake in a panic when I laid her on my bed and demanded I take her home.

Neither of us spoke as I drove her home, but she did ask me to park a street away, because her dad was furious at her for sneaking out without telling him.

Everyone told me to give her time.

I was giving her as much space and time as possible, but then she showed up at the manor drunk a week ago, while Base and Dez were there. Her words were jumbled, and her eyes were so glazed that Mum thought she was on drugs.

Tylar showed up; Dez had called her.

We gave Stacey water, and I was told to leave the room so Tylar and

Mum could change her into Luciella's pyjamas. Mum said she still had bruises on her legs and hips and doesn't know why they hadn't faded yet, though it wasn't impossible.

I wouldn't have known at the time, since it had been ages since I'd even seen her without clothes on. I understand why – I haven't been in the mood either.

But I knew she wanted to see me, so when she fell asleep in the guest room, I snuck in and held her to my chest and kissed her head and cheeks and nose until she fell back to sleep with mumbled words.

I wasn't giving a fuck if Tylar caught us – thankfully, for Stacey's sake, she didn't. I woke up the following morning to an empty bed: no message, no note, no nothing.

Not gonna lie, at that moment, I thought I was losing her.

That night, Stacey sent me a text – more like an essay – saying how sorry she was for failing me and our daughter, that she loved me and our angel more than anything. She wished she could have protected her and promised that if she's ever granted the chance to grow another life inside her, she'll do everything in her power to keep the baby safe. She said that when I'm ready, if I'm ever ready, that we should leave town and try again.

I told her she was my entire fucking world and it wasn't her fault – I'd also move to the moon with her and have a football team's worth of kids if she asked me to.

Ever since that message, I feel like I'm getting my Freckles back. She calls and texts constantly, and even stays over some nights. We don't have sex or get intimate, which is totally fine with me. Holding her and having her smile at me is more than enough. I'd wait forever for her to be comfortable with being physical.

We'll get through this. We'll survive this grief. We'll make our angel proud of us.

Dad breaks me from the trap in my head. "You said Doctor Turner had to up your meds again."

I nod, hands in the pockets of my shorts. "Yeah."

"How do you feel?"

I shrug.

"Are you still sketching?"

I shake my head, staring at nothing as we stop and sit down at the bench. My therapist was concerned about me and decided it was time to either change my dosage again or put me on different meds. I chose the former, because my body doesn't react well to any sudden change in medication. And no matter what I do, I can't draw. I can't even think about drawing.

I'm still undiagnosed, so she studies my every move and emotion during our sessions. I'm not like my dad, but I hold some of his ASPD traits. I'm aware of my surroundings and other's well-being, but there are moments that everything's black.

I've had those moments maybe three times, and once, it lasted for days.

It was like a mental barricade, forming armour around my mind. A dark shadow holding me back, dragging me into the abyss of my own self-destruction. I was trapped in a bubble, unable to be heard or seen. There were voices that terrified me, spoke to me about death and pain.

My therapist thought I was schizophrenic but ruled it out pretty quickly. That's when they introduced medication.

I had so many fucking uncontrolled thoughts. Urges. So much anger.

No, pure fucking rage. I put too many holes in my walls and smashed up my room. I was fifteen after all. There wasn't much I could actually do with my anger back then except break things and speak to my parents like shit.

But then I woke up and walked downstairs, and the tightness in my chest and the voice on my shoulder vanished when I saw Stacey sitting at the dining table. That infuriating yet infatuating human that I couldn't stop looking at whenever she was nearby.

She gave me the finger when no one was looking, and I smiled deep inside while glaring at her.

I haven't had a block since. Not that she's the reason why. That's not medically possible, according to my therapist. She mentioned that I spoke to her a lot about Stacey, and she wanted to make sure it wasn't an impending, out-of-control obsession.

It was, but still. She ended up mine anyway.

Can I love her and still be obsessed with her? Because I am.

"Are you sleeping and eating?" Dad asks, nudging me with his shoulder when I'm unresponsive and stuck in my head again. "You can talk to me. Everything is still fresh, so it's okay to be down and need someone to talk to. Who better to talk to than your dad, who's an expert in emotions after

studying the world and its fakeness for years?"

Snorting, I manage a half-smile and look at my dad. "It just sucks."

"It does," he agrees. "And it's alright to grieve a loss, as long as you don't lose yourself in the process. How is Stacey doing?"

In all fairness, the first few weeks were brutal with how much she withdrew from me, but she did reach out to me with that text.

I was with her before I left for the airport. Stacey was asleep in my bed before I had to catch my flight. She'd smiled up at me as I'd kissed her forehead and told her to dream of me as she fell back to sleep.

She'd called me a cheeseball and sandwiched herself between the dogs.

We're getting there. Day by day, we heal a little more, but I can't bring myself to burn the box under my bed. Filled with clothes and the little princess dress, it'll stay there until I have it in me to bin it.

When I get home, I'm gonna get a tattoo dedicated to our kid, right next to Stacey's nickname on my collarbone.

Stacey cries a lot, whereas I've struggled to shed a tear. Not that I'm not heartbroken about our loss, but I feel like I'm just broken in general. I'm battling that mental block – that fucking wall threatening to fall down. I've kept myself strong for us both. Whenever she breaks down, I keep her above the surface, even though I'm barely keeping myself afloat.

I tell Dad all of this, and he listens to every word, even as they strangle in my throat, and I have to keep stopping. I tell him that I wish I could go back to when we were happy and impatient about our future. I tell him that I was going to be a good father – I was going to work relentlessly to be everything my daughter wanted and needed.

He pulls me against him, and it's only when my head drops that I realise my eyes are burning and my cheeks are wet. My body is shaking as the tightness intensifies in my heart, and there's nothing I can do to stop it. Dad's hand is at the back of my head as he tells me repeatedly that he's got me.

He tells me it's okay to feel. It's okay to let it all out.

He's here.

A soft kiss to my lips pulls me from my slumber, and I open my eyes to find Stacey hovering over me, in my hoodie, face free of make-up.

"Hi," she says quietly, giving me a warm smile. "I missed you."

I squint and look at the clock beside my bed. "It's three in the morning, Stacey."

She shrugs and scrunches her nose. "Your mum picked me up. Can I sleep beside you?"

Despite the lamp being off, I can see her face. "Do you have a black eye?" I ask, sitting up and grabbing the back of her head to get a closer look. "What happened?"

"I walked into a door."

I narrow my eyes, and my heart beats harder in my chest at the idea of someone hurting her. "Don't lie to me. What the fuck happened?"

"Can I not be a klutz without you thinking I'm telling a lie?"

I search her face as her eyes start to water. "If you don't tell me, I'll find out. And whoever did that to you, I'll kill them."

She shakes her head. "No one did this to me, Kade. Can you calm down?"

"Promise me it was an accident."

"I promise."

I drag her to me, wrapping the duvet and my legs around her. "You know you can tell me anything, right?"

"Yeah." She buries her head into me. "Does this mean you missed me too?"

"Of course I missed you," I say against the hood then pull it down to bury my nose in her hair. "I tried to call you when I landed earlier."

"I know," she whispers. "I'm sorry."

I hold her tighter. "Don't be. You're here now. Sleep, Freckles."

"Can we try again?"

"Try what again?" I ask. "For a baby?"

She turns to face me, and even though it's dark in my room, the moon shines on her face, and I can see her undeniable beauty. "Yeah. Maybe not right away, but in like... a year? Six months? We could properly prepare, and I'll even stay on the couch the full nine months. I promise... I promise I won't lose our baby again."

Her eyes are watering, and I take her cheek in my palm, caressing the soft skin. "Hey, stop that. It wasn't your fault, okay? Please stop blaming yourself. We'll try again. Hell, I would start now if you wanted to."

Her chin trembles, but she nods anyway, and we shift so she's lying on my chest. "I love you, Kade. I don't think I'll ever not love you."

"Think?" I snort, my eyes closing. "You're stuck with me, because I know I could never not love you."

"I don't want us to hide."

Quietly, so quietly because I'm falling asleep again, I whisper, "Then we won't."

Two days later, I roll Stacey onto her back and pin her beneath me. "I don't want to watch this anymore," I say, burying my face into the crook of her neck and pressing my lips to her skin. "I think we should finish what we started last night."

She slaps my back with a giggle as I roll my hips, my cock rubbing against her leg, needing her to fucking part her thighs.

"I'm not blowing you while your dogs are in the room."

Our dogs, I correct in my head.

I laugh against her neck, trailing chaste kisses up to her jaw then pressing my lips to her cheeks and nose. She blushes, her eyes starting to dilate, and I grip her hips, my cock thickening as I slide it between her clothed legs and thrust against her.

She lets out a quiet moan that unravels my patience.

"Milo, Hopper." I jump off the bed and throw open the door. "Out."

I feel bad, but they hurry out and gallop downstairs like a herd of elephants. When I close the door and turn to my girlfriend, she's glaring at me.

But the top sliding off her shoulder makes my cock harder.

"That was mean. They were comfortable," she says, but my eyes are on the inked shoulder I want to sink my teeth into.

"You said you wouldn't blow me while the dogs are in." I shrug, lock the door and walk towards her. "I was simply finding a solution, Freckles."

Stacey presses her mouth to mine when I lie on her. "That nickname does things to me."

She rolls her hips, and I straighten my arms to look down at her. "You're good with this?" We haven't really been intimate except from her touching me last night.

She bites her lip and nods. "Just be gentle."

"Right, clothes off." I reach behind me, grabbing the top at the back of my neck and whipping it off. Her eyes are on my chest, larger from the weights I've been lifting and tanned still from summer.

"Pause the movie. Unless you want to watch it while you're inside me?"

I grimace. "I have no intention of watching a bunch of guys running around with guns while I'm inside my girl." I yank at the waistband of her shorts. "Fuck me, why did you tie these so tight?"

"To keep boys like you away," she teases, pulling me by the nape to kiss her again. "And I love seeing men run around with guns."

"You do? Will I find one from somewhere and fuck you with it?"

Not that I'd know how to actually do that – but still.

Her eyes go wide. "Kade!"

I chuckle with a smile, biting my bottom lip. "I love when you scream my name." The blush takes over her cheeks. My mouth presses to her throat, greedy hands travelling up her sides until my thumbs are under her tits as I lick and suck at her skin. "I wonder how fast I could make you scream it again. Maybe I'll use my mouth."

I love feasting on her cunt. Most of the time, even though I kind of know what I'm doing now, I love it when she tells me what to do. She usually has a grip of my hair and moves my head, grinding against my tongue while it's buried into her.

I would very much like to do it right now.

But instead, she slaps my shoulder to stop me from lifting her top over her braless chest and sucking a nipple into my mouth. "After this movie."

Did she just fucking tease me?

I need a new girlfriend.

I groan and fall onto the bed beside her, my shorts tented. "I hate you sometimes."

"You could never hate me," she says, which is true. "But, ah! Look, he just shot that guy in the head from away over there! Do you think you could do that?"

I twist a strand of her hair around my finger, tugging it to annoy her.

"I'd never touch a gun. People already have a grim view of me because of my surname. I need Nora's approval."

She told her dad about me, and he seems happy. He even wants to meet me next weekend. But her stepmother is strict as hell and probably won't like the idea of me being their future son-in-law.

Fuck them all.

"So, yeah," I add. "I'll pass."

"That was cute."

Completely out of my own control, I feel myself blush. Me, blushing – the fuck?

"Yeah? You know what else is cute?" I say with a smirk as I grab her leg, hiking it up to my hip, feeling the addictive heat of her pussy through our clothes. "Like... really, really cute."

She tries to pull away, but I hold tighter. "If you tickle me, I will—Kade!"

The tickle attack turns into passionate kissing, where I devour ever fucking inch of her until we're spent. Later, we walk the dogs down at the pier, but they run back in when I pin her to the small shack by the boat and kiss her until we're panting into each other's mouths and desperate for our clothes to come off.

Stacey smacks me.

I've given this girl countless orgasms today and this is how I'm treated?

"I do not snore."

I capture her wrists, pulling her to me. She straddles my hips, her tits pressing to my chest. "I'll record you next time."

Annoyingly, she rolls her eyes. "Then this is the last time I'll be in your bed."

"Liar," I reply with a grin, reaching up to press my lips to hers. "I'm afraid you're stuck sleeping in my bed for the foreseeable."

"How so?"

"When you come back from your night out tomorrow, we're going to sit Luciella down and tell her we're together. Then we'll break it to her

that we're in love, then add in some more by saying we're planning on moving away before trying for a baby." I shrug, as if it's a piece of cake. I don't even like cake. "Simple."

Luciella has been a fucking pain in this relationship. We can't put it off any longer. She's stressed with uni, but fuck her. I can't tell Base, because he'll tell her, so the only person I can talk to is Dez – fuck that.

"That's anything but simple. She might pass out," she replies, folding her hands at my chest, resting her chin on them. "I have a feeling I'm going to lose my best friend."

She looks sad. How can one person's opinion make her feel this way?

Instead of comforting her, I flip us over, nestling my cock between her legs. Naked as the day we were born, and I get hard.

"If you do, then she isn't a best friend, is she?"

She nibbles her lip, still swollen from her sucking my dick. I pull it from between her teeth with my thumb, dragging it down until it snaps back into place.

When I stop, she says, "I don't want to lose her."

"You won't. If she fucks you off, then she loses you."

"Stop having an answer to everything!" She gasps when my dick twitches, rock solid against her. "Again! Really?"

"Your tits are pressing against my chest, and I can feel your pussy against my cock. So yes, really."

It slides against her soaked entrance, and as I capture her bottom lip between my teeth, I thrust up into her, making us both gasp from how sensitive we are.

"She will accept us. Because I love you." Another thrust. "I'm always going to love you, Freckles."

Her nails sink into my skin as she sits up and moves her hips, grinding slowly against me while I palm her tits. I bite on her nipple, sucking hard to get as much of her breast in my mouth as possible.

"I'll stop birth control," she says as she rides me. "I won't take my pill today or any day after, and I want you to finish inside me, Kade. I want everyone to know. When I get back from my night out, the world will know who I love."

I drop my head back against the pillow as she bounces over me. I'm gripping her hips to pull her down as I fuck up into her tight pussy. "And who do you love?"

"You. Always. You're mine, and I'm yours." She gasps and caresses her own tits, and I grit my teeth to stop myself from finishing before her. Her voice is laced with pleasure as she keeps talking, her body like a fucking temple as she writhes above me. "You'll be the father of my children, the love of my life and the person I get to grow old with."

I mark her throat as I whisper the words. "There'll be no other ending for us, Freckles, because you're fucking it for me."

Fuck. After tomorrow night, I get to have it all.

I'll finally have all of her.

26

KADE

I blink against the bright light someone is shining in my face, my hands and ankles cuffed to a metal chair in the middle of my living room.

"Don't dose him with so much next time," Bernadette scolds someone. "We've already lost six hours." Then her heels click closer to me, and I lift my eyes to her. "I hope your night was worth it, because it's the last crumb of freedom you'll have for a while."

"Ask him," Cassie demands. "Ask him who she is to him."

"What?"

Bernadette hums, flipping through a folder. "Stacey Rhodes. About to turn twenty-two. Impressive dancer and aerialist. Instructor and choreographer. Her mother died when she was young. Dad remarried when she was fourteen to Nora Fields, and they moved in together. He died nearly three years ago."

I feel every drop of blood in my body turn to ice, but I try not to show it. "Never heard of her."

Bernie grins through her anger. "Don't lie to me."

"Pulling random names from your ass should be your talent. It's the only thing you're good at."

Her jaw tenses. "Careful, Kade. I control you, remember?"

"So you keep reminding me. Nevertheless, the name Stacey Rhodes means nothing to me."

Taking a deep breath, she slowly takes her glasses off, snapping them into her case and handing it to one of her guards. "A girl named Stacey Rhodes tried to report an assault not too long ago. She claimed her stepbrother beat her up in the back roads before killing someone in front of her."

My jaw ticks. "I don't fucking know who she is."

The front door of my apartment opens and closes, and I roll my eyes as Archie swaggers in with his shitty moustache and far-too-tight shirt that shows off that he's only skin and bones.

"Awesome," I mutter under my breath, but when a sting hits my cheek, I grit my teeth and count to three. No, ten, until I look up at the wanker who just slapped me. "One day, I'm going to rip that moustache off and scrub the ground with your fucking face."

"Keep threatening me and you'll see what happens."

I spit at his feet.

Archie tries to come for me but his wife puts her hand out – him being the little bitch he is, he halts and scowls at me as he hands Bernie a few folders. "Your days are numbered, kid."

She shakes her head. "Enough. Both of you."

I'd snap him with one hand if he wasn't such a threat. I wouldn't even need to open my eyes while I dislocated his spinal cord from his fucking brain, ripped the spine out and shoved it down his wife's throat until she choked and died.

The image in my head is a dream.

Bernie stares at me. Cassie looks on the verge of a mental breakdown.

"I don't know what you want me to say. Congrats on getting that info, but it still means nothing to me."

With narrowing eyes, Bernie gently opens the first folder and tosses the contents one by one to the floor at my feet. "Someone by the name of Christopher Fields tried to hack into our systems, and my team backfired it and downloaded some of his files. Pictures, videos, you name it. Very incriminating."

I look down, and my lungs stop working. In front of me, there are images of Stacey. Some of her sleeping in bed, eating at the dining table, scowling at the camera as she pulls down her underwear. There are also some of her out in a club, sitting on a guy's lap.

He seems familiar, but the pictures aren't clear enough.

She doesn't look happy in any of them, and once Bernie opens the second folder, I try not to burst out of my cuffs and wreck the place.

Screengrabs from CCTV footage show the guy punching her across the face, both her hands up to try to protect herself. She's wearing a Guns N' Roses top she used to wear when we were together, and her hair is a lot shorter.

Another is him slamming a car door on her arm, then one of him yelling at her in public and gripping her hand so hard she's wincing in the picture.

Pictures of her everywhere.

Swimming in their pool. Sunbathing. Crying. Covered in blood. Practising her dance routine in their ballroom.

There are images of the guy forcing pills into her mouth. Drinks. And making her dance in the club for him. And as my eyes land on the last picture, him gripping her face in a close-up, her nose bleeding and eye swollen, I notice him.

I pull so hard at my cuffs, my skin splits.

He's the one that tried to get her out of the manor months ago. He was sparkled at my gate and told her to go home. The same fucking prick who was at the party – he sold her to those guys and slipped her the blade.

He's her stepbrother. He's Christopher Fields.

She tried to tell me about him, and I walked away.

"This isn't half of the stuff we found between the two."

My throat tightens. "There's more?" I shouldn't be asking, or even conversing with Bernadette, but I need to know more. It seems that after we split up, Stacey's abuse escalated.

Bernie smirks at my anger, but I grit out, "Fucking tell me."

"Stacey Rhodes was your girlfriend. She was the one you were with in America. She was the one you fucked behind the club and then again on the bike. She was the one you rushed out of the country. She cheated on you, am I right? From the information I've gathered, that's why you split up."

I pale.

She chuckles.

"I don't find this fucking funny."

I need Stacey to get the fuck out of town – and fast. If I wasn't cuffed, I'd stab Bernadette in the eye with a pen and take her gun to shoot my way out of here.

"Seeing you get so worked up over a useless slut *is* funny. Want to know something funnier? A specific video was pulled from Christopher Fields' computer."

I slouch in the chair as I tug at the cuffs. If she mentions the video I was sent, I'll fucking explode.

"In fact, shall we watch it?"

I frown as Archie slaps his legs with a grin and gets to his feet, messing about with my flatscreen until the picture changes. Cassie is already out of the room.

The local nightclub comes into view. The date is from nearly three years ago.

I glare as her wanker of a stepbrother drags her from the booth, and Jason stops them, shoving a finger in his face as he pulls Stacey behind him – protecting her. Christopher raises both hands and laughs, backing away from them. Jason says something to her. I think he's asking if she's okay, and the clip ends.

Frowning, I try to remain calm.

My breaths come out in short bursts as the next clip starts. A camera is sitting in the corner of Jason's room, where three guys and Stacey's stepbrother make the bed and carry a barely conscious Jason in, sitting him against the wall opposite the bed.

He's wearing the top he borrowed from me. This is the same night.

One guy slaps his face, waking him, but his spit drips from his mouth, his eyes rolling.

The fuck?

At that point, Jason didn't do drugs. He hated them – hated smoking too. Fuck, he barely drank. Seeing my big brother in this state makes me physically ill.

My teeth clench as they inject him with something. He attempts to push them away, but he's too weak, and I want to smash their jaws off. He grips someone's top before taking a fist to the face.

My heart stops as they bring Stacey in, both arms over their shoulders – three of them I recognise right away. Stacey killed them at the hotel.

Her head drops to the side. "No," she slurs. "P... please, Chris."

I yank at my cuffs as Chris slides down her dress, her breasts falling out. One of the guys he's with twists her hair around his fist while the other slips off her shoes.

Bernie tilts her head. "This seems like the same setting as the clip you were sent. Doesn't it, Kade?"

I don't reply. I can't. They strip her and lie her on the bed as I watch. As her brother tells them each touch will cost them, I feel my stomach flip.

The big ginger one, the one Stacey stabbed, slaps notes into Chris's palm and unbuckles his belt.

I close my burning eyes as she begs him to stop.

He doesn't stop, and neither does the next one while Chris films it on his phone – as he tells her he decides when she feels pleasure, when she can sleep with someone else and that when she comes, she better scream his name.

"N-No," Stacey slurs, trying to scratch the guy's face, but he swears and headbutts her. Stacey goes limp instantly.

My knuckles turn the whitest shade of white. My heart is shattering.

You prefer them older, don't you?

You're fucking dead to me.

Stop fucking crying, Stacey. It's pathetic.

Please don't leave me.

No matter how many times we fuck, I will never ever *fucking forgive you.*

I'm so, so sorry, Freckles.

The first hour drags in. It's torture to watch. I know what it feels like to have your consent stripped away; to be used and fucked while you barely have a grip on reality. I know how it feels to want them to stop, to try to fight them off. I remember my own voice being like Stacey's – haunting me as she wakes and pleads. Cries. Even trying to hit back before being tied to the bedpost.

Tears soak her face, a bruise already forming on her cheek, her lip cut. "Please let me go home." Red stains her chin as crimson mixes with spit. "Please."

Her brother vanishes from the room, leaving her with Jason barely able to open his eyes on the floor and the other guy on top of her.

Chris comes back and tells everyone to get out as he strips himself. I'll kill him – I'll make it slow, and fucking make sure he feels every single bone I'm going to snap. I want him to be awake while I peel off all his skin and light him on fire.

Jason pushes to his hands and knees but falls down. I can't really understand what he's saying, but it sounds like he's telling him to get off her, that he's a sick fuck.

I agree, brother.

The brother I cut off and abandoned.

The brother who keeps trying to get to Chris as he forces open Stacey's legs, spits between her thighs and slaps her hard enough that she screams in pain.

He grips her face and kisses her, then says, "Do I get a big brother's discount, you filthy slut?"

When he enters her, she tries to kick her legs out.

My rage meets new heights, and blood trickles down my hands as I pull harder at the cuffs, both temples throbbing. Pain – I want to feel pain. I deserve to feel pain after what I put her through. What I put them both through.

Stacey stops fighting, and her body goes still, her eyes on the ceiling as her stepbrother keeps going. She isn't conscious – she's falling into a state where she's neither awake nor asleep. She's there, but she isn't.

A trauma response I've fallen into a few times. And now I'm

watching my ex go through the same.

I should have listened to her. I should have heard her out.

I'm a fucking idiot.

Stacey was everything to me, and instead of being a good boyfriend, I walked away. I fucking ran. Right into Bernadette's corrupted grasp. I don't deserve her forgiveness. I don't deserve to even look in her direction.

My skin splits more at my wrists as the metal cuts into my flesh, my teeth close to cracking with how hard I'm crushing them together, especially when he speaks.

"Next time you fall pregnant, sweetheart, it'll be *me* who fathers your child. Do you understand? You're lucky I found that ultrasound picture and dealt with the issue, so you wouldn't have a little bastard strapped to you."

My eyes widen in shock. She had two broken ribs here from apparently falling down the stairs, and bad bruising on her lower back, yet these sick fucks... I can't even say it. There are seven of them. Three are already dead. I'm going to fucking destroy the rest.

But how did they send me the clip of her and Jason...?

Before I can finish my thought, he pulls out and releases on her, then slaps her tit, grabbing her chin. "This is what happens when you try to fuck other people, Stacey. Bad things happen to bad girls. You are *mine*. You have been since you were fourteen. No more boyfriends. Got it?"

She stays still, her unseeing eyes on the ceiling, blank, her chest barely rising or falling.

Bernie decides to say, "She has a nice pussy at least. It's a shame we can't use her as a pet."

"Shut your fucking mouth. Turn this off."

"But the best part is about to start," she says. "Keep watching or I'll have *your* sister as my next pet."

I gulp down the lump threatening to strangle me, trying not to show emotion as Chris throws Jason on the bed, telling him his fiancée needs attention. He pulls his phone out again, sits on a chair in the corner of the room and watches.

Jason wraps his arms around her, and the part that was edited out is Stacey sobbing and saying with broken words, "K... Kade? Is that y-you?" She's touching his face, as if she's blind, then feels his shirt. My shirt. "I'm so... so sca-scared."

Jason grunts, unable to speak properly, and doesn't stop her as she breaks down into his chest, heaving and begging him to make it stop – the dream is too real, and she needs to wake up. Her words are incoherent, but that's what I pick up. She begs him to distract her.

"I've got you, baby," he whispers.

They kiss – I close my eyes again. I can hear everything happening, but I try to drown it out. A lot of the footage was removed, to make it seem like she wanted to sleep with Jason, but that's not the case. She's drugged up, far too high to realise that she isn't in my bed and he's on the same level.

"Watch. The. Footage." Bernadette slams her fist on the table with each word.

So I do. I watch – listening as she speaks to him like he's me, the sounds so clear as she weeps through the kissing, through him on her and inside her, to her on him, telling him she can't see straight, that the room is spinning. She feels weird. She thinks she's dying.

Chris is hard in the corner, stroking himself until he releases once again, and as he glances up at the camera, he fucking *smiles* before vanishing from the room.

He'll be at the Fields' manor. I'm going to burn it to the ground.

Sweat covers them both as skin slaps together, and I want to gouge my eyeballs out and stuff candle wax in my ears.

She keeps saying my name. Moaning it.

"I love you, Giana."

Stacey's eyes are glazed, slobber rolling down her chin from the amount of drugs she was given. "I love you, Kade."

I can't stop the vomit. It's out and down me before she can say it again, and I can't avoid seeing the smile he gives her, his eyes red raw.

The smile that I thought was for my girlfriend.

Bernie hums. "Interesting. Archie, go get the car ready."

"Fuck that. Can't we use his room?"

I pay them no attention – all I can do is watch the screen as they pass out and the footage skips to the morning.

The sound is off, but they're yelling at each other in double time as she covers herself, sobbing into her palm. He grabs his hair and paces, then gives her a change of clothes to cover her nakedness.

She keeps mouthing *sorry*.

Sorry. I'm so sorry. It's my brother. He's a monster. I thought you were Kade.

And Jason mutters a *fuck* and storms out of the room.

My body feels exhausted from watching all of this and the truth it holds, so I don't notice anyone has approached me until someone stabs something into my arm. My brain goes cold just as the footage skips one last time – to Stacey standing on the Erskine Bridge with tears pouring down her face, wearing what she had on when I told her to get the fuck out of my life.

My brother is trying to get her down.

Stacey was suicidal for something that wasn't her fault.

No.

27

KADE

FLASHBACK

Hours after Stacey leaves the manor, with a parting kiss and promising to see me tomorrow night, Jason shows up at my bedroom door.

"What do you want?" I hold the door open – confused.

"Going out with some of the guys from work, but my black shirt is too tight at the arms." He walks in, instantly going for my dresser to go through my tops. "I've been going heavy at the gym and can't button past my chest."

"What makes you think my clothes will fit you? I'm tall and you're..." I stare at him, gesturing to his height. "Not."

"I'm only three inches shorter than you, dickhead."

I shrug. But when he pulls open another drawer, I sigh. "Did you draw this?" he asks.

It's a sketch of Stacey. Her face. Her smile. Each freckle and imperfection on her skin detailed, her hair cascading all over the page. I only started sketching again a few days ago. I gulp. "Yeah."

"It's good. It's really good. I didn't know you could draw."

"My therapist pushes on it. I mainly design tattoos for me and Stacey." I snatch it off him and flip over the pages to close the sketch pad. "Here, this one." I hand him a black top, and instead of leaving, he pulls off his hoodie and goes into my bathroom.

He sprays my deodorant, then my aftershave, before slapping my shoulder on his way out. "Thanks, little bro."

"You need to stop calling me that."

"You're eleven years younger than me. Therefore" – he grabs my door handle – "little bro fits, asshole."

Once he leaves, I sit down and open the sketch pad and work on a new design. Stacey wants me to make her a tattoo to cover her thigh, and I think she'll love this one.

After an hour, I head downstairs to the kitchen with full intentions of making a snack and maybe a coffee.

I take one step in and turn back out.

Jason has his own fucking house – why is he kissing his girlfriend on the kitchen counter with her legs wrapped around his waist? Motherfucker knows fine well that my mum is in the next room.

I knock on the door heavily, three thumps with my fist – I hear her yelping and both of them straightening themselves. "Good to come in?"

Jason clears his throat. "Yeah."

"You idiot," Giana mutters to Jason as I push open the door.

I look between them. "Why are you trying to fuck your girlfriend in here of all places?"

"Fiancée actually," she replies, lifting her left hand to show off the diamond on her ring finger. "Jason proposed yesterday! And I said yes!"

He didn't mention this while stealing my clothes and emptying half my aftershave, but regardless, I give a genuine smile and pat his back as I pass him. I pull Giana in for a hug and turn to Jason. "Knew you had a set of balls on you. But please don't rub them all over the kitchen counters."

Giana slaps my arm, and I chuckle as I move towards the refrigerator, rummaging for ingredients to make a sandwich. They both stare at me as

I set up a chopping board and slice some bread.

I look up at them mid-slice. "What?"

Jason glances at his future wife. "We're going to try for a baby. I wanted to speak to you about it first."

"Why would you need to speak to me about it? You need my blessing or something?"

He sighs. "Stop being a sarcastic wanker. We want to know if you'll be alright with it if we do, or if you'd prefer we wait. I know things have been tough."

"I'd never stop you from doing something like that. If you want to have a baby then have a baby." I look at Giana. "You sure you want to birth his spawn? He's a dick."

I run to the other side of the kitchen island, knife in hand, as my brother goes for me. "I'll strangle you," he threatens.

I smirk. "I'll tell my dad."

He narrows his eyes. "I dare you."

"He'll kill you."

"Not if I kill him first," he replies, and he bursts out laughing as the words pass his lips – he knows he could never get near my dad to harm him. Instead, he goes deeper. "I'm no relation to Aria, remember?"

Giana groans. "This again? You're not going to screw your stepmother, for crying out loud!"

"My dad will hunt you down and tear you limb from limb, then your own dad will finish the job."

"Pair of idiots," Giana mutters as Jason throws a tomato at me, and I chuck it back. "Can we grow up please?"

We ignore her and keep our faces straight, until we lose it and laugh, him pulling me in for a hug. "I'm glad you're doing good. Keep your girl safe, and keep your chin up."

"I will."

Giana smiles and pulls Jason's arm. "Come on. I have a night shift and you have your work night out. Kade, I'm sorry. We shouldn't have brought it up."

"I really don't mind, and neither would Stacey," I say, stacking my sandwich with slices of tomato and different meats. "Just keep the baby-making to your own fucking house."

I know Jason's giving me the middle finger as they leave, and I munch on my snack, walk the dogs while texting Base and Dez, then head back to my room to watch the next episode of Still Game.

I look at the last messages from Stacey.

Freckles: I meant what I said. I didn't take my pill today, and I won't take it again. We'll leave and start a new life where no one knows us, okay?

Me: Okay, I'm already missing you. I love you.

Freckles: I love you more. I'm heading out in an hour, and my battery is low, so I'll message you when I can.

She'll be out now. I'm bored.

I was going to ask Dez and Base if they wanted to go out somewhere, but they're busy.

Instead, I lie in bed and look through our pictures together from holidays, lazy days in the indoor pool, our beds, and then I take a shower.

Kneeling, I pull out the box under my bed with shaky hands and place it on the mattress. I open it, letting the lid slide from my fingers as I stare at the contents.

We packed all the baby clothes we bought into it, along with newborn essentials, Stacey's pregnancy notes and weekly Polaroid pictures of me holding Stacey, waiting to keep going until I was holding a huge baby bump, then our daughter.

But we never got to do that, so we've locked all the memories and traces of the pregnancy into this box. We agreed to open it after we fell pregnant again, but I've caved.

The princess dress sits on my lap while I rub the material between my fingers, imagining a little girl giggling with the dogs and screaming as she leaps into my arms while we play in the pool.

Catch me, Daddy!

I love you, Daddy.

I want to be here forever, Daddy.

I sniff, stuffing all the things away and kicking the box under the bed again, before huffing and lying down.

Stacey's phone is dead. She's not been online and hasn't received my text telling her to have a good night and that she deserves it. I tell Dez and Base I'm having an early night, and they say they'll see me when they see me.

Me and Base are going to America for a few days for his birthday in two weeks, and I'm kinda dreading being away from Stacey.

I think I might be the clingy boyfriend. Most likely.

I close my eyes and hug the pillow Stacey sleeps on, falling asleep to the sound of her voice.

By the next morning, I've still not heard from her.

Usually, I'd get drunken calls from Jason, but there's nothing from him either.

Mum is making breakfast and offers me a coffee and a bacon roll. We eat in comfortable silence, then she drives me to my appointment, where I tell my therapist that things are getting easier, and that I'd like to start weaning off my high dosage, to which she agrees.

I tell her how I'm dealing with the loss – that we want to try again, and she said that as long as I feel comfortable, then she sees no issue. But I've to sit down and have a serious talk with Stacey about how big a responsibility it is to have a child, especially at our age.

We'll be twenty soon.

I'm fine with starting early, and Stacey has made it clear that she is too – I'll marry her, and our kids will be there. Our daughter will be the flower girl, and our son will stand by my side while Stacey's dad walks her to us.

By the afternoon, I've still heard nothing.

Me: Are you alright? Are you too hungover to enter the world of socialising yet?

An hour later.

Me: I'm going to order us Chinese food when you get here. It'll help the hangover.

Another two hours.

Me: I'm having withdrawals, Freckles. Want me to come to your house and nurse you back to health?

She replies instantly.

Freckles: No!

Freckles: I'm okay, just really tired. Me and Tylar are coming over later to go over plans with Ewan for the surprise studio he wants to build Luciella. We're going to stay over. I can come and see you once Ty is asleep? I need to talk to you.

Freckles: I miss you.

I smile at the screen despite not knowing what she needs to talk to me about. It won't be bad. We're good. I type back.

Me: Sure. I miss you too, Freckles.

Finally, Tylar and Stacey are here and downstairs with my mum and Ewan, but I wait. They're discussing whatever plans they're making for my sister's studio, since Tylar's family owns the studio they dance at. When they eventually go to their beds, I wait a bit more.

Milo and Hopper are lying at my feet as I pet them when my phone vibrates, and it's fucking embarrassing how fast I snatch it from the bedside unit.

Freckles: She's asleep now. Get you at the pool house?

I frown. Why the fuck would she not just come here?

Me: I'll race you.

She types and deletes a few times.

Freckles: I always win, remember?

I smirk like a psycho and get my shoes on, patting the dogs and telling them to stay in bed. The house is in darkness – unsurprising considering it's one in the morning.

When I push into the pool house, I roll my eyes. Of course I got here first. I pull my phone out, about to tell her she most certainly didn't win, when she rushes in.

My phone is tossed aside, and I scoop her into my arms without a word and crush my lips to hers. She whimpers but wraps her arms around me and kisses me back, sliding her tongue past my lips to tangle with my own.

I press her back to the door, closing it, and hum against her mouth as she tilts her head and deepens the kiss. Her legs wrap around my waist, and I grasp at her thighs and hips.

She tenses, and I loosen my hold. I'm so wound up, needing her, that I'm being too rough.

My phone dings twice, but I ignore it.

Stacey brushes her fingers through my hair, her hands on my cheeks, my neck, dragging down my chest, as if she's studying every inch of me.

I grab her ass and grind my hardening cock against her, and she flinches with a hiss, freezing in my arms.

"Stop," she cries against my mouth, and I pull back with confusion. "Please stop."

I settle her on her feet. "What's wrong?"

She breaks down into a sobbing mess, and I catch her as her knees give way, just as my phone dings once more.

I hold her to me as I glance down at my screen, which has lit up with three messages from a number I don't recognise. It dings once more as Stacey weeps into my chest, clinging to me for dear life and not telling me what's wrong.

"Talk to me," I say softly.

Nothing. All she's doing is crying and trembling in my arms.

I kiss her temple. "It's going to be alright. We'll try again. I promise. We're just hurting right now, but we'll work through this, okay? Me and you, Freckles."

She sobs even louder, and I grow increasingly concerned as I try to pull her back from me to see her face, but she keeps her head dipped.

"Do you want me to carry you to bed?"

She shakes her head. "I'm so, so, so sorry, Kade."

I hug her to me, my chest tightening. "Don't be. It wasn't your fault. Stop apologising for something that was out of your control."

Her hand grips my top at the back as she rattles against me, hyperventilating while repeatedly muttering "sorry".

My phone dings once more, and the message I get a preview of has me frowning and leaning down to grab it. I rest my chin on her head while I read.

Unknown Number: Not such a good girl now, is she?

Unknown Number: And with him, of all people.

Unknown Number: One video attachment.

Unknown Number: If you want any more details, let me know.

I release her and stand back as I click on the attachment. A video starts.

Bile rises in my throat instantly, and I feel my heart race in my chest, painful and swollen and fucking breaking as I watch Stacey in bed with someone else. They're naked and... I grit my teeth. She has her arms around him, kissing him as he fucks her.

The guy rolls onto his back, and then she's on him, and I drop my phone like it's burned me when I realise who it is.

I glare up at the traitorous bitch. "You fucked my brother?"

Stacey cries and holds the back of her hand to her mouth. "Please l-let me explain, Kade. Please. It's not what it looks like."

My vision is blurring as my entire body starts to shake, and so does my voice as I manage to speak.

"You slept with my fucking brother?"

She tries to come to me, but I back away from her like she's a disease. "Please," she sobs. "I was drunk in the club and—"

"Get the fuck out!" I yell, and she flinches and drops her head. "Leave. Right fucking now. We're done. You cheated. It's fucking over! Get the fuck out!"

"Kade. It's me. I would never do anything to hurt—"

I flip the coffee table, smashing all of its contents. "No!" I point at her, my eyes burning as my heart shatters into pieces, staring at the girl I thought loved me. "You're nothing. You're fucking dead to me."

She tries to grab me as I storm past her, but then she's on the ground, crying – begging me. I throw the door open and fucking leave her there, fighting against hot tears as I rush through the manor with a crippling pain in my chest.

As soon as I grab my keys, I storm past the dogs and get into my car.

My phone screen lights up with an incoming call.

Freckles.

I reject it and start the engine, just as messages start desperately pinging up on my screen.

Freckles: Please answer the phone, Kade. Let me explain.

Freckles: I want to fix this. Please.

She can fuck off.

Stacey cheated on me. She fucked Jason.

And now I'm going to kill him.

While I speed through the roads, nearly kerbing it multiple times, I punch my steering wheel until my knuckles bleed, my eyes and cheeks soaked, and pathetic tears spill onto my top. I'm so fucking mad and disgusted and goddamn hurt.

Stacey cheated on me. She actually fucking cheated on me.

I punch the steering wheel again and slam the brakes on, pressing my forehead to the wheel while I attempt to breathe, trying to calm my rage. I try to not think about all the times we've had together, all the firsts and I love yous and even the excitement that we were going to become parents.

I've never felt so betrayed in my life.

I pull out a joint I had pre-rolled in my glovebox – it burns my lungs on the first inhale.

I close my eyes and count to three, my forehead still pressed to the steering wheel. My jaw tenses, my chest fucking burns and it's not from the joint. My hand grasps at the back of my neck as I try to control my emotions.

I've never been good at control, but right now, with all the violent thoughts running wild in my head, I need to.

When I told Jason Stacey was pregnant, he was so fucking proud of me. I wanted him to be the first to know. Yet he fucked her.

Fucking bastard.

I stare blankly – images of my girlfriend and brother screwing, kissing, fucking all over each other like they knew each other.

They looked comfortable.

I grab my phone from my pocket and watch the clip again, torturing myself even more as I keep pausing it on their faces, nearly crushing my screen under the pressure of my thumb against her smile.

I hate her. I fucking hate her. Both of them.

She made me believe she loved me. She made me fucking believe we had a future and a plan. I stopped doubting myself, doubting what we had and how to deal with each emotion.

Was the baby even mine? How long have they been fucking?

I call Jason, but he rejects it, putting me to voicemail instead. She keeps fucking calling, and no matter how many times I reject the call, she keeps going.

Just fuck off.

I feel numb both physically and mentally, and the psychological wall is slowly starting to drop. That black veil of nothingness threatens to swallow me whole as I toss the joint out the window and start the engine.

Shivers snake around my arms and crawl up my chest as I pull into his street.

Jason's lights are on when I reach his house.

I don't hesitate to get out of the car, and as I reach the door, Giana, with swollen red eyes and a suitcase rolling behind, stops in her tracks.

"You know," is all she says, her lip trembling.

I nod, my anger hitting new levels when I hear him calling after her.

"Gi! Fuck. Please listen to me."

Monotone and blocking out my brother, she stares at me and says, "He told me he slept with your girlfriend. In our bed, where we've been trying for a baby."

She glances at Jason. "You're a vile piece of shit. Not only was she your brother's girlfriend, but she was a teenager!"

"It wasn't like that, Gi. Please, I'm fucking begging you not to leave me."

She gives me one last look and rushes towards the Uber waiting for her, but before my fucking cunt of a brother can run after her, I capture him by the throat and throw him into the house. The door cracks on its hinges as I shove it fully open.

He lands on his back, and I climb on top of him. "Fucking scum."

He doesn't get a chance to talk as I start hammering my fist into his face. Pain sears over my knuckles, but I'm blinded by the image of him sucking on Stacey's throat to pay attention to how hard I'm hitting him. "She was my fucking girlfriend! You're supposed to be my brother!"

Holding his hands up to protect his face, he barely gets a second to even breathe before I stand up and drive my foot into his side, ignoring the blood dripping from his nose and mouth.

"Kade," he chokes out. "Stop."

I grab his shirt collar, picturing Stacey all over him as I smash my fist into his face once more, his eye instantly swelling.

Giana is back now, dragging me away, telling me to stop, but with the roaring in my ears and the rate my heart is going, I'm blank to everything else around me. I shrug away from her and drive my knee into the side of his face when he tries to get up.

"How long?" I grab his hair, seething as I grit my teeth and yell, "How fucking long have you been screwing my girlfriend?"

Blood coats his face, dripping from his chin. "S-Stop."

"Please stop, Kade. He isn't worth it. Neither of them are!"

Giana yanks at my sleeve, and when Jason spits blood out on the floor and tries to get up again, raising his hand to block any more blows, he says, "I didn't know it was her."

He's on his knees, head bowed, his shoulders shaking. His face is bloodied as he looks up, eyes on Giana. "Please, baby. Please don't go. I love you."

"And did you love me while you were fucking a teenager last night?

You're thirty years old, Jason. Fucking act like it."

My brother tries to get to his feet to beg some more, but Giana manages to pull me away, shoving me into my car. "Go home." I'm not looking at her, so she grabs my face. "Go home, Kade. He's not worth it. She's not worth it."

My lip trembles as I stare at her. She's been crying for a while, by the looks of it. "She used to be worth it."

"I know, honey. I know. Just... go home. Please. Don't do anything stupid."

I nod, glaring back at Jason, who's sobbing in his driveway, muttering apologies and begging Giana to stay, but she slams the door of the Uber and vanishes.

He runs after the car, trips and sobs into the ground. Swallowing the lump in my throat, I start my engine and drive home, leaving him there.

Stacey's gone. Thank fuck. She's nowhere to be seen, and the guard at the gates said she left in a car an hour ago.

I feel numb when I reach my room, the dogs licking my bloodied and busted-open hands.

I feel numb when I look at all of our previous messages.

I feel like I'm dying when I watch the clip again, texting the number and asking for more details. But it bounces back – a sign that the person has blocked me.

Milo and Hopper follow me around the room as I collect all of her shit, pack it into a bag and get back into my car.

Jason tries to call me four times and sends a message begging me to pick up, but I block him.

I haven't blocked Stacey yet.

I want to hear her side. I need to hear what she has to fucking say for herself – to know if this has been going on for a while or if it was a one-time thing. It won't change the outcome, but I need to know.

I park down the street from her house, and my lungs completely seize when I walk up with a bag of her things and see the black Jeep sitting outside. I nearly fall to my knees when Stacey emerges from the passenger side and heads for her front door.

I drop her things on the ground and watch Jason's car drive away.

And there's my answer. To say I'm heartbroken is an understatement. I don't think I've ever felt this way or know how to control it.

I get in my car, staring into nothingness as I somehow make my way home. The organ in my chest squeezes every time I picture them together.

I bite my lip, and the burn in my eyes nearly buckles me.

No wonder Dad lost his mind over love. It sucks the life out of you.

A life I don't fucking want.

I don't remember being in the medicine cupboard, or grabbing the numerous bottles stored within it. I want to stop – it's like I'm being controlled by someone else. They want me dead. They want me gone. They want to eliminate the middleman.

Everyone wants me dead.

I guzzle every last pill then toss aside all the bottles – the glass of water smashing on the kitchen floor.

It's like a demon is sitting on my chest, telling me to go to the boat, to lie on it and watch the moon and the stars.

It rocks beneath me.

The stars aren't visible with the clouds. The moon hides behind trees.

This really isn't what I had in mind, but the dizziness and nausea is starting to take over. I'll fall asleep, and it'll all be over.

She was my girlfriend, and now she's not.

He was my brother, and now he's not.

They'll blame me. Luciella will blame me. She always does. They'll say I'm just like my dad.

Everyone thinks I'm the broken son of Tobias Mitchell, and I proved it by beating the shit out of my brother after finding out he was sleeping with the girl I'm in love with.

How many hours has it been? Why am I not dead yet?

My eyes close, and I try to sleep. Sleep will help. Maybe it'll calm the voices in my head that are egging me on.

Jump into the water.

No one loves you.

You ruin everything.

Drown yourself.

She prefers him.

She blames you for losing the baby, and this is her revenge.

Die.

You deserve this.

It's your fault.

It's all your fault.

I vomit while I'm lying on my back. The boat is spinning, and I struggle to tip myself to the side. Air fails to reach my lungs as more vomit gathers in my throat, suffocating me.

My legs don't move when I try to get up, my spine ramrod straight, and the only thing I can move is my left arm as I choke on my own vomit.

I want to breathe.

I need to breathe.

I can't fucking die.

Shakily, I fish my phone out of my pocket, my arm growing numb like the rest of my body, and open the chat box with my mum.

I manage to send her my location, and spit out as much vomit as I can before the next lot chokes me.

My eyes burn with the pressure of not being able to breathe, and the view above me fades every few seconds. My body tenses each time I try to inhale, bile rises and vomit spurts from my mouth.

Everything in me is on fire as I try to get up.

If I die, then everyone suffers. I'll be gone, and I'll leave my family in ruin. Stacey will blame herself. Jason will too.

My lungs sting, shrivelling from lack of oxygen, and my muscles go limp, the pressure in my head halting, and my vision goes blurry.

If I die, at least I'll get to be with my angel.

I hear my mum screaming my name, getting closer, closer, even closer as my eyes start to shut, and I stop fighting the urge to fill my lungs.

Someone grabs my head and turns me, forcing their fingers down my throat, but I don't know what happens next. I think this is it.

28

KADE

I wake up in my bed, Archie and Bernie spooning beside me. My vision is hazy as I rub my eyes, wincing at the pinch in my hand. I yank out the cannula, ignoring the blood dripping out as I shakily get to my feet.

What the fuck happened?

I glance at the window to see it's dark. The digital clock blinks 4 a.m. – and the date. Jesus. I've been out cold for two full days.

We're still in my apartment – and my keys are sitting on my dresser.

I need to get to Stacey. *Now.*

To apologise on my fucking knees and to get her the hell away from Bernie. As far as I can get her. I have a friend in Australia – I'll take her there and keep her hidden until I figure something out.

Whatever they gave me has knocked me for six, because it takes me five tries to get my leg in my joggers, and I give up on my socks before shoving my bare feet into trainers.

As quietly as I'm able, I stagger out of the room, hitting each wall I come into close contact with. Her guards are nowhere to be seen. And as I glance into one of my spare rooms, I see Cassie asleep in the bed.

I dodge my bike and fall into my car instead. The view of the nearby trees blurs as I make my way out of my garage and into the street.

I need to get to my girl.

My girl who didn't willingly fuck my brother and was raped by multiple men after being drugged. Who has a second brother who abuses her and is responsible for the death of our daughter.

Fuck the consequences. I'm hanging that bastard with his own tongue.

Freezing tingles take over my body, my stomach churning as I see them on her all over again. I punch my steering wheel, my eyes watering. I wipe them with the back of my hand, but it's no use. Tears drop onto my top from my chin, and each time Stacey's phone goes to voicemail, I die a little inside.

I nearly hit the kerb a few times, but that doesn't stop me from speeding.

The Fields' manor. Once I get Stacey away, I'll go there. Nora needs a fucking boot for letting this happen under her roof – and I'll punch Kyle for not noticing either. But if I get my hands on Chris? Everything my dad has done in his life will pale in comparison.

The twelfth time her voicemail sounds, I throw my phone off the dashboard, and it topples under the passenger seat.

I wipe my eyes again, regretting each word I've thrown at her over the years. I left her. I left her with a broken heart after being drugged and raped and abused, after losing our baby. Then her dad died two months later. She tried to contact me so many times, and I ignored her.

She needed me, and I let her down. The person who was supposed to love her – to make her feel fucking safe.

I'm a piece of shit, and she really does deserve better.

My phone starts ringing as I hit a long, narrow stretch of road with no lights, closed in by tall trees. I swear to myself and bend down to get it, but as I lift it to see it's Bernie, my wheel hits the kerb, my body jolts and I'm swerving the entire car to the side before it starts rolling.

Each time it hits the ground, glass shatters, my head bouncing off the frame, and my airbag explodes to protect me. I must flip about six times before colliding with a tree, and I'm not sure if I pass out, or if time just stops, but I'm upside down, blood rushing to my head, ears ringing painfully.

I choke, groaning at the rush of adrenaline shoving aside the pain. I unclip my belt, grab my phone and crawl out of the broken window. Palms cutting on the glass, I push to stand. My left arm is fucked – the bone is poking through my skin, and I'm limping as I hold my ribs. Blood is pissing down my face from my head, but I force my feet to keep moving.

I need to get to her.

I need Stacey.

Blinding pain mixes with deep emotions of regret and heartbreak, and I'm fucking crying again as I topple to the ground and cough up ruby red into my hand.

No. I need to keep moving.

I roll onto my back, hold my breath and lurch to my feet – only to fall again.

So I crawl. I'll crawl the entire fucking way to Stacey if I need to.

My vision is blurring – worse than any drug reaction I've had. I screw my eyes shut and try to focus. Block out everything. Focus on getting to my feet and walking; hell, running if I can.

But I fall onto my back once more and just lie here, staring at the moon shining through the treetops.

I like this. Us lying in the grass and watching the stars. You're usually a moody prick. Hey! I was kidding! I just mean it's relaxing. I think if I ever took my last breaths outside, I'd like to be able to see the moon. It's beautiful.

Stacey's voice is in my head. Surely I'm not already dead?

I'm so cold though.

A shaking, sliced-open hand pulls my cracked phone from my pocket as I dial Stacey's number one last time. I deserve this. I deserve it all. The excruciating pain, the karma, the blood spilling from my wounds so I'm lying in a puddle of crimson liquid.

"Hi, you're through to Stacey. Leave a message."

God, I miss her voice. I miss her.

My throat is tense, but I swallow blood and tears and make it clear, so she can understand everything I say.

"Hey, Freckles." I bite my lip and screw my face up as my ribs burn, taking a deep breath before continuing. "I'm so sorry. I'm so fucking sorry for not knowing what you went through or giving you a chance to explain what happened. I should have heard you out. I should have stayed. But you need to listen." I wince and pull the phone away, so she can't hear my groan of pain. "They know who you are, and what we were. They're going to come for you. Please. Please, baby, you need to run. Run, and don't you dare turn back. Get away from all of them. You... you hear m-me?" My eyes close, and my phone slides out of my hand, but I quickly grab it. "Please hide, please."

My vision goes dark, and the tremble in my bones stops.

"I n-never stopped loving you." My heart is fucking sore, but I need to get this last part out. I know I'm dying. But the only thing I'm worried about is her getting the fuck away from those evil pricks. "I will... will always lo-love you, Freckles. Go, live your life and be free. Meet someone who can tr-treat you ri-ight. For-for-forget me."

I can't hear anything, not even my heartbeat.

"Pl-please for... forgive me. B-Be safe and ha-ha-happy. I love you. I..." The phone slides again, and I have no energy left to finish my sentence, but as long as she knows I loved her, that she meant the world to me, that she is fucking special and deserves everything that makes her happy – then I've said all I need to.

A hand touches my face, but I can't see through the blood in my eyes from the gaping wound in my head.

Stacey? Is that you?

Mum?

But it's Bernie's voice in my ear. Faint, but enough that I can make out what she's saying. "Oh, silly me. Did I forget to mention Stacey fled the country? New phone. ID. *Everything.* You'll never find her, but guess what? I will."

She wipes my eyes with a cloth, and I can just make out a medic hovering over me.

Archie lowers himself beside me as I try to drag air into my punctured lungs. "I did some digging and was able to lift some messages between you both – and her nickname. *Freckles?*" He laughs, and blood drops from my mouth as I attempt to move, to get up and snap his neck. "I'll carve each freckle out of her skin."

"I'll k-kill y-you."

"Enough, Archie," Bernadette snaps, pulling him to his feet by the collar.

Someone else is by my side, tending to my head wound.

"I'll find out where she is, Kade. Your precious little girlfriend has no idea what's coming her way."

No. Fucking no.

Embarrassingly, my tears are still falling, and it feels like a knife is buried in my chest. This is a nightmare within a nightmare. I have no idea how to get out of it.

Archie looks down at me. "If you thought we had fun before, you're in for a ride from now on."

Archie chuckles as my eyes keep falling shut. "Your friend tried to intervene – did you know that? It backfired. We have Sebastian Prince."

What?

He smiles, and my vision blurs as darkness threatens to pull me under once more. I fight against it, but I'm too weak – I'm losing too much blood.

A medic shines a torch in my face and pulls back my eyelids, then gets to work on my side – which is still gushing blood. They place an oxygen mask over my face. I think they inject me with morphine, because the pain subsides ever so slightly.

"Clear up the wreckage," Bernie says to Archie, pointing to my mangled car. "And send the message to his parents. As far as anyone is concerned, Kade is doing work abroad. Do the same with Sebastian. They're both coming to Russia with us."

Panic seizes me – blood spurts from my mouth and into the oxygen mask as I try to speak and fail. I gasp in air as a wave of hot pain snaps through me.

Bernadette notices and leans down to me, a whisper against my ear that accompanies my vision blurring again.

Archie yells at someone to make sure the glass is cleaned up and any reports are deleted. All I can think about is Stacey, and how much I need to survive to get her out of this. Wherever she's gone, she needs to stay hidden.

And I need my dad.

Bernie strokes my cheek with the back of her fingers. "You'll beg for death, but you aren't allowed to die, my sweet boy. I'm not done with you yet."

29

KADE

THE FINAL FLASHBACK

Life kind of gave me a second chance.

Mum kept me close for days after finding me on the boat and forcing her fingers down my throat while she called for emergency help. In fact, she refused to let me leave the house.

My therapist visited me while I lay in bed on day one, staring at the wall in silence.

I wouldn't speak to anyone. Not even my dad.

My friends don't know what happened, but Dez knows I'm a mess.

He came over a few days ago and said I should get out of bed and at least wash, then forced me into a shower and refused to leave until I got ready and ate lunch with him. I told him Stacey fucked me over and I was done with her, but that's all.

Jason hasn't said a word, and Mum keeps begging me to speak to him, to see if there's been a misunderstanding. I refuse to even look at him. He was downstairs the other day, and all I wanted to do was fucking strangle him.

Ewan went ballistic at him. I overheard him asking what the fuck he was playing at and how long he'd been sleeping with a teenager.

Stacey has given up trying to call, so she's probably settled right in with him. Fucking bitch.

I'm just done.

"Hey, dickhead. Are you even paying attention?"

I look up at Base as we sit in the airport, waiting for one of his grandfather's men to escort us to our flight. "Sorry, I zoned out."

He tuts. "While you're visiting your dad, I'll go to this meeting with the old man. He wants me to take over one of his businesses, and I kind of want to decline."

"Then decline," I say, looking down at my phone, scrolling social media. She hasn't posted at all – hasn't been tagged in anything from her friends or the studio, and Giana has completely deleted all of her accounts.

My phone vibrates, and a message pops up.

Mum: Are you sure you want to go?

Me: I feel okay.

Mum: I want to give you your space, but I worry. All of your drawings are ripped up on your bed, and you left one of your letters on the kitchen counter too. When were you going to tell me you were moving away to study?

Me: I'll talk to you later about it.

Mum: Okay, sweetheart. Safe flight. I love you.

I close off the messages and click on Stacey's social-media account, hovering my thumb over the block button.

Then I turn my screen off.

By the time we get on the business-class flight and reach the States, Base is itching to get out for a night of clubbing. I don't want to go. I've barely spoken, and the last thing I want to do is pretend I'm enjoying myself. But since it's his birthday, I need to try.

He notices that I'm off and quiet, but instead of asking me what's wrong and forcing me to give him an answer, he tries to cheer me up with shots and banter.

I eventually tell him that I split with my girlfriend because she cheated with an older guy, dodging saying her name, and his response is that it sucks and I need to get laid.

I definitely don't.

My phone vibrates while we're in the hotel, getting ready to go out, and my heart stops when I see her name, even though I should be pissed off and should have blocked her by now. I can hear my blood rushing in my ears, and I hesitate before clicking on it.

Freckles: Luciella said you're moving out. Where are you going? Please talk to me. I love you.

After reading the last part, I take my first line of coke at a party Base drags me to, and the buzz knocks me on my ass, all thoughts of Stacey temporarily gone.

I take another. And another. Until the hours start blurring together.

Our bender lasts four days – four fucking days of going from party to party, club to club. I don't think I've slept a wink. My nose burns as I take another line a blonde neatly stacks, but I tell her to fuck off when she tries to put another line out, this time on her chest.

Luciella calls me on day four, and I struggle to listen to a word she says. I do lie in bed while Base gets a blowjob from two people, too exhausted and drained to move or even tell my sister to hang up when I drop the phone on my chest and fall asleep.

It's day five, and I nearly kiss a girl, but it feels wrong. She presses her petite body to mine, but I excuse myself and vomit my guts up in the alleyway of the club.

If I can't fucking kiss someone knowing how much she messed up, then how can she do that behind my back when we were good – when we promised ourselves to each other forever?

My friend claps my back, and we catch an Uber to the hotel to smoke a joint or two.

Base offers himself up on a plate – offers himself to me to keep my mind occupied while we lie on the bed, both stoned as fuck and trying to realign with reality. For a split second, I actually contemplate going for it.

I fall asleep somehow, with Base's head on my chest while he tells me that he thinks he's in love with my sister and only fucks around to keep her off his mind, so I should do the same.

I nearly text back so many times though – I only stop myself by thinking about what she's doing. Probably with Jason.

On the way to the institution, I eventually block her, and it makes me feel ill.

Dad is glaring at me during visitation, at my bloodshot eyes and messy hair – the number of times I sniff and drop my head in my hands.

I tell him everything about Stacey and Jason. He shakes his head and hugs me, but I don't feel anything. The numbness is returning, and the mental block falls fully into place.

I sent Stacey the clip of her fucking my brother in an anonymous email a few days ago. An immature move, but I needed her to see how much she fucked up.

When she responded by asking who I was, I blocked her.

Dad tries to calm me down by helping me set up five rules to keep me in check, all to do with Stacey. We write them down, and then he makes me repeat them out loud. Again and again and again. Until my eyes are watering with rage and the paper crumples in my fist.

Rule one: Stay away from your toxic ex-girlfriend.

Rule two: Don't unblock her number.

Rule three: If you're both in the same room, don't fucking look at her – it's a trap.

Rule four: Under no circumstances will you have any sexual interactions with her.

Rule five: Never forgive Stacey Rhodes.

In all fairness, he disagrees with most of them, but I'm holding to these rules – I'll never break them. I'll get them fucking tattooed into my skin if I have to.

"How do you feel now?"

I still love her, so all of this is fucking annoying. "I hate her," I tell my dad as I sit opposite him at the picnic table. "I honestly hate her."

"You don't hate her, son. You're just mad at her."

I snap my head up to glare at him. "Did you not fucking hear what I said? She fucked Jason. She's been fucking him for God knows how long."

"Language," he groans. "There must be a reason she's acting this way. No one changes overnight. What did she say about it?"

"I didn't want to hear whatever she had to say. She's nothing but a slut to me."

Dad slams his hand on the table between us, but I don't flinch – I think I still have drugs in my system. "Do not speak about any woman that way. Ever." When I stare at him in silence, he continues speaking. "You need to hear her out, Kade. If you love her, let her explain."

I lose my patience and flip the table before he can finish his last word.

"That's pretty fucking funny coming from you, don't you think? You have the cheek to sit there and tell me how I should deal with my fucked-up relationship when you did nothing but destroy my mother."

His eye twitches. "That's enough."

I shake my head, looking at him in disgust. "You're a fucking lunatic, a waste of goddamn oxygen, and you'd be better off dead after what you put Mum through."

I regret the words as soon as I say them, but my entire body is shaking, and I can't take them back. I want to apologise, to sit down and lower my head – the fucking dickhead of a son who treats everyone like shit.

Dad stands slowly, his eyes red – lined with silver as fury builds on his face. "You're right. Your mother deserves everything in life that doesn't involve me." A tear falls down his cheek. "I had no control of what I was—"

"That's no goddamn excuse for what you did!"

"Son, plea—"

I walk away from him before he can finish, storming through the artificial park and swiping my card. When I reach reception, the woman on the desk tells me that I'm banned from visitations for three months for vandalising property, and I tell her to go fuck herself.

Mum tries to call, but I ignore it. Four calls go unanswered, and I feel my chest tightening with each step. But I can't stop. I can't stop being mad.

My phone dings as I climb into Base's car, the one his grandfather gave him earlier for accepting the business deal – him being overruled by his family as usual. I slam the door and drop my face into my hands.

"Um, you good?"

Fuck off. Everyone needs to fuck off.

My head shakes, and I sit up, wiping my eyes with my sleeve. "Yeah. Just drive."

"Kade," Base says, nudging me. "What's wrong?"

I snap my head to him, eyes full of fury. "I said fucking drive!"

He blows out a breath and indicates out of the space. "Jesus, fine. Calm the fuck down, man."

He zooms into the busy road, and my back flattens against the chair as he accelerates. My chest heaves, and I breathe deeply through my nose as my eyes fill up again. I can't control it – the rage, the need to smash something.

I want to grab his steering wheel and make us crash. I want him to get faster so I can throw myself out of the car. I want to fucking scream.

But I don't want to die, so the thoughts need to go away.

My therapist said to talk – always talk. Staying silent and in your head just invites the bad thoughts inside, with no one to keep you on the right path.

Base is blasting "Pumped Up Kicks" by 3Teeth, singing along to the gravelly words as he lights a joint then pianos his fingers on the steering wheel. He glares at me when I turn it right down and clear my throat. "The fuck?" he says, inhaling a lungful of smoke.

"I tried to kill myself two weeks ago."

He frowns at me for a beat and pulls the car over, throwing the smoke out the window. "Say that again."

"Don't make this awkward."

He sucks in a breath and tilts his head at me. "Awkward? You just told me you tried to off yourself, mate. What did you do?"

I shrug as my chin shakes. "Swallowed a bunch of pills."

"Would it be acceptable for me to kick your ass right now?"

I manage a dry chuckle. "Probably not."

Base nods. "Do you know why you did it, or did you zone out like you used to?"

"Yeah," I reply, sighing. "I regretted it as soon as the pills started

fucking me up. I sent my location to my mum and woke up surrounded by a team of medics."

"That's where you've been? Why hasn't your sister mentioned this?"

I raise a brow at him. I knew he was close to her, but I had no idea they were on a level that she'd confide in him about something like that. My sister pretends he's a nuisance when she's around the rest of us. "She doesn't know."

I seem to be keeping everything from my sister nowadays.

"How do you feel now?"

I hum and pull a cigarette from the packet between us. "Shit happens. I kind of need to just move the fuck on, right?"

He grins. "Right. Well, you got me. The next time you even consider doing that shit, you fucking call me. And if you ever feel the need to tell me who your ex is, I'll happily send a few lovely words her way. She really fucked you up, didn't she?"

I lower my eyes. "You could say that. It was Jason."

"What was Jason?"

"The guy she fucked."

"What the fuck? What the fucking fuck? Jason? You want me to deal with him?"

I shake my head. "I don't want to talk about this anymore."

"Fuck them both. You're a handsome guy, rich and you have a big cock. You can get whoever you want." He swoops the cigarette from between my lips and tosses it out the window. "Spark that joint – I threw the other one away to be dramatic."

My friend is a dick, but he has his own way of being caring. Maybe, if Luciella ever gets her head out of her ass, he'd make a good, loyal replacement for the brother I thought I had.

Base starts the car, and it vibrates around me. We drive to his family's American estate and wait to be transferred to their private hangar. The entire flight home, Base drinks straight vodka and sleeps, and I scroll through pictures and videos, skimming social media.

My heart begins to race as I click on Tylar's account and find a sixteen-second clip of her recording Stacey while they're at a fairground with Tylar's niece and nephew. My ex is giggling as she chews on some candy floss, holding the little girl's hand. She presses her palm to the camera when her friend zooms in.

I watch it far too many times.

My eyes burn yet again, so I distract myself by staring out the window at the darkness and chewing a gash into my lip.

The need to talk to her is fucking pissing me off. I spoke to Stacey every single day for a year. I had her. I loved her and thought she loved me, but it was all a lie.

Our relationship was a fucking lie.

"Can you do me a favour?" Base asks as we descend the jet steps onto the tarmac. His family has a car waiting for us, and one of the drivers opens the door with a greeting to Sebastian.

"Sure," I say.

"Don't tell Luciella I took all those drugs. She keeps getting at me about doing coke, but she'd lose it if she knew I took ecstasy and acid."

"So you want me to lie to my sister?"

"Pretty much. In turn, I won't tell her you did them too."

Prick. "You do know that you two aren't together? You can do whatever the fuck you want."

"Would you want the girl you loved to know how much of a fuck-up you are?"

I stay silent.

He pinches the bridge of his nose. "Blin, izvini."

We get into the car and I arch a brow at his Russian.

He switches back to English. "Sorry. Forget I said anything. I'll have the driver swing by and drop you off at your place."

"Fine. I won't tell Luciella. Your dirty secrets are safe with me."

"Maybe don't mention all the sex either. I think my dick was sucked dry."

"Now you're pushing it."

He laughs deeply and smiles out the window. "Just living up to life's expectations for me. I am the family screw-up after all."

The car moves, and it takes an hour to reach our town. It's small, but all the houses are huge and spaced apart.

When we pass the studio, an idiotic, impulsive part of me speaks. "Let me off here. I can walk the rest."

Base looks confused. "You don't live near here?"

I raise a shoulder. "It's fine. I could use the breather."

Base instructs his driver, and they pull in a few streets from the studio.

I grab my suitcase and lean down to the window. "You're not the family screw-up," I say. "Don't talk down to yourself."

He nods – I can see how much he doesn't believe me. "Shoot me a text once you get in."

I tap the top of the car. "Right."

The studio is quiet as I walk by – my hood up, cigarette hanging between my fingers. The wheels of my small suitcase roll loudly along the road, and since there are no cars parked outside, no classes must be on.

It's ten at night on a Thursday. She always stays late. Maybe she's in there herself? Or maybe she's in there getting fucked by my brother?

I sigh and rub a hand down my face, going against the notion to walk in and confront her, demand fucking answers – or beg her to leave him, to take me back.

One foot goes forward, in the direction of the studio, but I stop.

No. She can't be trusted – neither of them can. They both cheated in relationships. Once a cheat, always a fucking cheat. They'll fuck each other up eventually.

I turn and walk in the opposite direction.

It starts to rain. Lightning flashes across the sky, and for a few minutes, I stop and stare up. Thunder growls around me, followed by another flash, and I hate myself for admitting this, but I miss her.

I miss Stacey so fucking much.

Almost to the point I'd consider forgiving her. If she promises to stay away from Jason, we could work things out. I don't feel like I can fucking survive without her.

I turn back towards the studio and take a few steps, but a car pulls up beside me, the window rolling down. "Kade Mitchell?"

Stopping, I frown at the older woman with wine-red hair and sunglasses. "Yeah?"

"My name is Bernadette Sawyer. I worked on your father's case many years ago. I believe you're trying to appeal so he'll be granted release for visitations, am I right?"

"Not interested." Fucking reporters and their constant need to post articles on me and my family. I turn and keep walking. "Fuck off."

The car crawls beside me as she pulls off her unnecessary sunglasses. "I'm not here for a story or to gather information from you. It's the total opposite. I have files upon files of evidence and witness statements that may grant your father's full release."

My feet halt, and I turn to her. "The last thing this world needs is Tobias Mitchell being fully released."

"We can both agree on that. But I can help with his other appeals. It would be nice for your parents to spend some time together outside the institution, wouldn't it?"

I stare at her. "What's the catch?"

"No catch. Just doing my old friend a favour. I have all the files at my home office, if you want to see them?"

"How do I know you aren't talking shit?"

She grins and pulls out her identification – Head of Police Scotland, Chief Constable Bernadette Sawyer. "I'm also an undercover detective for Scotland Yard. I have a lot of power to help your father, Kade."

I look around us, then at the white Porsche she's driving. My eyes lift to the middle-aged woman. "My dad is trying to get transferred to an institution here – could you arrange that?"

"I could certainly try. Come on – get in. I'll show you everything I have, and we can work together on a game plan."

I look around again, seeing the studio far in the distance. She could be there – an opportunity for me to demand to know what happened, to know if it's still happening. I want to fucking know why she felt the need to break my heart.

I gulp and keep my eyes on the studio doors. As if she's going to appear out of nowhere and cry for me to come to her. But then again, Jason might be with her.

Fuck it.

Bernadette opens the trunk for me to toss my suitcase in and smiles at me when I climb into the passenger seat of the car. She's wearing a tight black dress, driving in heels, and smells of over-the-top perfume. Her dress rides up her thighs while she drives, and she doesn't even attempt to pull it back down when her underwear is revealed.

I don't look – I keep my eyes forward, listening to her classical music.

When we pull up to her estate, I follow her through the manor. It's all white marble flooring and white walls. A man – tall and skinny – is watching us enter the main entrance. And when we reach the other end of the house, I notice he's trailing behind us with a dirty look.

She stops and places her hand on my chest. "This is Kade Mitchell,

Archie. The boy I told you about. I'm going to show him some of the files I have on Tobias."

His eyes spark, and he looks me up and down in a way that makes me want to ask him to look the fuck away. "You look like your father."

Everyone says that.

Bernadette's stilettos click across the floor, her hair swishing side to side. She glances over her shoulder at me as she unlocks her office and grins at me when I walk in. Her husband doesn't follow us.

Then she locks it.

She flirts with me while discussing the case. I'm certain she's flirting. Her tone and everything is seductive, and it does absolutely nothing for me. But she does have a lot of stuff on my dad, so I ignore her advances and sit down with each file.

The night after, she has me over again, this time introducing me to her eighteen-year-old daughter Cassie. She blushes when I nod at her, and Bernadette says we "look good together", but I shake off the comment and ask what the plan is.

For the next three weeks, I spend most of my nights in Bernadette's office, constructing a strong argument to have my dad transferred here. She has a list of top lawyers for us to use, and says she'll have a sit down with my mother when we have everything set. For now, it's to be between us, so I don't get her hopes up.

"He can't ever be released," I tell her. "He's not fit enough. He needs to be secured and controlled. He'll revert to his old ways, and I don't think anyone will be able to keep him from my mother."

"Agreed," she replies, sitting down at the table beside me. "I think we should celebrate how much we've managed to get through. Would you like a drink?"

Three hours later, I'm smashed, unable to read any of the documents properly. Bernadette is sitting on the table, leaning back on her hand as she drinks her whisky. "Do you have anyone special in your life?"

I look up from the papers. "What?"

"A girlfriend. Someone you turn to for... pleasure and fun?"

I shake my head. "No. I don't care for that stuff." And I mean it – I only ever wanted to have sex when I was with Stacey. The idea of fucking someone else makes me uncomfortable.

She smiles. "You really are like your father, aren't you?"

And then she leans down, her alcohol-ridden breath hitting my face as she tries to kiss me.

I pull back. "What are you doing?"

Sighing, she stands from the table and walks to her desk. "Forgive me. I... I must've read the signals wrong." She pours two more drinks then walks over and hands me one. "It won't happen again."

"Good," I reply, taking a gulp of the strong spirit. "Because I'm not interested. I'm only here for my dad."

"Oh, I know."

A few minutes go by, and sweat builds on my skin. I need to take my hoodie off. The place is like a fucking furnace. My vision blurs, and I can't stop closing my eyes. Then the glass slips from my hand, and my head hits a hard surface as I pass out.

My body jerks as I try to sit up in bed. Bernadette's beside me – naked – and I have a condom stuck to my dick, my hand chained to the bedframe. Archie, her husband, is sitting in the corner of the room, smiling at me as he sparks a lighter.

My head is fuzzy, and I want to stand up, to speak, to fucking yell at them, but I'm too weak, and I fall back into the bed.

They don't let me leave.

They touch me. He makes me touch her.

They inject me with drugs to keep me weak – they text my parents, pretending to be me, telling them that I'm fine and not to worry. I'm working on a project.

I have my first panic attack in ages, but she doesn't let me out of the house, even when I try to run. They catch me and beat me until I'm unconscious then drag me back into the building.

They won't stop touching me.

I'm sore. I'm confused. Why did I kill that guy?

My hands are fucking shaking. I can still see the blood.

I can finally go home, but now they hold a murder over my head, so they force me to do things. Nasty fucking things that make me thousands.

I try to escape them by moving away, but they find me.

My apartment in Stirling is far enough away that I'll never run into Stacey, but there's nowhere I can run to hide from them, no matter how much money I make from the evil pair.

Bernadette shows up and makes me fuck her. He sometimes watches.

They send me to other countries to work with highly skilled teams who train me in weapons and hand-to-hand combat. Months of training that nearly kills me.

My knuckles are permanently scarred.

Stacey doesn't reach out to me again. I blocked her, but I want to unblock her and beg her to run away with me – I'd run and never look back.

She broke my heart, but I want her back. I miss her. I love her.

I strangle someone until my hands cramp.

A Latvian man begs me to stop before I put a bullet between his eyes. I think I might be done – I might be free, but no matter how much havoc I cause, they always want more from me.

Another death. Another fuck. Another drug.

Another memory of Stacey holding me together.

When I screw up, Dad either gets the punishment – or I do.

Bernadette tells me to fuck her friends, and they pay me. I have to do it or they'll target my family, but each time I push into someone, I try to think of her.

I always think of her.

She's the only memory in my head that's holding me in place. My anchor.

My friends think I'm partying in Stirling and getting my head down with my studies – but instead, I'm slowly dying. I'm trapped in subspace, falling, falling, falling, and I can't find Stacey's hand to catch me.

For the next two years, I die a little more each day, until the version of Kade Mitchell I want to be turns into a ghost. My soul is shattered and broken, and I lose all the pieces, unable to glue it back together.

Look at me now, my little princess. Daddy's gone, and he's never coming back.

30

STACEY

TEN MONTHS LATER

"Wow! Look how pretty you are!" I clip a frilly pink bow into Eva's hair and straighten her bib, which says, *I'm Mommy's little princess.*

I fidget her baby shoes onto her feet and wipe her small hands, chuckling when she tries to take the cloth from me. Once I get my coat on and slip on Eva's, I check the nappy bag and make sure I have my purse and phone.

I walk over to the sitting room with Eva on my hip and grab my bank card – I left it there after making an online purchase last night while Lisa and Barry went out on a date.

Barry and Lisa own this place – it's on the outskirts of town so it's very private, and I live in the basement, which is probably bigger than the average UK house.

Although I'm his live-in babysitter while Lisa goes back to work as a teacher, Barry works for me now, but he's basically running everything. My bank account, thanks to Kade, gives me the heebie-jeebies whenever I check it.

The white SUV beeps as I unlock it, the lights of the garage flicking on. I fasten Eva into her seat then fold the pram and shove it in the back of the car. I got my full licence a few months ago, after failing the test three times. I'm still not sure how I passed, but here we are.

It took a huge debate and the threat of ending their marriage for Lisa to convince Barry to let me take their daughter in my car. The audacity of that man when it comes to safety baffles me, considering he drives like a lunatic. But when I said I was taking her to see Tobias? Barry nearly had a heart attack.

Lisa told him to shut up.

Smoothly, I pull out of the garage and set the satnav on instinct, even though I've done this journey twice a day for nearly a year. It says I'll arrive at my destination in twenty-seven minutes, so I play some Disney songs for Eva on the way.

She won't ever admit it, but she loves my singing voice.

Unlike some people.

Nope, I refuse to think about him. I've gone ten months without so much as a word from Kade. I wipe under my eyes and grip the steering wheel. I'm not going to cry; it seems to be all I've done since I got off that jet nearly a year ago.

I cried when I was handed a new passport. I cried when I saw all the money in my bank statement. And I bawled my eyes out when I chucked my old phone into a river.

Barry keeps me updated on the dogs. He hacks into the manor's cameras for me to see them with the staff, Aria cuddling Milo on the sofa while Ewan play-fights with Hopper. Getting their walks or splashing in the pool.

I've become a serial stalker though. I deleted all my social-media accounts as planned and made a fake account. But I only made it so I could watch what everyone was doing. The studio and all the girls are thriving and doing well. Kade's account is dead – Lu's is covered in stuff about deserving better and images of her schoolwork, and Tylar is always on holiday with Dez – travelling the world. They both took time away from life to live, and I'm jealous.

Base never posts anymore, which is strange. Any contact I've had with my friends, they've expressed their concerns, even though Base has said on multiple occasions he's with his family in Moscow. Not far from where Kade has been sighted, but from what I've found, there's no connection.

He used to message Lu every day, but he's only sent her two texts in the space of ten months, letting her know he's fine. As much as she claims she doesn't care that he's lost interest, I could hear the hurt in her voice when I called.

They assume Kade is still working, which in a way, he is.

A message pops up on the dashboard screen of my car.

> ***Barry****: For the last time, please inform me when you leave the house. Your stepbrother was last seen two towns over, or are you trying to put me in an early grave while you have my Eva in your possession?*

I'm not completely careless. I have two cars trailing me, and the car is tracked. The facility is secure – Chris isn't dumb enough to come for me when I'm protected this way.

Maybe it's that I'm used to his abuse, or the fact that I'm more protected than royalty, but I'm not scared. Chris has made my life a misery. He beat me until I lost my child, violently abused me and also allowed people to rape me. What worse can he do?

They say when you're faced with danger, your life flashes before your eyes. You see a glimpse of every happy moment, the parts of your existence that are the most important.

For me, that was watching the same movie or listening to the same song, over and over again. For me, that was experiencing all of my firsts with the boy I fell in love with; watching his face when I told him a song resonated with my feelings for him. For me, that was coming to terms with the fact we were going to be parents. Dancing. Laughing with friends. Spending time with the dogs. Making memories that will last a lifetime.

But in that haunting flash, it was all ripped away by Chris. Drugs and alcohol being forced into my body; being abused to such a degree I wished for death – I became a liar, secretive, a toxic person to be around.

I was terrified. I had been for a long, long time.

From the moment my stepbrother laid eyes on me, I knew life was going to be hard. But for that year, that wonderful, glorious year when I was in my late teens, I had something, *someone*, that made it worth sticking around, despite all those bad things.

I fell head over heels for Kade Mitchell. My best friend's brother. The guy who teased me whenever I was near him, who made my nerves shatter in both good and bad ways. He made me smile when I was sad, laugh when I felt like crying and warm when I felt so cold.

He reminded me of what it felt like to be alive.

The butterflies have never vanished. They've been there since he called me "Freckles" for the first time and stared into my soul like he wanted to fix me. Like he could see the fractures – the shards of glass that gradually fell from my heart with each deep breath. As if the danger I was in at home was written all over my face, and Kade wanted to keep me safe from it all.

And that's what I had for a year. When I wasn't in that hellhole of a house, I was wrapped in his arms. I was safe.

Until I wasn't.

He was everything I needed and more, but it's done. It's over. I've had time to come to terms with everything that's happened to me, and I honestly don't think I can ever forgive myself for never speaking out – Kade should've been told the real reason for our daughter's death – I should have forced the information on him.

Selfish – that's what I was.

I was grieving for the baby girl I'd lost, the life I had and the boy that was everything to me. My father died two months later, and Kade was gone.

As hard as it's been being away from everyone, I've been able to breathe. Lisa cooks with me. We shop. We watch movies while Barry plays with his daughter. I like to try living a little. There's a studio nearby that I teach at once a week, but it's nothing like the one back home. I go to the gym when I can, work out at home and try to eat healthily.

Sometimes, I get lazy and rewatch *The Greatest Showman* an unhealthy number of times with a tub of ice cream and a plate of sandwiches and a tissue of captured tears. Or I'll go out for a drive, walk around the park with bodyguards dotted around the place, and then order takeout food while Barry repeatedly tells me that I'm out of range.

He's always losing his mind with me, and sometimes, it's funny. Like how anxious he gets when I spend an hour with Tobias Mitchell, which I do twice a day. Much to Barry's dismay, I never miss a visitation with the father of the boy who broke my heart.

He hates Barry – like they're in competition for who can keep me the safest, but then again, I guess he hates everybody. I have no clue how he warmed up to me, even if there is the random day he doesn't speak, and we just sit in comfortable silence until visitation ends. I always notice a change in him when Aria's due to visit, though when she does, I usually stay at home to give them peace.

I've seen her four times, and each time, she hugs me until I break down. Then she kisses my head and tells me to keep my chin up. But also that she's happy Tobias has someone with him when she can't be by his side twenty-four-seven.

Don't get me wrong, he's a moody guy, but I've got used to him over the months of being here nearly every single goddamn day. He eats the lunch I bring along for myself, mocks my accent and tattoos – but he still thinks I want to sit in his presence.

I mean, I do, but that's beside the point.

31

STACEY

Once I arrive at the institution, I pop up the pram and place a sleeping Eva into it. I show my badge and tell the receptionist I'm here to see Tobias Mitchell.

She beams down at the little girl with Barry's eyes and Lisa's blonde hair then tells me she'll call my name once Tobias is set up in the room – the special room we always meet in, the one I went to the very first time I visited him, to ask for help with Kade. He managed to pull some strings a few months back because we felt like we needed more privacy for the subjects of our conversations, and it seems he's persuasive.

Or maybe he's a violent bastard who threatened the workers here? Who knows?

Once she calls my fake name, I head down the corridor, push the pram off the elevator and a guard opens the door to the room.

Tobias is sitting silently, arms crossed, glaring at the table, legs parted like he's thirty years younger.

His voice is deep as he huffs and says, "I've been waiting here for five minutes."

I sigh and pull off my scarf and jacket. "You say this every day."

"Because it's true and keeps happening." He turns, his face lighting up when he sees the pram. He gets to his feet and smiles down at Eva. "Hello, little princess."

I'll never tell anyone, but Tobias has the most beautiful eyes, especially when he smiles. They're blue, almost silver, and when the light shines on them, they glint. Despite being in his late forties, he's fit and has kept his chiselled features, the dimples and the straight white smile.

I get why Aria still isn't over him, even twenty plus years later.

Eva grins and kicks her legs as Tobias lifts her from the pram, sitting at the table and ignoring me while I set up the chessboard between us.

Ten minutes pass of him and Eva ignoring my presence, and I watch as he walks her around the room, telling her pointless facts about the books he's read from the bookcase.

He does this whenever I bring her, and we never get any work done. The man dotes on Eva.

Luciella always said that despite her father's illness and struggles, he was always so loving and caring when it came to her and Kade. I can see it, the side of him they got to see growing up. It makes me envious of my best friend, because although my dad died when I was nineteen, we were never as close as those two.

I smile as Tobias tries to read a passage from some ancient book to her, in the most babyish voice ever. She grabs the book and throws it, then breaks out in a giggle as he tickles her.

A few minutes later, she's cuddling into his shoulder as Tobias hums a tune to her, and he sways until she falls asleep then carefully places her back in the pram. Rolling it to the side, he pulls up the hood to shade her from the lamp light and gives me his full attention.

"I think I like her company more than yours," he says, stretching his arms above his head, his white top riding up ever so slightly to show that, even at his age, he has abs for days. "But that isn't much of a competition, since you're a pain in my ass."

"Shut up. It's because she has no choice but to tolerate you."

Telling Tobias to shut up is risky, but not for me. I've thrown every insult under the sun at him and he doesn't flinch – he just insults me right back.

He snorts and drops onto the single bed in the corner of the room – the room he has set up for visitations with Aria – the fact there is a bed here makes me question a lot, but I keep my mouth shut. He's lifting a book and pretending to read it. I cross my arms, lean back on my chair and glare at the older version of Kade. "Are you going to take your turn?"

He glances at the chessboard then back to the book. "No. I'm not in the mood."

I roll my eyes, making sure he can't see. He says it's rude when I roll my eyes, which I do a lot. "Remind me why I'm here? You're pissing me off."

Kade's father hums, flipping the page of his book and folding his arm behind his head. "I ask myself that same question every day." Then his narrowing eyes lift to me. "And watch your fucking language."

I toss a chess piece at his head, and even though it makes contact, he doesn't flinch. "Imagine I stopped visiting? You'd only have Aria and Luciella coming to see you once a month. And you get sad when I'm too busy to come."

He doesn't look away as he speaks with a smirk. "You always come, little one."

I groan and turn back to the chessboard. He taught me how to play, along with every other board game he could get his hands on. "I don't know how Aria has been able to deal with you for over twenty years. I can barely last one without wanting to strangle you."

"You could try. But that kink is specifically for one woman and one woman only."

I snap my head at him. "You said you stopped sleeping with her. Did you lie?"

"I don't lie. When my son told me to back off, I did. Maybe you should do the same. I'm starting to think you want a piece of me too."

I give him the finger without sparing him a glance.

He chuckles. "Very mature of you. Are you going to eat those chips, or do you plan on staring at them like they've offended you?"

I had no idea I was, but I grab the packet of Lays and toss it at him. "You owe me my entire lunch by the way."

"You'll live. Have you spent any of that money yet?"

Chewing my lip, I shake my head, but then I stop. "I bought a coffee from Starbucks the other day. I felt bad though."

"You have eight-six million in your bank and you felt *bad* for buying a coffee?"

"Hey, I said from the start I wasn't going to spend a penny!"

"Was it at least a large coffee?"

"No, the large wasn't worth the money."

"You are the worst visitor I've ever had in my life."

"Yet I'm still your favourite."

All he does is grunt like a damn dog while eating the crisps – or what he calls chips.

If I'm not here, he calls me on his secret phone. Sometimes I'm not able to answer, but his obsessive side makes him continuously call until I pick up. I know he doesn't mean to be overbearing, so I try to be as patient as possible with him.

"I'll be back later tonight, but I have a hair appointment tomorrow, so I can't come," I say, leaning my cheek on my palm, elbow on the table as I swing my legs. "Think you can handle a day without me?"

"Could you handle a day without me?"

"Stop answering my questions with a question! God, you're more like Kade than you think. Both idiots."

All Tobias does is chuckle and continue to read.

Once I knock all the chess pieces into the box and fold the board away, I grab my satchel and pull out two notebooks, an iPad and two pens.

I zoom in on the map I bring up and circle an area. "Okay, so based on our latest findings, Kade is in this small town in the west of Russia called Uglich. Barry thinks he's doing work there until next month."

That gets Tobias's attention. He tosses aside the book and joins me at the table. He stands behind my chair and leans over my shoulder. "Did he mention how he is?"

"No, just that he was with..." I gulp down a lump. "Bernadette has a daughter, and he's with her a lot. Plus, there was a transaction of two million between him and an unknown source two days ago, and the guy Barry has on the inside thinks it's Kade's way of trying to do undercover work without his boss knowing."

"I still don't understand why I've to stay here," he says, frowning and walking to his side of the table. "My son needs my help."

"What exactly are you going to do? She has an entire country, and you don't even have a passport."

"Do you think I've spent the last twenty-two years doing nothing? If I wanted to leave, I could be out of here within the hour."

I tut. "No, you couldn't. How would you escape, let alone get to Russia?"

He shrugs, and I have my answer.

"Barry is working on it. We'll keep tracking him."

Tobias chews his lip, sadness taking over his expression. "How many people has my son killed?"

"This month? Only five."

"*Only.*" He shakes his head and gets to his feet. "It's the fifteenth. Aria would be horrified if she knew any of this. I should be telling her. She could help him."

"You'd be putting her in danger."

"I know." He looks over at Eva then back to me. "And you still have all of your protection? Christopher can't get to you?"

I nod – he asks me this every day. "He'd need to survive multiple gunshots to get near me."

Tobias slouches in the seat in front of me, thinking to himself. "I feel useless. More useless than usual."

"You sent one hundred guards to Russia to watch Kade – I don't think that's useless." I had no idea he was as resourceful, considering he's locked up. But apparently, Tobias has a lot of connections.

"They all died within a day," he replies bluntly.

"And you paid someone to keep an eye on Luciella while she's at university."

"But I'm not there. I'm here, in this fucking..." He lowers his voice and glances at Eva. "I need to get out of here."

"Aria would never forgive you."

"My son is more important," he counters. "My kids are more important. Aria can just deal with it."

I stay silent, because I get it. It must be horrible to know your child is in the situation Kade is in and not be able to do anything about it.

"I need to leave now; I have two minutes left. Eva won't be with me tomorrow morning, so you might want to get some goodbye cuddles."

He cheers up instantly when Eva wakes and grabs his face. He tells her he'll see her soon, then pulls me in for a warm, caring hug. I love getting hugs from him. He doesn't always give them out, so when he does, I wrap my arms around him tightly and stay until he kisses my temple or the top of my head and tells me to fuck off.

"I'll bring you chocolates and popcorn for our movie tonight," I say. "Remember to keep me a seat!"

While I lie in bed, scrolling on my phone, I try to call Kyle, but he messages that he's at work and will ring me back once he's finished.

Barry and Lisa are out for dinner with Eva – I said I wouldn't be joining since I'm going back to the facility soon for movie night.

I click my screen off and toss my phone on the bed, heading up from the basement to grab a drink and fold laundry. I always help around the house. I think they've got used to me being in their space to the point that Lisa sometimes prefers me over her husband.

I turn on the speakers around the house. "Porcelain" by Moby plays as I pull my hair into a ponytail and tidy up. I fold a blanket, some dresses and Finding Nemo PJs and take them upstairs to Eva's room. It resembles a Disney princess room – her name is printed on the wall, her toys stacked up on the chest, her teddy bears all on her little sleigh cot.

Once her room is done, I grab a duster and get to work around the house. The living room is probably the messiest room, since we're always in it.

I freeze when I walk in and see someone standing there.

The duster drops to the floor.

I gasp out a *no* and back away until I knock over a lamp, just as he rushes to me and covers my mouth. "Shhh, baby. You need to stay quiet and come with me."

I'm frozen in place, my heart rate accelerating, waiting, needing Barry's men to barge through the door and save me. My lungs stop working, terror coursing through me as Chris snakes his arm around my waist and walks me out of the living room.

He drags along the hall to one of the spare bedrooms, and as much as I fight against him, kicking my legs and elbowing him, he doesn't let me go as he pulls me into a room.

"They're coming for you, you stupid bitch," he says, throwing open several wardrobes and swearing to himself. "If I let go, will you scream?"

"Screw you," I mumble against his palm, sinking my teeth into his hand and drawing blood.

He hisses and throws me to the ground. "Did you not fucking hear me?" He assesses the bite mark on his hand and shakes his head. "They found you. You need to hide."

My eyes water, my jaw rattling. "How did you get in here?"

Barry has this place heavily protected. Alarm system. Cameras. Security parked outside. Everything.

"Bernadette Sawyer found you," he says, and my heart sinks. "Her men are coming for you right now. There are two cars outside. We need to hide."

A tear falls down my cheek as I remember everything he did to me. I was free from him, and now that freedom is gone. "You ruined my life – what makes you think I'm going to listen to anything you say?"

"Because if they find you, she will torture you. Despite what you think of me, I'm all you've got."

"The house is protected. There are guards everywhere."

"You mean all the guys with slit throats and broken necks? They were already dead when I got here."

We both jump in fright as the front door crashes open and we hear what sounds like a group of men storming in.

Chris doesn't let me argue with him as he starts pulling up floorboards. He hauls me down with him, settling them on top of us. I want to scream, but he covers my mouth with force and warns me not to say a word – that he's protecting me.

The heavy footsteps come closer as they swarm through the hallway. I can see through the thin gaps that they're all dressed in black with helmets on, faces hidden beneath balaclavas. My body tenses as one of them fires a spray of shots all over the room, the window smashing, mirror shattered, bullet shells dropping above us.

I shake beneath the floorboards, unsure who's more of a danger to me – Chris or these armed intruders.

More tears fall as Chris keeps a firm grip on my mouth. One of them speaks in a different language, and then I hear a set of heels in the hallway.

"She must have run off. Search the woodlands and replace the tracker on her car," a woman says, and my nerves shatter when I realise I've heard that singsong voice before. "Try not to kill her, but you can mess around with her. I expect Stacey Rhodes to be in my facility by the end of the week. Preferably alive."

"Yes, ma'am."

Her wine-red hair curls down the front of her tight black suit, breasts spilling out where she keeps her shirt unbuttoned at the cleavage.

I hate her – despise this horror of a woman. I grit my teeth, digging my nails into my palms. I want to yell, to call her a filthy bitch and rip her hair out. If she's here with her team, and they're firing openly in my house, not knowing if they'll sink a bullet into my gut, where is Kade?

Is he here?

My inner questions are answered as she speaks again.

"Don't let him know why we're here. He thinks it's a regular contract. If you see Christopher Fields, shoot on sight. I'm not going to let him get away with stealing our data files." She's silent for a moment, then she adds, "Barry Lennox. The owner of this house. Did you find him? His wife and daughter?"

My eyes widen, but my shoulders unstiffen as he replies, "No. Do you want to give orders to look for them?"

"No need. Just kill the brother and bring me Stacey Rhodes."

"Yes, ma'am," the guy says again, and she orders everyone to leave – they've obviously assumed the place is empty.

I hear a few things smashing, and when we're sure the coast is clear, I elbow Chris in the ribs and push against the wooden slats. They lift, and when I get up, I turn around and punch him right in the nose as hard as I can, knocking him back into the hole he made in the floor.

"I fucking hate you!"

"Fuck, Stacey, stop!"

I'm impressed he bleeds so quickly, and when he doesn't try to hit me back like I expect, I punch him again, slapping his face and sinking my nails into his cheek.

I tumble back as he shoves me.

He wipes blood from his lip, giving me a deathly stare. "What the fuck was that for?"

When I turn and attempt to land another punch, he grabs me by the throat and shoves me against the wall, hard enough to hit the back of my head. My vision fogs, and painful pressure makes me groan as dizziness settles in.

"I'm sorry I left you," he says. "I was going to stop them, but I couldn't. Do you understand? I gave you the blade. Did you use it? I haven't heard from any of them since that night."

I spit in his face. "You made my life hell," I say breathlessly, my eyes stinging with tears and pain and exhaustion. "Why won't you just leave me alone?"

"Because I love you." Chris grabs my jaw in a tight grip. "Believe it or not, I'm trying to save your life. I'm trying to make it right, okay? Let me protect you. Pack your fucking bags and let me protect you. We need to run, Stacey. If not, they'll kill you."

32

KADE

Each day has been like an episode of a horror movie, and I'm the main character.

Unnecessary deaths. Receiving and giving excruciating pain. Unwanted and forced sex. Drugs that could kill injected into my veins. Being in a damn coma for two weeks after they found me near dead next to my mangled car.

I have scars on my ribs, the back of my head, a permanent dent on my forearm, and just to add to the mix of bullshit, no one knows where I am. My family thinks I'm working on a project for my studies – a message Bernadette sent to my mother before she had my phone destroyed.

Nearly a year – but it feels like a fucking lifetime of having my freedom stripped from me. I've been tethered to Bernadette since I was nineteen, but at least then I was given days, sometimes weeks of a break – now that's gone.

Staring into the mirror of the hotel bathroom, I fist my hands, wanting nothing more than to smash the glass and slice into an artery or toss myself off the top of a building. I'm exhausted, both mentally and physically.

I wet my lips, eyes dropping to the brand I wear – a deep scar from the corner of my mouth, down my chin and throat, stopping right where my heart is. It's becoming less purple every day, though it's still a bit itchy. I can still feel the sharp knife cutting my skin, the scream trapped in my lungs that I couldn't let out.

Another one of Bernadette's stupid games. I had to choose between hurting Base or doing that to myself, so obviously I chose the latter. It's ugly – annoyingly noticeable. I keep my hood up and my eyes down so people don't stare at me when I walk past them. I started doing that after a Russian lady asked me to cover up so I'd stop scaring her child.

She's dead now.

My rage got the better of me and I snuck out of my hotel, hunted her down, slit her throat and tossed her in a river. Her remains were found, and it hit the news before Bernadette could fix it. I found out she was abusive to her five-year-old son, so I guess I did him a favour.

To try to stay in the real world, I've snuck a few clients' phones while they slept. Checked social media – mainly. Luciella is back home and waiting for her final semester to begin. Safe. Constantly posting quotes – now and again trying to reach out to Base by posting stuff about him.

I have no idea what Stacey is doing, since she deleted all of her accounts and disappeared. She's probably, hopefully, partying and living her life as she should have been before meeting me. I hope she's happy, dancing, full of life and love and music.

Fuck, I miss her.

Bernadette kept me to herself for a month, but when people started offering her more money, she gave in and sold me to her clients again. The delusional cunt stopped me from offing myself a few months ago, saying with me gone, there would be nothing standing between her and my family. So, yeah. I'm still here.

Breathing. But not fucking willingly.

A knock on the door has my shoulders tensing. "You fly out in an hour," the high-pitched voice says. "Come back to bed for a bit."

I close my eyes.

A contract came in earlier for us to take out a family – husband, wife, little ten-month-old girl and their live-in babysitter, and I've been trying everything to avoid it. I even manipulated and seduced Bernie this morning to try to get her to drop the mission, but she caught on and sent me to her daughter's room instead.

The daughter I'm being forced to marry.

If I could cut my dick off, I would. But Bernadette would still find a way to fuck with me.

I hunt for my shorts in the dark, sneaking around as quietly as possible when I see Cassie's fallen back to sleep. If I wake her, I might strangle her to death.

So. Fucking. Tempting.

After I get dressed and make my way to the door, she sits up and holds the blanket to her chest. "When will you be back?"

"I don't know," I reply, almost robotically.

"I'm going to get them to stop using you for work. If we're going to get married, then I don't want you in other people's beds." She's said this before, but so far Bernadette refuses to agree. Not that it matters.

"I'm not fucking marrying you."

"You are. Mother will see to it that you do." She juts out her bottom lip, letting the duvet slide down over her tits. "Don't miss me too much."

Images of me slitting her throat infiltrate my mind. The sounds of her choking on her own blood would be so sweet. Before I can make it happen, I grab my bag and slam the door behind me on the way out.

On the plane, Base sits beside me, his pupils fully blown as his leg bounces beside me. "You good?" I ask, my voice quiet enough that only he can hear me.

"Great," he replies, closing his eyes and letting his head drop back. "Just fucking great."

I trace my finger up and down the scar on my throat, zoning

out. My fingers tremble. The shakes have been getting worse, and my mind goes fuzzy a lot. Sometimes, I black out.

That void swirls in and swallows me fucking whole, and I have no idea what happens when it does. It's kind of my escape. What better place could it be than nowhere?

By the time we reach the property, we're the second wave. I step over a body on the lawn, blood puddling from the head, and another to my left as I make my way up the footpath with my gun focused on the front door.

I take a deep inhale, closing my eyes. Hold it. Hold it some more, then let it out slowly. "Entering the building now."

Everyone gets into position. No one wants to be here, but they're all willing to kill men, women and children to protect their families. No matter how much they vomit afterward, hate themselves, beg for forgiveness from their God and even self-harm, they always pull through with the contracts.

Lights flicker as I push open the door, which is hanging off its hinges. It drops to the ground with a loud *bang*.

I wait for a second, listening for a cry or the soft whimper of a little girl, and silently beg that no one is here. I won't kill them. I refuse to. I'll try to help them escape before the rest can complete the contract.

But going by the mess of the place, the chance of them having survived is low. There are bullet casings everywhere. Why did they send us if the job was already done?

Before I can figure it out, one of the guys behind me radios in asking if the targets have been eliminated. A second later, a voice tells us that the babysitter is still alive. We've to keep an eye out for a short woman with dark hair.

They'll be hiding – hopefully somewhere hard to find.

I hope not to see blood as I gesture to the other men with me to continue, hearing the crunch of glass beneath heavy boots, the inhale and exhale of breaths through the earpiece, the ruffle of uniforms as we turn left and make our way down the narrow corridor to the garage.

I inch to the left and glance into the washroom. A pink blanket sits unwashed along with clothes, and a line of bibs and frilly white coat are drying on a rack.

I swallow a lump. "Clear."

Using the muzzle of the gun, I push open the main doorway to the garage, searching my surroundings, twisting left and right and leading the group behind me. An SUV is parked, the tyres all slashed, windows smashed, and the baby-on-board sticker lies on the ground.

"Clear," I say again, shifting past the guys as I take point position again.

Glass crunches under my boots as I take careful steps into the apartment. The torch from my gun shines around the floor and walls, as I inspect shattered furniture and torn sofas. I listen, trying to hear any voices or other signs of life. But the place is silent. I gesture for the guards to keep following me.

There are bullet holes all over the place – TV screens smashed, the coffee table and ornaments obliterated.

I step into the kitchen, keeping my aim raised. "Clear."

I make my way to a narrow hall, gesturing for Base to follow me while the rest of the men continue searching the ground floor. We open the door to the basement, and he shines his torch. "There's a bedroom down there."

I take two steps at a time until I reach the bottom, lowering my gun and turning on the light. "Are you hiding in here? I'm not going to hurt you."

Silence.

I examine the shelves, my eyes scanning the piles upon piles of books, then pull out all the drawers I can see. Some are empty.

Our radios buzz. "We have floorboards pulled up in one of the bedrooms on the ground floor. Some blood too. Bullet shells everywhere."

Base being Base, he tosses down his gun and sits on the bed, lying back and closing his eyes. "I have a headache."

I roll my eyes and head over to the walk-in closet, which has been ransacked. I duck under the bed, look into the bathroom and pull aside the shower curtain, chewing my lip as I stand in the middle of the room again.

A shift beside me as Base jumps off the king-sized bed and grabs a picture frame from the cabinet next to it. He whips off his helmet and pulls away his earpiece before shoving the image in front of my face.

It takes a second to process what I'm looking at, and I lift a shaking hand to take it from him. I don't blink as I stare at a picture of me and Stacey in bed. The first ever photo she took of us, when she accidentally fell asleep in my arms. I rub my thumb over her face, a smile tugging at the corner of my mouth.

Base snaps at me with his fingers. "Why is there a picture of you and Stacey in this house?" Then he frowns. "Wait, were we to kill Stacey? Who's the family? The kid?"

My wide eyes lift to my friend as the realisation sinks in, and I stop breathing.

The photo frame slips from my grip as I run, feeling like I'm going to pass out as I sprint up the stairs, stopping when I see a busted-up family photo canvas in the living room.

Barry, Lisa and their baby. Stacey was the live-in babysitter.

Barry got her out of the UK.

"Do we have any information on the family?"

One of the guys shrugs. "I think they were eliminated."

My blood runs cold. "No."

Base appears, grabbing my helmet to make me look at him. "Keep it together," he grits. "We have a target to hunt."

"There's a lot of blood in the baby room," someone says to my left. "Looks like there was a fucking massacre in there."

I shove one of the guards aside as I make my way up to the first floor, stopping when I reach the last bedroom. *Eva* is written on the door, and there are Disney characters painted everywhere.

As soon as I push the door open, my burning gaze lands on the pictures on the dresser, all decorated with blood. Barry, Lisa and Eva. And another one is Stacey with Eva on her shoulder, both grinning for the camera.

"Fuck, man. There's so much blood," Base says, his helmet dropping on the ground beside me.

I'm already on my fucking knees. They killed Barry? Fucking Barry? His wife and daughter?

Where the fuck is Stacey?

I lean forward on my hands, lowering my head, attempting to count to three. To figure out how to fill my lungs, to stop the pressure on my head and behind my eyes.

Base rests a hand on my shoulder, making me flinch as my eyes burn. "Breathe, man. We'll find her. Did you know the people she was living here with?"

"Yeah. Barry. He was my… friend. They can't be dead." I press a button on my radio, pushing my voice out as I try to focus. "Do we have confirmation if the other three targets were eliminated?"

"The only information we have is that the babysitter is still alive."

Base squeezes my shoulder. "I'm sorry, man. We… we can still find Stacey."

I'm shaking by the time Base helps me to my feet. He doesn't speak as I pull the picture of Stacey and Eva from the frame and fold it into my pocket, checking that the pistol in my leg harness is loaded.

I feel every fibre within me darken, my emotions void except pure rage as I walk past Base, shouldering into some of the men as I exit the building with nothing but murder on my mind. Base chases after me, and I get into the car and start the engine.

The passenger door opens and closes. "Where are we going? The mission isn't done yet. She'll punish us if we leave."

My eye twitches as I speed through the streets, nearly crashing numerous times but not giving a fuck. "Fuck the mission."

33

KADE

As soon as I reach our destination – the hotel Bernie is staying at – I slam my brakes on and pull off my seat belt.

"Fucking think about this for a second, Kade." Base swears under his breath as I throw open the door. I shake my head, making my way across the street towards the hotel entrance. "Kade!"

"I have no reason to think about it. She has a goddamn hit out on Stacey, and I need to know where Barry and his family are." I gesture to the car. "Go to the facility. I don't want you getting involved in this."

"You think I'm going to fucking leave you?"

I push into the reception, and the lady behind the desk takes in my all-black uniform, combats, bulletproof vest, the riot helmet hanging from my hand – then her eyes land on the pistol in the other.

Base rushes into the elevator just as the door closes, joining me inside. It'll take us all the way up to the penthouse. I stare forward while he bounces on his toes – nerves. He's a ruthless bastard, but he still gets nervous when it comes to confrontation. It's why he could never handle arguing with my sister, and whenever he did something wrong, he ghosted.

"You think they're dead?"

I close my eyes and count to three. Maybe ten. I want to smash him. "Stop talking."

He huffs. "You're a cheeky bastard when you're in a mood." Then, to be even more of an annoying asshole, he asks, "Where do you think Stacey is?"

My shoulder rises in a shrug, but deep down I'm in pieces. Whenever I've got someone out of a situation where they had a target on their back, it usually meant faking their death. And they'd need to stay invisible for the rest of their lives. Barry got lucky having a family and some normality outside of working for me – he was a low-paid contract I got on the side from Bernadette's client.

All I keep seeing is her name printed on a folder – Stacey Rhodes.

Stacey Rhodes. Stacey Rhodes. Stacey Rhodes.

I've kept her safe for the last ten months. I did everything Bernadette wanted. Everything. When a group of one hundred soldiers infiltrated her base in Moscow, me and Base had to kill them with a team, and then she blamed me for it. I spent weeks in a cell with stale food and warm water.

That had nothing to do with me, and nothing to do with Base. We've done everything we've been told. Our pain and suffering meant our families would remain untouched.

As we near the top, I check my magazine again – full. And then I crack my neck from side to side and straighten my spine while Base turns pale with anxiety. I sniff, roll my shoulder, twist on the silencer and wait.

The door slides open, and I put a bullet in the guard's head before he can raise his gun, his body dropping. The second guard follows when Base does the same.

I step over them with a deadly rush through my veins, adrenaline kicking in as I pull my blade from my thigh strap and shove it in the last guard's throat. A fountain of blood sprays over my face, but I don't flinch.

He falls and chokes like an animal just as Bernadette walks out with a glass of wine in hand. She looks at the bodies and the gun pointing at her. "Is there a problem?" she asks with an arched brow. Her eyes flicker to Base, who stays behind me, his weapon still drawn.

"Where are they?"

She gives me a fake smile, trying to warm her eyes as she tilts her head. "Who?"

"Don't fucking bullshit me," I snap with fury in my eyes, my pulse racing, blood roaring in my ears. "Where the fuck are they?"

"Oh, you mean the Lennox family. I have no idea—" Bernadette jumps with a squeak as I shoot the ground next to her feet. "Kade! Drop your weapon now."

"Fuck off," I counter. "I'm asking you one more time. They had a daughter – is she dead? Are they dead?"

"No," she says. "The contract was renewed and only Stacey Rhodes was to be eliminated. Mr Lennox and his family are unharmed and" – she glances at the clock on the wall – "most likely on their way home from their family dinner date."

I keep my aim on her, gritting my teeth. "Don't lie to me. What about all the blood?"

"I have no idea what you're talking about." She rolls her eyes and walks to a table full of papers. "You're being dramatic."

"Where is Stacey?" I don't remove my aim as she sits down on the sofa and crosses her legs. I try not to let my words break as I keep going. "Did... did you... did you kill her? Did you kill Stacey?"

"Would you like a drink, Sebastian?"

"No," he grits. "Answer the fucking question."

I cock the gun. "I'm seconds from blowing your fucking head off, Bernadette. Don't fucking test me."

She shakes her head and stands. "Drop your aim, Kade. You're not going to shoot me."

"If you've so much as harmed a hair on her head..."

Bernadette smirks and tips her chin. "Shame you didn't care this much for Stacey when she was drugged and gang-raped. Only weeks after losing your baby girl. And what did you do? You walked away from her thinking she cheated on you and never listened to her side of the story – the truth. You beat up your own brother and disowned him and your father. You came to me. I gave you a new lease of life. I gave you what you needed, and now you're going to do the same for me. Forget about Stacey – she's with her wonderful brother Christopher. Most likely spreading her legs for—"

I punch her into silence. I don't think – my mind isn't working or thinking about the repercussions as I drop the gun and smash a tight fist across her face, knocking her to the ground. Wine splashes everywhere, the glass cracking, and she's barely able to gasp before I'm over her – hammering my fucking fist into her face some more.

The elevator dings, and I hear Base in a scuffle – a gunshot, but the gurgling sound isn't coming from him.

Someone tackles me – then a taser to my side freezes me, sending jolts of pain through my body until I drop to the ground and stop fighting back.

I try to sit up and see Base is being held by two guards, one arm stretched behind his back.

"Bring Sebastian here," she orders her men as she wipes blood from the split skin on her cheek. "On your knees."

She gestures to the ground at her feet, pointing the gun at his head as he's forced down.

"Let me make this abundantly clear," she seethes at me, cocking the gun and digging it into his forehead. "I own you. I own you both. If you ever raise your fist to me again, I will make you eat his fucking brains after I blow them out of his skull. Do you understand?"

I glare at her, the after-effects of the taser still rolling through my body. I want to tell her to go fuck herself, that I'll fucking kill her, but I can see the panic in Base's eyes.

I might not give a fuck whether I live or die, but he's determined to stick around, hoping he'll eventually get a chance with my sister.

So instead of unleashing hell on her, I force out, "I understand."

"As I said, she's with Christopher Fields. And if we don't hurry, my plan will screw up, and I'll take it out on your friend here."

"What plan?"

She smirks. "You'll see." Then she steps back from Base. "You'll both see."

Archie barges into the room – not paying us any attention as he erratically pulls at his hair. "Fuck! Bernadette, fuck! We're so fucked!"

I'm yanked to my feet, and so is Base. We watch Archie hurry around the room – he finds the TV remote as his wife crosses her arms, bruises already blooming on her face.

"This better be important. We were about to have a little fun. Weren't we, boys?"

I grimace – her version of fun usually means she forces me and Base on each other. We'll be fine – we know what it is and what it means each time it happens. It's either that or he needs to get on his knees for someone else.

Will Stacey look at me differently if she knows that?

I want to take advantage of their panic – to slice their throats and run. I'll find her. I'll get her away from that prick and torture him till he forgets her name.

Archie turns on the news channel, and Bernie snatches the remote from his hand, turning the volume up while I help Base to his feet, scowling at the other guards as they step back away from us.

He mutters, "Sorry, man," and keeps his head down. "You should've just beat her to death. I'm sure my own demise would've been worth it."

"Shut up."

The remote drops to the ground when the young news anchor starts speaking.

"We have an emergency announcement. Reports say that Tobias Mitchell has escaped his institution this afternoon and is currently at large. The murderer and psychopath was given a life sentence over twenty years ago."

A picture of my father appears on the screen, and my lips part. They picked one that makes him look terrifying – his eyes burn through the screen.

"I would like to stress to everyone that this individual is *extremely* dangerous and may not be in touch with reality. Do not approach him. If you have any information on his whereabouts, please contact your local station."

Bernadette's eyes are wide. "Shit."

Archie can't get any paler – all the blood draining from his face as he nods and says, "This is not good. We have his son, for fuck's sake. What if he knows?"

I stare at the screen in disbelief, knowing my mum will be heartbroken and terrified. I want to call her, to be there for her. The dogs will keep her company. She'll be cuddling them every night. Ewan will probably take her to fucking Australia to hide her from him – he'll probably try to kidnap her again.

Dad might not have his meds.

I wipe a hand down my face and step closer.

Then a picture of a piece of paper with words written on it replaces the image of my dad, and I narrow my gaze to read it.

Save him. Save her. Save them. Save him. Save her. Save them. Save him. Save her. Save them. Save him. Save her. Save them. Save him. Save her. Save them. Save him. Save her. Save them. Save him. Save her. Save them. Save him. Save her. Save them. Save him. Save her. Save them. Save him. Save her. Save them. Save him. Save her. Save them. Save him. Save her. Save them.

34

STACEY

"Stop fucking fighting me!"

I kick his shin as I try to get away from him, slapping his face and managing to headbutt him in the nose. Instead of pulling me by my wrist or arm, Chris gets a fistful of my hair and hauls me to my feet while backing us further into the forest – we can see more cars driving up to the house.

Possibly a second wave. They'll hunt for me.

We get halfway through the forest next to Barry's house before he chucks me onto the ground and pulls a bag from under a bush. He unzips it and grabs a rope, before ordering me to press my ankles and wrists together.

When he advances on me, I kick him in the face, hard enough to hear a crack, and try to run.

But it's a lost cause. Chris is athletic and fast, so I only get a few steps before I'm tackled to the ground, his bloody nose dripping on my cheek as he backhands me, splitting the corner of my lip. I'm quickly bound and thrown over his shoulder for the rest of the walk.

His hands are still covered in blood. I have no idea what he did with it, but he was in Eva's room while I packed.

I wriggle on his shoulder, elbowing the back of his head, but when he grabs my ass cheek, I go freeze. He chuckles and returns his hand to the back of my thighs. "So easily controlled. If you aren't nice to me, I won't be nice to you."

"You don't know the meaning of the word."

"And you don't know the meaning of *behaving*, so why don't you start doing it and stop pissing me off?"

My head shakes. "I hate you."

My form is sliding down his body, and Chris pushes hair from my face when we reach the car – I guess stolen, with fake registration plates. He smiles at me as if I'm going to smile back and tells me that we've got a long drive ahead of us.

"Where are we going?" I ask as he shoves me into the car.

He gets into the driver's seat and slams the door. "I have a friend who stays upstate. We'll change there and fly from the airport nearby. I picked up your fake passport. We're going back to Scotland, to stay at the lodge. We can hide there until we know their next move – they'll never expect us to go somewhere so obvious. Just now, they're looking for us at—" He checks his phone. "Well, Bernadette and your ex are together in a hotel room screwing, but the rest are at the coast."

My eyes snap to him. "What?"

"You didn't know they were fucking?"

"They're not," I snap, tugging my hands, needing the ropes off my wrists. "He wouldn't sleep with a monster like her."

Chris chews his lip, clicks on something on his phone then, his eyes still on the road, shows me the screen.

My blood runs cold, and I quickly look away. My eyes burn as I try to rid the image of them from my head.

"See?" Chris says, adding to the building scream. "He fucks her. He also fucks the daughter, from what I've witnessed."

"Shut up," I reply, a tear sliding down my cheek. "Just... shut up."

Kade can do what he wants – we aren't together. But I can't believe for a second he's willingly doing that. Or do they pay him to sleep with them?

I feel sick. Cassie is beautiful. She might be the daughter of a monster, but she's drop-dead gorgeous. Kade would need to be blind to think otherwise.

The idea of sleeping with someone who isn't Kade makes my skin crawl. The most contact I've had with anyone else is when I fell asleep on Tobias's shoulder. And even then, he nudged me with annoyance and told me to stop drooling on his shirt.

Half an hour into the dreaded journey, I try to pull at the ropes, but I hiss as they cut into my flesh again. Skin raw and burning from my struggles, I give up and allow my tense body to sag in the passenger seat of the car.

My side smacks into the door as he swerves a corner, giving the middle finger to someone who honked their horn at him.

Chris seems to have road rage along with that ugly, tormenting, morbid fucking personality of his. I could also say he's more of a psychopath than Tobias, but having their names in the same sentence and comparing them feels like a crime.

Tobias would be offended, to say the least.

Plus, he hasn't driven a car in over twenty years, so maybe he doesn't even remember how to. Come to think of it, I'm missing movie night with him, so he's probably pacing the room and calling me every name under the sun in his very deep American accent.

When I get away from Chris – because I will – I'll give him the puppy-dog eyes as an apology. They *always* work. Then he'll hug me and talk to me about a book he read the night before, before commenting on how I need better sleep and food in my system.

The father I always wanted, needed and will keep forever, regardless of my position with his son.

However, I'll never hear the end of missing a visit. I'll probably have it carved into my tombstone.

"Your hair smells nice. I meant to mention it earlier. You know, before you hit me."

I grit my teeth, clenching my fists as Chris taps his fingers on the steering wheel, waiting for the red light to change. There's no point in me trying to run; I already did. The doors are locked, and only he can unlock them. And even if I did get out, my ankles are also bound together. I'm sure the skin is raw there too.

He really is a prick.

I glare at Chris. "I hate you."

The corner of his mouth curls. "You said that already."

He sighs and slouches in the seat, the red lights still glowing on his demonic, ugly, fucking annoying face. "You've been quite busy spending dirty money, haven't you? If you needed cash, I would have given you endless amounts. You didn't need to go fuck Kade Mitchell for it."

"Don't say his name," I snap, turning my head to stare out the window. "You took everything from me, so you do *not* say his name."

"You didn't have anything to take," he replies and pulls into the traffic as the lights turn green. "You were – *are* – mine, not his. So, technically, he tried to take everything from me and failed miserably. Was the baby his? I never got round to asking."

"She was a girl and I was sixteen weeks pregnant. And you killed her."

He laughs. "I saved you the hassle of raising a child so young. Really, Stacey, what were you thinking? Mum wouldn't have ever stood for it. She would have told you to get an abortion. I just made it easier for you."

"I hope Kade crushes your skull when he finds you."

"So it was his." Chris chuckles. "Would you still want him if he's fucking everything with a pulse into next Sunday?"

I roll my eyes, even though a hint of hurt hits me. "Stop talking to me."

"I wonder if he has any living children," he says thoughtfully. "I should look into that."

When I don't grace him with a response, he keeps talking, zooming in and out of speeding traffic.

"I hacked their system and found Bernadette Sawyer's plan. She's been hunting you for months; that's how I knew where you were and what you were doing." His head turns to me. "Oh, yeah, while I remember. Please tell me you aren't fucking the dad?"

"No," I retort.

"Are you sure? Did he manipulate you into bed like he did Dr Aria Miller? Does he know about us?"

I huff and ignore him. There is no *us*, the psycho.

"That little girl you were living with – I thought she was his; that he managed to knock you up again. I was going to smother her in her sleep... Until I saw her with her real mother. Lucky, I was minutes from eliminating her from the equation with a quick snap of the neck."

I feel myself pale. He's not a monster – he's *the* monster.

"I think I'd feel more comfortable with Bernadette."

"Don't be idiotic. Bernadette Sawyer was going to kill you," he continues, tutting when someone cuts him off on the road. "I couldn't have that. She was hunting for me and was going to use you as a bargaining chip, so now that I have you, we're going to be the most-wanted pair in her books. How exciting?"

He's insane. "And why would I be a bargaining chip to get to you?"

He smiles like he's just been presented with The Biggest Asshole of the Year award. "I have a lot of incriminating evidence against her and her husband, and she wanted to trade it all for the video she found in my files when I first tried to hack them. I said no obviously."

"What video?"

He gives me a look. "Over two hours of wank-bank material." Then he frowns. "But I'm not too fond of watching others fuck you anymore. Especially that fucking brother. I shouldn't have done any of it. That entire night was a blur, in my defence."

I glare at him. "Is that your version of an apology for letting people gang-rape me?"

"I was also a participant, or did you forget?"

When I just look at him, my heart breathing heavily in my chest, he laughs. "You were a little out of it by the time I got to you. I'll remind you soon."

I snarl. "You're not getting anywhere near me."

"But you need to be taught a lesson, baby."

"I'm not your baby."

"No, you're just *mine*. Now shut up, I like this song," he says as "Feel So Close" by Calvin Harris plays on the radio.

I close my eyes and beg for someone to crash into the car and put me out of my misery as he turns onto an interstate. Maybe I'll chew off my tongue and choke on my own blood, hold my breath until I pass out, or make sure my next bridge jump is successful.

I flinch as he lands his palm on my legs. "Let go." A demand – an order I spit out through my teeth. "*Now.*"

"Admit one thing to me," he says, licking his lips. "Who was a better shag? Me or Jason McElroy?"

"I'd rather stub my toe than think about that. Plus, if you remember rightly, you drugged me and I was unaware you even touched me, never mind violated me yourself with your pathetic excuse of a dick."

I dig my nails into his hand, making him swerve the car. I don't let go as I break the skin, blood gathering around my fingertips. He tries to pull his hand away, but I dig deeper.

"You're a sick rapist who killed my daughter, and if you think for a second I'll ever forgive you and play into this fantasy life where we're together, you've got another think coming. I am not attracted to you, and I never will be. I think you're ugly, with a personality to match. I will *never* love you."

For good measure, I punctuate the last five words by digging my nails in even deeper and throwing his hand off my knee.

He flexes his hand in front of his face. "You've made me mad," is all he says.

"The truth hurts, you psychotic dickhead."

I'm allowing my mouth and rage to take over. After all, what else can possibly go wrong?

Bloody crescents decorate his hand, and I feel a touch pleased with my handiwork as he sucks the droplets and stays extremely quiet. I wait for a punch or a slap, maybe my head smashing into the car window, but he indicates left and drives on as if he didn't hear my words.

After a few minutes, I groan. "Can you cut these ropes?"

"No," he says, not looking at me.

"They're hurting me," I say, raising my hands to show him the raw, tender skin. "And extremely unnecessary. Where the fuck am I going to go? You jammed the lock and stole my shoes."

Chris shakes his head once, emotionless, as if he's trying to zone out and imagine I'm not here. He leans his elbow on the door and rests the side of his head on his fist, the other hand tight on the steering wheel.

I huff and slouch back in my seat again.

35

STACEY

"I forgive you," he says an hour later as we drive along a road sandwiched between two forests.

I screw my face up with confusion. "For what?"

"Sleeping with Kade Mitchell. You can lie to me all you want, but I know he was your boyfriend. I saw the messages between you, and I got so fucking mad and acted out of spite."

"Acted out of spite..."

He looks heartbroken, but I don't care. I watch him until he sighs and elaborates. "When I found out you weren't a virgin anymore, and who took your virginity, I fucked someone to see if it made me feel better, but it didn't."

I'm about to tell him I don't give a shit when he waves his hand around.

"I know, I know, I'm sorry. I shouldn't have fawned over you and told you I loved you then had sex with someone else. It was wrong of me. If it makes you feel any better, I've only had sex with three pe—"

"Did you force yourself on her like you did me?"

"I swear to you I won't fuck anyone else. It's you. It's always been you, sweetheart."

"That doesn't answer my question. Did you hurt her? Was it consensual?"

Chris looks offended. "Why would it not be consensual?"

God, this asshole is delusional. "You know what? Never mind. You're more of a lunatic than I thought."

"It was consensual, I promise. I have a video, if you don't believe me." Chris catches my bound fists aiming for his face, and he lets out a laugh. "I'm kidding! I'm kidding!"

"I can't wait until you're in prison, or even better – dead."

"You'd be devastated, don't lie."

Sarcasm fills my tone as I say, "My heart breaks thinking about all the peace I'd get."

The music on the radio cuts out, and a steady voice takes over. "We have an emergency announcement. Reports say that Tobias Mitchell has escaped his institution."

I gasp, and Chris snaps his gaze to the radio. "The murderer and psychopath was given a life sentence over twenty years ago."

There's a short pause, and I chew my lip nervously while Chris turns up the volume.

"I would like to stress to everyone that this individual is *extremely* dangerous and may not be in touch with reality. Do not approach him. If you have any information on his whereabouts, please contact your local station."

There's a deadly silence between us, butterflies replacing the sickening feeling in my stomach. My heart restarts as a breath shudders through me, attempting to pump blood through my very still body.

Words like *dangerous* and *deadly* and *in possession of a firearm* fill the silence between Chris and I, echoing over the engine as Chris pulls over to pay more attention. Apparently, they found a note in his bed, a repetitive mantra about saving him, her and them, and the specialists have come to the conclusion that Tobias Mitchell is no longer on his meds and maybe hasn't been for a while.

I want to cry – he was doing so well with therapy and behaviour. He'd even started to accept that he and Aria would never be a couple again.

For a while, he'd believed that they could still have a happy, calm and carefree life together. That they'd watch their kids turn into parents, their grandkids running wild on the grounds while he told them the story he wished was theirs but wasn't.

He had photo books upon photo books filled with pictures of the twins over the years, and all the letters Aria had written to him when she couldn't visit. He let me read one once, and it was filled with all the praise and love that's kept him going for the last twenty years.

And now all of the progress he's made is gone.

"The individual is believed to have been planning this escape for many years and constructed an escape route by digging into the sewers from a broom closet."

I shake my head and tug at the ropes again, using the pain of my burning wrists to distract me from getting upset. Chris will only assume I'm in love with him or something equally insane.

I'm both terrified and disappointed, but what should I expect? His son is working for a disgusting woman and I've never missed a visitation. He'll know there's something wrong.

The first place he'll check is my house, and when he sees all the destruction, he'll assume I'm dead. And I have no idea what he'll do. Maybe he'll make sure Barry and his family are okay then try to find his son.

Chris wipes a hand down his face. "Jesus Christ. Is he going to look for you?"

I raise a shoulder. Chris looks deadly pale.

"Tell me the truth – are you sleeping with him?"

I scoff. "He's my ex's dad and over twenty years older than me – what do you think?"

"That means nothing to me. You fucked Kade's brother. But fine. I'll assume he has no interest in your whereabouts then. I already have Bernadette Sawyer on my ass – I don't need him hunting for me as well."

I don't say a word as the radio talks more about Tobias escaping.

A random woman I've never heard of is speaking to the host about her experience with Tobias and the signs she knew meant he was starting to spiral. In my opinion, these details are far too personal to be aired, and I want to slap them both for laughing that it *took him long enough.* She mentions that she's reached out to Aria, but Dr Miller has yet to respond.

Then they go into a big discussion about their history.

Aria must be devastated. I want to call her, to contact Lu – ask if there's anything I can do. But even if I could, all I'd do is make things worse.

I turn down the volume, and Chris lets me.

As much as Tobias is dangerous, he's also vulnerable. I called him my big teddy bear once, and he thought I was trying to offend him. He's a loose cannon when he's not under control and lets his dark side take over, but most of the time, he just wants to talk about his lost love and read a book.

His dark side – an evil motherfucker according to Aria – the Toby of Tobias – will stop at nothing until he has her to himself. He'll most likely look for her, maybe even put a bullet in Ewan's head, and then delude himself into thinking Aria will choose him – exactly how things played out over twenty years ago.

I have no idea how I manage, considering everything that's happening, but I fall asleep with my head against the window.

"Give me my phone," I demand, my hand out – waiting.

Chris looks at his friend, who's studying the burn marks circling my wrists, and lies, "I don't have your phone."

"If you think I'm getting on a flight with you without letting anyone know where I am, you can think again."

The guy, who has shaggy hair and a beard, steps forward. "So this is your girlfriend?"

Chris nods before I can say no, and his friend adds with an outstretched hand, "Nice to meet you. I'm Edgar."

I'm in such a snotty mood that I want to mock his name, but I hold back any immature response. "Give me my fucking phone!" I shout at Chris instead as he pulls on his jacket and makes sure our fake passports are in his bag.

He sighs. "As you can tell, she's on her period."

I punch him across the face, and Edgar pretends he doesn't see as he goes back into his gaming room and mumbles a quiet, "Goodnight."

I punch him again, and he grabs my throat and slams me into the wall. "Stop fucking hitting me!"

I snarl. "You're lucky that's all I'm doing!"

Two hours later, I'm sitting on a flight to Scotland with my arms crossed, Chris by my side, refusing to listen to a word he says.

I sleep most of the flight – or at least I pretend to.

Chris tries to take my hand when we get to the family lodge – tries to help me up the steps, but I push him. "Fuck off."

He sighs. "You need to stop being mad at me."

"And you need to accept we'll never work and let me go, but here we are."

He tosses down the bags with a temper. "Can you just fucking behave for one minute? Do you want her to get you? I might not be your knight in shining armour, but I'm the only person able to keep you safe. I'll give you my word that I won't touch you. I'll promise not to even think about it. But in return, I need you to let me keep you hidden without fighting me on it – preferably keeping you alive in the process."

He steps forward, and I stiffen.

"I'll make a deal with Bernadette. I'll reach out in a few days. Your life for her stupid files, and you'll be safe. Kyle will stop threatening me, I can go home to my mother and all will be good in the world."

"Why?"

He throws his hands out. "Why what?"

"Why are you trying to protect me?"

He chews his lip, grits his teeth and turns around with a shake of his head. "I looked into Bernadette Sawyer's files. She's demonic, Stacey. You think I'm bad? She has recordings upon recordings of shit I never want to look at again. If she gets her hands on you, she'll destroy you, and I'll never see you again. Despite your hatred for me and the stupid mistakes I'll continue to make, I do love you."

"You killed my daughter and raped me. That's not love."

He stays silent, hands falling to his sides.

I keep going. "I was going to have a beautiful baby girl. And you took her away from me. You robbed me of my daughter."

"The baby was his. I wanted you to have *my* kid."

"You've preyed on me since I met you, even when I was underage. I was a *minor*, and you still watched me shower with your dick in your hand. You still forced your way into my bed and made me hold you while we slept. You beat me for not loving you, for not wanting to love you, and then you took every ounce of happiness I had."

His brows narrow. "But you wanted me to watch. You wanted me to come to your bed. You told me you loved me."

"You *forced* those words out of my mouth. I was scared, Chris. I was fucking terrified because I was only fourteen and had a new older stepbrother who told me he was going to take my virginity and strangled me when I refused him."

"You were fifteen then."

"That's not the point!" I take another step to the lodge and stop, my lip trembling, but I refuse to let any tears fall. I feel the sting behind my eyes as I take a deep breath. "What would you have done if I actually wanted you, the baby was yours, and someone beat me up because it wasn't theirs and it died?"

His eyes turn dark. "I would kill them."

I nod. "I should've told Kade what was happening. He would have protected our child – that's on me. But I can't wait until Kade gets his revenge on you. You took his daughter from him, and even if he doesn't care about me anymore, he'll torture you for that. I hope he puts you through hell."

"Let's assume Kade does get his hands on me," he says as he follows me with our bags. "Would you help him, Stacey?"

I throw my head back and laugh. "He's the son of Tobias

Mitchell. He doesn't need help."

36

STACEY

Chris has always been smart when it comes to technology, but as I stare at all the computer screens and flashing lights on boxes I've never seen before, I think I may have misjudged just how brainy he really is.

Not that I want to praise him or anything – he's still a horrible human being.

After a week of annoying me, asking me every two seconds if I'm okay, he's finally exhausted and has fallen asleep on the couch. He'd lose his shit if he saw me in here. I tried to come in yesterday, but he pushed my face into the wall and told me that if he saw me trying to go in again, I'd regret it.

Being the loose cannon that I am – and apparently stupid – I'm standing in the middle of the room, staring at all the equipment and pictures decorating the walls.

Chris said a few days ago that he wasn't scared. Looking at this room, it's clear he lied.

He's trying to track Tobias and Kade. He has images of them on the wall, with a red string tracing Kade's movements, and a blue one highlighting Tobias's. The former's is considerably longer, with sightings all over the States, Russia, Spain and back to Scotland.

I narrow my gaze on an image dated the day Chris came for me that shows Kade fixing a scarf or snood to his face. He's wearing the same uniform as others who raided my place. His hair is longer – and for some reason he looks taller.

Maybe that's because I haven't seen him in nearly a year. Since he fucked me then threw me away.

The most recent sighting is of him leaving a black SUV and holding his hand out to the blonde. Written below the photo in messy handwriting is: *Edinburgh, 6:09 a.m., Cassie Sawyer – aged 23. Fiancée? Potential blackmail?*

There were only a couple of sightings of Tobias before the trail went cold – him wearing a cap and sunglasses at Barry's house and then him getting into a car at a gas station.

It's likely he's with Barry then. If so, I hope Lisa and Eva are hidden. I also hope Tobias is okay. I hope so much that he's on his way to find his son.

My hands shake as I lift up a plastic folder filled with pictures of me and others. Some of them are from my old phone – images of me and Kade, me and the dogs, me and my friends. Chris has crossed out everyone's faces aggressively except for my own.

I open one of the laptops, and my blood runs cold as the screensaver pops up – it's an image of me sleeping. I slap it closed and back away from the desk.

CCTV fills all the screens on the right-hand wall. Some of the footage is from the lodge, and I can see Chris asleep still, and some are from random areas around our town, the path that leads to the lodge. Three are around Nora's estate, and the rest are somewhere I don't recognise.

I stare at the screen nearest me, which displays a black-and-white image of a room with sterile-looking furniture and a four-poster bed with two people sleeping in it – a man and a woman. He has his arms wrapped around her, and my eyes widen. I recognise his face. He was the one who approached us on the pier a year ago and made Kade freak out when he took a picture of me. He was there that night I killed those three guys.

Archie Sawyer. Which means the woman in his arms must be Bernadette.

I step closer to get a better view, and as if they know I'm looking, the monster sits up, not bothering to hide her nakedness. She glances down at her husband, her mouth moving, but I can't read her lips. Then she stands, grabs a robe and walks to the door.

The adjacent screen shows her walking down the hallway, then she appears on the screen beside that, knocking on a door and pushing it open.

My stomach drops when the next screen shows her lifting the duvet on someone else's bed. And as the person turns around to see what's happening, I gasp.

It's Base.

What the hell is Base doing there? Kade never mentioned him working for her too.

Lu was right – there was something off about his apparent work in Russia. He was never there with his family, was he? Base left when Kade did.

When he sits up and shakes his head at her, she presses her finger to his lips and pushes him back down, and I can't stop the way my mouth falls open in shock.

She lets her robe fall, and I cover my gaping mouth as she climbs on top of him and parts her thighs while stroking him through his boxers. A few minutes later, she's sickeningly moving above him while he covers his face with both hands.

Chris showed me a similar image – her and Kade in bed. She's cheating on her husband with them both? But he… said no. He shook his head. She's raping him. That's non-consensual.

When I turn in revulsion with the back of my hand to my mouth, I don't even flinch when I find Chris staring at me, leaning his shoulder against the doorframe, arms crossed. "Do you ever listen?"

For a long moment, I try to control my rampant thoughts. I

drop my hand to my side. "To you?" I retort. "No."

He gestures to the screens behind me with his chin. "Kade is on screen twelve. Top-right corner."

I turn again, and my heart slowly shatters at the sight of Kade lying on his back with Cassie Sawyer in his arms, her head on his chest.

Her blonde hair sprawls over the pillow, her skin perfect – the total opposite of his inked body. I already know she's flawless, pretty, stunning, and she has Kade.

Jealousy burns in my gut.

"Every night, without fail, they share a bed. Sometimes he'll go to his own room and the mother joins him, but there hasn't been a night yet where he hasn't been inside at least one of them. Kind of sick, if you think about it."

I keep my gaze on the screen, and I notice Kade's eyes are open. He's staring at the ceiling, thinking deeply with the girl hugging into him. He doesn't seem to be hugging her back though.

Chris keeps talking. "You should know he agreed to marry the daughter. Some sort of deal was made – no idea what it was though."

I close my eyes, sinking my teeth into my cheek to stop my tears.

If he's sleeping with the mother and daughter, is he being forced like Base?

I feel ill as I watch Kade. I want to jump through the screen and pull him to me, to tell him that it's all going to be okay. He won't need to marry that girl if he doesn't want to.

"Did you love him?"

I snap my head to Chris. "What?"

"Kade Mitchell. Were you in love with him? Or was it a stupid crush and you accidentally fell pregnant?"

I swallow a building lump, a mixture of hatred and sadness filling me. "Why do you have access to these?"

"Answer my question and I'll answer yours."

I roll my eyes. "He was my boyfriend for nearly a year. He was the father of my unborn child, and we had a life ahead of us before you took it away. *Of course* I loved him."

Chris glares at me, his hands curling into fists. "And now?

Watching him in this life." He waves his hand to the screens, to Base and Bernadette, with the added audience of her husband Archie now, then to Kade on the other screen. "Do you still feel the same way?"

"Does it really matter if I still love him or not?"

"Well, I can assure you that he doesn't love you anymore."

I turn my body to fully face him, my arms crossed. "It's been four years since I started falling for him. I know he might not care for me, but I will *always* love him."

My throat is captured in a firm grip as he turns my face towards the screen. "Your love for him is worthless. He's not the same. I've watched every single clip of him. She has a folder filled with hundreds – and I mean *hundreds* – of videos of him doing horrific things. His hands are filthy." He pushes my face away. "A lot dirtier than his lunatic father's, that's for sure."

The resounding slap reaches my ears before I realise what I've done. But I don't wait for him to retaliate – I turn my back and train my eyes on the screen once more.

"You just fucking hit me again."

"As always, your observation skills are on point. Congratulations," I reply, watching Kade reach to the side to grab a cigarette – or maybe it's a joint? He lights it up, trying not to wake Cassie as he slides his arm free from beneath her head.

I feel like I shouldn't watch, but I can't stop. It's been so long – he's right there.

He sits up and takes a draw, blowing out a cloud of smoke that slowly rises to the ceiling before dissipating.

He grabs something from the bedside unit, twists it open then starts rubbing some sort of cream from the corner of his mouth, down his chin, all the way to the middle of his chest. I can't quite make it out in the video's low light.

Kade puts it back and studies his hand, which is very obviously shaking. I wish I was there to kneel in front of him and tell him it's okay. Tell him his dad is coming to get him out of the mess he's in. We'll do what we can. We care for him and love him.

Hold on a little longer. Please.

As much as he broke my heart in numerous ways, I'm going to

do everything I can to help him. Including ruining the deal Chris wants to make with Bernadette. Instead of my safety, I'm going to trade everything she wants for Kade.

I tilt my head, watching him stand and stare into a mirror, tracing the trail of cream with his finger again. I continue ignoring Chris, who's still holding his cheek like the dramatic idiot he is.

"Are you jealous?"

I tut. "Go away."

Chris chuckles. "You're the one in this room. The one I told you *not* to come into."

I tense all over as he comes up behind me and rests his chin on my shoulder, his hands on my sides. I try to shrug him off, but he digs his fingers into my ribs.

"If you want, we can send him a video of us doing the same. A little cuddle wouldn't hurt, sweetheart."

"I'd rather die."

Kade glances around the room, stubs out the smoke, then hunts for his clothes without waking Cassie. He looks like he has more tattoos and even more muscles.

I miss him. I miss him so much that sometimes I find it hard to breathe. My bedside unit had a picture of us. I looked at it every night before I fell asleep. It was a little obsessive, considering we were done and all, but I've never really been able to move on.

And like everything else me-and-Kade, that's also gone.

But I still love him.

Kade doesn't love me anymore though. Why would he? I'm the lousy one who's clinging to the emotions – he moved on. Once upon a time, we stood on a Greek beach next to a cave, full of laughter, happiness and alcohol, and Kade poured his heart out to me. He loved me then.

I remember every single word that made my heart beat faster, made it swell in my chest and gave me hope that I could have a happy ever after with him. We were teenagers, but we knew what we wanted.

"Are you going to be my forever, Freckles?"

What is forever if it's not with him?

It felt like everything had fallen perfectly into place when he asked me that. I had true love, friends, my passion for dancing, a chance at a life I never knew I'd get because of the prick standing right behind me.

I had it all, and Chris ruined it.

Instead of running for a knife and slashing his throat like I should, I glance over my shoulder and ask again, "How do you have access to all of this?"

Thankfully, he lets me go and walks over to one of the laptops, opens it to reveal another screensaver of my face and inputs my date of birth. "When I infiltrated Bernadette's database, I managed to pull everything, even the codes to all the CCTV she has set up. But I made sure to cover my tracks in certain areas, so she doesn't know how much access I actually have."

"She's going to kill you."

"Nah, she just wants what I've got, because it would put her away for life if it got into the right hands. She'll take the deal, or I'll send everything out for the public to see."

I cross my arms. "Then she'd kill you." Not that I'd give a shit. Chris dying would make my life easier. "Why not just release it all?"

Chris shrugs nonchalantly. "She'd retaliate by releasing what she has on me, and I can't be with you if I'm locked up."

I don't give him a response as my eyes fly back to screen twelve, where the girl lies in bed, Kade now nowhere to be seen.

I check the other screens and see him walk into the room Bernadette is currently fucking Base in. Archie tips a glass of whisky to him, but he blanks the older man and angrily points at Base and Bernadette.

He's saying something to them which makes her throw her head back in annoyance and climb off Base. I can tell they're raising their voices, but all Base does is lounge back in the bed and pull the duvet over himself. Completely unbothered as Kade pulls a gun out and points it at Archie.

I've no idea what's being said, and I ignore Chris typing on the laptop while they all shout – until Kade closes the distance between him and Archie and smacks his forehead into his face. The tall, skinny man grabs his bleeding nose. I still don't know what's being said, but Bernadette grabs her husband's arm and pulls him out the room.

As soon as the door is shut, Kade stands frozen for a second, making sure they're gone, before rushing over to Base and slapping his face hurriedly. He shakes him, and it's now I realise that Bernadette must've drugged him as he starts to vomit.

My eyes stay on the screen as Kade rolls Base onto his side and shoves his fingers down his throat.

"Where is this?"

"Don't sound so panicked – he'll be fine. They're in Bernadette's manor," he replies, not looking up. "They arrived three days ago. His little friend there seems to be a huge part of her control over Kade. She tortures him to make your ever-loving ex do shit. I even witnessed him sucking Kade's dick once." He fake shivers. "It was uncomfortable to watch."

I think all of the blood has drained from my face.

"She's disgusting. Why can't you send all of this to the police?"

"Because it'll go nowhere," he replies, closing his laptop. He nudges me with his shoulder and grins. "If you think that's bad, you have no idea what world your little lover boy is in."

"You think this is funny?"

He shrugs as he watches Kade dragging his friend to the bathroom, and once the door closes, we can no longer see what they're doing. "It's a bit entertaining, don't you think? We can sit here every night and watch them."

"You know what? I hope she gets you, and then Kade deals with whatever's left of your pathetic body."

His eyes light up. "If she gets me, then she gets you. I wonder what she'll make us do together?"

37

STACEY

Rain falls around the little shack in the middle of the woodland, and as much as I'd like to bash Chris over the head with something hard and heavy, grab a phone and run for it, I'd probably just end up lost in the woods. But since he stole my shoes and has CCTV everywhere, I wouldn't get very far.

The consequences aren't worth it.

He swaggers in and messes around in the kitchen, speaking then answering himself, then he comes in and asks why I look so grumpy.

He won't leave me in peace.

I huff and get up from the sofa, wrapping myself with a blanket as I go outside and sit on the back porch, in front of the fire pit.

"Stacey?"

"No," I snap. "Do not speak to me."

He mutters something under his breath about me being moody, and I prepare for the grab of my hair or smash of his clenched fist I've become accustomed to, but strangely, I walk freely into the autumn chill. Unscathed. Unharmed.

Chris hasn't fully kicked the shit out of me since we got here, but I can tell he's slowly losing his patience with me. I'm not sure what else he expects after kidnapping me.

I'm hardly going to roast marshmallows over the fire, share a bed with him and kiss him good-fucking-night, am I?

He has tried to come in beside me, but for once in his pathetic life, he left when I screamed like a banshee at him.

I tried to steal his phone from him this morning, but it resulted in him snatching my wrist and pulling me on top of him, onto his horrific, unwanted morning wood, before I slapped him and ran into the bathroom.

My belly grumbles, and I tighten the blanket around me as the wind whips up, lashing rain in at me. I welcome the cold, the shake in my bones, the redness of my nose as my body temperature slowly drops.

The only indicator that I'm not in hell – though being stuck with my rapist of a stepbrother is worse.

Waiting. For what, I don't know. He has everything he needs to make a deal with Bernadette Sawyer; her files for my safety, but he seems to be stalling on actually presenting the deal to her.

Maybe because he knows as soon as I'm no longer being targeted by them, I'll run to the opposite side of the world and make sure no one will ever find me.

Or maybe it's because Tobias Mitchell is loose. As much as I've tried to convince Chris he won't come for me, I know he will, given the bond we've formed over the past year.

Tobias will probably snap his neck without letting him speak a word. And I'd encourage it. I just hope he helps Kade first. Going by what I witnessed, he and Base need out of that mess more than I need out of mine.

Despite how vile Chris is, I can handle him. He's already did his worst.

So, yeah, Kade first. Then, if they have time, they can get this deranged dickhead out of my life.

Since Tobias escaped, Lu, Kade and Aria have been all over the news. The manor has been surrounded by protestors, and everyone in the family has been followed constantly by cars and reporters. Tobias's photo is being repeatedly shared on social media, though a large number of the posts are from people hoping he's okay and managing to stay hidden from the authorities. They're also the same people who want him to fuck their brains out.

I wish I could call Luciella and ask if she's okay. Hopefully Tylar is with her, keeping her sane during all of this. First Base – the realisation that she no longer gives a shit about their differences and wants to give them a chance – and now her father escaping prison.

Chris appears next to the fire pit, offering me a hot drink. He gives me a death stare when I knock the cup of coffee from his hand. "Fuck off."

"You need to drink something," he sneers, huffing and wiping the front of his clothes. Knowing him, it was probably spiked with a date-rape drug.

I pull my knees up, wrap my arms around them and keep my eyes forward. "Leave me alone."

"Fine. I was going to ease you into this subject, but I guess if you want to be difficult, then I'll be difficult too."

I glance at him. "Meaning?"

He lifts his phone, the screen bright. "The deal is in motion. It seems Bernadette is more than eager to discuss her options. I let her know I had you by sending a picture of you sleeping, and that I wanted her to leave you alone in exchange for the USB drive containing all the evidence I have on her."

I gulp. "What did she say?"

He hums as his phone dings again. "Ah, this will be fun."

"What?"

"She's having a party this weekend, and she wants me to attend. That's where the deal will be made."

I hope she shoots you then shoots herself.

"I'll give it another day to respond. I want her to sweat." He taps his leg with his phone repeatedly, looking up at the moon. "Maybe we should just stay here. It's quite nice, isn't it? I think I'd be able to worm my way into your heart."

"It's scary that you actually believe that."

He grins. "And you should too. Think about it." He throws his arm over my shoulders, and I bristle. "You're hot and so am I. We have cracking genes to pass down to our kids. I think Mum will be mad about it, considering she sees us as siblings, and Kyle will probably fold me into a suitcase, but they'd eventually be okay with it."

I frown. "You truly think after everything you've done to me, I'd ever go there with you?"

He truly is deranged.

"My dick has already been inside you. We've had sex, so why not?"

My frown deepens, and I glare at him. "That wasn't sex; that was rape."

"Tomayto, tomahto." He stares at me, dropping his gaze to my mouth. "I was giving you a break from the others. I went gentle on you."

I shake my head with a disbelieving laugh. "You're so incredibly sick."

"The only sickness I have is wanting you. Everything else has just been a mistake. I wasn't supposed to join in that night. I was just supposed to teach you a lesson. Letting them near you will forever be my biggest regret."

"You already said that, but that doesn't take away the fact that you raped me. Why?"

"Why what?" His brows furrow in confusion.

Gah! I hate him and his fucking obliviousness to how horrible he is to me.

"Why did you rape me?"

He sighs and attempts to tuck strands of hair behind my ear. I bat his hand away, and he says, "Have you ever let intrusive thoughts win?"

I shove him and stand. "Stay away from me, you monster."

"Ask me how many times I've fucked you."

My silence fills the air, but my heart rate is accelerating.

"Nine times," he says, and my face drops. "You were so easy to drug. You always had a bottle of water next to your bed." He stands, towering over me. "I saw opportunities to take what I wanted, so I did. I tasted you – kissed between your legs, licked, fingered." He gets even closer, and I'm shaking. "Did you know a person can still have an orgasm while drugged? Feeling your pussy gripping my cock only made me want more."

Tears slide down my cheeks, and I somehow manage to breathe. My bones are rattling, and I look away from him. If he was doing that when I was with Kade… was my daughter his?

"When I was with Kade," I manage to push out. "Did you drug me while I was with him?"

He shakes his head. "No. It wasn't until later. I waited for so long – you were so young and small and innocent; I didn't want to hurt you. But when I found out you'd already been broken in, there was no more reason to wait. You will learn to love me, Stacey. And as soon as you do, I'll be good. I promise."

I flinch as he strokes hair away from my wet eyes.

"Say you already love me."

Delusional. Absolutely delusional.

I don't respond.

He sighs and drops his hand. "I need to buy you a dress."

Of all the things I thought he might say, that was way down the list. "A dress?"

"A fancy one. I'll go into town and find one. I know your size. Can I trust you to shave your legs with my razor, or will I do it?"

I grimace. "Are you serious?"

"I want you to look your best," he replies, trying to stroke his knuckles down my arm. When I raise a brow, he pulls his phone out and shows me Bernadette's message. It's an invitation. "You're going to Bernadette's birthday party, sweetheart."

I nearly choke. "Why me?"

"It was one of her conditions. She wanted you personally to hand over the USB, and she wanted you as an audience. I'm not allowed to go, but she gave me her word you'd be safe and her permission to drop you off and pick you back up."

He can't be serious. "And you actually believe she won't do

anything to me? Are you *insane*? No, I'm not doing it."

A smirk, then he sits up. "It was either that or she said she'd run a trace on my email, shows up here and take you anyway. I agreed to her conditions, Stacey. You're going. Plus" – he clicks his tongue – "Kade will be there."

38

STACEY

I massively overestimated my stepbrother's intelligence. He's smart and nerdy but has no common sense whatsoever. I reckon a ten-year-old has more goddamn sense. I'd say it had something to do with him being a blonde, but that's a ridiculous stereotype. My best friend is blonde, and she's brainy as hell.

Chris is just… *urgh.* I huff into my glass of wine and cross one leg over the other, trying to block out "Eleven Minutes" by Yungblud and Halsey blaring all around the lodge.

He's singing in the shower, his voice screeching like nails on a chalkboard. Then his tone turns high as he does the girl's lines, and I down the rest of my glass while wishing for a quick death or for my eardrums to blow.

I walk to the kitchen and refill my glass. I checked to make sure the wine bottle was sealed when he offered it to me earlier to help calm my jitters. Killing the nerves with alcohol is both stupid and really stupid – but here I am, downing another glass.

My eyes fall on the bag Chris usually keeps in his bedroom. After a second of listening to check he's still showering and singing, I lunge for it.

His phone password is my date of birth, which he seems to use for everything, and I let out an excited sound as I get access, immediately scrolling through the contacts and pressing Kyle's name.

Four rings, and then a voice I've missed so dearly: "You better have a good fucking reason for calling me."

The low sob is covered by my palm. "Hi. It's me."

"Stacey? What the fuck?"

Silence descends for a second as I try not to ruin the make-up Chris bought me by crying. "Wait. Wait. If you're calling from his phone… that means… *No.*"

My bottom lip shakes. "He got me, Kyle." My voice breaks on his name. "Chris got me."

"Where?"

"The lo—"

"I'll be taking that," Chris snaps, swiping the phone from my hand. "As usual, you don't behave." He presses it to his ear. "Howdy, big brother. What can I do for you?"

Fuck it. "We're at the lodge!" I yell as loud as I can, smacking the ground after Chris backhands me hard enough to make me dizzy, the searing pain slicing my cheek where the blow connected.

"Shut the fuck up!" He hangs up and tosses the phone aside. "Why did you just do that? Why are you always choosing him over me? *Why?*" He grips my throat and pulls me to him on my knees. "You fucked up."

I struggle against his hold, feeling pressure behind my eyes and tasting blood. I should be scared, but instead, I spit blood in his face. "Fuck you."

Grimacing as he wipes his face with his free hand and licks his palm clean, I try to pull away from him, but his fingers squeeze my throat tighter. "Tempting, but we're going to be late. I'll fuck you later."

I try to swallow, but his hold on my throat tightens. "N-No, th-thanks, asshole."

He brings his face closer to mine, and I battle against him as his lips hover over my own. "I'm trying to be good; don't you see that? I want to do so many things to you, hurt you, *fuck* you, but I'm holding back until you want me just as much."

I drag in air as he releases his grip a touch, and although his grip on my throat is still painful and harsh, I manage to speak. "You'll be holding back until your last breath then. I will *never* want you."

Chris shoves me away, my ass hitting the floor again. "We'll see. Get the fuck up. We need to leave, and you look like shit. Clean the mascara off your cheeks and fix your hair. I reckon my brother is on his way here, and we need to be gone before he shows up."

With the police hopefully.

But then, Bernadette runs the police.

This is a disaster.

A huge part of me hopes Tobias is hiding in the woods ready to slit his throat and take me somewhere safe. But I'm not his priority. He'll either be hunting Kade or obsessing about ways to win Aria over.

Chris marches me to his bedroom and orders me to sit in with him while he gets dressed, and I listen. I keep my blank gaze on the wall while I absently wipe the mascara from under my eyes and fix my hair.

He's intentionally walking around naked. Asking me if I think he has a decent-sized cock, if his balls are smooth enough and if his abs are more defined since the last time we were close to each other.

I was unconscious the last time, but I ignore him anyway.

"Your tits look great in that," he tells me as I fix my dress back into place. "You've got them, so you should flaunt them. The wire will hide there too."

Urgh.

The dress he bought me is annoyingly flattering. Black silk hugs my every curve, my right leg exposed from the slit that runs all the way to my hip, but with every move I take, the nakedness I feel only grows.

"I saw a video of you and Kade having sex, by the way. Made me mad."

The hairbrush freezes in my hand. "What?"

"Yeah. I told you I knew about what you did in America. Behind a club. Bernadette has the footage too. Kind of makes me want to kill him that little bit more."

"You won't be able to kill him," I say, tutting. "You only hit women."

"We'll see."

That was the first time we'd had sex in two years. And I was stupid enough to do it behind a goddamn nightclub. We didn't even kiss. I swear, everything in my body becomes mush when I'm around Kade.

Our first actual time sleeping together was in a hotel in London when we were teenagers. We went to see the live version of *The Greatest Showman* before he took me back to the room, and he was so respectful and gentle and made sure I was okay. I was already in love with him then, but it took weeks for me to admit it.

The difference between those two encounters is drastic.

Chris finally gets his clothes on – casuals, because he isn't allowed inside the building. He fixes his golden hair in the mirror, sprays breath freshener in his mouth and starts flossing his teeth.

I screw my face up and drink from the wine glass.

"You look beautiful again. Good touch on hiding the redness on your cheek. I didn't think I hit you that hard."

I glare at him. "I hope Bernadette shoots me in the head."

"Strange thing to hope for, but okay. Ready?"

Without nodding, I stand and walk out, Chris following behind me. I flinch as he slaps my ass and tries to grope it, but I shove his hand away and turn to him. "Stop it. I swear to fucking God, Chris, you better stop touching me."

Raising both hands, he smiles. "Fine! I like when you're all pushy and angry. I get why Tobias Mitchell was so drawn to you."

"Oh, shut up."

"No, I'm serious. Why would he have so much time for you? You're a nobody. All you have are your good looks, a cracking set of tits and a nice ass. Your dancing gets me hard, so maybe that's it too. Fuck, wait. Did you dance for Kade's dad? Will you dance for me?"

"Delusional," I mutter and walk into the sitting room.

The little USB drive sitting on the coffee table in front of me has everything I need for tonight. The images of Bernadette and numerous others taking part in illegal activities, a letter of gratitude from Chris for leaving me alone and an invite to Chris and I's wedding, to be apparently confirmed at a later date. He also tells her she can bring Kade as a plus one.

I want to smash it to pieces, but I already did that with the last three.

The plan will fail.

I either need Kyle to show up right now, or I say goodbye to my life and await whatever torture Bernadette has planned for me. There's absolutely no chance she's letting me leave that building.

I hate Chris.

Since he still has access to everything, he's made me watch Kade every night before bed. For five nights straight, I've sat tied to a chair, forced to watch him in bed with Cassie. One night, he was sleeping beside Base and Bernadette joined them.

She watched. Base watched. Kade watched. I watched.

Chris laughed.

"Right, drink up. Time to go."

The glass of wine Chris forces down my throat leaves a nasty taste in my mouth, or maybe it's the unwanted kiss he smashes to my lips before telling me to go to the car – who knows? All I do know is that tonight is going to be brutal and I need to do everything he says through the earpiece he slides into place to make sure I stay safe.

I'm weighing up the pros and cons here. Who's the lesser of two evils?

Chris, someone who's been abusing me since I was a little girl, who's raped me, killed my unborn baby and ruined my life? Or this psychotic woman who seems to be the devil in disguise?

I'm undecided.

Chris tells me he'll get me out of there the minute anything looks dodgy.

I'm not sure how the hell that's going to work with him not even at the party, and me being surrounded by Bernadette and her guards, but I have no other option. If I refuse to go, she'll come for me regardless – and I'm still unsure which is the best option.

When we drive out of the woods and onto the main road, I feel deflated that Kyle hasn't made it in time. If he had, he'd have punched the living daylights out of his brother, taken me somewhere safe and Bernadette would never get her hands on me.

"You're killing me – I hope you know that."

He narrows his eyes. "She gave me her word."

I let out a "pffft" and look out of the window. "And then they'll come for you. Or Tobias will. You're screwed." I look over with a fake smile. "I doubt you'll see your next birthday."

He audibly gulps and turns on the radio. "Shut up."

The drive takes over an hour, and when we reach a long, narrow road through trees that open up to reveal a large manor, I can't help but look in awe.

White bricks. Pillars. A driveway full of flowerbeds and party lights. Classical music is playing inside, and workers stand by the gates and ask our names.

"Christopher Fields. I'm here to drop off Miss Rhodes." He shows the screen of his phone. "There's the invitation email with my car registration."

The man studies the phone. "Very well. You have ten minutes to drop off, then be back ten minutes before midnight."

Chris drives around the large fountain and parks to the side, tapping his fingers on the steering wheel to the beat of the song we can hear through the manor entrance. "Right, tell me the plan again."

I huff. "We've gone over the plan thousands of times. I go in, introduce myself to Bernadette, hand her the USB drive, then you come for me when I say the code phrase."

"Which is?"

I flatten my lips at the ridiculousness. "*Stacey Fields.* By the way, you're a child."

"Smart and beautiful," he says with a smile. "I'll be able to hear you, so don't worry about trying to get in contact with me before that moment, okay?" He reaches forward and tries to tug the wire hidden between the cleavage of my pushed-up breasts. "I'll be able to hear you and know where you are, so if anything goes wrong, I'll find you."

"That's... unsettling." I fidget my hands, cross and uncross my legs, and chew my lip. "I don't think I can do this. Isn't there another option? We can post it to her, or you could just let me go into hiding."

"You were in hiding, and she still found you. These are her rules and terms, Stacey. We need to abide by them."

My teeth chatter, and my eyes sting with a burning sensation. Fear. Bad adrenaline. Terror. Impending death and doom. I've endured trauma for years at the hands of this guy – I should be used to this. I should be able to zone out like I have millions of times.

But I can't even fill my lungs without making a guttural sound. "I really don't want to go in. I-I'm scared."

I flinch as he cups my swollen cheek in his palm. "I won't let anything happen to you, okay? Stay under the radar and don't speak with anyone. Stay with crowds. Don't go anywhere they can attack you without witnesses."

"None of this is helping."

"If I didn't make this deal, she would have come for you. This is the only option left," he says, stroking his thumb under my eye. "Be a good little lamb and listen to me."

I manage a nod as I shake, unable to move or tell him to let go given how scared I am.

"Don't trust anyone. None of these people..." He points to the guests entering the manor with dirty grins. "They're all bad people. They are versions of *her*. In her circle – evil and vile and corrupt. You understand? This isn't a normal party. I don't believe for a second that it's even a celebration."

"You're making it worse."

More cars appear, and Chris glances at the time on his watch. "I need to go. I'll be right outside. I know ways to get in if you need me. Go." He leans forward and shoves the door open. "Behave."

I get out and hug myself as the breeze smooths over my exposed skin. Clutching a purse that contains a folded envelope with the

USB drive inside and a small can of pepper spray, I walk away from the car shakily and ignore him driving out of the courtyard.

I'm offered a glass of champagne, but after Chris's warning, I kindly decline the drink.

"Stacey?"

I freeze halfway up the steps at the sound of my best friend's voice, then turn around, my eyes wide. She should *not* be here. "Lu?"

39

STACEY

Wearing a navy dress that hugs her body, hair pinned up with blonde strands falling down the sides of her face, Luciella takes two steps at a time until she reaches me. Without any more words, she pulls me in for a hug, and I instantly melt into her arms.

I haven't hugged my best friend in so long.

Being away from her and Ty and everyone else has been hard but necessary. I haven't gone a day without thinking of them all. The sleepovers and dances and days out. The group chats and social-media tags and late-night phone calls that lasted hours.

"I missed you," I choke out, fanning my eyes to stop my mascara from running for the second time tonight. "God, I missed you so much."

It feels good to be in the arms of someone who cares. I haven't had that in a while.

"I missed you too," she replies, hugging me tighter. "Nearly a year! I hope the break helped." She giggles as I snort, and we both pull back and fix each other's hair. "You haven't aged at all."

I chuckle with an eye roll. "It's been ten months, not ten years."

"Feels like it. We have a picture of you on the studio wall as a remembrance."

I let out a soft laugh. "Those fucking girls." Then I pull back, and my face falls at the realisation of where we are. "Why are you here?"

"Base asked me to come." Lu narrows her eyes at me in confusion. "Wait, did he invite you too?"

From what I know, thanks to Chris and his snooping, Bernadette has both Kade's and Base's phones. They have no contact with the outside world.

I don't think it was Base who invited her.

"You should go," I say quietly. "Please. Go. It's not safe here."

"What? What do you mean?" She looks around then near the manor entrance to see more waiters standing with trays of alcohol. "Is it because of my dad?"

I want to hug her again at the sadness in her eyes, but there's no time. I shake my head. "You need to leave."

"Why are you here?"

I flatten my lips, Chris in my ear telling me to stop making it obvious and to get inside. "I was invited," is all I say.

As if she can hear my brother yelling, she hooks her arm in mine and turns us towards the entrance. "At least we can hang out. When do you leave again? Or are you staying?"

"How did you get here?"

She tilts her head. "Jason drove me. He's just out of rehab."

I should ask her about him, ask if he's okay, but instead I ask, "Can he come back to get you?"

She sighs. "It'll be fine. Let's go find Base."

I hold the side of my dress as we take the rest of the stairs together.

"The place is beautiful, isn't it?" she says.

I try to pay attention to the decor, but my eyes are flying all over the place, hunting for a tall, dark-haired man I can't get out of my head. I want to both dodge and run to him. To beg him to run away with me. His boss is the devil, and we're both in danger being near her.

"Though it does look a little weird... Can I see Base first then we can go? I haven't seen him in months. He's been... ignoring me. I just want to make sure he's okay."

"Is this you finally admitting to your feelings?"

She looks down at her feet. "Four years too late, right?"

"Why didn't you give him a chance before?"

Lu shrugs. "I wanted to."

My gaze flickers over the crowd gathering, everyone being instructed to follow the servers. "Then why didn't you?" I ask, needing to keep on the subject to not ruin my nerves.

She sighs as we walk down a corridor. "Base has a big personality and a very dominating lifestyle. He parties like he'll die tomorrow and fucks anyone with a pulse. He's close to being a billionaire, an heir to the entire family fortune with huge responsibilities. His grandfather will arrange a marriage for him; another rich man or woman who can offer way more than me. I... I'm not good enough for Base. I never have been. I would just bring him down, and he's not that type of guy."

I listen as she blows out a breath and sniffs. She accepts a glass of water, but I take it from her and place it on a nearby window ledge. "That's so far from the truth, Luciella. Don't ever belittle yourself like that."

"Even if I tell him how I truly feel, nothing can come from it. I'm not right for him. I just want to make sure he's okay, then I'll ask Jason to pick us both up." She eyes me warily. "Will that be okay? You and Jason are okay after everything, right?"

"Yeah," I lie. We haven't spoken at all. Whenever I was over at the manor and he was in, he'd leave within seconds. He lost his relationship with his brother, his job went downhill due to him turning to alcohol after Giana left him, and from what Luciella has told me, he's lost his spark.

We're both victims – dealing with it differently.

When the time comes, we'll talk.

Luciella keeps her arm hooked in mine as we walk into the main ballroom, both stopping in the entranceway. "I thought this was a birthday party?" she asks, confused, and I think I might faint.

I knew this wasn't a party.

Loads of seats are lined up, facing a stage with a platform, a large screen behind it. Workers are setting up as more guests fill the room, all with glasses of champagne and chatting between themselves.

There's no dance floor or DJ, no balloons or birthday banners. This isn't a party. People are holding paddles with numbers on them, stickers on their clothes with their matching numbers.

They all look filthy rich.

I have no idea what this is.

"Did Base mention why you were to come tonight?"

She shakes her head beside me. "No. Just that he wanted to see me."

Guests begin to take their seats, the classical music quieting, the lights dimming. The workers start to disperse, and bodyguards with black suits move to each exit, some to the stage, a few others just dotted around.

"Take your seats, ladies," one says to us, gesturing to the seated crowd. "It begins in five minutes."

Lu and I give each other an unsure look. Regret is painted all over her face as she bites her bottom lip and stares at the exit. She won't leave. She wants to see Base. I'm not sure we actually can leave at this point.

"Can you hear me?" I whisper, basically breathing the words as Luciella takes her seat, placing her bag under the chair and looking around. "Chris?"

Nothing. The stupid gadgets he covered me with aren't working. I'm on my own here. What if they find wires on me? What if I accidentally curl my hair behind my ear without thinking and expose the earpiece? Nervously, I sit, keeping my purse in my lap as the main doors close.

We flinch as the other exit doors slam closed.

Luciella takes my hand as the music stops completely. My chest tightens when a tall, skinny, bearded man takes the stage. Archie

Sawyer.

"Good evening, ladies and gentlemen. Thank you for being here at such short notice."

I gulp. "Kade works for him."

She looks at me, dumbfounded, then frowns at the stage. "Really? He looks… sketchy."

"He is," I say quietly. "He took a picture of me, then Kade rushed me out of the country. He's horrible."

"When?"

"When we all went to the States a year ago," I whisper.

"He's a bad man?" she asks, and I glance at the spooked expression on her face.

I nod once, and both of us move our eyes forward. "His wife is worse."

And as the door next to the stage opens, my heart sinks. The older woman enters, wine-red hair cascading behind her, boobs nearly falling from her white dress, her heels clicking as people trail behind her wearing fitted black suits with blank white masks.

No faces. No designs. Just white. I have no idea how they can see or breathe.

Then a smaller version of Bernadette appears, only blonde. Cassie. I avert my eyes to the purse in my lap. He must be one of those masked people. Base too.

She smiles at her mother as they stand on the stage, all the masked people in a line behind them. She has a huge rock on her wedding finger. An engagement ring. My eyes burn, pressured, but I battle against the need to scream as I sink my nails into my palm and hold Lu's hand tighter.

Bernadette Sawyer sucks on her teeth and looks around the room. Proud of herself at the turnout. With a clap of her hands, my blood starts to boil, screaming in my ears.

She's a monster. I despise her as much as I hate Chris. She's a rapist too.

I pale when her eyes land on me, and she winks and walks over to the podium, saying something into her husband's ear before she takes the stand. "We haven't had one of these in a while, have we? It's been some time, my friends, but let's not take longer than necessary. Bring the first four in."

My eyes narrow as one of the masked people is shoved forward, the mask then ripped off to reveal a young man with sweat all over his face, his eyes wide with fear. He tries to back away; a guard grabs his arm and shoves him forward.

The screen lights up behind him – two more people with the same masks are standing in an office, a guard behind them with a gun out.

Luciella gasps as soon as they start the bidding.

I don't blink.

Is this what I think it is? A human auction?

"Stay calm," says a voice in my ear. Chris. "Don't stand up. *Please.* Nod once if you understand."

I lower my chin ever so slightly.

"Good," he says. "Kyle's with me. We're going to get you out of there. I'm sorry – I didn't know what this was."

At the same time, I hear Kyle smack him and say, "Motherfucker. Why is she there? I'm coming to get you, Stacey. Fucking prick. You're lucky I'm not punching fuck out of you right now."

There's a rustling, and then nothing, indicating that Chris has muted his microphone.

This isn't good. And it's not just me – my best friend is here too. Someone who has no idea about Kade's and Base's situations and what's transpired over the past year. What Kade has been going through for nearly three years.

I try to breathe normally. I try to not look at Bernadette and Archie, at the masked people being auctioned off like meat, the guards and all the exits.

Lu tightens her hold on my hand, and when I glance at her, her eyes are red and her chin has a noticeable tremble. *I'm scared,* she mouths.

I know. Me too.

Archie keeps looking at her.

I want to slap him as he licks his lips and smiles at his wife.

All four are done within minutes and taken off stage.

When four more people reach the stage, they're forced onto platforms, so they're standing higher than everyone else.

A spotlight illuminates the first one on the left. She looks my age and has bruises around her throat. To my horror, the guests seated around us start lifting their paddles, bidding for their new pets.

They are the silver packages, as Archie explains. Instead of only being available for a set duration, these girls can be kept indefinitely.

The bids go higher, and when the person in front of me places the highest bid, I want to punch them in the back of their head.

"I want to leave," Lu says beside me, visibly shaking, her hand grasping mine. "Please. I feel sick."

She tries to stand, but I grab her wrist and pull her back down onto her seat before she's spotted. "They have the exits guarded. We can't leave. We can't attract attention." They've already seen us, but causing a fuss will make it worse.

I just want to give her this USB drive and leave.

"Oh God." She closes her eyes and lowers her head, refusing to watch.

For the next hour, we sit through hell as the auction continues. Men and women sold like cattle. Dehumanising. Mortifying. Now I know what Chris meant by all the other shit he had on her. She's corrupt and horrific and… a monster.

"I have something a little different tonight. You're all aware of the services I provide, and I want to give you all a chance to purchase a full week with some of my most precious men."

She gestures to the screen just as the guard shoves one of them forward, bringing them closer to the screen. Whoever it is can barely stand – he's stumbling to the side a little.

"No," Lu breathes as the mask is removed.

Base.

Slowly, I feel the pressure releasing from my hand as Lu tries to get to her feet. I pull her back down and beg her to stop, but she fights me as people stand in excitement, raising paddles to bid on him.

A woman two rows in front of us bids one million. Someone else bids two million.

Lu sobs into her hand as I wrap my arms around her. "Please make it stop," she cries. "None of this is real. None of this is real."

The bidding ends at five and a half million. Sold. Done.

Base isn't even slightly lucid as he struggles to put his mask back on, his hair soaked in sweat. A guard drags him back from the camera, and the other one is pushed forward.

I already know who it is.

"Do *not* stand," Chris orders in my ear. "You'll make it worse."

Most of the guests sit back down with their paddles ready, but some remain on their feet, waiting like vultures. I want to take one of their paddles and smack them with it.

I can't save him from this. I don't know how. I'm helpless.

He removes his mask on the fifth attempt, and Luciella freezes in my arms.

"What?" she lets out as more tears fall, ignoring the married couple giving us strange looks beside us. "What is happening? Why is this happening?"

"I don't know," I admit quietly as I watch the love of my life be humiliated and sold.

Although he's taken off the mask, he has black material covering his mouth and neck. His hair is probably the only thing normal about him. He's covered in sweat too, his fringe falling down his forehead. He has bruises on his cheek and a black eye, a drugged-up gaze as he squints under the blinding light on the screen.

"Please bid on him," Luciella begs the person beside us. "I'll give you triple what you bid. *Please.* I'm begging you. That's my brother!"

When they don't give her a response, just a dirty look like she's a piece of shit, she taps the person in front's shoulder and says the same thing.

"Make her shut the fuck up," Chris seethes in my ear.

"That's against the rules," an older woman snarls and wipes her blouse. "Please refrain from touching me."

Luciella sits back, lost, eyes wide, staring at her twin brother as he struggles to stand still, swaying on the screen. Base falls into the camera shot, and the guard drags him out of the way.

Kade lifts his hand to try to shade his eyes from the light but misses completely, his hand flying to the side.

I want to find him and hug him, to drag him away – bid billions on him. He gave me enough, but I don't have a number or board or anything.

Instead, I raise my hand, and not once do I get noticed as the bids start from three million. Four. Five. When they reach eight million, I lose hope and drop my hand.

Kade, the boy I fell in love with as a teen, who had all my firsts and planned a whole future for us, the one person in the entire world that kept me going while Chris put me through hell, is now sitting at eight million for bids.

I gulp and cover my mouth as the blonde daughter argues with her mother down front when she calls the bidding to an end. An old, overweight man is handing his board to Archie.

Just when we think it's all over, Bernadette stands at the podium once more, smiles at the crowd and says, "We have two special guests with us tonight, and I want you all to put your money where your mouths are." She gestures in our direction, and the spotlight moves to us. "Stand, chair forty-nine."

Luciella grips the chair in front of her, and I swallow and glance around us. Everyone is staring, waiting, and when a guard walks over and presses a gun to Luciella's head, I gasp, and she whimpers and stands.

Kade and Base are forced into chairs in front of the screen and ordered to watch.

But when Base manages to lift his head and sees the girl stepping onto the stage, he jumps to his feet. "Fuck no!" His voice comes through a speaker. Base steps towards the camera just as Kade starts fighting with a guard. His words are slurred and forced out. "We had a deal. You let her go, right fucking now. Me for her, that was the deal!"

"Things changed, Prince." She nods to her men. "Sit them back down."

Kade drives his fist into someone's face, but the butt of a gun hitting the back of his head knocks him to his knees, and I wince, wishing this was a nightmare I could wake from.

"Chris," I whisper.

Nothing.

"Don't fucking touch me! What the fuck are you doing there?" His words are aimed at Lu, who stands in tears, trembling. "What the fuck!" He punches one of the guards and when Lu is shoved forward with the barrel still to her skull, he raises his hands and stops. "Fine! Fine! Lower your fucking aim!"

Kade's drugged gaze is back on camera. The rage in those eyes... He's silent, letting Base do the yelling, but he's mad. Really fucking mad as he fists his hands and grits his teeth.

They drugged him – both of them. They both sit, begrudgingly.

My friend looks terrified.

Bernadette tips her head, and the guard lowers the gun to his side and forces Luciella forward. "And chair forty-eight, please stand."

"Stacey Fields," I whisper. "Stacey Fields. Stacey Fields. Stacey Fields," I keep saying, repeating it like a mantra, but there's no response from Chris.

The guard drags me up, and I hold the purse containing the USB drive to my chest as I'm hauled to the stage, standing beside Luciella in front of the packed room of sickening faces staring at us – studying us.

My heart is racing, the lights bright in my eyes, everyone watching us be positioned on the platform like Barbie dolls.

The screen is silenced behind me as a chair goes scattering, and I glance over my shoulder to see Kade trying to tackle three guards, yelling so harshly his face is red, veins bulging on his temple. The black cover is gone from his mouth and neck, and I can see a scar there.

"Kade," I say, a tear sliding down my cheek.

Cassie gives me a look as I face forward. "Why is she here?"

"Be quiet," Bernadette snaps.

Cassie is sitting at the front of the crowd, her eyes red and swollen as she covers her mouth. Probably upset from Kade being sold – even though it was her mother who caused it. She trains her gaze on me, studying me as the bidding begins.

At the back of the room, a few guests walk in, down the side, having shown the guards their badges to grant entry. They're wearing masks, the same ones the unwilling participants wore. They stand at the back of the chairs, waiting.

Bernadette grins when she sees them. "Ahh, now we have the

billionaires," she whispers to me like it's the most exciting thing ever, and I glare at her.

One of the billionaires wins Luciella's auction, and I reach for her as Archie grabs her by the nape and whisks her away from me. I try to go to her, but someone else grabs me.

But then Luciella lets out a harrowing scream, her eyes on the spot behind me with her hands against her mouth. I turn to see Base on his knees, blood seeping from a wound in his chest, and Kade trying to catch him when he falls forward.

With shallow breaths, I turn to face the crowd, slowly taking them in and wishing Chris would appear. As Bernadette announces the final auction, one more billionaire enters. He's tall, well built, and he shows his badge to the guard but falters in his steps when he sees me.

Bernadette showcases me.

A well-used toy with experience in staying silent.

I think I might be sick.

"I believe you have something for me," she says as she walks towards me, letting Archie register each bid. She snatches the purse from me, emptying its contents to retrieve the USB drive. "Shame. He must have been special to have broken into my system. He would've been a valuable member of my team. But you wouldn't care if I killed him, would you?"

She can kill him all she wants – after he gets me the hell out of here.

There's buzzing in my ear, as if the signal between me and Chris is being tampered with. He's talking again, but his voice is fuzzy, my name desperately broken, until it cuts off.

She smiles, and I recoil as she strokes my arm and lowers her hand to open my dress further at my hip to show my underwear. I shift from her, and she releases the material. "Stay away from me."

"You would like to see him dead, right? After all, he did kill your unborn baby, rape you – along with many others – and ruin your relationship. No matter, my dear, we'll make sure you birth as many bastards as possible while you lie in a comatose state for the rest of your useless life."

One second, I'm standing like a statue as people bid for me; the next, my hand is tangled in red hair as I yank Bernadette towards me, smashing my forehead into her nose. The snap is louder than the gasps in the room, and blood instantly gushes out and down her dress.

She leans down, and I see the opportunity to drive my knee into her face.

A hand around my throat yanks me back.

She laughs and tells her guards to lower their guns and encourages everyone to bid higher. The newest member of the billionaire clan wins me for ninety million.

I'm dragged away, pushed through the side door Lu was taken through, while Archie comes up behind me and snatches my shoulder. "I want some time with her before she goes."

Bernadette tuts. "Stop playing with the package. Send her to the loading room. She belongs to someone else now." She fakes a smile at me. "It was lovely to officially meet you."

Then she slaps me across the face, the sting nearly as bad as Chris's blows. "While you're lying in your owner's bed tonight, spreading your legs like you always do, I want you to think of this moment. The last few minutes of your freedom."

I try to go for her again, but the guards pull me away with a firm grip of my hair.

Her daughter comes into the corridor, but Bernadette orders her to go back, that she'll come for her soon. She listens, giving me an uncertain look as I fight against the guard. As if she hates this and wants to help but has no idea how to.

I'm pushed into an elevator on my own, and the metal doors slide closed as I try to catch them and fail.

"No! Chris! No! Please hear me!"

I punch against the metal doors taking me to a floor named "loading". I let my tears flow as I pound and pound and *pound* against the hard surface, the skin of my knuckles splitting. "Stacey Fields!" I scream at the top of my lungs.

The helplessness and depravity of this entire night attacks me in one go, and I throw my body against the elevator wall over and over again in desperation, mascara dragging down my cheeks again as I scream, "Stacey Fields!"

Nothing. I don't have his voice in my ear, just the sound of static.

"Stacey Fields," I sob, seeing images of a random billionaire man claiming me, chaining me to a wall and drugging me. "Please. I'll do anything. Please, Chris. Please come get me. Stacey Fields." I punch the elevator door until my knuckles crack and blood splatters on the metal, and I slide down against it, hunched on the floor as I mutter two words over and over again.

"Stacey Fields. Stacey Fields. *Stacey Fields.*"

CONTINUE THEIR STORY IN

RESTITUTION

NOW

AUTHOR BIO

Leigh Rivers is a Scottish Biomedical Scientist who has ventured into the world of writing dark, morally grey characters with rollercoaster storylines to drive her readers wild.

When she isn't reading, writing on her laptop, or gaming until ridiculous hours, she dances at the pole studio, goes to the gym, and walks her dogs with her sons and husband.

Email: authorleighrivers@outlook.com